"LAKE
—Spur Awa

UNTO

LAKE
OF
FIRE

Gold Imprint
Medallion Press, Inc.
Printed in USA

Previous accolades for the Yellowstone series
from the WILLA Award Winning Author,
Linda Jacobs:

"SUMMER OF FIRE is at once a beautiful and disturbing voyage through the type of hell that only firefighters understand. Human, brutal, wrenching. Clare Chance is as genuine a character as they come — brave, vulnerable, well-trained and thrown by her own act of escape into a forested hell. Beautifully crafted and shudderingly real."
— *NY Times Bestselling author, John J. Nance*

"Linda Jacobs will keep your heart pounding as she describes the fires that tried to destroy Yellowstone in 1988 and the work that was done by the brave men and women who fought this fierce dragon."
— *Romance Junkies*

"Linda Jacobs has produced a gripping novel about one of the most electrifying events in the annals of American wildfires — the great Yellowstone fires of 1988. Through her fictional characters, Jacobs has captured the essence of the emotional coaster, high drama and the outstanding performance of America's finest wild land fire fighters. She has done her homework well and the setting is completely accurate. This is a compelling work and I had difficulty putting it down."
— *Bob Barbee, Yellowstone Superintendent 1983–1994*

"RAIN OF FIRE by Linda Jacobs is exciting, poignant, and puts you on the edge of your seat, which is why it is my honor to award RAIN OF FIRE <u>a Perfect 10</u>. Run out and pick up your copies of RAIN OF FIRE and SUMMER OF FIRE today; you won't be disappointed."
— *Romance Reviews Today*

DEDICATION:

*To the late Professor Venkatesh Srinivas Kulkarni of
Rice University, winner of the 1984 American Book Award,
consummate teacher, and citizen of the world.*

And always, to Richard.

Published 2007 by Medallion Press, Inc.

The MEDALLION PRESS LOGO
is a registered tradmark of Medallion Press, Inc.

Typeset in Adobe Caslon Pro
Printed in the United States of America
10-digit ISBN: 1-9338362-1-0
13-digit ISBN: 978-1933836-21-8

10 9 8 7 6 5 4 3 2 1
First Edition

ACKNOWLEDGEMENTS:

One summer, I visited the Yellowstone Lake Hotel and picked up a copy of the book *Plain to Fancy, the Story of the Lake Hotel*, by Barbara Dittl and Joanne Mallmann. The rest is history – I was so fascinated by the place and its story that I felt compelled to create a fictional cast of characters to come for a visit in the year 1900. I have altered history by eliminating the real E.C. Waters, who lived in a house next to the Lake Hotel and ran a steamboat concession on Yellowstone Lake from 1889 through 1907, replacing him with my character of Hank Falls. The Northern Pacific Railroad did attempt to sell the Lake Hotel around the turn of the twentieth century – my rival factions are fictional.

In addition, the renovations to the Lake Hotel, adding the wonderful porches with Ionic columns and some additional rooms, did not take place until 1903-04 – the hotel in my story was plainer, but still a fabulous place to while away the time at Yellowstone Lake.

Other books that helped me understand the history of the early years of the park: *For Everything there is a Season* – Frank Craighead, Falcon Press, *Old Yellowstone Days* – edited by Paul Schullery, University Press of Colorado, and *F. Jay Haynes, Photographer*, Montana Historical Society. On the Nez Perce and the War of 1877: *Soun Tetoken*, Kenneth Thomasma, Grandview Publishing Co., and *Following the Nez Perce Trail*, Cheryl Wilfong, Oregon State University Press.

Thanks to my husband Richard Jacobs for consulting on firearms and other details, and to Dr. Lee Whittlesley, of the Yellowstone archives, for showing me around on my several visits there. Thanks to my agent Susan Schulman, my publisher Medallion Press, and to the following for giving critical input on all or part of the manuscript: Deborah Bedford, Carolyn Lampman, Elizabeth Engstrom, Kathleen O'Neal Gear, Sarah Lazin, and my Rice University writer's group — Marjorie Arsht, Kathryn Brown, Judith Finkel, Bob Hargrove, Elizabeth Hueben, Karen Meinardus, the late Joan Romans, Jeff Theall, and Madeline Westbrook.

CHAPTER ONE
JUNE 20, 1900

Above a scarf of morning mist, the Grand Teton blazed in a rose glow that would not touch the valley floor for another half hour. Though the snow-capped peak towered above Jackson's Hole, it looked so sharp and close to Laura Fielding she thought she might brush the snow from a wind-sculpted cornice.

The Snake River's willowed bottomland and the jagged mountains were like nothing she knew from life in Chicago. If she were home at Fielding House, she'd be basking before a banked fire.

Laura wrapped her coat closer and stepped away from the red-painted coach into snow-muffled silence. In last night's sudden storm, swirling darkness had forced the driver to give up searching for the stage station. As the only passenger left on the Yellowstone run, she had passed a restless night on hard-sprung seats, wondering if she'd been wrong to defy her father and travel alone.

1

With rising light revealing the ramparts, she breathed deeply and exhaled a little cloud. Beneath a nearby cottonwood, a moose rubbed antlers in velvet against bark. Behind him, next to a white-flocked spruce, three more of the stately animals nosed aside the snow to reveal spring shoots.

Postcard perfection, until a snort from the nearest moose signaled alert. The others raised their heads. In the same instant, Laura detected the drumming of horses' hooves. Perhaps it was the stage scouts, searching at first light for the overdue coach, but she could not see through the snow-draped brush.

She looked to the high driver's seat. Angus Spiner, a mustachioed man in the khaki duster of the stage line, threw off his snowy poncho and reached for his Smith & Wesson lever-action shotgun.

Laura dropped to her knees behind a willow and peeped through thick spring foliage. When the hoof-beats grew louder, the tethered team of four stage horses surged in restless motion.

Two men rode into the clearing. The lead horse-man reined in his palomino and shifted his eyes to his stocky partner astride a handsome chestnut. Bandana masks over both men's faces sent a clutch through Laura's gut.

Without a word, the men on horseback snapped their rifles up.

Angus raised his weapon; too late, for a pair of sharp cracks echoed over the snowy plain.

He tumbled from the high seat, falling . . . in

macabre slow motion to land with a thud.

Laura suppressed a gasp.

Not thirty feet away, Angus lay facedown, his hand limp on his gun stock. A red stain spread from beneath his coat; another bloomed in the snow beside his head.

Bile rose, burning Laura's throat. In her twenty-six sheltered years in the city, she'd never seen anything like this.

The leader called, "Dismount!" in military style and swung off his palomino. He was very tall, with dirty blond hair straggling over the collar of his black duster. Though his mask kept her from getting a good look at his narrow face, his eyes were dark as coals.

His partner obeyed, sliding to the ground. He bore a hungry look, but his protruding stomach, along with the well-fed look of his horse, told her he didn't want for food. His plaid cloth coat looked unsuitable for the cold Wyoming morning.

From her hiding place, Laura tried to memorize what the men looked like.

The tall outlaw approached the coach, rifle at hand. Searching for passengers, no doubt, and after what happened to Angus, she suspected she knew the fate of anyone they might find. It was only a matter of time before they detected her tracks in the snow.

Off to her left, a twig snapped. It must be one of the moose; she preferred their company to cold-blooded killers. Then another noise, this one closer, like a boot crushing snow.

In a blur of motion, the blond leader whirled and shot toward the sound. The ball buried itself in the trunk of a cottonwood, three feet from her. She crabbed sideways toward a narrow ravine, where a stream ran beneath a skim of spring ice. Rolling down, she pressed herself into the snow.

Silence reigned in the copse. From where Laura lay beneath the spicy-smelling cottonwoods, she could see the untracked perfection of the far creek bank.

How she wished she had never heard her father utter the word "Yellowstone." That she had not changed her plans without his knowing. Not taken the southern stage route rather than the Northern Pacific direct to the park.

She should be home safe in bed, just thinking of shaking off slumber. Instead, she lay on a blanket of snow, shivering so hard her teeth chattered. Here, she could cower and wait for the outlaws to follow her trail, or she could try to save herself.

Pulling her wide-brimmed hat down over her knot of hair, Laura crawled to the lip of the ravine and peeped over. The outlaw's palomino, his reins looped over the saddle horn, side-gaited away from the coach to within fifteen feet of her.

No good. Though she was an excellent horsewoman, the men would see her mount up and shoot her down.

Angus's gun lay in the snow beside the coach wheel. If she could get it, she knew how to use it. Against her father's orders, she'd persuaded the coachman at Fielding House to teach her to shoot bottles and cans on the Lake Michigan shore. Her own weapon, a tiny brass-framed, four-barrel pepperbox, bought without Father knowing, was in her valise.

Another faint shushing to her left, but she ignored it, dug in her elbows, and pulled forward. Scanning the hummocky bottomland, she planned her path to stay behind the coach until the last moment. Then grab Angus's gun and stand for a clear shot.

Two shots.

The lead outlaw, apparently confident he and his partner were alone, jerked his mask down from his nose and mouth. Angular planes of jaw were revealed, along with deep creases from his nostrils down to the sharp chin. He opened the stage's boot, dragged Laura's luggage out onto the ground, and unlatched her valise. She cringed as her clothes came out in a ragged pile. And again when he bent and retrieved her pistol with a chilling smile.

Something grasped her ankle; her heart began to race. A jerk and she was dragged back down the slope.

Breath gathered in her throat, but a large hand choked off her scream. She kicked out and tried to bite the callused palm.

"Quiet, boy." A rough male whisper.

Damp seeped through the trousers Laura had purchased from the Marshall Field's men's department for the trip. At the time, she'd kept it secret from Father and Aunt Fanny, but figured people on the Union Pacific train and the stage would be less likely to bother a boy. With her captor's weight lowering onto her body, she felt fortunate to be mistaken for a male.

She twisted her head, and a man's hard face filled her vision. With untamed black hair and a ragged beard, he had eyes of glacial blue. Wearing a thick sheepskin coat and trousers matching the willows' bark, his weight pressed her to the cold earth.

Her chest heaved. Scrabbling through the snow and down into the dirt, she grabbed fistfuls in an effort to gain traction.

"Want to get us killed?" His hand clamped down harder, obstructing her nostrils.

She continued to struggle until reason won out. Whoever this man was, he wasn't with the outlaws.

Though she forced herself to go limp, he held his grip a moment longer. "Will you be quiet?"

She gave a jerk of a nod.

He released her and rolled away. She took a ragged gulp of air, trying not to gasp out loud.

"Where's your piece?" he whispered with a furtive glance up the bank. His gloved hand drew his own pistol and held it before her eyes. Thick-barreled and heavy, it bore a grip of creamy bone, with "Colt" lettered on the side.

He inched his way up the embankment to peer over the edge, and a fine trace of lines appeared at the corners of his eyes. Laura crawled up beside him.

Behind the coach, both outlaws rooted through the mess of her belongings. Thankfully, her leather-bound journal was secure in her coat pocket, but she despaired for her fine cameo, sharp white on black onyx, one of the few things she had left from her mother. Dirty fingers parted the carefully packed tissue paper, and she wished she held the Colt.

"Lookit," said the plaid-coated one and pointed to her tracks.

The leader pocketed her pistol and drew a large handgun from a holster beneath his coat. His partner brought up his rifle.

Less than a foot from Laura, the Colt roared. Her left ear twanged and commenced a piercing ring.

Plaid-coat was down, blood spreading from his stomach.

The man beside her fired again.

The leader's gun cartwheeled into the snow. With a single glance at his bleeding partner, he rushed for his palomino and leaped to the saddle. The chestnut spooked and ran, hoofbeats accelerating until both horses and the single rider disappeared into the brush.

The man with the Colt leaped up and dodged through the trees. Laura scrambled to her feet and followed, staggering through a snowdrift to keep up.

When they reached the coach, his sharp blue eyes took in the driver's limp form. Angus's head lay turned away as if he were sleeping; the pool of blood had melted a patch of snow beneath his temple.

Crumpled amid the scattered clothing, Plaid-coat didn't look hungry anymore. His face was slack and his eyes muddy. Keening like a child, he tried to press his intestines back inside.

"Gut shot," Laura's rescuer murmured with a shake of his head. She watched him raise his Colt in a hand that trembled, so slightly she wondered if she imagined it.

The blast reverberated through the vast cold wilderness.

Cord Sutton lowered his gun, his pulse pounding as though he had run a long way. Though the outlaw richly deserved to die, killing a man still made him sick inside.

He turned on the boy, who sagged against the coach wheel, face pale with shock. "What were you thinking? Hiding in the woods while they killed the driver . . ." Cord spat into the snow.

The kid shoved small fists into the pockets of a brown woolen coat and looked away toward a stream running to join the torrent of the Snake. He looked even younger than Cord had thought, not old enough to shave. A glint of tears shone in hazel-flecked green eyes.

"Name's Cord," he offered.

The youngster bit his lower lip with even white teeth. Something in his manner suggested a city child; no doubt, he had never seen anyone die. For that matter, Cord had never killed a man.

How he wished he could turn back the clock to when he'd risen in the predawn darkness, eager to embark on his journey.

With another appraisal of the frightened boy, Cord put two fingers to his mouth and let loose a piercing whistle. A vague movement in the willow bottoms became his well-muscled black stallion trotting into the clearing. "There, Dante." He stroked the horse's flank.

Cord needed to be on his way, but he turned back to the kid studying the snow. Without warning, the child dove on a black velvet pouch beside the steel-rimmed wheel. Trembling fingers shook out tissue paper that floated to earth, and he went onto his knees and pushed piles of snow aside with cold-reddened hands.

"What are you looking for?"

"A cameo on a gold chain. My mother's."

"All this belongs to your mother?" Cord gestured at the scattered clothing. "Is she here?" He hoped there wasn't another body.

The kid shook his head and kept searching.

Relieved, Cord knelt and sifted snow alongside. He lifted a blue-green ball gown trimmed in black lace and shoved aside a gold satin wrapper. After a few minutes, he realized the pendant might be beneath the body of the outlaw he'd killed. He'd never realized a gut-shot man would smell like a deer or elk carcass, a rank, sweetish stench.

Cord pushed to his feet. Reaching down, he touched the kid on a slumped shoulder.

"I have to go," he began. "As we shouldn't steal the stage horses, and mine can't carry you and your mother's bags, I'll have to leave you."

"No!" The boy's tone went shrill. "There might be more of them." He looked at the man Cord had shot in the head and then away.

"The stage company scouts will find you soon."

The last thing Cord needed was a greenhorn to slow him down. If he waited or took the kid back miles to the small town of Jackson, he'd be late for his appointment in Yellowstone. The deal waiting in the park promised to be the most important thing he'd ever done.

The child in the snow looked up and, for the first time, met his eyes. "I need to get to Yellowstone."

Cord saw himself at age six, ragged, homeless, dependent on charity. They could ride for Menor's Ferry; he'd speak to Bill Menor, who was a friend. He'd leave the kid there and report the outlaw.

Before he could speak, something in the way the youngster moved, rising lithely to stand before him, set off alarms. Cord's eyes narrowed, and he studied the smooth jaw. The whisper of suspicion grew stronger when he looked at long-lashed eyes and the generous curve of smooth lips.

This was surely no boy, but a young woman. A lady of wealth, from the look of her belongings spread in the snow.

"Please." Her voice was not a beggar's.

Of all the times to play Good Samaritan, this was the worst. But there was something appealing about traveling with this spunky and mysterious female. Her green gaze was wary while she awaited his verdict.

"I'll take you to Yellowstone," Cord agreed.

For the first hour riding on a folded blanket behind Dante's saddle, Laura sat numbly, aware of nothing but the impossible fact she had survived.

Then, with the rising sunlight, she began to notice her surroundings. Her skin prickled in the chill air; her ears tuned to the scrabble of the black stallion's hooves in the cobbled bottomland. With her nostrils flaring at the pungent mix of sage, horse, and male perspiration, she realized she also stank from the sweat of fear.

It flashed her back to the stream bank, counting the seconds she had to live before her tracks were found. Cringing in anticipation of bullets tearing into her flesh, heart racing, breath cut off when Cord covered her mouth and nose. The sharp concussion of the Colt going off still had her ears ringing.

Tears welled so quickly she couldn't blink them back. She stifled a sob, and her chest felt as though it would explode. Shoulders shaking, she pressed her lips together.

Don't think about it. Wait until you're alone and can write it all down. Then you can fall apart.

Pressing a fist to her mouth, she held her breath until the sharpest agony abated. Though the immediate danger seemed past, she had to keep her wits about her. Would Cord believe a young man sobbing like a girl?

Laura wiped the tears from her cheeks and studied

him. His profile might have been carved from brown sandstone, with a hawkish nose and a sculpted jaw his beard could not hide. High and prominent cheek-bones might have belonged to an Indian, but she'd never heard of one with blue eyes and thick facial hair. Though the set of his jaw conveyed he was still angry at a boy who'd done nothing to defeat the outlaws, he seemed to have accepted her story about the valise of women's things being taken to her . . . his . . . absent mother.

Laura sighed. If only there had been a chance to know her own mother better.

The rustle of skirts and the scent of lemon ver-bena had always preceded Violet Fielding into a room. On the hottest August day when the breeze off Lake Michigan died and flies droned, Violet's hands always felt cool. During her life, Forrest Fielding's rigid de-meanor had been tempered by his wife's unquenchable lightness of heart. When she died, he turned from merely wooden to stone. Pushing ten-year-old Laura into the role of hostess and supervisor at Fielding House, he had set exacting standards for everything.

In the years since, she'd yearned to break free, but stayed with him because she had no better place to go. A woman's options were limited: entering a convent, for which she had no vocation; becoming a nanny or companion, preposterous with the Fielding wealth; or getting married.

With deft motions of his knees, Cord steered Dante several hundred feet down a pair of steep river terraces. In the innermost valley, the Snake River sparkled in the sun. Although it rushed smoothly past, boiling eddies revealed its turbid depth. Born in Yellowstone, the spring torrent flowed south forty miles from its headwaters.

"Menor's Ferry," Cord said.

A wooden frame on each riverbank supported a metal cable works strung across the flood. Tied to the far shore, a board platform topped two flimsy-looking pontoons. She couldn't imagine Dante balancing on the raft and riding the current.

"Halloo!" Cord called, his voice coming back in an echo. The wind stirred the squat willow bushes and wild roses.

All was silent. A whitewashed cabin near the boat looked deserted.

Cupping his large hands, Cord shouted again for the ferry operator. There was no answering hail. "Menor said you couldn't work it from this side," he explained. "It keeps people from crossing without paying their twenty-five cents."

"Now what?" Laura asked in her little-boy voice.

With a look at the river, Cord concluded, "We'll have to ford."

"What?" Floating snags of trees demonstrated the current's power.

"Not here." His tone made her feel stupid.

He turned Dante upstream to a place where the river spread a hundred yards wide, separated into three channels by gravel bars. "He ought to be able to carry us both across this."

Knee-deep, then belly-deep, the horse followed Cord's urging into the rush. Dante's feet left bottom, and the river poured into Laura's boots and climbed her calves.

A few strong strokes, and the horse trotted up onto the first bar. Water streamed from his flanks. Though the second channel flowed deeper and wider, Dante took it easily. Laura almost relaxed, but the farthest stream appeared the swiftest and deepest.

She took a grip on her precious journal, making sure it rested in her coat pocket.

Dante waded in and began to swim gamely, but the current caught him. He stretched his neck and pulled harder, swept downriver faster than he could move across. Laura watched the far bank recede, feeling the water's cold transmitted through her bones so her pelvis ached.

The horse's head surged up. Kicking frantically, he began to founder.

Water came up around Laura's waist, and she began to shudder. Try as she might to hold fast, she found her hands free of the solid strap of Cord's belt. Her fingers brushed the hem of his sheepskin coat; a fleeting touch, and the Snake River seized her.

Wet clothing dragged Laura under, intense cold numbing her from head to toe. She kept her lips pressed together and forced her eyes open. Ahead, she made out a blurred tangle, but before she could fend off, she slammed into something solid. The air she'd been holding in expelled with a whoosh.

As she was scraped along through a twisted jumble of jammed logs, a thick trunk caught her across the middle.

All her muscles clenched, and she hung motionless, while the swift current pressed her against the log. Seconds passed like hours, and she fought the rising urge, first a sly whisper, that perhaps she might be able to breathe underwater. It gave way to a raging scream in her chest.

Then slowly, she felt her head and shoulders pushed forward until she tumbled free. Upside down, water seeping up her nose, she looked for the light and couldn't see her way.

Something seized her leg.

In a rage, she reached to tear at whatever held her. Slippery evergreen branches, covered in algae, bent in her hands. Her eyes were still open in the rushing water, but sparks of light like diamonds began to break up her vision.

Once more, with waning strength, she reached to break the branches.

Free again, she exhaled the last air in her lungs and followed her bubbles. When her head broke the surface, light exploded into her eyes.

She opened her mouth to breathe, but her chest muscles had seized in the cold. Flailing, she felt her boots brush bottom.

Though the shore was just there, the rounded cobbles gave no purchase and she fell back into the current.

The numbing cold was almost benign, the temptation to lie back and let herself float insinuated itself into consciousness.

"No!" She spat water. She hadn't watched Angus and the outlaw die just to lose her own life.

Arms and legs slapping, Laura fought her way into an eddy close to the bank. She grabbed an eroded ball of tree roots.

For a long moment she lay gasping, with cold water pouring over her legs. Her brain as empty as her reservoir of energy, she was loath to move . . . but oddly, what made her was the man who had rescued her at the coach.

What if he needed help?

Step by painful step, she staggered up the cut bank of the Snake River. Hand over hand, she grasped the pungent pale sage to pull herself up. At the top, she fell to her knees.

River water rushed from her mouth. Though she was shivering, sweat peppered her face. Doubled over with her forehead touching the ground, and her wet hair hanging in strings around her shoulders; streaks of bright light seemed to stab at her. Helplessly, she retched.

Clamping her tongue between her teeth, she forced herself to breathe evenly, in and out through her nose. The richness of earth dampened by melting snow rose, redolent of dung and the decaying leaves of last season.

She pressed her palms to the ground, anchoring herself until the maelstrom passed.

After what felt like a long time, she lifted her head.

The mist had burned away to reveal the mountains. They lifted their proud heads, as though the granite mass strained to reach the sky. If she could stand, just there, on the highest peak with wind whipping around her, this valley would surely seem green and warm, the raging Snake subdued to a lazy-looking, sluggish stream.

Wiping her mouth with the back of her hand, Laura got to her feet and stood unsteadily.

On instinct, she reached for her pocket, where she expected the wet weight of her ruined journal. Laura wrote her deepest thoughts down daily, had done so ever since those terrible days after Violet died. Volumes of Laura's life rested in a plain and dusty carton in the Fielding House attic, labeled as "canning jars" so her father would not be tempted to read her true thoughts. This latest book chronicled her decision to undertake this trip alone, along with the wonders of prairie and mountain vistas. Last night, she'd curled up in the coach and written by candlelight, describing the crystalline snowflakes sticking to the windows.

It couldn't be lost, but an exploratory hand in her wet pocket encountered only slivers of bark and gritty sand.

She looked around the lonely valley of the Snake. If Cord had been swept away, she'd have to make her way back to Menor's Ferry and hope someone came along before she got too hungry.

But there he was, a hundred yards upstream on the

steep inner bank, scanning the river. She almost called out, but realized her hair hung around her shoulders.

To her surprise, her leather hat still dangled from a rawhide cord around her neck. She'd bought it from a stable boy at Fielding House, not wanting to go west with a hat that looked new. Hastily, she pulled her hair up and covered it.

Wending her way through sage that exuded aromatic scent each time she brushed gray-green leaves, she worked her way along the high bank. When she approached Cord, he raked his gaze from her slender, shivering shoulders to her squishing boots. In five swift strides, he climbed up fifteen feet to join her on the terrace. His coat and pants were drenched and dripping.

"Are you all right?" he asked.

"I'll make it." She crossed her arms to hide her breasts beneath sopping flannel. "You acted like you knew what you were doing. I should have waited for the stage scouts."

His nostrils flared.

"Why did we have to cross here?" she challenged through chattering teeth.

"It saves a day's travel. I thought you needed to get to Yellowstone."

"I do."

"So do I." The hard note in his voice said he was having second thoughts about her slowing him down. His gaze dropped to her body and his tone softened, so she feared he knew her sex. "You're quaking like

18

an aspen."

She hugged herself harder to hide her female curves.

Cord nodded toward Dante, standing with his neck stretched to sniff a tuft of coarse grass. "Let me give you something dry to wear."

Looking around at the thigh-high scrub, she imagined taking off her shirt beneath his scrutiny. She pointed to the saddlebags hanging sodden. "There is nothing dry."

Cord began to gather gnarled branches of dead sage. Still shaking, she moved to help. He knelt to brush aside the last of the melting snow from a clearing and used a flint to strike and kindle a small smoky fire.

The blaze established, he rummaged in a leather pack and withdrew a pewter flask. When he unscrewed the cap, drank, and passed it to her, the familiar smell of bourbon her father sipped along with his cigars rose to her nostrils.

She had never tried it neat, only in Christmas egg-nog and punches. Trembling as she was, she lifted the flask to her lips and drank after Cord, though Aunt Fanny would not have approved.

It burned and sent a trail of warmth through her middle.

Wiping her mouth with the back of her hand, she handed the spirits back.

As they hunkered down to get warm and dry, she gauged Cord—six foot two, no less, with broad shoulders and tapered hips. His brimmed leather hat showed signs of wear, as did his sheepskin jacket and boots. His hands were nut-brown, his nails clean.

Laura watched with interest as he reached for his rifle, opened the lever action, and shook out the water. Then he pursed his lips and blew down the barrel, sending water droplets flying. From his pack, he removed a rag that looked and smelled of oil. "Got to get out the river muck and hope my bullet pouch is waterproof." He ran the cloth down the barrel using a string with a small metal weight to pull it through.

"What takes you to Yellowstone?" He set the weapon aside and focused on her.

Laura cast about for an answer, knowing her world could not be more different from his. On instinct, she decided to keep her family's wealth a secret.

"Work." She hoped the half truth came out naturally. She did work for her father; he would probably have her take care of his personal correspondence while they were in the park.

A skeptical look suggested Cord wondered about her so-called mother's expensive things. She could make up a story about her mother working in the park, too, a hostess in a hotel dining room perhaps, but deception was best kept to a minimum.

"Work," he repeated into the lengthening silence.

She wondered if he were passing through the park on his way to do ranch labor, perhaps in Montana.

Half an hour passed in uneasy silence until her stomach growled. Torn between delicacy and hoping Cord heard her audible hunger, she planted herself with her back to the flames, her legs spread the way she imagined a boy might stand.

Cord rummaged among the things he'd spread out to dry. From a metal tin, he handed over some jerky.

At Fielding House on Lakeshore Drive, Giselle would just now be setting out breakfast on the walnut sideboard. Laura imagined biscuits hot from the oven, crisp bacon, and link sausage mingling their aromas with the tart smell of stewed apples.

She fingered the tough dried meat Cord gave her, thinking of the curling leather she had seen at the cobbler's when Aunt Fanny took her to get her dancing slippers resoled. Laura had been eleven, big enough to carry the satin toe shoes in to the proprietor on her own and count the change before it disappeared into her aunt's reticule. Old enough to know the things you counted on, those implacable finalities like family, were not as permanent as you imagined. She'd never expected her mother would die giving birth to a baby brother who lived for a day and a night.

How easily Laura might have been the one today to lie ruined while vultures spiraled.

She tried to take a bite of jerky, but her teeth slid off. Another effort managed to rip a small shred from the edge. When Cord offered his canteen, she took it and drank.

Once their clothes were dry, they remounted Dante and headed north along the base of the mountains. She gazed at the rugged cirques and boulder fields adorning the heights. Even from the bottom of the valley, she could see long, linear tracks of avalanche on the glaciers.

Rather than dwell on what had happened this day, she tried to focus on her journey's end, when she would meet her father at the Lake Hotel. His efforts at matchmaking usually fell flat, as he pressed her toward the sons of the wealthy who turned out to be largely indolent, or introduced her to young men he considered worthy to be his successor in the Fielding Bank.

Perhaps, because she would rather have been the one groomed to succeed him, she had run through a string of suitors and declined them all. If she must accept the shackles of the nineteenth century, hers would be nothing less than a love match.

She was well along toward being labeled a spinster.

Fortunately, her father's latest business partner, Hank Falls, sounded different from the men of the Midwest. He had not only built the Lake Hotel in Yellowstone, but he managed it for the Northern Pacific Railroad. Notwithstanding rumors of opposition from a rival buyer, with the help of Fielding Bank, Hank hoped to own the hotel.

Laura smiled, imagining Hank with Cord's understanding of this rough country, yet with a grace and wit a mountain man must lack.

Gradually, the rhythm of the horse became hypnotic, and the sun's warmth lulled. Though she fought it, her eyelids grew heavier, until she drifted into a somnolent haze.

CHAPTER TWO

JUNE 20

You say she's one hell of a gal," Hank Falls chuckled, "but can she cook?" He shook his head at Forrest Fielding's latest attempt to interest him in his daughter, Laura.

"She makes biscuits like lead." Forrest furrowed his broad brow. "But she organizes the house and sees the servants lay a feast at every meal."

Hank's gaze went to the drifts of steam wafting from Old Faithful. The geyser topped a rise at the head of a grassy valley, set in among ridges studded with dense, lodgepole pine forest. The evergreen hills looked dark, in contrast to June's pale shoots beside the Firehole River. All traces of the snow that had blanketed Yellowstone the previous night were gone.

Forrest warmed to his topic. "My Laura will make someone a wonderful wife."

"Providing the fortunate gentleman can afford a cook," Hank agreed jovially.

Forrest pulled his gold hunting case watch from the pocket of his black suit and opened the lid, embossed with a leaping stag. "The geyser is late," he announced, causing a murmur to spread through the clutch of perhaps twenty waiting tourists.

Though Hank had met Forrest only a few days before, when the stout and balding owner of the Fielding Bank in Chicago had clambered awkwardly from the stagecoach, they'd been in correspondence for months. However, until today Hank hadn't realized that having the bank behind him came with the pressure to pay court to the owner's daughter.

Forrest had mentioned Laura several times over a lunch of tinned beef, biscuits, and beer at a trestle table in Larry Matthews's Lunch Station near Norris. And while everyone was washing their pocket handkerchiefs in a geyser pool after the meal, he pointed out how Laura's exacting standards with the servants ensured the linens at Fielding House were always white and crisp.

Forrest looked up at Hank, who towered over his five foot seven. "How old are you, thirty-five?" He didn't wait for an answer. "Well, I'm sure you know how to manage a woman, but Laura needs a firm hand."

Hank suppressed a smile.

"You must promise me," Forrest insisted, "if it ever comes to a contest of wills between you, you'll be sure to make Laura see things your way."

"Mr. Falls." Hank found a gloved hand light on his arm.

Turning, he recognized one of the guests at the Lake Hotel, a woman on the ripe side of forty. The hem of her crimson velvet gown was rimed with soil from riding the stagecoach around the Grand Loop Road, in spite of the dusters provided by the touring company.

"Mrs. Giles." Hank put on his hotel-manager's manner and made a gallant bow.

"Esther." Her coiffure of black hair hung awry, and she reached to secure her Spanish comb studded with glass rubies. As women often did, she appeared to inventory him, from blond hair and narrow but handsome face, down his spare frame clad in tailored gray wool, all the way to stylish leather boots.

"Can't you do something . . . Hank?" Esther looked with bright blue eyes toward the unimpressive mound of sinter forming the cone of Old Faithful.

Hank felt a secret amusement. Captain Feddors, of the Lake Soldier Station, had told him over a hand of poker that tourists often asked the park's military custodians to make the geysers erupt, as though they were man-made fountains in an exposition. In fact, it was well known that some people, including soldiers, threw soap into the geysers for a lark to make them foam. Thankfully, enforcement of regulations protecting the formations had made that less common.

"The geyser is a natural phenomenon," Hank reassured Esther. "We will just have to wait."

Her hand pressed his arm a little more definitely.

Breathing deeply, he drank in the sights he had

loved ever since coming to the park twelve years ago. Afternoon light shone on the valley, where meandering streams and hot pools glowed in the clear air. Steam from hundreds of thermal features rose and floated away on the breeze.

With a clatter of hooves, a stagecoach pulled up and began to discharge passengers. The Monida and Yellowstone ran regular tours, bringing guests to the tented camps and park hotels.

Three men on bicycles pedaled up and dismounted, removing flat caps with short bills in front. Long socks with garters displayed their muscular calves below short riding breeches.

Several soldiers in the uniform of dark blue blouses, light blue trousers, and peaked caps watched the new arrivals. One of their major duties was to prevent tourists from defacing the formations by writing or scratching their names into the travertine. Anyone caught was forced to eradicate all evidence of his vandalism and marched to Headquarters at Mammoth Hot Springs for a hearing before the military superintendent. Swift expulsion from the park was certain to follow.

Old Faithful spit suddenly, a gush of water no more than two feet high; a gasp spread through the watchers. When only steam roiled away from the geyser's neck, the excitement subsided.

Hank saw Forrest look around at the waiting crowd with appreciation. "After we buy the Lake Hotel, we ought to convince the government to let us build a new place here."

Hank agreed, with a disparaging look at the small plain hotel near Old Faithful. When he could manage Lake without the Northern Pacific's penny-pinching, he would be able to turn around the losses they'd seen on the property, perhaps even expand within the park.

Old Faithful sputtered again to a rising chorus.

Hank smiled, for it would be at least a full minute before the geyser rose to its height.

"I wish Laura were here," Forrest said.

Fielding was surely pushing that daughter of his. Hank reckoned she resembled her father, built like a fireplug, with a broad face that wore a constant look of assurance.

"When we get back to the Lake Hotel, Laura should be waiting," Hank told Forrest. The stage would bring her south from the Northern Pacific terminal in Cinnabar, Montana, only a few miles outside the northern park boundary.

Old Faithful blasted again, a crest of white water blowing ten feet in the air. Then steam boiled beneath the earth and the geyser blew, fifty feet, a hundred. As the hissing rush became a roar, a blowing white veil blotted out the green hill behind.

"That's a regular stunner," Esther said, adjusting her hair comb as a gust of wind hit.

A little girl of perhaps four years, dressed in a striped green dress, escaped her mother. She rushed toward the fairyland of spray, her tousled brown curls streaked with gold in the sun.

Hank shot out his long arm and pulled her back

before she could go farther toward the torrent.

"Laura looked like that when she was little," Forrest said.

Old Faithful reached its full height of almost two hundred feet, a drapery that whipped in the wind, like the little girl's hair.

Hank suddenly wished that Laura Fielding might truly be a prize.

The three men overtaking the stage on horseback wore the blue of the United States Cavalry. Forrest leaned forward to look out the open window, braving the dust on the grade that wound down from Craig Pass to Yellowstone Lake.

They had traveled nearly seventeen miles east over mountain roads and were approaching the West Thumb of the lake, where passengers had a choice. Those going to the Lake Hotel could stay with the coach for the final nineteen miles of sandy road, or transfer to the steamboat Hank Falls owned for a ride across the blue lake in the breeze. The driver had recommended the boat; Hank had confided to Forrest that he offered all the drivers, or "savages" as they were known locally, a little additional "tin" as incentive to add to his business.

The cavalry hailed the stage driver, and he brought the coach to a halt with a jingle of harness. A final jolt and the springs bottomed out.

The lead horseman dismounted. Forrest reckoned the red-faced, sweating officer at no more than half his fifty-seven years.

"Gentlemen, I am Sergeant Larry Nevers." He nodded to the woman holding the child Hank had rescued at the geyser. A look of apprehension clouded the youngster's eyes as he advanced toward the coach window. "I'm looking for a Mr. Fielding."

"Right here." Forrest opened the coach door. With care, he let himself down from the high step into dust that rose in twin puffs, laying another layer onto his boots.

Nevers turned and walked to the side of the Grand Loop Road, removing his black worsted gloves as he went. Forrest followed, and the two men looked out over the tops of the pine forest. A mile away and a few hundred feet below, wind etched a herringbone pattern into the cobalt surface of Yellowstone Lake.

With a grave look, Nevers adjusted his thick-lensed glasses that were slipping down his nose. "I'm afraid, sir, that the stagecoach carrying your daughter was attacked in Jackson's Hole."

"My God." The sun had receded behind clouds, and the wind whipped up cold in the late afternoon. "She was supposed to be on the train to the north entrance."

Forrest found that his hand rested heavily on young Nevers's arm. He remembered the waiting silence, a spare last second when he'd stood in the doorway of Violet's bedroom. Her dark hair, still damp with the sweat of childbirth, spilled over the pillow. The doctor's ponderous bulk hid the crimson bloom, leaving Forrest the length of the flowered carpet to live in the time before his wife died.

Please, God, not his daughter, too.

Blood pounding at his temples, he managed to speak. "Is Laura dead?"

"The scouts found the coach, with the driver and another man dead," Nevers answered in a low voice. "Your daughter's valise was there. She wasn't."

At the unmistakable press of feminine flesh against his back, a slow smile curved Cord's lips. This young woman was obviously clever and scared to death he would press his advantage.

She wasn't off base. He knew men in Jackson's Hole who would have thrown her on her back and then left her.

Though that was not his way, he couldn't help wondering what she would look like in one of those lacy gowns left behind at the coach. She was slim hipped, but her wet clothes hadn't hidden the curve of the breasts moving against him with the rhythm of Dante's hooves. He turned, as though to look back the way they had come, and stole a peek.

She was asleep. At his motion, her head lolled awkwardly on his shoulder blade. He shouldn't be surprised after what she'd been through, but he was somewhat astonished at his reaction to her innocent touch.

The journey would no doubt be easier if he continued the charade that she was male, but it was several days' ride to the Lake Hotel.

He didn't believe he could keep up the pretense.

Laura came awake to find her arms around Cord's chest.

She jerked away. "Where are we?"

"Jenny Lake." His voice might have been tinged with emotion.

Afternoon shadows lengthened across a perfect jewel of tarn, lapping gently at its graveled shore. Evergreen, paler aspen, and a profusion of wildflowers grew down to a beach crisscrossed by gnarled ghosts of trees. Mirrored in the water, a craggy peak was haloed by the setting sun.

Holding Dante's reins slack, Cord looked over his shoulder. His sleek black hair shifted over his collar. "Those were your clothes at the coach, girl."

She pressed her lips together.

Sliding to the ground, he dragged her down after him. To her chagrin, her hat fell off and revealed tousled hair her mother once said matched the color of brown sugar taffy.

Cord grabbed her hand and turned it over, looking at the rough spots on her palm. "This morning, when I helped a young boy onto Dante, I thought at least he didn't have a woman's hands."

Incensed that her penchant for riding and tending

her Chicago rose garden without gloves had left obvious signs, she flashed, "A gentleman would never admit he noticed."

The lines at the corners of his eyes crinkled, and his laugh came out hearty. "Got a name?" His gaze raked her body in a too-familiar way.

"My name is Laura," she said through gritted teeth. "And if you touch me, I will take your Colt, shove it down your throat, and pull the trigger."

He blinked. "You expect me to believe you can shoot?"

"I can shoot."

Cord reached for the bone-handled gun at his hip and held it out. He pointed at a piece of driftwood on the lakeshore about fifty yards away. "Hit that, if you can."

Laura hefted the pistol's gleaming weight. She checked that it was loaded and raised it, clasped in two hands. From the corner of her eye, she saw him watch her pull back the hammer.

It took four clicks, that some said spelled, "C-O-L-T."

She sighted along the barrel, drew in her breath, let out half . . .

Held it . . . and squeezed the trigger.

The gun kicked and stung her palms. A chunk of her driftwood target went flying, and the sound of the shot came back twice, echoing in a canyon on the far side of the lake.

"You can shoot . . . Laura." His look was speculative.

She lifted her chin and smiled.

Cord set his jaw. "It doesn't mean you have the guts to kill anything."

The cold came down fast after sunset. Clouds scudded past the high crest where snow blew in arching veils. Laura helped Cord gather firewood, piling the twisted lodgepole logs. The way he'd spoken of killing made her uneasy; it reminded her of the bottomless cold in his eyes when he sighted at the outlaw and pulled the Colt's trigger.

The next time they arrived back at the woodpile together, she ventured, "That man this morning, had he gotten to a surgeon he might have lived."

In the lowering darkness, Cord turned on her. "You know anything about how a gut-shot man dies?"

She swallowed and shook her head.

"First, infection sets in from the shit inside him," he said with a harshness that sounded deliberate. "Then fever, shakes, unimaginable agony from the putrefying wound . . . it takes days."

Laura shifted her weight from one foot to the other.

Cord went on, "We were a half-day's ride north of Jackson and the sawbones there doesn't have a modern operating room. He'd have given him whiskey and morphine, but the outcome would have been the same." The anger went out of his voice. "What I did this morning was the humane thing."

She sighed. True or not, hadn't she planned on shooting the man herself when she tried to go for Angus's gun? When the outlaw had fingered her mother's cameo, hadn't she wished she held the Colt? The memory of the kindly driver's blood on the snow made her believe she could have pulled the trigger.

She gave a tight nod and went for more wood, taking the private opportunity to relieve herself in the forest. Upon planning this trip, she had never expected to end up a "sage brusher," what folks called people who camped wild.

When she came back, Cord had lit the fire. Pine logs snapped and crackled. While he cooked beans in a pot and added jerky, she was glad he hadn't expected her to cook. No working girl would be unable to boil water, as she was, though she could plan a menu for a hundred.

After they ate, Laura perched on a boulder. The fresh aroma of evergreen and an undercurrent of spice hung on the air the way light lingered in the sky. How different this frigid land was from Chicago. Back home, summer brought the fecund aroma of algae and other water plants off Lake Michigan. Here at Jenny Lake, the chill air on her back and the fire's warmth reminded her more of October than June.

She turned to Cord. "What's it like here in the winter?"

"Cold." His voice conveyed the depth and breadth that cold could reach. "The lakes are frozen. Elk and moose come down from the high country by the thousands. The wind blows and blows, and the snow is a weightless dry powder that doesn't even stick to your clothes."

He looked up at the peaks. "For weeks on end, you can't see the summits because they're shrouded in clouds. When you catch a glimpse of the high country, it's blinding white. Dante here," he gestured toward his stallion, "spends stormy weeks in the sod barn."

Odd that a cowboy would be well spoken; he must have had a good teacher in some mountain school-house.

"It sounds very difficult," she replied.

"It's beautiful." His husky voice bespoke his love for the high country.

"Do you think it will snow again tonight?" She huddled closer to the fire and surveyed the clouds against the blacker sky.

"No." Cord's breath came out smoky. "The air is dry, and I don't smell a hint of snow."

Laura knew what he meant. She'd tried to describe the biting aroma in the wind to her cousin Constance and hadn't been able to make her understand. Of course, Constance, with her delicate airs, tended to stay inside when it threatened snow in Chicago.

Cord threw more wood onto the fire, his shadow looming on a boulder. Then he pulled a bedroll from the items he'd been drying. Made of waterproof tan duck with a sheepskin lining, it carried the label of Sears and Roebuck. He went back for blankets. "This is all we have for bedding; we'll have to share."

She hoped the firelight hid her flushed cheeks.

Cord stirred the fire once more and lay down. She waited until he breathed with the even tempo of sleep before she climbed atop her side of the still-damp bedroll and pulled up the blankets. Keeping her coat on, she turned her back to him.

After a while, the fire burned down. Hard diamonds of stars appeared, except for where the bulk of mountain blotted out the sky. Beyond the clearing where they slept, the blackness seemed absolute. Minute by minute, the night grew colder, tempting her to move closer to Cord.

But Aunt Fanny had cautioned her and Constance that even a simple thing might drive a man to take liberties.

Though Laura hugged herself, she continued to shiver. If this was June in Wyoming, she wondered how Cord could possibly love the winter here.

Unless he was as hard as the land.

Long after midnight, Cord drifted in and out of sleep. The woman beside him had threatened to shoot him if he touched her, but perhaps that had been bravado. The clothes he'd seen spread on the snow had either been a rich woman's or those of one who made her living on her back.

What would a wealthy woman be doing disguised as a boy on the Yellowstone stage?

Cord shoved back the covers, sat up, and pulled on his boots. Laura stirred briefly, then settled, while he shrugged on his coat and rose. Picking his way with care through the rocks, and stepping over deadfall, he walked down to the dark shore.

He needed to keep his focus on his business in Yellowstone. It could fall through for a number of reasons, if another party tried to bid things up . . . or if anyone discovered the truth about him.

He stared out at the blacker peaks on the far side of the water. As he had put aside thoughts of Laura, he now refused to delve into his past.

Yet, when he returned to his bedroll and settled into slumber, he found no respite from his roots.

Outside his parents' cabin, six-year-old Cord heard the wolves, a large pack calling each other home across the night. The wind whistled through the crack beneath the cabin door, and the draft ruffled his hair.

Rolling over in his flannel nightshirt, he removed a loose chink of mud from between the logs over his bed. Outside, a wash of moonlight turned sage to silver and the gray granite spires of the Tetons to pearl. The wolves howled again, closer.

Across the cabin, Cord's mother, Sarah, sat up in bed, one slender hand at her throat. Even in the dim light, her hair shone like a silken curtain. "Franklin!" she hissed at her husband. "Wake up."

Cord's father reached beside their bed for his Remington.

Knowing he was on alert made Cord feel better, for Franklin Sutton was a man who made other men look small. The child of a French Canadian mother and a Maine woodsman, he had a big glossy head of hair and a thick black beard.

A prickle of fear went down Cord's spine as one of the wolves howled again, just outside.

Sarah had told Cord the Nez Perce revered the wolf, believing it to be an awesome spirit with the power to change the seasons.

Sarah shuddered, too, but oddly enough, Cord saw her run a finger over the brightly painted elk hide draped over the foot of his parents' bed. She'd told him magical stories, of how her young man of the Nez Perce had come courting with stringers of freshly caught salmon, wreaths woven from mountain daisies, and finally the betrothal gift of the hide he'd painted himself. That was long ago, she had told him, before Cord's father came and took her to live with him while he prospected the Teton wilderness for gold.

Turning to Franklin, Sarah went into his arms, and Cord saw his father's large hand stroke his mother's hair.

The front door of the cabin crashed back against the wall; a tall man stood silhouetted against the silver moonlight. He wore a breastplate of bones over a flannel shirt and trousers. Braids lay over his shoulders, and his hair swept up in a startling dark wing from his broad forehead.

Two shorter men crowded into the doorway behind the first one.

"Stop!" Franklin shouted, pointing his rifle at the man in the lead.

Sarah gasped, "Bitter Waters."

Cord had seen her older half brother when he and his parents had traveled to the Wallowa Valley of Oregon, named for its winding waters . . . where Sarah had been raised . . . seen him from a distance. Bitter Waters had refused to receive his sister and her husband and son who were not of the People.

Yet, in the middle of the night, wearing the striped paint of war, Bitter Waters turned to Sarah. "Two moons ago, I stood helpless and watched our mother, Seeyakoon, die."

Cord sucked in his breath. In his mother's beloved valley, surrounded by snowcapped peaks less rugged than the Tetons, his grandmother had shown Cord her special touch with animals, from the smallest scurrying pika to the wild yearling horses being broken from the Nez Perce's breeding herd. How beautiful Seeyakoon had been, with her supple white deerskin dresses and black hair softly blurring to gray.

"We have been driven off our land," Bitter Waters said. "Burned the white man's Bible and seek a new life." He spoke of war as he if were about to spit from the bad taste in his mouth.

"Then go to your new life," Sarah returned, "and leave my family in peace."

"The army pursues and kills us at every turn. We need everyone in whose veins flows the blood of the People to stand with us. Leave this white man, bring your child, and come." He reached toward his trouser pocket.

"Don't move!" Franklin warned.

Bitter Waters shrugged and drew out a much-folded and grimy piece of paper. "Tarpas Illipt wrote this for you, Sarah, when Colonel Gibbon laid siege to us at Big Hole last moon."

Sarah did not reach to take the offered letter, but she seemed to hesitate, glancing at the painted blanket. Bitter Waters's moccasins made no sound on the earthen floor as he moved toward her.

Cord's father raised his weapon and placed his cheek against the stock. He growled, "Get out," and reached to chamber a round.

"No!" Sarah leaped in front of her brother.

Cord would never forget the shock that transformed his father's face as the hammer connected and the Remington slam fired without a finger on the trigger. The explosion of sound filled the low log house.

Sarah clutched her side and brought her hand away, dark with blood. She muttered something in Nez Perce that Cord did not understand.

One of the two warriors with Bitter Waters reached to his belt. A blade flashed in the firelight.

Arcing through the air, it struck flesh, a dull slicing thud.

"No!" Bitter Waters shouted.

Cord bit back his own cry as his father staggered, trying to grasp the wooden handle protruding from the center of his chest.

Sarah screamed. The sound seemed to bubble in her throat, a liquid agony.

His father went down.

Rushing to his mother, Cord tried to grasp her hands, but she fell silent and slumped across the body of her husband, mingling their blood where they lay. Cord gaped at the impossible sight, wondering if Jesus was holding it against him that his mother's people had burned God's Book.

Suddenly, smoke assailed Cord's nostrils. Through a blur of tears, he saw one of the Nez Perce had stirred up the fire's embers and scattered them. Flames climbed Sarah's lace curtains and licked at the bark on the log walls. Bitter Waters snatched the painted elk hide from the foot of the bed and dragged Cord outside by the back of his nightshirt. Despite his struggles, his uncle wrapped him in the blanket and took him up with him onto a big gray horse.

Fueled by the wind, fire turned the silver night to blood. The Nez Perce leaped astride their horses and barked as they had before, the sounds echoing over the terraced river bottom. Cord looked at the full moon that seemed to fall endlessly through a bank of scudding clouds and listened to the unearthly howling that had wakened him only minutes and a lifetime before.

His home collapsed in a shower of sparks.

CHAPTER THREE
JUNE 21

"Are you going to sleep all day?" Cord called to the slender woman in his bedroll. Dawn barely grayed the eastern horizon, reflected in the smooth surface of Jenny Lake.

She did not answer.

The fire he had built blazed merrily. He dumped coffee into cold water and put it on to boil, his hands still shaking from the nightmare. No, not a dream, but the unvarnished truth that came back to haunt him when he least expected it. He had awakened gasping, while scalding tears poured across his temples. Quickly, he'd bitten his lip to silence himself.

He looked at the sticks being consumed by the campfire and closed his eyes.

His life forever divided into the time before and the time after . . . Riding to a neighboring ranch in the wagon behind the team. His father handing over the reins to Cord's small hands, even though his mother said he must pass another snow before he was big enough. Sarah coming in from her garden, a paring knife in one hand, a bowl of cabbages and carrots propped on her hip . . . a smudge of mud on the tip of her nose. The warming scent of a winter stew, made with dried vegetables held over from summer's bounty.

How could fate have let his father's gun malfunction and kill his mother . . . How could hate between white men and Nez Perce have driven Bitter Waters to think Sarah would leave her husband? What a terrible fortune was Cord's; his mixed blood set him up to be despised by members of both races.

A raven's harsh call from a nearby fir was answered by another across the dark surface of Jenny Lake.

Cord left the fire and went to check on Dante. He rubbed the soft black nose, and the horse bent to sniff his pockets. "Sorry, fella." He wished he'd brought some of Dante's favorite molasses candy.

Although Cord had taken his saddle and tack off, he hadn't tethered him for the night. The stallion wouldn't wander, and he wanted to give Dante a fighting chance if a bear happened along. Plucking his bridle from a nearby aspen limb, he slipped the bit deftly between the horse's lips and adjusted the straps.

The simple labor pleased him. No matter how much time he spent in cities, his heart would always be in these mountains.

Catching a whiff of coffee on the pungent, pine-scented air, he was tempted to break out his rod and catch some breakfast trout. Grilled over hot coals until the skin crisped, the fish would make a succulent meal.

Unfortunately, the rising light reminded him daylight was wasting. He walked back to the patch of soft sand and the bedroll where the woman . . . Laura . . . still slept. The curve of her lashes shadowed her cheek.

How much easier it would be if he still believed she was a boy.

"Time to get up!"

Laura gasped at the deep voice and at the needles and lances of pain that struck her body from riding all day yesterday. Another not-too-gentle prod in the side, and she realized Cord stood over her, his long legs spread.

"What's the rush?" she snarled. "It's not even sunrise."

"I don't know about you, but I need to be on the road." Though his tone was curt, a little curl of his hair stood up from sleeping on it; the errant strand made him look vulnerable.

"All right, all right." She'd slept in her clothes, so she was decent enough to push back the blankets and stagger to her feet. The insides of her thighs and her buttocks felt as if she had been flayed from hours riding bareback on Dante's rump.

Cord knelt and rolled the sheepskin bedding with

swift efficient movements. Scooping up the blankets, he headed toward his horse.

Stiffly, Laura moved to open the pack he'd taken food from yesterday, finding jerky and dried fruit, as well as a cloth sack of cornmeal. Digging deeper, she came up with a comb made of bone. With haste, while Cord was loading Dante, she untangled the knots in her hair and smoothed it over her shoulders.

She walked down to the shore, cupped shockingly cold water, and washed her face. The clear lake lapped gently at her boots. Atop a nearby boulder, a striped chipmunk chattered.

This time yesterday, she'd been sleeping in peace while Angus bedded down on the high driver's seat. Today, she appreciated how easily she could have died, at the coach or in the numbing rush of the Snake. This land was truly as violent as the man who'd dispatched the gut-shot outlaw.

If she had her journal, she would capture every detail.

Her ablutions complete, Laura followed the aroma of coffee to the fire. Cord still occupied himself with the saddlebags, while she put the comb away in his pack. When she reached deep to replace it where she'd found it, her hand brushed something sharp.

Carefully, her fingers traced the contours of the object. Not a knife; it was cold and smooth, almost slick to the touch. The ragged edge opened out into a thicker girth with almost-squared ends. It felt like an irregular piece of broken glass, but it was too weighty to be a chunk of even the finest crystal.

Laura drew it out and recognized the material as obsidian. A professor friend of her father had a drawer of the black volcanic glass, each piece in a tray labeled with the locality and date he had collected it. She raised the stone and rubbed the smooth side against her cheek where it warmed perceptibly.

"May I?"

Laura jumped. She looked up, but Cord's eyes were as opaque as the black glass he gestured her to hand to him.

She placed it on his palm.

Cord looked down at the obsidian and heard the ring of Bitter Waters's voice. "Your spirit is weak. You were raised far from the People."

His uncle's wife, Kamiah, burst out talking from where she prepared dinner on the other side of the rough canvas shelter in Yellowstone . . . the place they had ridden to after his family and home had been destroyed. Although Sarah had taught Cord the Lord's Prayer and some other words in Nez Perce, most of what small-boned, fragile-looking Kamiah said was unintelligible to him. Thankfully, Bitter Waters spoke a stilted formal English that sounded as though he'd been taught by a Britisher.

Kamiah gestured at Bitter Waters in apparent anger, a dusting of camas flour falling from her hands onto the tule rush mat on the earth. The starchy root was one of their staple foods. Boiled and mashed, baked in a pit of hot coals, or dried and pounded into flour, the roots of the camas were harvested in summer but used year-round.

Notwithstanding his wife's protest, the hard expression remained on his uncle's sun-beaten features. "She thinks we should not send you out into these mountains, that we should wait until we have reached safety in the land of the Crow . . . or in Canada." He did not speak of the prospect of being captured by the Army of the United States. "But women and children of the People have died on this journey, many on the battlefield at Big Hole where we had to abandon our tipis."

Leaning back on his heels, Bitter Waters delivered his verdict. "As no one is given tomorrow, you will seek your guardian spirit tonight."

And so, alone in the backcountry, Cord had hugged himself against the night wind and watched the moon rise over the jagged tops of Castor and Pollux, the highest peaks in the Absarokas. From the place Bitter Waters had left him, on a bare mountain peak covered in loose cinders, the enormous coin of moon appeared tinged red by the smoke of late summer forest fires.

Could that bloody orb be his *wayakin*?

His mother had taught Cord that in the Nez Perce way, a spiritual protector revealed itself in many and varied forms. A jackrabbit might pause to sniff at the wind, a distant mountain peak might catch the illumination of the setting sun, or a *hohots*—a grizzly—could happen by.

Sarah had told Cord how Heinmot Tooyalakekt, or Chief Joseph, as the white men called him, had discovered his *wayakin* in the hills overlooking the Wallowa Valley. After ten-year-old Heinmot had watched and waited for five suns without food or water, a storm poured fury upon the peaks, sending down jagged lightning bolts and rain that soothed his parched throat. Thereafter, Heinmot was known as Thunder Rolling in the Mountains.

Twelve-year-old Sarah Tilkalept had wandered alone for a day and a night on her own pilgrimage, until the crisp tinkling of water pouring over a ledge of sandstone attracted her to a crystal pool. From that day forward, she adopted the name of her guardian spirit, Falling Water.

Hours passed. Cord watched and waited for a sign.

He steeled himself against his hunger and thirst, and tried to stay awake, lest the spirit pass him by while he slept. Repeatedly, he nodded, his head falling forward with a jerk that brought him back to that twilight between wakefulness and sleep.

Suddenly, before his widened eyes, flames belched from the surrounding mountains, great pillars of fire rising to heaven. Liquid lava, cherry red, ran thick and viscous down the broad slopes, cooling and breaking into great blocks. Violent explosions threw vast clouds into the air, to the very edge of the inky night.

Ash and rocks rained on the green valley, burying

even the tallest trees beneath a deep suffocating blanket.

In a single heartbeat, more than a thousand cubic miles of earth blew up into a roiling gray column that seemed to have a life of its own. Pyroclastic flows filled the canyons and valleys while smoking lava poured into the vast vacant chamber left by the explosion.

More eruptions followed, though not as great as the first cataclysm.

Cold winds came to the land, blowing down from the Arctic. Snow fell for many years. Vast mountains of ice ebbed and flowed, carving out valleys and leaving streams cut off to cascade to the valleys below. The glaciers left great grooves and dragged boulders hundreds of miles, only to leave them behind like a child's forgotten building blocks.

Beneath the earth, hot magma continued to roil. Sounds of steam hissing and whistling, and the rumbling and splashing of geysers punctuated the simpler sounds of the wind soughing in the trees.

And falling water.

Young Cord awakened with a start. Below him in the moonlight, the broad central plateau of the park spread beyond the foothills of the mountains. Yellowstone Lake filled the center of the depression he had dreamed was a lake of fire.

The vision must have come from his *wayakin*, but what form did the spirit take? A jay calling a warning? The thundering bison herd stampeding before being buried by superheated ash? Perhaps he was guarded by the cold, blue sheen of glacier ice.

Cord dreaded going back to Bitter Waters without finding his *wayakin*. His mother had told him some lost children never found a spiritual protector.

Suddenly, the moonlight fell onto a pair of yellow eyes glowing in the darkness. Cord stared into the night for a long time, until the rough shape of a wolf emerged. Hackles raised, the animal crouched and began to stalk.

Cord shouted, leaping to his feet and waving his arms.

The wolf flinched, but only for an instant. The rest of his pack appeared; at least ten animals surrounded Cord.

He fumbled on the ground for a stick, a rock. There was nothing, and his wild heartbeat threatened to burst his chest, until his hand closed over an angular sharp stone.

Drawing his arm back, he threw the rock as hard as he could.

With a sharp "*kiyah*," the wolf leapt from the rocks and disappeared.

Cord picked up another missile. Although one of the animals had slunk away, the others paused, watching warily.

He shied another stone at the nearest predator and missed. Crouching, he picked up another.

Like smoke, the pack seemed to evaporate into the night.

Only then did Cord feel the sharp edge of the stone he clutched and look down to see what he held. Black and glassy, and glowing like a diamond, the obsidian reflected the light of the full moon.

Laura watched Cord close his fingers almost reverently, as if the simple stone were a thing of great value, and stow it in his trouser pocket. Then he turned away and poured steaming liquid into speckled tin cups. He handed one to her, his rough fingers brushing hers.

Sitting on twisted logs close to the fire, they drank the strong hot coffee. Cord said nothing more, but as they shared dried apples and jerky, he kept glancing at her.

Aunt Fanny said not paying attention would discourage a man. A widow for over twenty years and determined to love no one else, when Fanny's still-black hair and buxom figure attracted unwanted attention, she kept men firmly at bay.

Laura found her gaze wandering back to Cord and looked away with a little jerk.

"If I didn't hurt you last night," Cord said evenly, "I'm probably not going to."

Laura started, wondering if he read minds. "Probably," she repeated, and kept her head averted, pretending to study the gray shapes of the mountains.

Cord exhaled in a way that might have been amusement.

She gave him a sharp look. He returned it.

Eyes that challenged looked out from a face whose lines made him look older than Laura thought he really was. Perhaps he was thirty, but living in the mountains seemed to have toughened him.

Without finishing his coffee, Cord stood and threw the last of it into the fire. With a sigh, Laura watched the hissing rise of steam and got to her feet, as well. The morning was more blue than gray now, and as she stretched her aching back, a rose finger of light touched the highest spire of the mountain peak. It reminded her how far she had traveled since yesterday's sunrise.

Cord kicked at the burning brands, scattering the fire over the rounded rocks and gray sand of the beach. "I guess I should be glad you're just going to Yellowstone to work," he announced. "What if I'd rescued one of those spoiled rich girls who are good for nothing?"

In a broad willow bottom at the base of the square-topped peak Cord pointed out as Mount Moran, he reined Dante in and called a halt for the night. Though the summer sun was still above the western range of the Tetons, he estimated aloud that it was around nine o'clock.

Then he turned to Laura in a matter-of-fact manner. "Seems to me it's your turn to cook."

She asked herself how difficult it could be to soak and boil some beans and add jerky to season them. Cord had surely never sampled the kind of delicacies that routinely graced the table at Fielding House.

With the sun sinking fast, he unlimbered his rifle and sat upon a boulder to clean it. Laura assumed he was doing routine maintenance until he rose, placed the weapon over his shoulder, and began walking through the marshy flats like a stalking cat.

"What are you doing?" she asked.

"Hunting."

"What?"

"Birds."

She knew a little about bird hunting from listening to man talk in Chicago drawing rooms, most notably that it was accomplished with a shotgun, not a rifle.

A moment later, the distinct flapping of wings accompanied a flock of plump birds bursting into the sky. Cord threw his rifle against his shoulder; sound cracked. He pumped the lever to chamber another round and fired again.

A pair of feathered bodies dropped to earth.

Cord turned to her with white teeth flashing. "Ptarmigan."

He strode out twenty paces, bent, and retrieved the birds. Then came back to her with the same confident walk and held out the game.

She recoiled at the bright ruby blood drops on the multicolored feathers.

"Aren't you going to cook?" The limp masses hung from his strong fingers.

"Perhaps," she ventured, "you could clean them."

A vertical line appeared between his black brows.

She drew in a breath and reached for the birds, her

hand closing over the scaly legs. "I'll need a knife."

Cord reached to his hip, pulled a horn-handled hunting knife from a sheath, and offered it to her.

With the birds dangling from one hand, she took the knife in the other. Even as she did, she knew her best intent wouldn't pluck, gut, and prepare these birds in a proper manner. Every piece of meat she'd ever seen had been cut at the butchers, or by one of the servants. She didn't have the first idea where to make incisions without slashing into intestines and exposing her and Cord to the foulest of diseases.

"I'm sorry," she admitted. "I don't know what to do."

He jerked birds and knife from her. "You're not a tart, you're not a cook, but you can shoot." Blue eyes bored into hers. "Well, so can I, lady. What good do you do us?"

Upon awakening the next morning, Laura lay beside Cord on his spread-out sheepskin, a stone poking the small of her back. Even at dawn, this day promised to be warmer than the one before, as insects were already crawling on the long blades of river-bottom grass.

Forty-eight hours since she'd risen to a summer snowfall and watched men die. The memory, sharp and vivid, of Cord leveling his Colt at the outlaws, still had the power to make her breath come shallow.

Laura turned onto her side and looked at him. With his eyes closed, black lashes trembling with each inhalation, he once more looked vulnerable, something she knew he was not.

No, he was hard-edged and completely at home in this country that had a way of suspending the rules she'd chafed at in Chicago. Thinking of it in those terms, she almost wished she were the kind of woman who felt at ease in the wilderness. Despite the looming night shadows, no matter the yipping cry of coyotes, she breathed the cleanest air she'd ever known and gazed into the clearest sky.

Cord stirred and his eyes opened, their focus unerringly on hers. A small shock seemed to go through him; his pupils dilated. They studied one another across ten inches of bedding, the warm gust of his breath upon her cheek.

Should he choose to force his will upon her hundred-pound frame, she would be at his mercy.

He threw back the covers and heaved his big body up to crawl out the opposite side.

This morning there was no bonfire, no coffee. Laura went to the river's edge among the willows, dropped her dirty trousers, and managed to relieve herself without splashing her boots. She knelt on the bank, dipped up water to drink, and cupped handfuls onto her face.

When she came back, Cord had rolled the bedding into a tight bundle. Without a glance at her, he whistled to Dante and saddled him.

"We can't both ride all the time or we'll wear him out," he said. "I'll walk this morning."

She refused his offer of a hand and mounted without assistance. Gathering the reins before he could try to lead the horse, she earned a look of grudging respect.

Though it shouldn't matter, it helped make up for his telling her she was good for nothing.

As they set out north toward Yellowstone, Cord walked ahead through the green willow bottoms. After a few miles, they began to climb into a dense and darker forest. In places, the trees grew so close together that the horse had to be turned back to find a wider path.

In early afternoon, they came upon the brink of a steep-walled canyon.

Cord stepped to the edge while Laura dismounted. The verge overlooked vertical black lava walls studded with pines wherever there was enough soil for growth.

"Is that the Snake?" She pointed to the mesmerizing silver ribbon of river below.

"The Lewis. It feeds into the Snake."

Lewis Canyon . . . They'd managed by traveling cross-country to enter Yellowstone without passing the military station at the south entrance.

Cord paced along the precipice. Being in the park was both a relief and a worry. The fewer checkpoints he had to go through, the less likely someone would detect he was part Nez Perce. Part was as good as all for some, and he'd seen everything, from the sly rapier of ostracism to the blunt bludgeon of assault. The farther he got without running into anyone, the less likely he'd be interrogated about the dead men at the stagecoach.

On the other hand, when he arrived at Lake, he'd be questioned about not checking his weapons at the park boundary.

He took off his hat and ran his hand through his matted hair. Usually fastidious in his grooming, after their dunking in the river he'd let things go. It would make it easier later for him to turn into someone Laura wouldn't recognize.

Staring down hundreds of feet at the river, he thought he heard a twig snap in the thick stand of trees. He looked over his shoulder, but saw nothing save the straight trunks of lodgepole and the soft brown duff underfoot.

It was peaceful here, with the wind sweeping up over the canyon rim and a raven soaring on the drafts. The midday sun shone through the branches, making a checkered shade that shifted and moved across Laura's face.

She took a half step back from Cord, but she wasn't afraid of him anymore. His eyes reminded her of the highest part of the sky at midday, with a midnight blue ring around the iris. He had shed his sheepskin coat, and his denim shirt lay open at the neck, revealing a pulse in the hollow of his throat.

Behind them, Dante shied. In the same instant, Laura caught the stench of decay.

"There." Cord pointed to some mounds of flesh and fur at the base of a tree.

The carcasses lay piled, their arrangement assuring there had been no accident. Deer; she knew them from the woods north of Chicago, and elk, which she had seen only in books. But the massive antlers she expected upon their heads were absent; empty sockets crawling with green flies all that remained of former glory.

"Poachers." His hand near his holstered Colt, Cord scanned the woods, then returned his focus to the fallen.

"But why?"

He bent and pulled back the dead animal's lip to show a gap in the jaw where the eyeteeth had been removed. "Elk ivory. It makes into jewelry and trade goods."

What kind of person would kill a magnificent animal for such a small prize? The tall blond man who had ridden away from the stagecoach leaped to mind. Might a person who would kill Angus Spiner and get virtually nothing but her pistol and her mother's cameo also commit such an atrocity?

She surveyed the area again, noting that Cord was also edgy. "Do you suppose that outlaw . . . ?"

He spat onto the pine straw underfoot. "If not him, then the same kind of scum."

Suddenly, Laura's nostrils were assailed with a new

odor that was far viler than the dead before them, like a mixture of rancid grease and vomit. She gagged.

Cord whirled away. "Bear!"

She didn't see one. Lodgepole grew thick to the canyon's edge, and none of the trees were thick enough to hide a large animal. But Cord must have recognized the stench, and the poachers' leavings were excellent bait for large predators.

As she ran behind Dante, he caught the scent and whinnied. She looked underneath his belly and saw Cord about ten feet away with his back to her, his Colt drawn.

A low growling and the bear lumbered into her line of view. Big and shaggy, the grizzly padded toward Cord on broad paws studded with claws at least four inches long.

Dante reared. The grizzly took a look at the horse and appeared to decide the man was more interesting.

Cord raised the Colt and fired into the air.

Rather than retreat, the grizzly lumbered toward him.

He fired again, this time into the animal.

It didn't even flinch, but came on. Before Cord could get off another shot, a swipe of paw sent the Colt tumbling.

Cord dropped to the ground and curled into a ball, his arms over his head. "Mount up, Laura!" he shouted. "Ride!"

Dante danced and plunged. Laura reached for the reins, but the stallion rolled his eyes and tossed his head. As she struggled with the horse, her hand fell onto Cord's 1886 Winchester, sheathed in its scabbard behind the saddle.

Laura pulled the long gun free and ran out from behind Dante.

The grizzly swiped a paw at Cord's back, covered by thin cotton.

"Over here!" Laura screamed.

The bear looked at her, and then pulled up onto its hind legs to a height of at least seven feet. Clearly a huge male, he opened his mouth with a curl of snout and roared.

Raising the rifle to her shoulder, she fired. The gun kicked viciously, and her thumb caught her nose. Nearly blinded by instant, painful tears, she jacked another round into the chamber and fired again.

The bear fell to all fours and lumbered toward her, covering ground at an astonishing pace. She fought the impulse to drop the Winchester and flee. She'd heard a bear could outrun the fastest horse.

"Shoot him again!" Cord leaped to his feet and scrambled for his Colt.

Laura lined up the sights and wavered; she might kill Cord with a wild shot. While she hesitated, the bear rushed her.

Cord darted left.

She stood her ground, firing. The grizzly hit like a train, throwing the rifle up into the air and her onto her back. A vile greasy smell filled her head as she was crushed by dead weight.

With the air knocked out of her, she heard a shout. "Dante!"

A rough shambling of hooves, more commands. "Back. No, go again."

Was it her fate to die in this rough land? Each attempt at breath refused to lift her lungs against the weight pressing her into the earth.

"Dante. Pull."

The sharp tone cut into her fading consciousness. If this were her end, how much better here than in some Chicago drawing room where every move and word was measured?

Then, as though no time had passed, or a thousand years, Laura opened her eyes and looked into sun radiating through the trees. It reminded her of a painting her mother had pointed out in her white leather Bible when Laura was small. Had the sky been any different back when Baby Moses floated in the bulrushes beneath rays of shining light?

Something touched her arm. "God, Laura . . ."

Cord knelt beside her on the litter of pine needles, his bronzed face pinched looking. Dante stood nearby, a slack rope hanging from his saddle. The bear lay a yard away with the same boneless look Laura had seen in Angus, the outlaw, and the poachers' victims.

"Are you hurt?" Cord gestured at the mess of blood on the front of her flannel shirt.

Besides a lingering dizziness, she felt no pain. "Must be the bear's."

"You killed him." Cord grinned.

"Did he hurt you?" she asked.

"I'm going to be black and blue where he swiped at me." He rose, went to Dante, and retrieved his pewter flask of bourbon. Once more, as she had beside the raging Snake, she lifted it to her lips and drank. Cord twisted the top back into place without taking a sip.

His eyes sought hers. "I'm sorry for insulting your nerve."

Laura found herself smiling. After twenty-six sheltered years as her father's daughter, she felt a sudden fierce joy at being filthy, at smelling of bear.

And at simply being alive.

CHAPTER FOUR

JUNE 22

Cord didn't return her smile, but looked around the canyon rim with a listening air. Although the bear threat had been neutralized, not a bird sang or a chipmunk chattered in the still afternoon.

Even so, Cord put out a hand as though he had heard something and was waiting to learn what it was. Something disturbing in his expression made her quietly accept his hand to help her up.

Putting a finger to his lips, he kept his Colt in one hand and picked up the fallen Winchester. Still scanning the area with a wary eye, he reloaded his rifle, mounted Dante, and pulled Laura up to the saddle in front of him.

Riding hard, they pressed on to the north. Jolted against Cord, she managed to ask over her shoulder, "Do you think there was another bear?"

"One of the two-legged variety."

Hours later, they forded the Lewis River in a

broad meadow above the head of the canyon. Turning east from the river valley, they began climbing the northern base of what Cord called the Red Mountains. There, the steeper slope forced them to slow their headlong rush.

With the danger seeming to be behind them, she had time to think. No one in her family, not her father, not his sister, Fanny, and not Laura's delicate cousin Constance, would believe she had raised the Winchester and fired into the approaching bulk of bear. They wouldn't recognize her, riding this stallion in her boy's clothing, a sense of pride swelling her chest beneath the stain of bear blood. Even Cord had apologized for thinking she didn't have nerve.

They climbed higher, first encountering snowy patches, and then rode into a blanket covering the ground, deep and soft. It was last winter's snowcap, not yet melted in the divide at the headwaters of a rushing creek. A few yards downstream, the heat had melted the snow, and she saw the pool of the hot springs.

"Witch Creek," Cord said, "named for the boiling cauldrons on its banks." Pointing up the steep slope, he showed Laura the steam rising from at least fifty craters. "The early explorers named this Factory Hill. All that smoke made it look like a New England manufacturing town."

She wondered if they were safe this close to the hissing vents, but risk was part of the fascination.

"We'll make camp here," Cord declared.

It seemed a hundred years since she'd awakened

this morning. The long ride, the wasted carcasses left by poachers, the bear . . . how she longed to collapse into a dreamless slumber.

But that wasn't possible, for Cord was unpacking gear, letting Dante out to graze, laying a fire, and placing his deadly Colt upon the nearest rock where it was in ready reach. She helped as she could, pulling out the cooking pot and mess kit, and filling his canteen with water from the rushing stream up current from the vents.

While she worked, Laura became more aware of her filthy state. Her blood-encrusted shirtfront felt sticky against her chest, and though the evening chill was settling in, her scalp prickled from where she had perspired earlier.

"You look as though you could use a bath." Cord's gravelly voice made Laura jump.

"What bath?" She thought of her claw-footed tub in Chicago, with the option of water falling from above like rain, and pointed at steam rising from the nearby hot spring. "That would parboil me."

Cord gestured at the woods. "There's a pool over there that should satisfy any lady's desire."

A few minutes later, Laura smelled the faintly corrupt odor of sulfur beside the spring to which Cord escorted her. He handed her the rough shape of a bar of homemade lye soap. "Made this myself at my cabin."

He walked away.

Laura looked around at the forest, wondering about bears and outlaws. She could call Cord back to stand guard, but privacy won out.

Only a little steam rose from this clear water, blowing away and constantly renewing itself. Just as she felt that she would have an unobstructed view of the blue depths, a tantalizing veil blew back.

With the water inviting at her feet, she slipped the buttons of her blood-encrusted flannel shirt, took it off, and laid it on the terraced white rock that rimmed the pool. Beside it lay a clean blue cotton shirt Cord had offered.

Even with the bloody garment off, Laura had never felt this grubby. She smelled so bad that she offended herself. Her face felt grimy from where she had sweated in the midday sun, and she itched where her ivory silk camisole had been plastered against her back. Her hair was matted with dust.

She untied the delicate ribbons that held her camisole together in front and took off the rest of her clothes. The evening air felt cool on her skin. Easing her bare foot into the pool, she found it temperate and inviting. Wading in naked, she submerged to the top of her head.

She couldn't help but compare this to bathing at Fielding House. There, her tub was in a small room without windows. In Yellowstone, sculling with her hands, she breathed the almost-impossible freedom of being nude in the open air.

She reached for the soap Cord said he had made and imagined him in a log room before a fireplace, stirring a kettle of lard and ashes. Did his soap making mean there was no woman to do for him?

Though his bar of lye was harsher than the lavender-milled variety she was used to, she shampooed her hair and lathered her body. After sluicing the suds away, she washed her lingerie.

Once she and her underclothes were clean, Laura started to rise but decided to linger, floating on her back.

A moment later, she opened her eyes with the sensation that someone watched her. Surely Cord would not . . .

Heart pounding, she scanned the darkening woods.

A man stood on the hillside, not fifty feet from the pool. His hair hung lankly over his brow, but even in the dimness Laura saw that it was a lighter shade than her own brown. He wore a long coat over his tall form.

She scrambled up, sheeting water as she struggled through the thigh-deep pool. Her feet slipped on the algae-coated travertine.

Cord splashed water over his shoulders and took up a handful of sand to scrub his skin, having given Laura his only bar of soap. The pool in which he bathed wasn't as warm as the one he'd offered her; nearly nonexistent tendrils of steam teased its surface.

He could be a gentleman when he wanted to.

In Salt Lake, where he was generally known as

part Indian, mothers drew their daughters aside and let them know he was not suitable marriage material. Having lived there since he was six, he'd given up believing he'd find a wife and start a family.

But in the spring, when he went to St. Paul to meet with the Northern Pacific Railroad, he'd been welcomed like a king in the city drawing rooms. No one had looked past his blue eyes and fine clothing to see a ragged breed.

Especially the curvaceous pale beauty, niece of one of the St. Paul city fathers, who had danced and taken the air with him and gazed on him with admiration. Passing for a man without Nez Perce blood was the sheerest folly, but he was trying it anyway. First, to be certain his business in Yellowstone was concluded without question, and second, to have a chance at seeing the lovely young woman again. Strangely, this was the first time he'd thought of her since he'd heard gunshots in yesterday's dawn.

Running his hands up through his hair, he held his breath and ducked his head. No matter how rich the food, how well appointed the drawing rooms of St. Paul or Salt Lake, there was nothing like breathing the damp sulfurous scent of a hot spring. Out here, he came alive.

Surfacing, he wiped the water from his eyes. And blinked.

Was that a shadow in the forest or a man? Because if it was a man . . . he reached for his shirt, dried his face, and looked again . . . the bastard was stalking the pool where Laura bathed.

Cord surged out of the water and reached for his Winchester. His hands tensed on the stock, and he strained to see into the gathering darkness. He was nearly certain that the man skulking through the brush was the outlaw who had escaped him at the stagecoach.

He ran toward where he'd left Laura, scanning the woods as he went.

Not a branch moved on the hillside, but Cord started up, his legs pumping. He saw again the lifeless form of the stage driver, and his blood heated with the determination to finish what he'd started.

"Cord . . . be careful." Laura's voice, and he realized the foolhardiness of rushing into the dusk and making himself a target.

He slid to a stop not ten feet from her.

She wasn't a thing like the boy he'd first mistaken her for, not with that tiny waist and rose-tipped breasts she brought up her hands to cover. Her foot slipped, and she grimaced as she stepped on something on the bottom of the pool.

Cord started to go closer, to put out a hand and help her out of the clear water that hid nothing, then realized what he must look like to her, naked and dripping.

"I . . . thought I saw something," he explained.

"You did." She gave him an even look. "I think it was the outlaw."

With care, he picked up his clean shirt, handed it to her, and turned away.

With trembling hands, Laura jerked Cord's shirt on over wet bare skin, and pulled on her still-dirty trousers. She gathered her camisole, step-ins, and the ruined shirt, being sure not to leave the lye soap behind.

Back in camp, Cord brought out a waterproof tin of matches from his saddlebag.

"Do you think he's gone?" she asked, handing over his soap.

"I have no idea." He stowed the soap in a metal tin and knelt to start the fire he'd laid earlier. As he straightened, he looked down at her. "I should have told you earlier . . . At the canyon rim, after you shot the bear, I thought I heard something . . . like a gun being cocked."

She stared out into the dark woods. Though sparks danced skyward while hungry flames consumed the kindling, she felt a coldness deeper than damp skin and night air could account for. The outlaw knew he'd been seen by both her and Cord, and here by the fire, they made the simplest of targets.

"Shouldn't we hide out in the dark?" She put on her woolen coat and buttoned it.

"We could," Cord agreed. "But he's had ample opportunity to shoot us down from cover; he could have plugged either one of us while we were bathing in the hot pools."

"It doesn't make sense."

Cord reached for the pack where he kept food.

She knew there were the inevitable beans, jerky, and dried fruit, but hadn't she noted a small sack of meal when she'd looked inside at Jenny Lake? Recalling that one day at Fielding House, Giselle had served a chicken casserole with a cornbread topping, Laura figured she might impress Cord by putting a layer over the beans.

"You said it was my turn to cook?" she offered.

He looked dubious, but crouched back on his heels.

In an hour, she wasn't feeling so positive. The beans had started out all right, she'd remembered to add salt and jerky, and dug around and found some dried onions. However, when she mixed up the cornmeal and water and placed it on the surface of the beans, something disastrous happened.

Instead of cooking up into a layer of golden cornbread, the paste sank into the beans, creating a mass of starch that stuck to the bottom of the pot no matter how quickly she stirred.

Aware of Cord behind her, she dipped up the food and turned to offer him a plate.

"Your dinner," she murmured, ashamed.

Cord took his plate and spoon, and ate with relish. When he made no comment on her mistake, she thought he might have been hungry enough not to notice.

Her hope was dashed when his lips curved into a smile that peeked out from his mass of black beard. "Ah, Laura, one thing . . ."

"Hmm?" She tried to force a sticky mouthful down.

"The cornbread-on-top thing only works with the lid on. You have to get it hot in the pan like an oven. Works even better if you put some coals on top of the lid."

She swallowed and nodded.

Cord gathered their dishes and scrubbed them with sand in the stream. He took the small pack containing food and roped it up into a tree a distance from their fire. "No sense tempting another bear."

Laura remembered her bloody shirt. If food were a bear magnet . . .

She retrieved the soiled flannel and flung it into the fire.

Cord stretched out on the ground against a log and watched the cloth burn with a listening alertness in his posture. His hands were in constant motion, worrying the piece of obsidian she had found in his pack at Jenny Lake.

She looked into the darkness, wondering if the tall blond man lurked just beyond the circle of light. He might not have shot them, but what if he was more sadistic? What if he preferred to sneak up in the night and slit their throats while they slept?

As though he were reading her mind, Cord proposed, "I'll stand guard until dawn. Tomorrow I'll put you on Hank Falls's steamboat; it'll take you safely across Yellowstone Lake to the hotel."

She'd traveled over a thousand miles to meet Hank, a man she'd imagined might meet her on her own terms, but tonight the sound of his name failed to interest her.

Laura wrapped her coat tighter and looked up at the sky. The waning moon would not rise until after midnight, but the starlight was nearly bright enough to read by.

Behind them in the dark woods, Dante whickered softly.

"Have you read *The Divine Comedy*?" She thought Cord remarkably well spoken for a mountain man. Perhaps he really had named his horse for the author of the epic depiction of hell.

"I love Italian literature," he rejoined, leaving her to wonder, as she wondered so many things about him. A little later, he rose and pocketed his obsidian with care.

As he moved to spread the bedroll and blankets, Laura's face grew warm. It felt different now that she had seen the muscles of his broad chest and he had seen . . .

He came and offered a hand to help her up.

She let her own be taken into his clasp, and he pulled her to her feet. His eyes looked black in the deep forest night. The glow of the firelight emphasized leaping shadows.

Without warning, the intensity in Cord's gaze extinguished. He released her hand, stepped back, and dropped his hands to his sides. Though he did not bow, she imagined that he did, so formal was his posture.

"I'll keep watch while you sleep."

Cord leaned against a log and watched Laura's eyes close.

Reaching to his trouser pocket, he removed his precious talisman of obsidian and watched it come alive in the light from the dancing flames. The glass, born of fire, warmed in his fingers, as it had done when he first plucked it from the earth.

As a child, he'd returned to the Nez Perce camp at dawn. The smoke from cooking fires rose, and Cord's stomach growled as he found his way to his uncle's camp. Approaching with his *wayakin* clutched in his fingers, Cord had found Kamiah alone beside the breakfast fire.

She raised her head from where she worked over a wooden bowl of camas flour, wiped the back of her hand across her snub nose, and left a white smudge. The front of her beaded deerskin dress was also liberally sprinkled.

Though she did not speak English, she raised her brows to ask about Cord's quest for his guardian spirit.

He answered by opening his hand and showing the piece of stone.

She smiled and reached to touch the glassy surface.

Cord gestured to ask where his uncle was.

Kamiah pointed across the main fire in the center of camp toward the largest makeshift shelter, draped with a mosaic of soft-looking hides.

On swift feet, Cord made his way toward the enclosure. When he drew close, he heard voices raised in acrimony. Holding tightly to his *wayakin*, he put his eye to a space between skins and looked inside.

Bitter Waters was in council with the elders. The air was thick with pipe smoke, as the chiefs and their lieutenants continued a discussion that seemed to have gone on a while.

"We did the right thing when my mother and the others were killed by white men," Bitter Waters insisted. To Cord's surprise he spoke in English, but then he noticed the older white man in their midst. He had heard this man, Cappy Parsons, was a miner who had been captured in the park and was being forced to guide the tribe through unfamiliar country.

Bitter Waters went on, "We rallied the young warriors . . ."

"It is not your turn to speak," White Bird interjected. His square shoulders still looked sturdy, but his chestnut hair was streaked with gray. Small eyes in his long face admonished, and his chin, scarred from skin eruptions, lifted imperiously. "You forget that some of our youths, full of themselves on fire water, went on their own killing spree among the white men."

Cord made a face. This was the first he'd heard the tribe might also be at fault in starting the war.

Though Bitter Waters had been told not to speak, he went to the center of the circle, wearing ceremonial feathers in his braids. "After the thief treaty of 1863, when the United States took much of our land, many began to question the wisdom of keeping the peace."

Quiet descended. The only sound was that of

Looking Glass puffing on his pipe. Younger than White Bird, he was nearly six feet tall.

"Joseph!" Bitter Waters turned to the chief. "Your own father renounced the white man's religion, as well as his government."

Joseph nodded. "I watched him tear up his copy of the treaty with the United States and his Gospel of Matthew, a gift from the missionary who baptized me." He stared into the fire. "The hate is high on both sides. Knowing we are pursued by both General Howard's soldiers and the Bannock Indians he hired, we are pitted against both white men and red."

Cappy Parsons, who had been sitting silent, raised his head. "That's no excuse to kidnap me."

One of the younger braves started to move toward the miner, but Joseph lifted a hand. "Do not harm him. He will help us through these mountains, and then we will let him go."

Parsons subsided back into silence.

Joseph went on, "It no longer matters how this war started. We are on the run from the United States Army and must not stop until we reach Canada."

Cord walked away from the council.

How could he live among these people after he had seen his parents' mingled blood? He hated his uncle and all these strange warriors, even after Bitter Waters had spoken to him in his formal English: "Sarah was my sister. I grieve for her, even as you do."

He might be Cord's uncle, but if he had not come like a thief in the night, how different things might have been. While Cord's home burned with his parents' bodies inside, he had sat stiffly in the saddle in front of his uncle and hardened his heart.

"You are of the Nimiipuu, the People." Bitter Waters's strong arms kept him from tumbling off the tall gray horse.

"I will never be one of you!" Cord had declared.

CHAPTER FIVE

JUNE 23

With the first pearling of dawn, Laura raised her head to see the clearing and the surrounding woods. The campfire had burned to pale ashes, and the pines loomed large against the mist rising off the hot pools. Cord sat with his back against a tree. The collar of his sheepskin coat was turned up; he held his Winchester across his knees.

She started to stretch her cold, cramped muscles, but stopped. A pale shape crouched at the edge of the trees, about forty feet away.

Gooseflesh prickled her arms, and she peered through the rising light, thinking how she might warn Cord without sounding an alarm. She could try to whisper.

The apparition resolved itself into a large boulder.

Her stomach tense, she lay back. Cord was on guard, and he apparently had excellent instincts: knowing from just the scent that a grizzly approached, hearing the click of a gun being cocked, and somehow divining that the outlaw spied on her while she was bathing, even as he was in another pool.

Studying his profile, she had to admit that beneath his rough beard and thick hair he was a handsome man. And last night, when he had turned away from her, the expression in his eyes had been something she recognized. She'd seen the same look of lust . . . or longing on men's faces before and elucidated the encounters in her journal.

Only two months ago in the soft Chicago spring, the warm breeze had sighed through the gazebo on a long green lawn sloping to Lake Michigan. Just Laura and Joseph Kane, heir to the Kane Mercantile Fortune . . . Laura's father would have loved it. Though she had opened her mouth to Joseph's and run her hands across his broad shoulders and through the gold of his hair, she'd felt nothing more than a peculiar woodenness.

Aunt Fanny had told her a lady need not necessarily expect to enjoy the act of love, but the restless stirrings Laura sometimes felt had led her to expect more, although she could not say exactly what it was that made her spurn Joseph's offer of marriage.

Perhaps it was the same spirit of wanting more that had induced her to travel alone by stage through the wilder parts of the West, something her father did not yet know. Had she known what that decision meant, would she make it again?

She closed her eyes against the coming of morning.

Cord stared down the boulder near the edge of the woods for the fortieth time. His eyes were scratchy, and he had to concentrate to keep them open.

A few minutes ago, he'd thought Laura lifted her head and looked around, but maybe it had been another figment of his overactive imagination. If the outlaw from the stage was shadowing them because they'd seen his face, why had he passed up a dozen or more opportunities to kill them?

Here Cord was, inside the national park, with his Winchester at the ready when it was against regulation for him to be carrying weapons that hadn't been sealed by army inspectors.

He looked again toward the bedroll. Laura appeared to be sleeping.

At times she seemed a dirty transient on her way to do menial labor in the park. But then he would reconsider: those clothes she'd left behind had cost a pretty penny. And what was that remark about reading *The Divine Comedy*?

He had, in fact, named a new colt Dante because the rambunctious fellow had been a perfect little hellion.

As dawn began to brighten, Cord rose from his cramped position and stretched his legs. Keeping his rifle close, he stirred up the fire's embers, added wood, and put water on to boil.

Laura opened her eyes to the welcome smell of coffee and exhaled a puff of white. Rolling over, she stretched her arms above her head and found her gaze meeting Cord's across the morning campfire.

He poured coffee into the mug she had used before and brought it to her. She pushed back the covers and sat up to take her drink. Sipping the strong black liquid, she studied him over the rim.

He smiled. Though he often appeared content, she sensed sadness in him, some empty place needing to be filled.

Or she could be wrong. Perhaps, in spite of his claim to soap making, he did have a woman somewhere in a mountain cabin. Maybe he loved this woman, who was more like him than Laura would ever be.

At midday, beneath a sky of almost-impossible blue, they came to West Thumb Geyser Basin. Moored alongshore, a stern-wheeled paddleboat stood two stories tall, painted a gaudy red and black. The forward and upper decks were open-air, with a large rear cabin. Gilded metal flames decorated the rims of the smokestacks, and gold letters a foot high proclaimed the boat to be the *Alexandra*. Passengers from a nearby stagecoach climbed the planks laid from the dock to the lower deck.

Cord shifted his weight behind Laura on the saddle

and brought Dante to a halt at the edge of Yellowstone Lake. Framed against the snowcapped Absarokas to the east, cobalt water stretched away to the horizon. A warm wind frothed the surface into waves that flung themselves onto the rocky shore.

Located at the southwest corner of twenty-mile-long Yellowstone Lake, the hot springs of Thumb filled pools of steaming water. Brilliantly colored algae streamed like long hair in the conduits that overflowed and ran down from the hot pools to the lake. Farther from shore, gentle eddies swirled, while strings of bubbles marked where additional springs mingled warm water with the cold lake. A few yards out, a pair of flat, travertine cones broke the surface of the clear, shallow water.

Cord pointed to the larger of the two, which looked like a miniature volcano of pale gray sinter, three feet high. Steam escaped its mouth. "That's Fishing Cone. You can catch a trout in the lake and cook it in boiling water without taking it off the line." His smile crinkled the skin around his eyes.

The boat's steam whistle blew, a long, shrill call.

"Hank Falls will charge too much, but he's got the best boat on the lake."

She'd practically forgotten Hank.

"You'd better hurry." The vertical furrow between Cord's brows became a deeper slash.

It was time to return to being Miss Laura of Fielding House, to wearing sweeping skirts and sleeping alone in a bed with crisp, clean sheets. She got her balance to dismount.

The whistle blew again.

She moved to sling her leg across, but Cord reached forward and put a stilling hand on her thigh. "Why don't we ride the rest of the way to the hotel?"

Laura looked at the boat where the gangplank was being raised. There was money in her pocket for passage, bills that had been wet and dried several times on the trek, but still legal tender. There was time, if she hailed them, dismounted, and ran for it.

Silently, she watched the plank secured on deck. Smoke poured from the stacks, and the *Alexandra* began to pull away from the bank.

Cord turned Dante's head away from the shore and urged him along the rock path, pointing out where spring deposits glowed in a hundred hues—emerald, olive, brick, orange, ochre—from mineral staining and more algae. Pools lay filled with the clearest turquoise water, as well as opaque concoctions of pink and gray mud.

They left the geyser basin behind, riding not at the water's edge where tree trunks felled by storms made passage tortuous, but farther back in the woods with a filtered view.

"There was once a great volcano here. The lake fills its crater," Cord observed.

She'd seen obsidian here in the park and other once-molten rocks of the type called igneous but hadn't expected him to know such things.

"My father studied geology," he went on. "He

always carried a pick and bag for samples, on the look-out for color in every streambed."

"Gold?"

"Mostly, a little silver. But his efforts at prospecting in Jackson's Hole barely saw his family through the winters."

"Does he still . . . ?"

Cord shook his head. "He died in 1877, along with my mother."

"I'm sorry . . . You must have been very young."

He cleared his throat. "Yellowstone once had grand volcanoes, with eruptions bigger than Mount Vesuvius when it buried Pompeii and Herculaneum."

That was easy to believe; the evidence was everywhere. Heat from within the earth escaped to warm the pools she and Cord had bathed in at Witch Creek, to boil the colorful mud pots at Thumb. Why, it was even possible that someday this land, which lay deceptively lovely beneath its mantle of evergreen, would again erupt into inferno.

A few hours later, they rounded a point, and Laura spied a long yellow building across an arm of water.

"The hotel," Cord said unnecessarily, for she recognized the accommodation from postcards.

He drew rein and made a move to dismount. "We'll rest a little while here."

Once on the ground, she strolled away to the base

of a bluff where winter storm waves had undercut the lakeshore. Great festooned cross beds of sand stood out in sharp relief in the fifteen-foot-high cliff that headed the beach.

She traced her fingers along a row of pebbles that must have once lain on the bottom of an ancient stream. Though she did not look at Cord, she was aware of him putting together a fishing rod, attaching a metal hook to a line, and digging into the sandy soil for a worm.

Casting far out into the crystal shallows, he began reeling the line in, keeping his thumb close to the guard to apply more drag if necessary.

Laura wandered a circuitous route and sat on a flat rock near Cord's elbow. Far away, Hank Falls's steamboat cut a white wake through blue water, and she was fiercely glad she wasn't aboard.

Rolling up the sleeves of the shirt Cord had given her, she lay back on the sun-warmed rock, propping herself on her arm to follow the hypnotic dance of man and fish. Each time Cord cast, he sent the bait flying toward a deep pool beside a fallen log. It might have been her imagination, but she believed she could see the shapes of fish in the shadows there.

Suddenly the fishing pole jerked. Cord pulled up sharply on the tip. Laura leaped to her feet and stood close enough to see beads of sweat on his brow.

As he worked, she watched the clear water for the first sighting. Flashing in the shallows, the fish was a deep spotted pink and green with a bright orange slash beneath his head.

Cord waded into four inches of water and captured it. "Cutthroat trout," he announced, holding the flapping fish between his hands. "Now you catch one."

"Me?" Laura laughed. "Catch a fish?" Something she'd never tried, though people fished all the time in Lake Michigan.

Cord shook his head, the sun glinting on his ebony hair. "Lady, if you can shoot a bear, you can hook a trout."

He bent and dug around until he found another worm and offered it to her on his open palm. The shiny pink segments twisted and curled as the primitive animal sought escape to the soil.

A few seconds passed.

Cord nodded toward the pole lying on the sand. "Pick that up, find the hook, carefully, and thread this fellow onto it."

Laura's lips set in a line. He was toying with her, and she shouldn't care to impress him, not when she would never see him again after this afternoon.

She reached for the pole.

Hook in her left hand, she extended her right toward Cord's outstretched palm and its wriggling burden. Was that a hint of merriment at the corners of his mouth?

Before she could lose her nerve, Laura grabbed the moist worm, slammed the point of the hook through its narrow body—and into the pad of her thumb.

"Ow!" Pain and a drop of blood's welling were

simultaneous.

Cord's chuckle, which had begun when she seized the worm, choked off as he took in her misfortune. "Let me have it."

"No."

Laura put her thumb to her mouth and sucked the salty blood. The puncture smarted but not as much as her pride. "Stand back," she instructed. "I'm going to catch a fish."

Thirty minutes later, Laura lay in the sun and watched Cord through half-closed, sleepy eyes. The trout she had pulled in lay beside his, the larger of the two.

"Just my luck," he said, "to have rescued a woman who not only kills a bear but shows me up fishing."

With efficient sharp strokes of his knife, Cord sliced open the bellies of the fish and gutted them. A pair of gulls seemed to materialize from nowhere to quarrel over the entrails, strutting and pecking at one another.

Cord gathered wood and built a bonfire on the sand. He cut a strong green sapling from the thicket behind the beach and skewered the trout on the stick. Sitting on his heels, he fed the fire larger sticks until it blazed hotly.

Across the lake in the high mountains, a plume of smoke rose lazily in the afternoon light. "What is that?" Laura pointed.

"Forest fire on Mount Doane. Some of the soldiers are probably trying to put it out. Bit early in the season, but last year's snowpack was only half that of the year before."

"You know a lot about the park."

"Gustavus Doane is the military man who escorted the Washburn Expedition in 1870. His journal of their trip gave him the credit for naming Wonderland." Looking at Laura, Cord cocked a brow. "Those of us who lived in these mountains before they were 'discovered' take issue with some people's terms."

"You said your father was a geologist?"

"Trained at some college in the east. I don't know much about it. He never went back there after he married my mother." Cord prodded the fish with a fork.

"His family didn't approve his choice of a wife?"

Without answering, he removed the stick, beheaded and boned each trout, and served fillets on tin plates.

Laura decided not to question him further and turned her attention to the meal. Tender and flaky, the pink fish reminded her of both salmon and trout.

When they had eaten, Cord set the plates aside.

Time was running out. He would douse the fire and kick sand over it, whistle up Dante from where he cropped grass, and they'd be on their way.

Moving deliberately, Cord came and straddled the rock behind Laura. They'd been as close, closer, when sharing Dante's saddle, but this was different. His hands slid gently over the tops of her shoulders.

For an instant, she thought of pulling away, but the decorum she'd learned in Chicago felt as far away as the city itself. The sun made diamond facets on the lake, shining in her eyes until the beauty made her ache with mingled joy and sadness.

Cord drew her closer, and she thought he might have murmured her name. The afternoon breeze calmed and turned Thumb into a mirror. His arms came around her, and they watched the play of ripples lapping the sand.

"Why did you ride away from the steamboat?" she asked.

"Fishing," he replied solemnly.

"Fishing!"

"You're fishing." Cord turned her to him, put a hand beneath her chin, and tilted her face up. "You want to hear me say I wasn't ready to give you up yet."

For the rest of her life, Laura promised, she would remember this, that little halting space between knowing Cord was going to touch her and feeling his lips, warm against her temple.

"You want to hear me say how beautiful you were when I saw you rising naked out of the pool like Venus."

Cord couldn't decide whether her indrawn gasp was one of innocence or the calculated art of a practiced harlot. They'd been through so much in such a short time, cheated death and shared the incomparable beauty of his land.

He told himself it didn't matter who they were or where they went tomorrow. He wanted to take her down with him on his sheepskin bedroll, to keep her with him all of another night and another, to watch warm cherry light flicker over the smooth-looking skin he'd seen at the pool last evening.

The soft cotton of his shirt enveloped her, a powerful intimacy that made him want to protect her, from outlaws and anyone else who might challenge his claim.

She clung to his shoulders, and Cord heard what might have been a sob catch in her throat. The little breathy sound reminded him of another who had whispered his name on St. Paul's spring air.

One who waited for him at the Lake Hotel.

Laura had never wanted anything more than to have Cord teach her what happened between a man and a woman, but she felt him hesitate again, the way he had last night.

More of that mystery boiling beneath his surface.

She drew back and watched his expression alter, the proud ascetic planes turning harder.

"Cord . . ." Her voice came out trembling and husky; she'd never heard it that way. The sun slipped behind a cloud, and the shade in the pine-smelling woods deepened.

He closed his eyes, as though they stung. For a fleeting instant, Laura thought his emotion might have been pain.

Reaching a tentative hand, she touched his denim-clad thigh.

He jerked his leg away, though he still touched her shoulders.

Laura looked at the silent forest and the still mirror of lake. The two of them alone for days, her nerves on edge from the savagery of the outlaws and being in the backwoods. Had she imagined he wanted her?

Her woman's instinct believed he did, but he would never beg or steal a kiss the way her Chicago suitors had. No, Cord would be hopeless at drawing-room games. Not for him the niceties of courtship; with him it would be all or nothing.

Well, at least she knew the answer to the questions cascading through her. There was nothing for them, no meeting place for a mountain man and the mistress of Fielding House.

And though he had been the one to pull back, she could at least hold her head up the way Aunt Fanny said a woman must.

"Let us go, then," Laura said in a low voice.

Cord took his hands from her as if his palms had been burned, rose, and stalked away. Like a nightmare in which her arms and legs were too heavy to move, she sat where she was and watched him go to Dante. The sun reappeared from behind the clouds, slanting through the pines.

She heard Cord speak gently to his horse. The contrast was more terrible when he spoke to her in a distant tone. "It's an hour to the Lake Hotel. I'll have you there by dark."

Cord guided Dante toward the shoulder of the well-traveled road along the lakeshore, while Laura held on behind him with her hands at his waist. His rigid posture made her feel as though he were made of wood.

Across royal blue water, the Lake Hotel stood on a promontory. Three stories high, its yellow made a bright contrast to the forest.

Though their last moments together were slipping away like the sun from the afternoon sky, Cord's eyes remained on the wheeling gulls. "Not much farther."

With a drumming of horses' hooves, a group of blue-coated cavalrymen overtook and passed them at a gallop, casting a cursory glance in their direction. Fishermen walked up the shoulder of the road carrying rods and buckets. The youngest of their group, a boy of perhaps six, had the honor of carrying their stringer of trout.

Laura looked away from this reminder of their angling expedition.

A horse and wagon passed with a load of sight-seers chatting about their tour of the Grand Canyon of the Yellowstone. Cyclists pedaled in the gathering darkness.

Dante reached the stretch of Grand Loop Road that ran along the shore; a rustic wooden sign indicated the hotel. Beside a dock that stretched a hundred feet into the lake, the *Alexandra* was tied up alongside stacks of wood for stoking her firebox. Adjacent, a group of smaller piers were home to a flotilla of canoes and wooden rowboats outfitted for fishing.

The lake faded from ultramarine to purple.

Cord turned Dante up the hotel drive. Atop the widow's walk on the third-floor roof, a man and woman stood with their heads close together, silhouettes against the darkening sky. In the drive alongside the long wooden verandah, a stagecoach discharged passengers. The glow of electric lights beckoned inside the glass doors to the main lobby.

"I don't even know your last name," Laura said.

Cord reined Dante in. "I'd take you to the servants' entrance," he was polite, correct, "but I don't know where it is."

Laura slid to the ground.

"That won't be necessary." She managed to match his impersonal note and marched through the main entrance into the brilliantly lit lobby.

CHAPTER SIX
JUNE 23

Forrest Fielding regarded the hand he'd been dealt with disgust. The card table in the lobby of the Lake Hotel had been in the sun when he had rounded out a foursome for poker; now night had fallen.

He had entertained such hopes on the train west, playing and winning the big pots in the paneled parlor car on the Northern Pacific, thinking his recent spate of bad luck had been about to change.

Until three days ago when Sergeant Larry Nevers had hailed the stage.

How could his proper daughter have deceived him? Well, perhaps *proper* wasn't the word for Laura. He often saw in her a longing for adventure that might have been acceptable in a son. Like the plainspoken way she rejected Joseph Kane and other suitors, and the fire in her eyes when she viewed photographer Henry Jackson's studies of Wyoming.

"Look at these mountains." She'd held out the

book and pointed to the Teton Range. "Black and white can't even suggest the myriad colors there must be. And a frozen image doesn't convey the way those clouds must form and disappear."

Forrest looked again at his hand: a two, five, and nine of hearts; a jack of diamonds; and the ace of spades. He could discard and draw, but somehow he didn't have the spirit to do more than fold.

From across the table, Hank Falls's piercing dark eyes fixed on Forrest, his cards fanned loosely in his long-fingered hands. The tulip-shaped electric light mounted on a redwood column shone on his blond hair.

Hank had talked him into playing, after Forrest had spent the last three evenings rocking on the porch, waiting for news while he watched the light die over the lake.

"I guess this wasn't such a good idea," he told Hank and the two men from Memphis who'd joined their game.

Pushing his cards away, he rubbed his chest. His roast beef dinner lay like a rock in his stomach, the same as everything he'd sent down lately.

Laura should be here, dressed in that red brocade she'd worn on New Year's Eve to receive at Fielding House, with Violet's exquisite cameo at the neckline. They'd ushered in 1900 with fanfare.

Forrest closed his eyes, while he tried to push away the image of sparkling green eyes turned sightless, vultures pecking and stripping away his daughter's flesh. Manfred Resnick of the Pinkerton Agency, who had arrived yesterday to investigate, had told him about the bodies beside the abandoned stagecoach. Thankfully, Laura had not been with them, but where could she be?

The orchestra of hotel employees, who waited tables and made beds during the day shift, played "Lorena," that haunting tune, and he imagined Laura dancing with Hank Falls. The top of her head would not reach Hank's shoulder.

Forrest sighed. It would take a forceful and forthright man like Hank to tame his daughter, if only she were found safe.

He excused himself from the card table and trudged across the lobby toward the small barroom, built in the hotel in spite of general prohibition in the park. He ordered Kentucky bourbon, neat, and studied with approval the selection of liquor behind the bar. It was really quite remarkable how good the hospitality was, considering the wilderness outside the front door.

Draining his glass, Forrest contemplated having another and rejected it. A rocking chair on the hotel's front porch called to him; he would spend the hours between now and bedtime torn between wanting to cry for Laura and wanting to pinch her head off for putting herself in danger.

Ten feet from the door, he swerved to avoid a young boy hurrying precipitously into the lobby. The kid wore trousers and an oversized blue shirt with rolled sleeves, and carried a dirty brown coat under one arm.

As they collided, the boy's hat tipped from his head. Brown hair spilled in untidy waves over slender shoulders.

Laura recognized her father when he gasped, "I thought you must be dead!"

He threw his arms around her, and all she could think was that he must have been terrified, or he would not let his silk waistcoat contact her filthy jacket.

Thinking how many years it had been since they embraced, she closed her eyes and pressed her cheek against the scratchy lapel of his wool suit coat. He smelled the same as she remembered, of cigar smoke, bourbon, and a violet-scented preparation he used after shaving. Funny, she had watched him age day by day, but after just a few weeks apart, she noticed his paunch from Chicago steaks and his matching round bald head.

When they broke apart, she blinked in the bright electric lamps that decorated each dark post in the wide lobby. The big room was all wood, redwood paneling and dark beams holding up the white-painted ceiling. Polished yellow pine gleamed underfoot, reflecting the orchestra and couples dancing to the lively rhythm of Scott Joplin's "Maple Leaf Rag." The men wore dark suits or army dress uniforms, while the ladies were decked out in colorful silks.

Laura thought of Cord riding Dante on through the night.

Forrest snapped his fingers for a waiter. "You must be starving."

"I had something earlier." She had trouble reconciling the image of trout roasting over an open fire against the aspics, pastries, and frozen dainties she'd heard were served here.

"Nonsense," he insisted. "You'll eat something."

Before she could demur, a man approached Forrest from behind. Rapier-thin, with dark blond hair and a sharp nose, he seemed vaguely familiar.

An equally slender blond woman in a purple satin gown, a match for her eyes, walked up with him. She looked with disdain upon Laura's grimy trousers and Cord's too-large shirt that hung on her. "Where in the world did she come from?"

In the silence that fell in the crowded lobby, the tall man ignored the question. A moment later, the woman stalked away, her heels tapping.

Laura hadn't been able to comb her hair after the wind had knotted it, and in her unconventional dress, she was sure she looked frightful to guests who'd dressed for dinner. Her father was also taking in her sunburned face and arms, as if he wished she'd stumbled in out of the wilderness in a brocade gown. He hadn't even asked how she'd gotten to the hotel.

"Your father has been very worried," the thin man said in a tenor voice that grated on Laura's nerves. "We sent a military posse out looking for you days ago. Tonight, they rode in empty-handed." He looked down his narrow nose, as if she were at fault for the cavalry not finding her.

She thought of the cloud of dust raised when the soldiers had passed her and Cord on the road; they'd been looking for a helpless woman rather than a wiry boy on a sleek black horse.

Laura's father also bore an impatient look. "We are going to have a discussion, young lady. I never authorized your traveling alone by stagecoach through the backwoods."

How could she have thought things might be different? As soon as the initial shock of seeing her safe was past, he was back to his high-handed ways.

Laura straightened her spine. "I am not such a young lady." Her gaze swept over her father, the imperious man, and the considerable audience their altercation had gathered. "If you will excuse me, I am very tired."

The interloper bowed from the waist. "You and your family have the Absaroka Suite on the third floor," he said smoothly, "with the best breezes. There's a view of the lake and the mountains from your window, along with the ravens that roost in the tops of the pines."

"How charming." She was too exhausted to sound pleasant.

"And how thoughtless of me," Forrest's hand closed on her wrist, "for failing to make a proper introduction. Laura, this is Hank Falls."

She gasped.

Hank bowed again and tried to snag her hand. She drew it back and stared up at him in disbelief. How could this haughty stranger have taken the place of the man she had manufactured in her mind?

As though he read her thoughts, her father slid his grip to her elbow and pointed her toward the stairs. "Here. As you are tired, you're to go right to bed."

He guided her up to a third-floor bedroom with a brass bed, heavy wardrobe, and bureau topped by a mirror. Pale champagne striping accented the wall-paper. She assumed the door on the opposite wall opened into the suite's parlor.

"It will be better if we talk in the morning about how you came to arrive here." He barely brushed a kiss on her cheek. "Rest well."

He closed the door.

She leaned against it.

How could he have no more curiosity about what she had been through? How could he not ask what she had seen at the coach and after?

She looked at the bed, longing to collapse into a sleep so deep she might forget the past few days. But nature called, so she went back into the hall to find the bathroom.

Above the lavatory, a posted sign indicated that for a nominal charge of fifteen cents one might order a tub and hot water brought to their room.

Back down the wide hall, she descended the stairs and went to the front desk. The orchestra still played, and a young man with a baritone voice sang.

A pair of strong-backed boys, probably some of the college students working for the summer, carried a heavy tin tub up to Laura's room. Then they ferried up buckets of cold water until the tub was three-quarters full. Last, a steaming teakettle of hot water was delivered, and Laura was left alone.

She unwrapped a cake of lavender soap that smelled gentler than the harsh bar of lye Cord had given her at the hot spring.

Her mouth twisted, and she stripped off his shirt and threw it on the floor.

Blinking fiercely, she shampooed and washed herself with vigor. She would not think about him, not now or ever. Not imagine that he stood in her doorway, taking in her nakedness with eyes that appreciated it. Not wish the trail from Jackson's Hole to Yellowstone had gone on forever.

Tears teetering behind her eyelids, she rose from the tub and toweled off as roughly as she had washed. Throwing back the chenille bedspread and wool blanket to expose clean white sheets, she prepared to climb into the luxury of a real bed.

The linens were surprisingly soft for a wilderness outpost. Though she never slept without a nightgown, tonight she slid between the covers naked. Her father had not even commented on her lack of luggage, and she had been too preoccupied to mention it.

Tired as she was, she expected to fall asleep immediately. Instead, she lay staring at the square of light on the ceiling above a glass transom. The clock on the heavy wooden dresser ticked, marking the minutes toward midnight.

Each time Laura closed her eyes, she saw Cord's blue eyes against an even bluer sky. After an hour, she gave up fighting it and allowed herself to remember. Moving her arms and legs restlessly on the smooth sheets, she felt a heavy fullness in the palms of her hands.

Tears welled again, rising behind the dam she'd built. For as much as she hated to admit it, she longed to be with Cord tonight.

The dam broke.

Laura lay on her back, shaking while tears ran into her hair. How could she still want to see him when he'd turned away without a backward glance?

If only she had not lost her journal in the raging waters of the Snake. If she had her leather-bound book, she would get up, find pen and ink and nib, and pour out everything that had happened since leaving the Union Pacific train and boarding the stage.

A soft tap at the bedroom door brought her up with a start. She retrieved Cord's shirt from where she had dropped it beside the bed and used it to dash at her wet face.

Another knock. God, not her father, after he had promised to leave her alone until morning.

"Who is it?" Laura padded across the room and pressed her ear against the heavy dark wood, while she wrapped herself in the shirt.

An indistinct voice murmured something she didn't understand. Slowly, she pulled the door open a crack, peering out into the hallway.

A warm soft shape nearly bowled her over, and she smelled the floral scent of too much Stolen Sweets perfume.

"Constance!"

"Laura!"

Opening the door wide, she fell into the arms of her cousin from Chicago, Constance Devon. Both only children, they had grown up playing together.

As feminine and fragile as Laura was tough, Constance was two years younger and at least four inches shorter than Laura's five feet, five inches. In the glow of electric light, Constance's dark hair made a silken veil around her porcelain face. Her blue eyes were not the clear sky blue of Cord's . . .

Laura clamped her teeth together.

. . . but pansy blue, the purple blue of winter flowers against snow, a shade that matched the silk wrapper belted snugly around Constance's ample curves. She was a devotee of The Princess Bust Cream, "unrivaled for the enlargement of the bosom."

"Father didn't say you were here," Laura groused. "Of course, I shouldn't be surprised, for he seldom has much to say to me besides giving me household orders."

"I went to bed early with a headache, and Mother took a dyspepsia powder," Constance declared. "We've been so worried for you since we heard about the stage attack. I just overheard Uncle Forrest telling Mother you were here safe."

"Then why didn't she . . . ?"

"Because he told her to let you sleep. You know she listens to him the way he wishes you would." Constance's expression conveyed her own frustration. Since her father had died when she was very young, Forrest Fielding's influence had been the dominant force in her life, as well as his daughter's. Even his younger sister, Fanny, lived largely underneath his shadow.

As though there was no point in reopening an old wound, Constance began to speak of other things. "How on earth did you get away from the stagecoach robbers? I heard the driver was killed." Her eyes were bright with a mix of trepidation and vicarious excitement.

Laura sat down heavily on the woolen blanket, feeling it scratch her bare legs. How like Constance not to notice that she had been crying, to assume she was all right because she always had been before.

She'd even held her head high when some people assumed Joseph Kane had thrown her over early in the spring. After all, what woman would turn him down? That had been just before Constance left for St. Paul for a long visit with Aunt Florence and Uncle David.

Laura knew the couple well, short and round like two peas that had occupied the same pod too long. Their staunchly Presbyterian attitude would never have allowed someone even remotely like Cord to sweep in on their niece's life.

With a sinking feeling, Laura realized she couldn't talk about Cord. The Victorian age might be out of vogue, with a new century of progress ahead, but it was quite another thing for an unmarried woman to spend three nights alone with a man in the mountains. The idea would shock Constance, Aunt Fanny, and her father so profoundly that none of them might ever look at her the same way again.

"I managed to hide out during the attack at the coach," she said slowly, knowing she would have to tell whatever story she wove many times. "Then I walked thought the woods and a man and his wife picked me up and brought me. They weren't stopping here, just going on to Montana."

Constance sighed. "I imagined you on some great adventure. You were always the one who wanted things wild while I . . ." She blushed, ducked her head, and fiddled with a ring on her left hand.

Laura had not seen it before, a garnet set with seed pearls on a gold band.

Constance smiled and turned the stone; it sparkled. Her manicured hands made Laura want to hide the nails she'd broken on the trail.

"I met a man in St. Paul," Constance confessed with a shy sort of rapture.

"Tell me!" Laura suppressed guilt at her own lack of candor.

Constance took a breath. "William is very handsome and such a gentleman." She toyed again with the ring. "Aunt Florence and Uncle David said it was unseemly the way he gave me a betrothal ring so quickly, but who cares what they think? William asked Mother to bring me out to see his country, and she said yes."

"You've turned down many proposals. What's different about this William?"

Constance's expression grew even softer. "I've been kissed before," she mused, "but when William held me, it was as if he were more alive than all the rest."

CHAPTER SEVEN
JUNE 24

After Constance returned to her room, Laura still could not sleep. The little clock on the bureau ticked loudly, marking the hour as midnight passed.

Part of her felt betrayed that her father and aunt did not care enough to welcome her back with tears and hugs. Especially Aunt Fanny, who was the closest thing to a mother she had. It was as though they suspected some terrible violation a woman would keep to herself.

All right, it would make it easier to hide her secret. With each hour, she grew more determined never to reveal the complex and confusing experience meeting Cord had been.

When morning came, she would borrow clothes from her cousin and her aunt and face the world with shoulders straight. She would relate how kind the couple from Montana had been when they found her wandering after she fled from the stagecoach. But should she say she had witnessed Angus Spiner's murder and the outlaw's demise, or pretend she had run blindly into the willow bottoms?

No, she should describe the outlaw and have him caught before he came after her here at the hotel, attacked some other unsuspecting person . . . or hunted down Cord.

She almost wished her invented story were true. If she'd never met him, she would not be imagining fanciful ways they might meet again.

Though she had not believed she could sleep, she realized she'd drifted off when a tapping inserted itself into her consciousness. It took a moment to swim up from a dream of fishing beside blue water.

Her eyes felt gluey, but she forced them open. The third-floor window she'd raised last night was still open. Instead of the evening breeze that had soothed her, this morning it let in cold air. "What is it?" she called to whoever knocked at her door.

"There's a man here to see you!" She recognized Aunt Fanny's voice.

"What man?"

Naked, Laura rolled over and pushed herself to a sitting position on the side of the bed. A black-and-white photograph of the Grand Canyon and the Lower Falls of the Yellowstone hung opposite, signed by photographer F. Jay Haynes. Looking at the river, tumbling as white and fast over the rocks as her emotions, she swung her bare feet to the cold hardwood floor.

"Let me in," Fanny insisted across the open transom.

"A minute." Laura reached with a trembling hand to the floor where her dirty trousers and Cord's shirt lay crumpled. Banishing the thought of him, she covered herself and ran a hand through her tangled hair.

Then she stood a moment more, postponing the inevitable. Outside, a raven perched in a pine, its dark head cocked to one side. Beyond, Yellowstone Lake lay silver-gray like poured metal in the cloudy morning light.

"Laura!"

Barefoot, she went and opened the door.

Aunt Fanny smothered her in familiar softness and the scent of tea roses. "Land sakes, I was so afraid for you."

With a sinking heart, Laura realized that despite Fanny's acquiescence to Forrest's wish not to disturb her last night, this morning her aunt would insist on knowing everything.

"I'm here, safe, and that's what matters." She hoped her tone was reassuring.

Laura's aunt was even more buxom than her daughter. Still a pale-skinned beauty at forty-seven, Fanny had dark hair virtually untouched by gray. Dressed in a morning gown of black satin with a white collar and cuffs, she tossed her scarlet, fringed shawl onto the bed.

Squinting, she took in Laura's trousers and wrinkled shirt. "Laws, but you could be arrested for wearing men's clothing." She looked into the empty wardrobe. "You have nothing to wear."

"My suitcase was ruined in the stage robbery."

"Thank goodness Constance brought two trunks." Fanny recovered briskly, shaking her head and setting her gold ear drops in motion. "I can alter her dresses to fit you."

She gauged Laura's slender waist and hips to see how much she would have to take in the dresses designed to fit her daughter. In anticipation of dressing her niece, she seemed to have forgotten Laura's male visitor.

"Who was it that wanted to see me?" Not Cord, for he thought she was a serving girl, and he didn't know her last name.

A line appeared between Fanny's black brows. "A man with the Pinkerton Agency."

Before she could tell her aunt to put him off until she had time to work on her story, a little man broke the bonds of good manners and slipped through the door Fanny had left ajar.

"I'm Manfred Resnick, Miss Fielding." No more than an inch taller than she, the youthful agent wore a suit with a chalk pinstripe over his wiry frame. "I'm investigating the robbery and murders near Jackson for the stage line." He looked around at the blue-and-white china washbasin and the unmade bed. Next, he appraised Laura with the same analytical expression.

It took her a few seconds to realize that Manfred Resnick was blind on his right side, his useless walleye dull as if there were a film over it.

Thinking only of getting him out of her room, she

bent and pulled on her boots without stockings, then walked toward the door.

Aunt Fanny gathered her scarlet shawl. Beads of black jet tapped together as she followed Laura and Resnick down the hall.

At the top of the stairs, Resnick paused and ran a hand through his slicked-back brown hair. "Thank you, Mrs. Devon," he said, with an air of finality.

He started down, apparently assuming Laura would follow.

She gripped the carved wooden rail and looked out through the oval glass window at the park visitors queuing for morning tours. In the rear yard, wagons and stages waited, while horses stamped restlessly. With a sigh, she went down the stairs behind Resnick.

He evidently did not think of offering the restorative cup of coffee Laura longed for, but led the way to a windowed alcove. A felt-topped gaming table and straight-backed chairs were the only furniture.

The investigator sat down and shuffled a pack of cards. The smooth whir of the deck falling into place was hypnotic. "You saw them die?" He spoke without taking his eyes from the cards.

Laura looked out the window at a lone rower on the lake. Something about the powerful shape of his shoulders was reassuring.

The detective waited.

"I saw two men ride up to the stagecoach," she allowed.

"Descriptions?" She'd thought he would take notes,

but he continued to handle the playing cards.

"One of them was tall, thin, blond, wearing a long coat, he rode a palomino horse. The other, shorter, stouter, in a plaid coat and riding a chestnut. They shot the driver, Angus Spiner."

"Did you see who killed Frank Worth?" Resnick's tone was more kind.

"Who?" Was this the man she had watched Cord shoot?

"Your man in the plaid coat."

"I . . ." She looked down at her hands. "No."

"If you saw the tall man again, would you recognize him?"

"I'm not sure," Laura murmured. In the same instant, the strange aversion she'd felt last night in the lobby became clear. "I'll tell you, though . . . " She leaned forward. "Even with a bandana mask, he looked a lot like Mr. Falls."

"Falls?" Resnick pulled a pad and well-used pencil from his breast pocket.

"Hank Falls. The manager of this hotel."

He wrote something illegible and raised his good eye to meet hers. "Who brought you to Yellowstone?"

"A man and woman." Laura gained conviction in the telling. "They were traveling to Montana."

"Names?"

"Oh . . ." She cast about, looking at the common objects surrounding them, a table and chairs, playing cards, and bright stacks of poker chips. Paging through all the names she'd ever known and trying to choose some for the faceless people he would next ask her to describe.

"Miss Fielding?" Resnick's pen poised.

The little room seemed stuffy, and Laura was glad for the window and the slow progress of the rower on the lake.

"I'm sorry." She put her hands over her face. "I was so distraught I cannot recall."

Cord stopped rowing and laid the oars in the bottom of the boat. His shoulders and back burned from the self-imposed exertion.

He wiped his brow on his blue cotton sleeve and found his tired eyes stinging from salty sweat. It didn't help that dawn light had penetrated his room at the Lake Hotel and found him still awake, angry and resentful at having tossed for hours.

It was Laura who had kept Cord from sleep; or rather the lack of Laura, as he had drifted off repeatedly, only to awaken and find himself reaching for her. In his comfortable hotel room, bathed and sleeping on clean sheets, he had wished he were still on the road with Laura in his bedroll.

Lifting the oars, he pulled toward the dock. When the wooden boat bumped against the pier, he climbed out and secured the painter to a metal cleat.

On the dock, he took advantage of the opportunity for a closer look at Hank Falls's gaudy steamboat.

Forward of the paddle wheel, velvet curtains covered the windows of a private cabin where he'd heard Falls lived aboard after the days' excursions.

Cord walked across the Grand Loop Road between the hotel and the lake and tried to put things into perspective. He needed all his wits to deal with business, and a serving girl like Laura could not figure into his plans. He couldn't imagine the midwestern beauty he was to meet shooting a bear or fishing with him. No, she was the consummate definition of a lady.

Cord pushed open the door into the Lake Hotel lobby. Last night he'd put off asking at the front desk, telling himself he was too exhausted. This morning, he had no more excuses.

With resolve, he approached the high mahogany counter and made his inquiry.

The eager desk clerk rummaged in a metal box that held a card for each of the guests. He raised his dark head. "I'm sorry, sir, but I don't believe your party has checked in."

Cord thanked him, shocked by his profound sense of relief.

The day stretched before him like an open meadow where he might give Dante his head.

He considered a shave and haircut; the barbershop off the lobby had been closed last night, but he really must take his weapons and register them as required at the army post down on the shore.

Instead, he stepped outside.

The morning clouds lifted further, and the sun

shone onto his face. Its warmth brought back the memory of checkered light filtering down through the trees onto Laura's hair.

Turning toward the cabins that housed the serving staff, he found his feet moving faster along the well-worn path. At the head of the row, a larger frame building wore a sign that labeled it as the laundry and administration building. Opening the door, Cord caught the aroma of starch.

Laura was probably already at her first day's work. He imagined her in the blue-and-white striped uniform of a maid, changing linens somewhere inside the hotel or loading trays with breakfast to be taken into the dining room.

"Excuse me." Cord approached the desk where a matronly woman sat copying figures into a ledger. "I'm looking for Laura . . ."

"Laura who?"

Indeed. He had been so secretive on the trail that of course she had not volunteered a last name. Nor had he asked.

Cord held out his hand near shoulder height. "About this tall, brown hair . . . came in last evening."

The woman's faded blue eyes softened, as he blundered on, "A little slip of woman . . ."

"I'm sorry," she said. "I know all our workers, and we don't have anyone named Laura."

"She's lying."

Captain Quenton Feddors listened to Pinkerton man Manfred Resnick, who faced him across the desk in the Lake Soldier Station. "I don't know about what or why," Resnick went on, "but Laura Fielding's story doesn't ring true."

Feddors spit tobacco juice into a tarnished brass spittoon and wiped his sparse goatee. He balanced his straight-backed wooden chair on two legs and looked out the post window. The log building fronted an open field overlooking Yellowstone Lake, a short walk north of the hotel.

"Lying?" At last, there might be some excitement on his watch as commandant of the First Cavalry's garrison. Since Superintendent Oscar James Brown had left the park and his replacement, George William Goode, was not due until July 23, Feddors was enjoying his month of power.

"How do ya know she's lying?"

"The hesitation." Resnick shrugged a thin shoulder. "The way she won't look at me straight."

Perhaps Laura Fielding was just trying not to stare at the bad eye. Feddors was having trouble with that himself.

Resnick crossed his arms over his chest. "At Pinkerton, we're trained to question people."

"If you're so good at reading folks, suh," Feddors said, "I should get you to help me out with the men heah." In the months since he'd come out from Tennessee, he was finding the Yellowstone post to be the most frustrating of his twenty-year career.

"What's wrong?"

"What's not?" Feddors rejoined.

He had found the soldiers, spread over the park in twelve remote stations, to be an undisciplined and untrained lot. And though every man carried a red book of regulations that forbade the use of alcohol, it was rampant.

"The enlisted men go AWOL to the saloons and whorehouses in Gardiner." Feddors referred to the small rough town four miles north of Fort Yellowstone, down the Gardner River named for a different pioneer family with a distinct spelling. "The troops even bring women into the park to the stations. They know females are forbidden, except for tourists viewing the facility."

Feddors could see by the dull look on Resnick's ferret face that he wasn't interested in the garrison's troubles.

As he leaned back, Feddors's uniform blouse gaped between brass buttons over his stomach. Reaching to smooth the blue wool together, he advanced his theory about the stagecoach murders. "Did Laura Fielding at least get a good look at them Injuns?"

"The stagecoach wasn't attacked by Indians," Resnick protested. "There were two white men. Frank Worth was found dead. Miss Fielding said the other one was tall and blond."

"You said she was lying. They had Injun troubles down in Jackson. In '95, folks left their homes and circled up their wagons at Wilson Ranch."

Resnick paced with small rapid steps.

Feddors went on, "One of the reasons they brought in the cavalry in '86 to oversee the park was because the Nez Perce came through in '77 killing tourists and ranchers for no reason."

"If that were so, why did it take them nine years? The Nez Perce War is ancient history."

Feddors's cheeks heated. To him, it was yesterday; he'd been a boy of fifteen the summer he'd watched the Nez Perce sweep through Yellowstone.

Resnick stopped pacing. "Twenty-three years is long enough for people to forget the Nez Perce lost their homes in Washington and Oregon Territory. They've never been allowed back on those lands."

"Are you defending them?" It gave small comfort to know he outweighed the young detective and could throw him over his shoulder if he cared to take the trouble. "The Nez Perce would never have been driven from their homes if they hadn't been killing white men with their bows and arrows."

"Worth wasn't killed with a bow and arrow, but a forty-five," Resnick drilled. "Maybe his partner shot him."

Feddors dropped his chair legs to the floor with a thump. "Maybe the Indian had one."

Cord pushed open the door of the soldier station. With

his Winchester over his shoulder, he showed his pistol to a soldier behind a desk. "I need to declare these."

"Nice-looking Colt." The captain, by his insignia, sounded pleasant enough, but his smile did not extend to his dark eyes. He wore a waxed mustache and straggling dun-colored goatee that failed to offset his thinning hair.

Beyond him, a wiry man in a pinstriped suit leaned against the chinked log wall, hands in his pockets.

Cord placed the Colt on the table. The captain lifted it and checked the chamber. "A forty-five." He raised the weapon and sighted at the lake through the open door. "Feddors," he said abruptly. "Quenton Feddors. In charge of all army personnel in the park."

With a whole sentence on the air, Cord detected a drawl, Tennessee or northern Georgia. He also noted how Feddors's eyes followed him as he unshouldered his Winchester and set it on the desk.

"Sutton," he offered, "William Cordon Sutton," giving what he thought of as the double-barreled version.

The other man observed both Cord and Captain Feddors without introducing himself.

"Any particular reason you didn't stop by the south entrance and have these weapons sealed according to park regulations?" Feddors sounded sharp.

"My horse got lost," Cord related with a straight face.

He was immediately sorry, for Feddors let his Colt down onto the wooden table with a clatter. "Nevers!"

he called.

A young sergeant stuck his head in from the rear room. Of medium build with a broad open face, wavy brown hair, and thick glasses, he nodded briefly at Cord.

"Fix these weapons," Feddors ordered.

Nevers turned away and came back with a roll of red tape. He picked up the Colt.

While Cord watched, the soldier tied the mechanism with the tape. Then he lit a wooden match and melted a dollop of red sealing wax onto the knot; if anyone took off the tape, it would be obvious. "Sir, anyone traveling with weapons can be stopped by a soldier at any time for an inspection."

Feddors chuckled. "Anyone failing inspection will be marched to Mammoth for a hearing before the acting superintendent. That's me, suh. Or if anyone leaves a campfire burning. Or defaces the formations. The penalty begins at expulsion from the park and goes up from there." He gestured toward Nevers. "Tell the man what happened to that poacher we caught a week ago."

"He was force marched from near Yellowstone Lake up to Mammoth. The captain presided at his hearing and then personally horsewhipped him before expelling him permanently from the park." He spoke in a monotone.

Cord kept his expression grave. "I don't think you'll have any problem with me." He hated being obsequious, but it seemed the best way to handle the little captain's Napoleon complex.

Feddors was studying him. "There was a stage-coach attack down near Menor's Ferry in Jackson's Hole a few days ago. Couple of people killed."

Cord hesitated, then figured it was safe to admit; the man who'd rented him the rowboat this morning had talked of little else. "I heard," he said. "A terrible thing."

"One of the outlaws was killed with a forty-five." Feddors aimed a stream of tobacco juice at a brass spittoon. "Gun like this." He ran a finger along Cord's Colt.

"I bought that in Salt Lake." Cord noticed that the man against the wall was on alert. "Andrew Stanislow had maybe fifteen guns that would shoot that same kind of bullet." The big Russian had laid out piece after piece onto the worn wooden counter for inspection. "Not to mention all the other weapon sources in the world."

"Yeah." Feddors shot a look at the man beside the fireplace.

Cord nodded at a Cavalry Model Colt hanging in a holster on the wall. "Don't all the men in your garrison carry a forty-five?"

Feddors became absorbed in watching Sergeant Nevers securing the trigger of Cord's Winchester. With a jerky efficiency, Nevers pressed a pad of paper with carbons toward Cord for his signature. He gave him a smudged copy of the acknowledgment that unsealed weapons were prohibited in the national park.

Cord pocketed the paper.

"By the way," Feddors said, "while you and your horse were lost, you didn't happen to engage in some poaching with those unsealed weapons? Some of my men found a mess of dead game down south . . . including a grizzly."

Hot words rose to Cord's lips, but he managed to speak in a mild tone. "Poaching is illegal."

"Last I checked." Feddors placed a hand on the red leather-bound book he carried in the breast pocket of his blue tunic. Gold letters indicated that the book contained the park regulations.

"I didn't shoot a bear or any other game," Cord said truthfully. He'd killed a man, though, albeit one who'd behaved like an animal.

Through the open door, he saw sunshine on water and grass waving in the summer wind. He took up his useless guns and moved toward the bright day.

As he passed through the doorway, he heard the man against the wall say, "Don't ask me how I know, but that one's lying, too."

Cord shook hands with banker Edgar Young outside the Lake Hotel barbershop. Edgar's boyish, freckled face was topped by a head of wild russet hair that would defy the cutter's craft. Rubbing the beard he'd decided was about to come off, Cord wished he'd had a chance to get to know his backer better before coming to the negotiating table.

"I've been wondering where you've been," Edgar said.

"I checked your room earlier." Cord did not acknowledge that he was a day or so later than he'd expected.

"Things are not going as smoothly as we had hoped." Edgar's tone was grave.

"We knew this was an uphill battle," Cord said. "The railroad's managed to control the park concessions through dummy corporations run from eastern drawing rooms for the past twenty years."

Edgar nodded. "While they lobbied Washington for permission to build branch lines into the park."

Only recently had the executives of the Northern Pacific become sufficiently frustrated to want to lay off some of the properties.

"Is Norman Hagen representing the railroad?" Cord had been introduced to the big red-bearded blond beneath high chandeliers in the paneled lobby of St. Paul's Ryan Hotel. "He and I hit it off well in the spring . . . that is, I thought so."

"He's here, all right. With a nasty fellow by the name of Hopkins Chandler."

Cord led the way into the small shop, empty save for a barber in a black suit, stropping his straight razor while waiting for business. Edgar climbed into a barber chair, and Cord took the one adjacent.

Edgar's dark eyes were serious. "The news is that Lake Hotel manager Hank Falls wants to buy the place out from under you."

Cord swore an oath that made the barber flinch. "When you approached me in Salt Lake last spring and offered to finance out of your bank in Great Falls, you made it sound like we could buy the hotel without opposition."

"My sources didn't know then that Falls would make an offer. He's making it sound like you don't know a thing about managing a hotel."

"Did you tell them . . . ?"

"Of course I told them about the Excalibur." Edgar's voice rose, and Cord was glad there were no other customers in the shop.

He thought of driving up Temple Square in a four-in-hand, amid the streetcars and clouds of dust in Salt Lake City. Pulling up under the porte cochere that accommodated at least a dozen carriages, while the liveried doorman made order out of chaos. Inside, the tall marble lobby of the Excalibur would have echoed save for the fine rugs and tapestries strategically placed to mute the voices of hundreds of travelers.

The pride Cord felt in owning half of the finest hotel in Salt Lake City had palled lately with the realization that the business was not big enough for both him and his adopted brother, Thomas Bryce. Cord loved Thomas's father, Aaron—Cord's father now, too—the man who had taken in a young refugee of the Nez Perce War and treated him as his own. But Thomas, a fervent Mormon who stored food against the apocalypse and kept his plain-looking wife, Anna, constantly pregnant, had never approved of anything Cord did, from the day he arrived in the big town house in rags.

Though Excalibur was Cord's creation, the banks had refused to loan money to a man who was one-quarter Nez Perce. Therefore, the hotel officially resided in the name of Thomas Bryce, a fact that filled Cord with more bitterness and humiliation each day.

The barber approached with a warm towel in his hands. His chocolate-colored face wore the blank, thousand-yard stare that Cord had taught his hotel employees signified a good servant.

"Cut it short and shave all but the mustache," Cord instructed politely. It would make the scar on his face more prominent, but he wanted to appear as well groomed as possible.

"I'm thinking of growing one." Edgar fingered his clean-shaven upper lip. "Maybe it would make me look older."

Cord ignored him, still seething at the news he had competition.

"I needed you here days ago." Edgar tapped his leather boot on the foot rail of the barber chair.

Preoccupied, Cord let the truth slip out. "I'd have been here sooner, but I met a woman on the road who needed help."

"You were a fool for letting anything slow you down getting here."

As Cord exited the barbershop, he almost ran into a statuesque older woman with too-black hair and a

Spanish hair comb set with fake glass rubies.

"Pardon me," he murmured.

Rather than move aside, she blocked his path, her blue eyes evaluating him.

From that familiar expression, he recognized her.

Though the eligible girls of Salt Lake stayed out of his way at their mother's behest, the women who overnighted at the Excalibur were another story. He'd lost count of how many times he'd been offered a few hours' dalliance.

"Mrs. Giles." He kept his voice neutral. Esther Giles had taken it particularly hard when he'd indicated no interest in helping her cuckold her older husband, Harold.

"I beg your pardon?" Her expression turned frosty, and she sidestepped him, heading for the stairs to the upper floors.

The woman knew damn well who he was. Especially after he'd forcibly unwrapped her arms from around his waist in the Excalibur serving pantry. She'd followed him there and ambushed him while he waited to discuss the week's menu with the head cook and Thomas Bryce.

As soon as he'd set her aside, he had wished he'd not reacted violently. But she was older, married, and her sly overtures repulsed him.

"Who needs you, then?" Before he had realized what she was about to do, her hand came out of left field and cracked smartly across his cheek.

"Hold there." Thomas had grabbed Cord's arms

and held them at his sides. "What's all this?"

Cord, who had not raised a finger to retaliate, almost fought free of his brother's grip. But before he could, Esther Giles, with a face as scarlet as her satin blouse, slipped past Thomas through the door.

"What were you doing to her?" Thomas demanded.

Cord flexed his arms and was free. "Nothing."

Thomas, staid and pompous, sniffed. "A woman doesn't strike a man like that unless he has behaved like a savage."

CHAPTER EIGHT

JUNE 24

"Is there any word on your young man?"

Laura fumed while her father bent solicitously toward Constance. He dug into the pocket of his too-tight vest for a Havana Rosa Bouquet, put a match to the cigar, and blew a wreath of smoke.

Constance lifted her chin. "William should have been here days ago."

Even with her obvious distress, she looked resplendent in blue satin with bands of darker velvet at her wrists and neck. She placed her small hand on her uncle's sleeve and stretched on tiptoe to kiss him on the place where his forehead and bald spot met.

Forrest patted Constance's arm. "May I get you a glass of sherry?" Too late, he included his daughter by sending an inquisitive look her way.

Laura set her jaw, half-surprised he didn't ask her to fetch their drinks.

"I'll take care of your daughter, Forrest." Hank

Falls appeared at her elbow, his blond hair slicked back. "You look lovely this evening."

His gaze swept over Laura, clad in Constance's green-and-white striped dress. The sweeping skirt was newly trimmed at the bottom with rows of black braid to make it long enough. Though Constance's figure was more full, her feet were tiny. Thankfully, Laura and Aunt Fanny were the same shoe size, so a pair of the older woman's satin slippers peeked from beneath the hem.

His perusal complete, Hank took Laura's fingers in his. Instead of air kissing above the back, as style would have it, he turned her wrist and kissed her palm, letting his lips linger too long.

Laura pulled her hand away and darted a glance at her father to see if he'd noted Hank's familiarity. He was again inquiring about Constance's missing betrothed.

Everyone seemed to have accepted Laura's safe arrival as she related, a simple uneventful journey . . . back in her place as "dutiful" daughter, niece, and cousin, just plain Laura who always did what was expected of her. Traveling with Cord had made her realize she was truly unhappy in her role as mistress of Fielding House.

Well, perhaps she had known, or she would not have canceled her Northern Pacific train ticket and taken the southern route with its necessity of traveling by stage. Her gaze went to the window and the lake. Inside the lobby, all was formal, proper, gentry with the trappings of civilization. What if she told the assembled company about Angus Spiner's blood on the snow?

"Miss Fielding?" Hank looked toward the bar. "Will it be sherry?"

She remembered Cord's flask. "I'd like a glass of bourbon."

"We have ice, cut from the lake during the spring."

"Neat."

Hank raised a pale brow. "I like a woman who knows what she wants."

Laura looked away from his direct gaze.

Across the lobby, two men stood outside the barbershop. She passed over the shorter, younger one, with curling brown hair, to the more striking fellow. Tall and trim, he wore an expensive-looking black suit; his freshly cut ebony hair waved above his brow. Clean-shaven save for a sleek mustache, he had a whitened scar that slashed from the corner of his mouth up across his cheek. Despite his handsome profile, the three-inch stripe of pale flesh made him look dangerous.

He turned his head; sharp blue eyes roved over the crowded room. For a heartbeat, Laura thought he looked right at her, but his gaze moved on smoothly to her cousin.

That was nothing new, men were usually drawn to Constance, but her pulse began to pound. A moment later, she knew there was no mistaking it.

"William!" shrieked a woman across the lobby.

With a shock, Cord discovered that Constance Devon was just as lushly lovely as she had been in St. Paul, sparkling at him from across the floor. He left Edgar behind and cut a path through the guests enjoying the cocktail hour.

Surrounded as Constance was by a group that included her mother, Cord did not embrace her, but bowed from the waist.

Ignoring his formality, she lunged at him. Plump arms went around his neck and drew him down for a kiss the like of which they had never shared in St. Paul's spring gardens. Her full lips clung to his.

It should have been the ultimate greeting for two people who yearned to be reunited, and perhaps it was for her. As soon as he could, Cord straightened to greet her mother, Fanny, who looked at him with familiar violet eyes and a subtle boldness he believed was not for herself but to advance her daughter's position.

Constance clung to Cord's arm. Her sleek, satin-covered bosom grazed his sleeve. "Where have you been? I've worried so."

Cord set his teeth against the memory of Laura. "I asked for you at the desk this morning. They said you weren't here."

"That must be because we're in Uncle Forrest's suite." She tugged at Cord's sleeve, her face turned up. "You remember I told you about my cousin in Chicago?"

He didn't, but turned to accept an introduction.

In the hubbub of Constance's greeting, he hadn't noticed the other woman who stood a few feet back.

The instant he looked at her, blood rushed to his cheeks. Green eyes glared at him from a sunburned face that managed to seem drained of all color.

"This is Laura," Constance burbled.

He could barely hear through the roaring in his ears. Constance's cousin, in the Lake Hotel lobby dressed for dinner.

"William?" Soft, but with steel in her tone. She gripped a glass of amber liquor so tightly her fingers whitened.

He bowed again. "William Cordon Sutton, at your service, miss." He hoped she'd accept his cue and pretend, at least for the moment, that they had not met.

"Sir." Laura extended her free hand.

He took it, feeling her fingers tremble. He hesitated and settled for a handshake, as though she were a business associate. She rewarded him with a faintly mocking look that suggested he was a coward for not kissing her hand.

Cord bit off telling her how beautiful she was, with her tawny hair piled on top of her head, faceted green glass drops at her ears, and black velvet rimming the neckline that accentuated her slender shoulders.

"So you are going to marry my cousin," Laura said.

"I beg your pardon?" He'd proffered the garnet ring to Constance as a simple gift . . . asked her to meet him here in the park as a trial, to see if they were suited once she saw his land. Above all, he had never in so many words asked Constance Devon to be his wife.

Constance reacquired her grip on Cord's arm.

"You're Sutton." The sharp voice came from the tall, thin man Cord had already noticed watching him. He stopped himself from offering his hand in time, as the man closed both of his onto Laura's elbows.

Everything was out of whack, as Constance hung on him and he wanted to smash this fellow's face for touching Laura. "And you are?"

"Hank Falls. I built the Lake Hotel, and I'm the manager." His thin-lipped smile verged on a sneer.

Cord knew he'd really hit bottom when Falls indicated a stout and balding man nearby. "This is my backer, Miss Fielding's father, Forrest."

Laura fought the urge to gulp the bourbon in her glass, then considered flinging the contents in Cord's deceitful face. Instead, she sipped the pungent liquor and watched him greet her father in a guarded tone.

How different Cord looked. His curling hair had been tamed, razor precise to the edge of his starched collar . . . she had never imagined he carried this fine suit in his rough leather saddlebag. Though he wore a neatly trimmed mustache instead of his wild black beard, the scar thus revealed reinforced his exotic air.

"It's time we went in to dinner," Hank announced.

Lips pressed together, Laura watched Cord's bent

head, while he listened to a murmur from Constance. Her raven hair blended almost perfectly with his.

With a hand at Laura's waist, Hank led the way to the dining room. He pulled out a ladder-back cane chair for her at a table covered with snow-white cloth and took the seat beside her. "The view of Yellowstone Lake is tremendous from every table," he said with pride.

Golden afternoon light poured in through the windows. Outside, a moose lay placidly on the ground, its palmate antlers turned toward the setting sun.

Across the table, Cord sat by Constance. She touched his arm and made doe eyes while they discussed the menu. Her garnet flashed in the glow of electric chandeliers that seemed to grow brighter as the light faded from the sky.

"The trout is caught fresh every day, Miss Fielding," Hank explained. "I would be honored if you would let me order for you."

She strained to hear what Cord was saying to Constance while Hank went on, "Our wines are brought in on the train from St. Paul, nothing but the best French vintages for a civilized meal."

Laura's bourbon glass had somehow gotten empty. Hank poured a Sauvignon Blanc into a crystal flute set at her place and ordered jellied consommé, tomato aspic on a bed of shredded lettuce, and the trout.

"I will enjoy showing the park to you, Miss . . ." his thigh brushed hers,". . . Laura."

Cord laughed at something Constance said. Laura

missed her cousin's reply, for she was affecting a sultry tone that seemed to thrill men to their toes.

Hank moved his chair closer. "You must come aboard the *Alexandra* some evening. My quarters are quite well appointed; I would enjoy showing you my collection of Persian rugs." His thigh made another pass at hers.

The waiter placed a dish of chilled consommé before her. Across the table, Cord and Constance both smiled at the arrival of their shrimp cocktails.

Unable to contain herself any longer, Laura sent Cord a direct look. "Mr. Sutton, how come you by your interest in owning a hotel? I might have taken you for a cowhand or a member of some other rough profession."

Cord met her hard gaze with one of his own. "It happens I do own a ranch, in the valley of Jackson's Hole." He bit off a shrimp with white teeth, chewed, and swallowed. "I am also a principal in the Excalibur Hotel off Temple Square in Salt Lake City."

Laura felt as though she'd been struck. She noted, however, that Constance did not show surprise.

Giving up, at least for the time being, Laura wet her spoon in the consommé and gave it the barest taste. A few minutes later, the dish was removed and replaced by the tomato aspic. Though Hank dug in with relish, she stuck her fork into the quivering red mass and set the implement aside.

Cord and Constance both dipped into a cream of chicken soup. Aunt Fanny and her father conversed over hearts of lettuce dressed in creamy mayonnaise for him and French onion soup for her. Hank refilled Laura's wineglass and she drank deeply.

The wait staff—Cord had thought her a member—took away the plates of their second course. Hank's thigh grazed Laura's for the third time.

She moved away, grateful for the arrival of their entrée.

The waiter placed a gold-rimmed platter before her. The pink meat of the cutthroat trout glistened in a lake of butter sauce. She broke off a piece of the firm flesh and conveyed it to her mouth.

She dared a look across the table and found Cord also raising a forkful of trout to his lips. Their eyes met, and the succulent meat turned tasteless.

Hank wanted to tell Forrest he'd been a fool for doubting him.

He found Laura exquisite, seated beside him at table while the last light off Yellowstone Lake reflected onto her face. Her green eyes were boldly inquisitive one moment and demurely downcast the next. Striped satin accentuated her waist, her small breasts swelling the material of her dress.

Hank found his palms sweating. He wiped his hands on the snowy napkin across his long thighs. Raising his wineglass, he toasted his banker partner.

Forrest broke off conversing with his sister, Fanny,

to lift his glass; he waved an expansive hand at the roomful of chattering diners. "Let's drink to the day when Hank will be the owner of the Lake Hotel."

Hank recalled his elation when he'd first heard the Northern Pacific was selling, but in the midst of his triumph, he suddenly felt as though he'd been dashed with cold water . . . Cord Sutton was giving Laura Fielding a heated, speculative gaze. The hell of it was that she appeared to be responding with a look that made Hank's mouth go dry.

He raised his toast. "To our mutual success, Forrest."

Sutton turned away from Laura. His blue eyes hard as flint, he placed his palm over the top of his glass. "I'm afraid, sir, that I cannot drink to that."

The assembled company went silent.

Hank met Cord's stare. "Then shall we toast this?" He looked around the table. "That the best man wins."

CHAPTER NINE
JUNE 25

By dawn, Laura felt as though her world was upside down. Cord, not a simple cowhand, but a rancher who also ran an elegant hotel . . . She'd been right to think he was too well spoken to be who he pretended to be.

And pretense it had clearly been.

With the horizon graying, her head felt muzzy from the strong spirits and the wine Hank had pressed upon her.

No, she had lifted her own glass and drunk every drop.

But she could accuse Cord, or William Cordon Sutton.

She threw back the covers and got out of bed. She wished she could wear her trousers, but they were in the hotel laundry, in defiance of Aunt Fanny and her father's edict that the pants and Cord's shirt be relegated to the rubbish bin.

Laura pulled on a camisole, step-ins, and a thin petticoat—Constance would have worn layers of crinolines—and studied the dresses Fanny had transformed with her needle yesterday. Finally, she selected a pink creation trimmed in white lace, conscious that it was in her cousin's more delicate taste. She studied her face and hair in the bureau glass, ran a borrowed tortoiseshell comb through her sun-ripened locks, and called it good.

Hoping her father and Aunt Fanny were still asleep, she tiptoed to the hall door and went downstairs.

The night clerk looked younger than Laura, probably another student. When she paused in front of the desk, he kept his dark head bent over a dime novel. The slender magazine bore a cover picture of a bronco trying to buck off a cowboy in fringed chaps.

She could not blame the clerk for enlivening the lonely graveyard shift.

Laura cleared her throat.

The clerk started. "Excuse me, miss."

"I'm looking for a guest." She tried to sound matter-of fact. "His name is William Cordon Sutton."

"William Cordon Sutton?" he repeated, reaching for the metal box that held the registration cards.

She'd thought it would be hard, but it was simple, really, standing there with her palms pressed on the high mahogany desk, while the young man said politely, "He's in 109."

She wasn't going to his room. Not at an hour when he might reasonably still be abed.

If she did, what would she say? He had met her cousin first, had chosen her to be his bride. It was Laura's tough luck to have encountered him under impossible circumstances.

She headed toward the first-floor hall. With hands knotted before her, she placed one foot in front of the other down the carpeted corridor. And stood outside the portal labeled "109."

Her hand rose. She watched her knuckles rap the panel; any second Cord would open the door and glower at her. "What are you doing here?" he would snarl. "I was well shed of you when I thought you were headed for the servants' quarters."

She waited on rubbery legs but with her chin lifted to face him. Seconds passed, and she knocked again.

The sound echoed in the hall, followed by silence within and without.

Either Cord was not in his room or he had decided not to answer.

Or . . . what if Constance had slipped away from the family suite and was with her betrothed? A man with the virile appetites Cord had shown on the trail would surely claim a woman before they marched to the altar.

Her face hot, Laura turned away. Though she wanted to retreat in a dignified manner, she moved faster and faster down the corridor and out into the rising morning light.

She shouldn't be surprised. Things were as they had been from the time she and Constance were girls.

The far shore of Lake Michigan had always been beyond the horizon, even when Laura peered through a spyglass from the widow's walk atop Fielding House on Lakeshore Drive. Seven miles north of Chicago's State Street and the growing downtown, the mansion and grounds formed a placid island, well back from the busy road.

Constance, twelve to Laura's fourteen, already had the figure of a young woman, though her hair was still caught up in pigtails. She gave the spyglass a bored spin, rotating the brass and mahogany instrument on its tripod. Gripping the rococo wrought-iron railing, she called, "I spy."

Laura looked around the slate roof with bronze lightning rods topped in colorful ceramic balls. They'd already spied the sailor on the weather vane today, and though Constance sometimes picked the same thing twice, she didn't have the secret air of smugness that usually went with it.

Laura peered over the rail, down at the long green lawn that sloped to the lake. Scattered islands of roses and camellias decorated the way to a white-latticed gazebo near the shore.

"Venus," she guessed, pointing at the statue of a life-sized woman in a clamshell atop the terrace wall. She dreamed that someday her slender-as-a-reed body would resemble that sculpture.

"Try again." Constance chuckled.

"It must be Apollo." Laura gestured toward the bronze god, naked in the garden save for his fig leaf.

"No." Constance's giggles lifted above high C, and she pressed a plump hand to her Cupid's-bow mouth.

"That ship," Laura crowed, when Constance cast her blue eyes briefly toward an ore boat. The vessel plowed its way across Lake Michigan with a load of copper or iron from the North Country.

"What about the ship?" Constance teased.

In their version of the game, once Laura had guessed, she was required to make up a story about the vessel.

She took a deep imagining breath that barely swelled her tiny breasts beneath her pink peppermint-striped blouse. "They come from the iron mines," she said. "Almost everyone onboard is a poor, hard-working sailor, but on the captain's deck there's a special passenger."

Laura closed her eyes against the summer sun and tried to describe the perfect man. "He's tall, with eyes as blue as Lake Michigan, and black hair." She smoothed her own hair, which she thought of as plain brown, and imagined the dark-haired man combing it with his fingers.

"His beard is glossy," she embroidered. "It makes his lips look full and red and ready to kiss someone. His body . . ." Laura smiled wickedly, "is like the statue of Apollo."

"And he's mine!" Constance claimed.

Why should Laura be taken aback that life was turning out the way the signs had portended?

Though Laura had to endure arch suggestions that she was becoming an old maid, along with the suspicion that Joseph Kane had been the one to throw her over, Constance seemed immune. Though she was twenty-four, everyone acted as though her single status were the result of her impossibly high standards.

Only Laura knew her cousin secretly longed to be married.

It looked like she was getting her wish.

Turning away from the Lake Hotel, Laura walked along the shore. Though she knew the family expected her to join them for breakfast, she kept moving, putting distance between her and what she didn't want to face.

She'd been a fool to think there was something between her and a man who had rescued her in the back of beyond. He had business to deal with here in Yellowstone and a woman waiting to marry him.

When she approached the soldier station, smoke poured from the stone chimney above the log walls. A few uniformed men stood outside holding mugs of steaming coffee.

"Good morning, miss." The speaker had an earnest face and lively eyes magnified by thick spectacles. "You're out early."

Something in his sincere appearance caused Laura to confide, "I slept so poorly it feels late rather than early."

The soldier smiled. "Some nights the demons keep me from sleep, and I wake with the same feeling." He gestured with his cup. "Coffee?"

"Perhaps." She looked at his insignia without knowing how to read his rank. "Corporal?"

"Sergeant Larry Nevers, at your service." He clicked the polished heels of his boots together. "Cream, miss?"

"Black. It's Miss Fielding."

Sergeant Nevers gestured to another soldier, who moved briskly through the door into the station. He turned his attention back to Laura. "You're staying at the hotel with your father?"

"Yes."

"With all its luxury, you cannot find rest there?"

The other soldier returned with a battered tin cup.

"Miss Laura Fielding, this is Private Arden Groesbeck."

The red-haired young man with a freckled face pressed the cup into Laura's hands. She hooked her fingers through the side handle to protect them from the heat and inhaled the rich aroma that reminded her of the coffee Cord had brewed on the shores of Jenny Lake.

Though Private Groesbeck moved away, Sergeant Nevers waited in a listening pose. Laura lifted the cup, blew on the hot liquid, and sipped. Fortified, she gave him a level look. "I shall remember your kindness, Sergeant. Perhaps it shall help me find the rest I need."

He raised his drink in salute. "Please, call me Larry."

Laura smiled. "Very well . . . Larry."

The sun was full up when she decided to take her leave. As she started to walk away, Sergeant Nevers detained her.

"The soldiers come to the hotel, nights when the orchestra plays." He ducked his head, and she detected a blush on his cheeks. "We, that is, the military, are encouraged to dance with the ladies who have traveled far."

Laura decided she liked this stalwart young soldier. Extending her hand, she touched his callused palm briefly. "Then when we meet again, we shall dance."

As full sun brightened the park, Laura had no watch to tell the time. After returning the coffee cup to Sergeant Nevers, she walked for what must have been hours.

Sergeant Nevers . . . Larry, had spoken of night demons. Hers were now of the day variety.

The falling arc Angus Spiner's body had defined when he toppled from the driver's seat. A stranger's hoarse whisper, "Where's your gun, boy?" Sparks spiraling from a campfire. Witch Creek's cauldrons boiling while the outlaw spied on her bath. Now that she had described him to Pinkerton's man, there would be handbills posted, leaving no doubt that she had been the informant.

She tried to ignore the clutch in her chest.

It must have been ten o'clock when Laura decided she was hungry enough to turn back toward the hotel. Just as she did, she spied a ruined cabin, set inside the forest.

Built of pine logs, the tired building bore a luxuriant growth of summer grass atop its flat roof. The windows were boarded, and Laura imagined the former owners taking care to put the place in good repair, but knowing they were leaving it forever to the national park.

She went suddenly still. A man approached, cutting obliquely through the woods, from the general direction of the hotel. As he came closer, she recognized Hank Falls.

He looked different this morning, wearing a suit of buckskin instead of the gray wool he'd affected at dinner last night. His blond hair was no longer Brilliantined, as though he had dressed in haste.

She almost raised her arm to hail him, but stopped, curious to see what he was up to.

Hank stalked toward the cabin, looked in all directions, and slipped inside. The leaning structure looked as if it could be no more than one room, the door hanging on its hinges.

Laura waited, but he did not come out. She considered going up and knocking, but the thought of being with him alone after he had pressed his thigh against hers made her turn away.

Hurrying toward her was another of the hotel guests, apparently out for a morning constitutional. As he drew nearer, she recognized the young man who'd been outside the barbershop with Cord last evening.

He saw her and started, then seemed to recover and tipped his hat. "Good morning, miss."

With a murmured, "Good day to you, sir," Laura passed him on the trail.

She walked on, over a hundred feet. There, she paused and looked back to see if Hank had come out of the cabin. He had not, and the man she had seen with Cord was not in sight, either.

This evening she'd ask Hank what a man who managed a fine hotel and owned a luxurious steamboat could want in a disintegrating hovel. She had encountered this same mystery in Cord, who seemed at home in both the forest and the drawing room.

As she drew closer to the hotel, her pace slowed.

When she returned, Aunt Fanny would no doubt scold about her running around with her hair hanging freely over her shoulders. Father would probably grouse about her wandering alone.

Laura looked toward the stables. If Cord were a guest, then Dante must occupy a stall. Perhaps the horse, at least, would be happy to see her after the journey they had shared.

Cord walked with Constance in the woods near the hotel. He'd asked her to accompany him after breakfast, thinking he needed to set her straight about their so-called betrothal.

"I had no idea you and Uncle Forrest were both trying to buy the hotel." She shivered as the wind in the tops of the pines dropped down. "That was terrible the way you and Hank acted last night."

"When I met you in St. Paul," he replied in an even tone, "I thought I was the only bidder."

He felt as though a stone lay across his chest, while he studied the meadow stretching from the forest down to Yellowstone Lake.

"I saw a postcard of your Excalibur in Salt Lake, with its white marble portico. The crystal chandelier looked as though it came from Versailles." Constance placed her hand on his arm. "Will you take me there when your business is concluded?" Her burgundy satin skirts whipped against his legs.

As he hesitated over an answer, she reached up to tend her hair. The wind ruffled the long grass and whipped up whitecaps on the lake.

While he was wondering how to tell her things had changed since St. Paul, her hand slid down to his. "When are we going to set a date?" She extended her other hand, showing off the ring he'd given her. "Mother and I could probably find what we need for the wedding a lot faster than the traditional six months to a year."

She raised her face, as though hoping he would take the hint to kiss her.

A bell sounded nearby.

Cord turned toward the sound. Beneath the trees, a split-rail corral had been built to contain six black-and-white dairy cows, their generous udders full. The wind brought the smell of the animals and their droppings.

Constance wrinkled her nose.

"They're for the tent camp," Cord explained. "Wylie's advertises that no tourist camper shall go without milk or cream."

"Wonderful," she muttered.

Looking toward the untidy cluster of small sleeping tents arrayed alongside the big striped dining tent, Cord thought of Laura, camping out with him beneath the stars. He tried to imagine Constance in the same circumstance.

But Laura had deceived him about who she was, and last night she had shown every evidence of letting her father make a match for her with Hank Falls.

Constance frowned and pointed toward a tipi at the edge of the Wylie Camp. "What's that? Indians?" Something in her tone tipped him that she would not take kindly to knowing his grandmother Seeyakoon had been a full-blooded member of a tribe.

Cord examined the construction of poles and skins that looked remarkably like the style used by the Nez Perce. "Who knows?" He shrugged.

Constance's hand pressed his arm; her cornflower

eyes rose tremulously. "William . . ." Her voice was lower and sultrier than he'd heard it, and he couldn't help but remember the quicksilver mystery of her laugh in springtime.

If Laura were going to be with Hank Falls, he should pull Constance into his arms like he'd done the last night before he left St. Paul. See if he couldn't forget her green-eyed cousin.

Laura stretched her arm to offer Dante one of the withered apples she had found in a barrel inside the stable door. He whickered and lowered his great black head.

"You big baby," she crooned. Seeing him brought back everything that had happened on the trail to Yellowstone. How deep was the bond between this noble animal and the man who trusted him enough to leave the stallion untethered when they camped.

Down at the other end of the long aisle, the tackies, as the stable help were called, saddled a pair of horses for tourists. But it was largely quiet since the morning wagon tours and the stage had departed.

A scraping sound announced someone opening the stable door at the near end.

"Dante?" Cord's voice.

His horse tossed his head, and the apple Laura had offered rolled away into the hay.

Cord and Constance approached, walking into a beam of morning sunlight that streamed through a crack in the roof. Laura saw that her cousin's pale face seemed to glow above her burgundy satin dress.

"I thought I knew who you were," Constance teased in a low tone, "but this cowboy stuff is a side I never expected."

Laura gritted her teeth.

The couple moved closer. Laura scurried into an empty stall next to Dante's. In the muted dusty light, she pressed her eye against a half-inch gap in the boards.

While Cord stroked his horse's nose, Constance stayed well back in the middle of the wide aisle, hands clasped behind her.

"Hello." Cord spied the fallen fruit and bent for it.

In the dimness, Laura could have sworn he looked right at her.

He offered the apple to Dante, who took it between his lips almost delicately. But after Cord's fingers withdrew, he crunched with enthusiasm.

Constance grabbed Cord's arm with both hands, and he turned toward her. Her rosy lips pouted, and she wrinkled her nose. "It smells like the dickens in here, but we're all alone . . ."

She brought her arms up and wrapped them around Cord's neck.

Laura's face went hot, and she gripped her borrowed skirt. She wanted to rush at them, but she felt frozen. Her fingernails cut crescents on her palms, and the flush that had begun on her face suffused her whole body.

My God, she would have to sit at table with him on Thanksgiving and Christmas, and watch his children grow up. She'd have to watch his lovely dark head turn silver, so near and yet forever far.

Wildly, she looked for a way out.

Lifting her skirts to prevent them rustling, she fled. Cord's back was to her, and Constance's face wasn't visible behind his shoulders. Expecting that at any second one of them would see her, she kept going. The twenty feet to the exit seemed to stretch a mile.

Reaching the big wooden door, she ratcheted the metal latch. For a few interminable seconds, she struggled. Finally, she wrenched the door open and stumbled into the sun.

Outside, a family was loading their wagon with picnic supplies from the hotel store: a whole ham, loaves of bread, and a sweating jug of drink. The young mother, wearing a worn sunbonnet and carrying a baby on her hip, watched Laura's flight with curiosity.

Without slowing, Laura rushed across the road ahead of the clattering hooves of a four-horse team. The driver atop the red-painted stagecoach sawed on the reins and swore.

Reaching the cool shade of pines and the footpath along the lakeshore, she wished she'd never left Chicago.

In the ripe warmth of the stable, William's hands gripped Constance's shoulders and his mouth plundered hers.

All the remembered tenderness had turned dark and somehow desperate. It did not seem possible that this man had walked with her beside the lily ponds in St. Paul's Como Park, bending his head attentively like a perfect gentleman.

A door slammed, and rapid footsteps approached. "Halloo!" a man called.

William raised his head and stepped back from Constance so quickly that she nearly fell.

The man in army blues and braided cap took in her heaving breasts. Stepping forward, he placed the flat of his hand on William's chest and pushed him back against the creaking wood of the stall gate.

William stood perfectly still before the shorter, barrel-chested man in uniform, but a muscle in his cheek jumped. "Feddors," he said quietly.

"Are you all right, miss?" Feddors asked without taking his eyes off William.

"Of course." Her face flamed, and she reached to smooth her hair with trembling hands. "Mr. William Sutton is my betrothed."

Constance saw Feddors's dark eyes narrow above his wide, waxed mustache. He studied William's bronzed face with its high cheekbones, and she got the distinct impression that Feddors wanted to hit him.

"Is there anything else we can do for you?" William asked.

"No." Feddors stepped back and gave Constance a little bow she thought might be ironic. "It's just a might strange that a fine young girl like you would take up with a . . . person like this."

Grabbing her hand, William pulled her with him down the stable aisle. Her high-heeled boots nearly went out from under her as she struggled through the thick straw.

When they reached the door, William shot the latch and went through. Stunningly bright, the sunlight outside seemed to stab her eyes.

The golden grass waved; the sun made the pine smells rise just as it had before they went into the stable, but nothing felt the same.

CHAPTER TEN
JUNE 25

L aura entered the dining room late for dinner, for she dreaded seeing Constance and Cord together. Even more, she did not want to have Hank dance attendance on her.

To her surprise, she found that this evening's meal would be shared with only her cousin, Aunt Fanny, and her father.

Forrest glared at her from beneath his graying brows. "You have missed the appetizer."

Laura slid into a seat and unfolded her linen napkin. "Thank you for waiting."

"Beg pardon?"

She raised her voice. "I said, thank you for waiting dinner for me."

"Why, Laura." Aunt Fanny sounded aghast.

She could have taken her cue, but since she'd come through the wilderness with Cord, Laura wasn't willing to settle back into her old submissive role. "What's the matter, Aunt? I am so insignificant that no one waits on me, while in Chicago I am expected to wait on you all."

Constance gave her a level look across the boards. Laura couldn't tell if she offered support.

"Where is your . . . William this evening?" Laura offered her own challenge. The memory of her cousin's arms around Cord made her want to throw plates, to scratch Constance's delicate cheeks until she drew blood.

Constance took up the gauntlet, gritting, "Perhaps he and Hank are out dueling over the hotel."

"Girls!" Forrest's voice cracked like a whip.

The elemental idea of Cord and Hank coming to blows did not seem far-fetched to Laura in her present mood. Unable to help herself, she went on, "Or perhaps William is waiting for you in the stable."

Constance's blue eyes went wide, then seemed to narrow into slits.

"What's this, child?" Aunt Fanny looked from Laura to her daughter. "You know it is not seemly . . ."

Her face whiter than usual, Constance shoved back from the table and fled the dining room.

Blood pounding, she hastened away from the hotel into twilight, following the beaten path past the employees' quarters. How could Laura know she and William had been in the stable, unless she'd been spying on them? Her face hot, she imagined her cousin peeping at them while they kissed.

Wishing she had brought her blue woolen cloak, Constance crossed her arms and hastened on, her thoughts turning from Laura to that embrace. It had been all wrong, rough and somehow forced when she'd expected tenderness. It dawned on her that William had dodged speaking of their betrothal. How dare he court her in the spring and then turn into this hard man once he returned to the West?

It really was getting cold out here, but as she started to turn back, she saw a crowd of people gathered in a clearing. Though she had fled to the woods for privacy, curiosity drew her on toward the unmistakable stench of garbage.

At the hotel dump, two grizzlies and four smaller black bears snarled and waved their paws at two soldiers bearing buckets of kitchen scraps, backed by three with rifles.

One of the soldiers flipped a pork chop toward a shaggy grizzly female with a humped back and a blond muzzle. On her hind legs, she neatly caught the tidbit, put it into her mouth, and raised her claw-studded paws in renewed appeal.

A few feet away, Constance noticed Hank Falls, standing quite close to a dark-haired woman of at least forty. His hand rested on her silk-clad elbow; her hair appeared to have been hastily pulled up and fastened by a Spanish comb.

Hank leaned closer and murmured something in

the woman's ear. She laughed, and Constance recognized Mrs. Giles, the woman she had breakfasted with her first morning in the park, having risen earlier than her mother or Uncle Forrest. Esther Giles seemed too youthful for her husband, Harold, a rotund, florid-faced man of at least sixty. Yet, despite his age, Harold seemed hale, as he planned his day fishing with a guide.

On that morning, Constance had believed William would never leave her alone like that.

Mrs. Giles giggled like a girl at another of Hank's apparent witticisms. Maybe Harold had not been too smart to go fishing without his wife.

Several of the black bears crowded closer. Constance retreated a step, colliding with what felt like a very large person behind her. "I beg your pardon."

"Certainly." With that single word, Constance was reminded of the Swedes she'd met when she visited St. Paul.

As one of the grizzlies lunged toward a black bear, she recoiled once more and made a misstep on the uneven ground.

A hand on her arm steadied her. "Be careful, for I do not fancy carrying you back to the hotel."

The sense of familiarity grew stronger. Constance turned to look up into the broad face of a blond giant whose beard was much redder than his hair.

"Or perhaps it would not be unpleasant to carry you."

Her face grew warm.

"Norman Hagen," he said genially, bowing over

her hand in a gallant manner. "We . . ."

"Met in St. Paul," she finished for him.

"It's a pleasure to see you again, Miss Devon." Norman's fair skin looked flushed, even with the evening breeze. His hand, still holding hers, was as broad as a board; his fingernails cleaner than those of men who made a living with their hands.

"Are you still with the railroad?" Constance remembered, while his clear eyes held hers with what could only be admiration.

"The Northern Pacific." He spoke as though he restrained his tone to avoid scaring people. "You do remember."

At the home of Uncle David and Aunt Florence, a string quartet had played the drifting notes of Bach. Everyone at the party was older than Constance, except for Cousin Fiona, nineteen and already sadlooking like her mother.

Constance had sought the solace of the terrace.

"Do you mind if I smoke?" The deep voice had startled her, and she'd turned to find Norman looking down at her from his great height. A man of apparently few words, he had lit a cigarette and stood next to her by the balustrade, enjoying the garden view. Golden daffodils and purple crocus cups promised spring.

When the dinner chime sounded, Norman escorted her in, his big hand placed politely at the small of her back. Whenever she looked up from her plate, his eyes met hers with a kind of emphasis that made Constance have to force her focus away.

The next afternoon she met William.

"Hello, what's this?" Norman lifted Constance's left hand with the garnet ring.

"I'm betrothed to William Sutton," she said staunchly.

"Cord Sutton." Norman nodded. Everyone but her seemed to call him that. "He was in St. Paul talking with the Northern Pacific about buying one of our park hotels."

"Is that what you're doing here?"

"Yes, two groups have put their name in the hat."

"Won't the highest bid win?"

Norman looked thoughtful. "I wish it were that simple. The railroad's board is concerned that the best possible candidate manage the hotel, since we will still be bringing folks here by train. Though the Northern Pacific has been stymied in their attempts to build branch lines into the park, we continue to have hopes."

"Always progress," Constance observed.

"After all, it is nineteen-hundred." Norman shifted his weight from one leg to the other.

"For the past few days, I and the other company representative, Mr. Hopkins Chandler, have been getting to know Hank Falls and his banker, Forrest Fielding. Tomorrow, I will talk with your fiancé, and then we may have some joint sessions to see how each side will plead their case."

Constance met his eyes. "I'm also the niece of

Forrest Fielding."

"Oh dear." Norman smiled ruefully. "I guess that puts us both in the middle."

Cord pulled the plats of the Lake Hotel closer, and his obsidian paperweight fell from the table and rolled. He bent and retrieved it, rubbing it between the fingers of his left hand as he scribbled rapid notes.

He'd worked through dinner, using his bed as an improvised table.

Though Cord had been discouraged by Hank's incumbent advantage at the hotel, the documents Edgar had brought him this afternoon were the ammunition he needed. With them, he could show the railroad that Hank had not managed the hotel maintenance properly.

Eager to look at some concrete details of the construction, he checked the nickel alarm clock on the bedside table and found it nearly nine.

A few feet down the hall, he tapped on his banker's door.

After a few minutes without an answer, he continued down the long corridor and outside. Over the hills the western horizon still glowed. It reminded him of the light fading behind Mount Moran as he and Laura ate ptarmigan, seasoned with salt from his pack and sage from the meadow.

Beneath the pines and darker firs that loomed only

a few yards from the hotel walls, the day's heat had dissipated. No attempt had been made at carving a lawn out of the rough earth, but there were footpaths, worn tracks that crisscrossed their way through the trees and volcanic boulders.

Cord stopped to examine some ugly places in the foundation. Extracting his pocketknife, he peeled a little paint from some boards and smiled, then struck out walking.

The evening fire at the tent camp blazed. Silhouettes of people crowded around to listen to a storyteller or watch a short play.

Cord cursed the proximity of William Wylie's permanent tent camp, hoping that if he bought the hotel, the camp would not eat into his business. On the other hand, the "Wylie Way" meant the cheap opportunity for those who couldn't afford the hotels, so perhaps it would be all right.

Drawn to the laughter and applause, Cord approached the entertainment. Taller than most, he stopped at the outer ring and looked over others' heads.

In front of the tipi Constance had remarked upon this morning, the Wylie Camp barker waved his arms for silence. An expectant hush fell, and just as the group began to become restless, the tipi flap was thrown back.

An older man emerged, bending his back to clear the pole. His crown of dark hair was streaked with white at the temples, and a pair of long braids fell over a bare and bony chest. Bright dark eyes, his strongest feature, flicked over the crowd and came to rest unerringly on Cord.

It couldn't be, but Bitter Waters's arms rose over his head. Gazing at his nephew, he began a chant Cord recognized from the night he returned to camp with a hunk of obsidian in his small hand. All the elders had gathered, even Chief Joseph, to honor one of the smallest, who had braved the wilderness to find a guardian spirit.

Outrage swelled Cord's chest. How dare Bitter Waters remind him of their past?

The chant ended.

Bitter Waters motioned for silence, the firelight casting his hawk nose in prominent shadow. "Tonight, I speak a story—no, not a story, but the truth."

Cord sucked in his breath.

In a mix of pantomime and words, his uncle began in his peculiar precise accent.

"Seeyakoon peered round the door frame at me and my great friend Tarpas Illipt. We sat on her front porch beside Oregon's Wallowa River, playing poker and drinking whiskey."

Cord's nostrils flared at the name Tarpas: the man who had loved his mother before she chose his father. The one who had brought the painted hide that occupied a place of honor in his parents' home. Franklin Sutton must have been secure in love to let her keep the piece as a memento of her prior life.

Bitter Waters paced the edge of the fire ring. "My mother claimed her name of Seeyakoon, 'the spy,' came from her keen eyesight." He smiled. "But everyone said she had been caught listening at the flap of the smoking lodge by Chief Joseph's father, Tuekakas, when she had but four snows."

Cord could not have achieved four snows of his own when Sarah had placed him on Seeyakoon's lap. He could still recall the smell of his grandmother, of summer flowers dried in the sun and apples from the trees on her land.

Bitter Waters seemed to be speaking directly to Cord. "The first day of May, 1877, was unseasonably warm. Seeyakoon carried out a dipper of well water that she added to the pitcher on the table. Small droplets made dark patches on her white deerskin dress. Still slim for a woman of fifty snows, she moved deftly to drink from the whiskey bottle."

Bitter Waters rolled his eyes, and the Wylie crowd chuckled in appreciation. Cord moved forward a few feet, heedless that he was blocking others' view. As the story continued, he imagined his grandmother's homestead beside the Wallowa, where he'd been put down to sleep near the fire.

Bitter Waters continued to spin his tale of two young men at cards.

Tarpas crowed and threw his straight flush onto the table. "Luck is not with you today, Bitter Waters," he observed slyly, "or skill."

Bitter Waters folded his own hand without revealing it and looked up at Seeyakoon.

She reached to ruffle both men's hair as though they were still small boys coming up to her porch from fishing in the river. Tarpas's rich mahogany hair fell in waves over his strong shoulders, while Bitter Waters's raven braids hung to his lean hips.

Seeyakoon looked at the whiskey bottle and scattered playing cards. "Kamiah want you home," she cautioned.

Bitter Waters already knew he had best start winning and sober up before his wife saw him and started asking about the money that had gone into Tarpas's leather pouch. It would be months before cash came in from this season's crops.

Tarpas stretched, scratched his broad bare chest, and looked pleased.

Seeyakoon studied him with a serious air. "You need to marry, like Bitter Waters and Kamiah." Her words echoed what Bitter Waters had told Tarpas before.

But he suspected Tarpas still carried a torch for his sister, Sarah, even though she had gone away years ago. As his half sister with the blood of a white father, it was for the best that she traveled away with white man Sutton, the odd one who picked up rocks and studied them as though each told its own story.

Tarpas shrugged off the talk of matchmaking.

Seeyakoon sat on the step in the shade looking out over the sandbar in front of the house where she lived alone. Two of her men were buried on the hill beside the river.

Bitter Waters's father, Isa Tilkalept, known as Yellow Wolf, had married Seeyakoon through the arrangement of families and died young of the fever and ague during the winter of 1837, before Bitter Waters's birth. Though their marriage was not unhappy, Seeyakoon fell truly in love but once, with Sarah's father, Andrew Brody, whom she met after Yellow Wolf's death. They never married, though they loved each other. When he was shot while hunting in 1869, some said the tragedy was no mystery. With tensions rising between tribal people and the United States, the shooting might have been a message that white men were not welcome to the women of the Nez Perce.

Behind Seeyakoon's cabin, the sound of an ax rang out in the woods.

A jay fluttered down from a nearby tree and landed on the porch rail next to her. Chattering, it moved closer, then perched on her shoulder while she reached to smooth its feathers with a fingertip.

Tarpas gathered the cards and dealt. Preoccupied with arranging his hand, Bitter Waters failed to notice that Seeyakoon got up and wandered barefoot across the yard, the bird on her shoulder.

"I will have to loan your money back, or you will not dare go home," Tarpas crowed, laying down three twos against Bitter Waters's pair of queens and jacks.

"Damn!" Bitter Waters swore in English, for the Nez Perce language lacked profanity.

"What are you doing cutting my timber?" Seeyakoon demanded. The jay flew to a tree and scolded.

Bitter Waters and Tarpas were off the porch in an instant.

"I am building an orchard and vineyard," a man's deep voice said. "I need fence rails."

Bitter Waters recognized Raymond Harding, a miner from the Florence district who had lately settled a short way downstream from Seeyakoon. It had been rumored that the rough-looking man in his forties had been to sea; tattoos on his forearms seemed to bear this out. Sweat stains darkened the armpits of his blue work shirt.

Before Bitter Waters could order Harding to leave, his mother stepped into the dirt track before the team of horses. Her white skirt swung as she pointed toward the river. "You go now!"

Harding leaped onto the wagon seat. His splotched and sunburned face seemed to turn even redder, as he pulled a pistol from the waistband of his trousers.

Bitter Waters and Tarpas were both unarmed.

Seeyakoon stared at Harding, her face devoid of expression. The green scent of trampled grass rose from beneath the team's hooves.

Harding held Seeyakoon's gaze for a long moment. Then he slowly replaced the pistol at his waist. "Hiyah!" He gathered the reins. "Out of my way!"

Seeyakoon stood her ground in the rutted track.

She raised both arms and extended her hands toward the horses.

Although Harding snapped the reins smartly onto the horses' flanks, they did not move. One flared its nostrils and sniffed, and the other twitched its ears toward the murmuring sound coming from the woman before them.

Seeyakoon swayed as though in a trace, her eyes half-closed. Bitter Waters felt himself relax. His mother was using the power of her guardian spirit, her uncanny ability to communicate with animals.

"There!" Harding shouted. "Go, you bastards."

The horses danced and side-footed in their traces, but did not pull forward. Harding pulled a whip from a slot beside the seat and raised it.

Seeyakoon sang softly, a sibilant "Sh-sh-sh."

The whip whistled through the air, landing with a crack on the back of the horse on the left. "Look out!" Tarpas shouted.

Seeyakoon's eyes snapped open, her trance evaporated.

The whip fell again.

Bitter Waters began to run, but it was too late.

The team surged forward and trampled his mother. Wagon wheels ran over her limp form.

Cord might have been a child once more, so clearly did he hear in memory the announcement Bitter Waters had made when he burst into the cabin. The news that his grandmother Seeyakoon was dead had been mere words then. Words swallowed by the terrible deeds of that night when his mother and father were killed before his eyes.

Tonight, listening to Bitter Waters, it was as though he watched Seeyakoon die, saw a vivid image of a white man's wagon running her down like an animal.

Caught up in his own reaction, it took Cord a moment to realize what was happening around him. His last words spoken, Bitter Waters retreated with swift steps to the tipi. He left behind a restless crowd that seemed unsure how it should react.

A smattering of uncertain applause mixed with commentary.

"He said a white killed her . . ." a man's angry tone, "but everyone knows those Injuns went on the warpath and started the trouble."

"Damn right." Cord looked over his shoulder and saw that the last came from a uniformed soldier. "We don't need this old man stirring up more."

Not needing any trouble of his own, Cord almost turned away into the night.

Behind him, he heard a female voice. "But it's too bad about that woman . . . his mother."

Before Cord could change his mind, he strode toward the tipi his mother's brother had entered. He drew back the flap and found the tent empty.

CHAPTER ELEVEN
JUNE 25

Down toward the lake, it was dark and quiet. Cord half-slid down the fifteen-foot bluff to the beach and watched waves slap the shore.

Though he'd made a cursory search near the Wylie Camp, he had not been able to detect which way Bitter Waters had gone. The tipi was obviously a stage prop rather than the place he slept.

Perhaps it was for the best that Cord had not confronted Bitter Waters this evening. What would he have said to the man who brought about his parents' death and destroyed his one true home? Though adopted by one of Salt Lake City's most prominent families, Cord had never felt the sense of peace he'd experienced each night in his parents' cabin.

When Franklin Sutton was not panning or digging, he had spent a lot of time "in the field." Evenings he would turn up the lamp, bring out pen and ink, and make notes and drawings in a leather-bound book.

Cord would climb onto a chair next to him and gaze at fascinating images, cross sections of rocks that had been folded or faulted.

When Cord was older, his father was going to take him to see Yellowstone's geological wonders: great waterfalls tumbling over cliffs, glacier-carved valleys, and geysers greater than the fountains in Franklin's books showing London, Paris, and Washington, D.C.—the capitals they'd also visit.

Tears stung Cord's eyes, while the white-capped waves of the lake blurred. What was the use of thinking back? He had taught himself through the years to keep his past locked up.

Bending, he chose a flat stone to skip across the water. The rocky beach reminded him of being on the point with Laura, where they had fished together.

Taking Constance into the stable this morning had been a test of his feelings. He knew the dark and quiet would permit them to renew their association in a way that would answer any question about which cousin he favored.

How he'd dreamed of Constance, a shining symbol of all that was unattainable to him. Her exquisite porcelain skin against his own bronze, the way her black hair shimmered like his mother's. The dream had been worth having.

Until he met her cousin.

Cord cast the stone into the lake and climbed the hill with swift strides.

The hotel lobby and dining room were ablaze with

lights. Through the open doors, he heard the orchestra tuning up. Going closer, he saw the after-dinner crowd waiting for dance music.

Near the fireplace, Esther Giles smiled up at Hank Falls, her hand on his arm. He gave an answering smile and a nod . . . and moved away as an older man Cord recognized as her husband, Harold, approached.

The orchestra swept into "There Is Only One Girl in the World for Me," a hit song from about three years ago. Couples formed, and the dance floor became a swirl.

Laura stood alone beside a wooden pillar, her hands clasped in front of her. She watched the dancers with the eager sparkle of a child, but the teal taffeta dress she wore accentuated a woman's slender curves.

Cord strode toward the lobby door.

"May I have this dance?"

The voice of Sergeant Larry Nevers startled Laura, who had been waiting for a glimpse of Cord.

When she didn't reply, he went on, "You did promise me a whirl."

She looked up into his bespectacled face. With his blue dress uniform and neatly combed brown hair, he looked more presentable than he had when she'd spoken to him earlier. His hand extended, his manner was formal like all of the army officers who made sure no female guest sat out a round.

"Certainly, we shall dance," Laura agreed in a pleasant tone.

Nevers drew her onto the floor, one hand at her waist. Right away, his lack of rhythm began to wreak havoc upon their steps.

"Do you ride, Miss Fielding?" he asked.

"Quite passably," she allowed, thinking of a certain spirited black stallion.

"Then perhaps you might favor me with the pleasure of your company on an afternoon ride?" He sounded nervous. "There is a quite nice filly from the bloodlines of the Nez Perce, a new addition to the military stable, that I believe you might enjoy. White Bird is a much better piece of horseflesh than the nags they usually rent to tourists."

"She sounds very nice, Sergeant."

"Larry." He cleared his throat. "Tomorrow afternoon? I could stop for you in the dining room after lunch."

Laura considered. His eager attention made her feel better about herself after seeing her cousin in Cord's arms this morning. "I will try to borrow some appropriate clothes."

Knowing Constance's fear of horses, she could only hope Aunt Fanny had come west prepared to do some riding as she did weekly in Chicago.

The orchestra swept into another tune. Though some couples left the floor, Larry kept up his dogged rhythm. Laura tried to follow, her lips curving in a smile. She had been on the receiving end of this kind of admiration before.

"Have you been long in the park, Sergeant?"

"Larry."

"Have you been long in the park, Larry?"

His pleasant countenance darkened.

Ordinarily, she would not have pursued an inquiry, but with her father's bank about to invest in a park hotel and Cord opposing him, she looked up at Larry. "What's wrong?"

"For a start, the officer in charge while we wait for our new commandant. George Goode can't get here soon enough."

"What's the trouble with the man in charge?"

A muscle in Larry's jaw worked; she saw the boy beneath the soldier's brass. "Captain Feddors is what you would call a martinet. He is drunk, not on the alcohol he abhors, but on power."

"Aren't there other officers in the park?"

"There's Lieutenant Stafford, the superintendent's second-in-command." He nodded toward a mustachioed man with a deeply tanned face, brown hair, and incongruous pale gray eyes. Stafford was laughing at something one of the female guests said, and Laura thought he looked too nice to stand up to a man like Larry described. At his other elbow, she noted the red-haired, freckled young private Arden Groesbeck.

The music ended.

Before either Larry or Laura could speak of having another dance, a caustic male voice intruded. "If you can tear yourself away, Sergeant, I have need of a soldier to stand night duty."

Larry dropped his hands from Laura and turned toward a short, stocky man in uniform, who bore the ugly expression of a despot. Larry's face took on the hue of a nearby crimson lampshade. "I would be pleased to assist you, Captain."

Laura was left on the dance floor, wondering how much Feddors had overheard. The orchestra swept into "The Blue Danube."

"May I have this dance, Miss Fielding?"

Vaguely, she heard a voice behind her while she watched Larry Nevers led away by his dreaded commandant. She turned and found she had to look up . . . into Cord's eyes.

"Miss Fielding?" she echoed the formal address that felt strange after all they had been through.

Cord bowed. "I meant to convey respect."

"Respect?" When he had dallied with her beside blue water, while Constance waved his betrothal ring beneath the nose of anyone who would look?

Though she had not accepted his invitation to dance, Cord put his hand on Laura's waist. The place where his fingers touched her bodice warmed, and she wanted nothing more than to swing into the waltz with him.

But she held back.

He bent closer and put his lips to her earlobe. "If

you tell me to walk away, and if you mean it from your heart, I will."

Her knees nearly buckled.

"Dance with me," he went on.

The music swelled, Strauss played inexpertly, yet enthusiastically, by the amateur orchestra of employees who made beds or worked in the laundry by day.

Laura tried to dredge up her anger, but all she could manage was to stare at Cord.

Without further coaxing, he led into the waltz.

He was an excellent dancer, moving his tall frame with the grace of a beautiful animal. "You dance divinely, Miss . . . Laura," he murmured.

Her taffeta skirts rustled as they moved together.

"You look lovely in that dress," Cord went on, a compliment she'd heard thrown out on dozens of dance floors.

Constance had said it was the last she was willing to give up, and Laura knew she'd only gotten this garment because it fit her cousin too tightly. As if he were reading her mind, Cord glanced over his shoulder and Laura saw his focus on his fiancée.

Across the room, Constance held court in a beige lace dress Laura hadn't seen before. It made her look naked, her curtain of black hair rippling like silk in the firelight as she nodded to Norman Hagen of the Northern Pacific. The burly Swede spoke with great enthusiasm, gesturing expansively with his large hands.

Anger swelled inside Laura as she remembered Cord's hands on Constance in the stable. She made her own right hand intentionally wooden in his.

Cord swept her on, one two three, turn two three. Round and round they swirled until the redwood paneling and pine floors made a blur.

She steadied herself on Cord's shoulder. His hand holding hers tightened.

Slowly the distance between them narrowed. Laura's taffeta-covered breast barely brushed Cord's suit jacket, then he pulled her more firmly against him until the length of their bodies pressed together.

Constance glowered at her and Cord's closeness.

Laura started to push away. "I should think you would be on the other side of the room protecting your interests."

"Let me worry about where my interests lie." Something in his tone brought back the moment on the lakeshore.

But there was Constance, still glaring.

Without thinking it through, Laura slid her hand up from Cord's shoulder into his crisp hair and cradled the back of his head. Let Constance be slashed with pain as Laura had been in the barn.

"Good God!" Cord exclaimed.

Leading strongly, he waltzed her across the polished wood of the dance floor, through a swinging door, and into the hotel's kitchen.

Cooks and servers rushed in all directions shouting orders. A massive, wood-burning stove as well as electric burners and kettles blasted out heat. Sweat rolled off the cooks' faces.

Cord's polished mask vanished. He dodged a buxom waitress carrying a tray above her head and shoved Laura against a long wooden table. "What in hell kind of game do you think you're playing?"

"You are the one toying with two hearts."

"I am not speaking of Constance. I'm talking about you." His blue eyes turned dark. "You were coming to work in Yellowstone?"

"You didn't tell me who you were," she came back, crossing her arms over her chest. "Why did you pretend to be some kind of mountain hermit?"

Cord rolled his eyes toward the ceiling hung with rows of stainless and copper pots. "It seemed to suit your fantasy of being swept off your feet in the forest."

Laura trod on Cord's foot and managed to hit his instep with Aunt Fanny's borrowed dance slipper.

Cord swore and hopped back, crashing into a tuxedoed waiter with a tray of salads. A bowl slid off the edge, scattering lettuce and tomatoes and leaving a pool of Roquefort dressing on the waiter's black jacket. The bowl hit the floor and bounced once, then smashed, splashing more creamy liquid onto a Chinese cook's shoes.

Cord grabbed Laura's wrist and pulled her down the long aisle between worktables. Reaching the rear door of the kitchen, he pushed it open.

Cool air rushed to greet them, and he guided Laura down the short flight of wooden steps and across the hotel lawn. Halfway to the lake, they startled an elk in the shadows beneath a tree. With a snort and a clatter of hooves, the animal ran across the crushed stone drive and disappeared in the woods near the small square cabins of the employees' quarters.

Cord's grip on her wrist softened, but he kept towing her toward a pier built out high over the water.

Hank Falls's crimson-and-black steamboat, topped with golden flames, rested at anchor beside a larger dock at water level. An oil lamp burned in one of the cabins on the lower deck, and Laura could see Hank and the same slender woman he'd been with the night she'd met him. She looked younger than Laura remembered, not more than twenty. The same purple dress set off her figure; lamplight gleamed on her golden hair.

Hank stood with his long arms akimbo, his cheroot planted between his lips. He raised a brow at something the woman said, shook his head angrily, and drew the curtain over the window.

Cord released her arm. "Did I hurt you?" His tone was gentle.

She walked away, rubbing her wrist. Tonight was the dark of the moon, and the stars shone brightly in the black sky.

"Back to the business at hand," Cord said dryly. "I don't think the best way for a man and woman to begin is by deceiving each other."

"To begin what?"

No matter that she'd given her cousin a bloody nose when she was eleven, she couldn't let Cord play both ends against the middle. "Constance cares for you."

He caught both her hands in his.

She tugged at them. "Let go!"

He held on. The taffeta dress of Constance's was cut low and square at the neck, and Laura felt sure he could see down her bodice.

"How could you, how can you act as though there is something between us, with you engaged to Constance?" Laura got free. "You thought it was all right to use me because I was a poor woman."

"You could have told me you were rich."

"You could have told me you weren't a mountain man."

Cord loomed over Laura. "Why were you spying in the stable?"

She turned away and saw the light go out in the cabin of Hank's steamboat.

"I was paying a visit to Dante," she said stiffly, "when you and your betrothed came waltzing into the barn. Not wishing to interrupt your little tryst, I left at the first opportunity. I must say I got the distinct impression that everything is going very well between you and your future wife."

His mouth set into a taut line. "I took Constance to that stable thinking I could get you out of my system . . ."

Laura's stomach fluttered. "It looked as though you were trying quite hard."

"I was, and for good reason. You have not exactly shown an aversion to Hank Falls."

A board creaked on the dock behind her.

"Thank God that Miss Fielding shows no aversion to me." Hank sounded smooth on the surface, but an undertone said he would like nothing better than to call Cord out.

Laura whirled. "Hank . . ." She'd believed he had gone to bed with the woman in purple.

His smile looked forced. "Your father has been wondering where you are. I believe he may have seen your rather unorthodox exit from the dance floor."

"I don't need my father to speculate on my whereabouts."

"Perhaps I should tell him you consort with the enemy."

"Perhaps you should not intrude where you have not been invited," Cord countered.

Both men bristled.

"Stop it." Laura stamped her foot and felt the pier shift. "If you want to fight over . . . the hotel, you can do it without me."

She gave a single glance toward the bright lights of the lobby where her father waited and swerved away into darkness. Her steps speeded until the black trunks of trees seemed to rush past her.

How dare her father send Hank to be her watchdog? Or had Father been the one to seek her out tonight? Hank might have heard her and Cord's voices. If so, he might have taken up this "rescue" mission on his own.

Were those footsteps behind her? It really was black out here.

Her breathing sounded harsh in her ears, and the

foot beats behind her grew louder, boots thudding on the earth.

What if it were Hank? He had pressed his thigh against hers at dinner last night and claimed that by virtue of her father's business, she must automatically view Cord as the enemy.

What if it were the outlaw chasing her? Her heart thudded as she imagined the gaunt form from the coach.

Laura looked over her shoulder and saw a looming shadow.

Her outstretched hands hit first. Her chest, cheekbone, and temple slammed into something upright and unyielding. Pain exploded in her skull, and she found out the expression "seeing stars" wasn't an old wives' tale. The breath whooshed out of her, and her head felt as though somebody had swung a fist and decked her.

Hands grabbed her elbows, steadied her. She drew in a shuddering breath.

"God, Laura. Are you all right?" In the dark, she couldn't see the color of Cord's eyes, but sensed their intensity.

As the first shock of impact started to subside, she twisted in his grip. "Let me go."

He released her. "Your attitude says you're not hurt."

Laura raised her hand to her throbbing temple. Warm wetness said otherwise. "I'm bleeding."

Cord touched her cheek in the tender place. "So you are." In the shadows, she made out movement, hand to trouser pocket. Then soft linen patted her wound and pressed to staunch the flow.

She stood trembling, while the pain continued to subside.

"My instincts tell me," Cord murmured, "that a tough gal like you will survive."

"Tough?"

"Shooting a bear, catching a fish . . . cooking over an open fire in the forest."

"And all you want is my hothouse flower cousin."

"Very well." He grabbed her fingers for the fraction of a second it took to press his handkerchief into her hand. In the dimness, she detected that he crossed his arms over his chest.

"Just one question, tough gal. Are you running from Hank, your father . . . or me?"

"That's none of your concern."

"I'm making it my concern." His hands, which she had demanded he remove from her, were back, sliding up her arms to her shoulders.

"But . . ." Her voice came out a whisper. Through the sleeves of Constance's dress, which was rapidly becoming inadequate to warm her in the evening chill, she felt heat radiating from Cord's palms.

"Isn't this better?" He pulled her against him. "The two of us in the woods again instead of putting on airs beneath the chandeliers?"

Her hand was caught between them against his crisp shirt. She knew it was white, but in the dark, it was merely a paler shade of night.

Before he moved, she knew it would happen. Knew it despite Constance, no matter her father and Hank, knew that she wanted it, just as she had wanted a mountain man with nothing to offer.

His mouth came down. She lifted hers to meet him.

For such a large man, his touch was unexpectedly gentle. The scent of his skin filled her head and brought a wave of longing for everything else she associated with him. For the rich aroma of pine, fresh-cut with Cord's small hatchet, for campfire smoke and the crisp chill of dawn when she woke beside him. For all the memories she knew would haunt her, long after she returned to Chicago.

How easy it would be to pretend nothing stood between them, to go with him deeper into the forest.

But if she did, she'd be a fool. No matter what Cord said, her cousin wore his betrothal ring. And as long as Constance believed in Cord, that meant he had not broken off with her.

The sweet ache in her turned to the burn of anger, and Laura shoved him away. "Stop behaving like a savage."

Cord froze at the word that had the power to make him crazy.

Though he should keep Laura with him, make sure she was all right after hitting her head, his history rose before him . . . for the moment more vivid than the woman who whirled and disappeared into darkness.

"Savage! Savage!" He imagined he could hear the boys screaming.

Cornered on the playground in Salt Lake after school—Cord could still see that faraway yard, hard-packed earth without a blade of greenery to relieve it.

"Half-breed bastard!"

He'd run as fast as his shorter legs could carry him, but they'd headed him into a corner beside the white wooden schoolhouse.

He dove at them without even thinking that they were both sixteen to his eleven. Levi Price was thin and wiry, and he might have been able to take him, but Carey Phillips was a blond ox. Cord raised his small fists to fend them off, standing with his back against the wall. Carey could have finished him with his bare hands, but instead he pulled a knife.

As soon as she realized Cord was not following, Laura slowed to avoid any more collisions with trees. Though the lights on the hotel porch helped her see the black silhouettes, they also blinded her to what was under-foot.

When she reached the lakeside stairs below the lobby, her focus was on the ground.

"Did your cousin's betrothed catch up with you out there?"

Laura jumped and looked up to find Hank in a waiting pose. He nodded toward the forest, and lifted a hand toward where her cheekbone throbbed. She imagined the bruise that must be forming, though she thought the bleeding had stopped.

"Did he, ah . . . ?" Hank paused.

"I ran into a tree in the dark."

A raised brow said he didn't believe her. "I can settle the matter with Mr. Sutton for you."

"I'll thank you to keep your insinuations to yourself. He never touched me." As soon as the words were out, she heard their untruth and flushed.

She lifted her chin. "While we are on the subject of clandestine things, Mr. Falls . . ."

"Hank."

"You might tell me what you were doing sneaking around in the woods this morning wearing buckskin. Playing native?"

Hank apparently had the presence of mind to appear dumbfounded. "In the woods? Can you imagine me wearing some crude costume?"

He broke off, his brow beetling. For a moment, he was silent, then went on, "Whomever you saw, you may be certain it was not me."

He took her arm and guided her up onto the outdoor deck. She smelled tobacco smoke on the gray suit that hung on his tall frame and had trouble imagining him in buckskin.

As they entered the hubbub of lights and music of the lobby, Laura scanned the group. "Where is my father?"

Hank did not look around. "I believe Forrest has retired for the night."

She planted her feet. "How dare you tell me he was looking for me?"

Sliding an arm around her waist, Hank drew her toward the dance floor. "That was quite a while ago when he was looking for you, as you will recall. Since then, he mentioned feeling fatigued."

"I must go and check on him." Laura started to pull away.

"He gave explicit directions to Mrs. Devon that he was not to be disturbed." Hank pulled her against his starched white shirt and gray waistcoat. "Dance?"

She gave in. Now was not the time to confront her father and have him ask about her leaving through the back door with Cord . . . if he had seen their exit as Hank suggested. And if Cord came back to the lobby, let him see her with Hank.

Another waltz and it was different from being with Cord; none of that wild dizziness that made her want to be carried along.

While they moved to the music, Hank reverted to pursuing her. "You must dine with me some evening aboard the *Alexandra*."

Laura didn't answer.

"Within my quarters, she is no simple vessel. There are Oriental rugs and Limoges china."

Across the room, Laura noted the young blonde she had seen aboard the boat. "It sounds as though you enlisted a woman's touch at decorating."

Hank nodded. "My sister had the china made up especially for the boat."

"Your sister?"

"You've seen Alexandra." Hank inclined his head toward the girl. "I failed to introduce you after she was rude the evening you arrived."

"The lady in purple," she breathed in surprise. "I thought . . ."

"Quite rightfully," Hank agreed, "you thought she was my mistress." His dark eyes met hers directly, hotly. "There is no other woman in my life, Laura."

As though it were his right, he snugged her even closer.

Automatically, she fended off the advance, the way Aunt Fanny had taught her. With downcast eyes, she murmured, "You would not want me to think you were making a declaration, sir?"

Hank laughed.

An undertone of bitterness chilled her. Recalling the predatory stalk with which he had moved through the woods this afternoon, she suddenly suppressed a gasp.

It wasn't possible. Hank could not be living two lives. He must have an alibi, he must have been here at the hotel when the stage was robbed, but . . . in spite of his gentleman's airs, could there be a darker side to Hank?

Something that might motivate him to rob a stage-coach?

CHAPTER TWELVE
JUNE 26

Morning had Cord wishing he'd slept better and hoping someone would cancel the meeting with the Northern Pacific reps. The scene with Laura last night had him on edge, though her calling him a savage must have been a lucky guess.

He tried to rationalize that he hadn't told a direct lie to anyone, but didn't the sin of omission make him just as guilty?

When he entered the conference room, he found another reason to worry about his position. On the wall, a prominent poster publicized the Northern Pacific with a caption: "The story of a railway in Wonderland, 1900, shows the changes time has made in this old Indianland." Advertising the "crack train of the northwest, the North Coast Limited," the poster depicted a fallen Indian with black braids, fringed buckskin, and moccasins. The route of the rail from the Pacific Coast to Duluth followed the contour of his feathered headdress, along his prone shoulders and back, and down his leg to the end of the line. The first to arrive for the meeting, Cord took a single look and averted his eyes.

Edgar Young followed him into the room. "When you went to St. Paul, the railroad set you up with Hagen as the nice guy. This Hopkins Chandler will be the one who calls the shots, especially now that there's competition."

Cord fingered his leather portfolio. "I looked over the documents you gave me. There are some pretty damning things here against Falls."

Edgar nodded. "I thought you would be able to use them."

"I can, but you never said anything about the hotel being in disrepair. Though on the one hand it works in my favor, I'm going to have to spend capital on repairs and take that into account on the price."

Edgar cleared his throat. "I didn't have the information until recently."

"When . . . ?"

He trailed off as Norman Hagen, looking like a painting Cord had once seen of the Norse god Thor, entered. With a smile, he extended a hand. "Morning, Sutton."

The man behind Norman did not smile. In fact, with his too-black hair and beard, his dour expression, and an undertaker's suit, he appeared ready to hawk a cemetery plot. "Hopkins Chandler, the fourth," he announced, without offering to shake hands.

Forrest Fielding and Hank Falls came in next. The banker's stout body contrasted sharply with Hank's lanky frame.

Cord gave Edgar a sidelong look. "I thought . . ." Today was supposed to be his chance to present his position to the railroad alone, as Falls and Fielding had been doing for days before he arrived.

Chandler took the seat at the head of the table. Everyone else sat with a scraping of chair legs. Cord, by virtue of arriving first, had the place at the opposite head.

He pressed his advantage. "This morning, I'll present my case for why the present management is not the best choice to take over the hotel."

He withdrew a piece of paper from his file and offered it to Norman Hagen, who sat nearby.

Norman pulled out a pair of half glasses and placed them on his nose.

"That letter was written by a team driver who hauled rock for the foundations of the Lake Hotel in 1889," Cord said. "He claims that he and a number of other workers were cheated out of their pay by Hank Falls, who supervised the construction."

"Impossible!" A lock of Hank's normally controlled hair fell down across his forehead.

"Next we have an inspection report from 1890." Cord pushed more paper toward Norman. "It states that there were many places in the hotel's foundation that one could push over with one's foot."

"All of it fixed," Hank insisted. "In the spring of

that year I had the rubble stone foundation remortared."

Hank's banker, Fielding, appearing unconcerned, drew a fresh cigar out of his vest pocket.

Norman studied the documents and passed them down the table to Hopkins Chandler.

Chandler fingered the letter from the worker, smoothing his finger over the ink. "This is an original, not a copy, yet it's addressed to the Northern Pacific."

Hank's fingers drew into fists. "Where did you get those papers?"

Cord didn't answer. In his eagerness to make the case Edgar had prepared for him, he hadn't wondered that the documents were originals.

Resisting looking at his banker, he suggested, "What say we go on a little tour of the hotel? I'll show you firsthand where the troubles lie."

Hopkins Chandler continued to review the documents. "Before I left St. Paul, I made certain to look over all the railroad records of the building of the hotel. There was nothing like this in the files."

Edgar shifted in his chair. "It seems obvious to me, then, that someone," he placed an emphasis on the last word, "must have intercepted the worker's letter. Someone who also made certain the inspection reporting faults did not make it to the railroad files."

"See here." Hank rose. "That's preposterous."

Now, Forrest Fielding appeared dismayed.

Chandler and Norman exchanged a look that raised Cord's spirits, even as he struggled to contain his confusion at Edgar's change of story. He distinctly remembered Edgar saying the letter and the inspection report had come from the railroad . . . but how would that have worked? Had Edgar hired someone to steal from the files, thereby explaining why Chandler had not seen them?

Cord gathered his composure. "Mr. Chandler. It seems obvious from Mr. Falls's consternation that something is amiss." He gestured toward the door. "Shall we see the condition of the building?"

With a thoughtful look at Hank and an exchanged look with Norman, Chandler nodded.

Cord led the way out of the meeting room. When he shoved open the main door to the parking area, he noted from the corner of his eye that someone small and feminine fell into step behind the men.

He glanced over his shoulder; Laura shadowed them.

Outside the hotel, he stopped, facing the wall. "Watch this." He kicked the mortared foundation with the tip of his brown leather boot.

Both Chandler and Norman looked amazed as a puff of dust appeared, and several small rocks rolled to the earth.

"Ten years later, we're back to the same problems." Cord spoke to Norman as though they were on the same side.

"How can I help it if the railroad refuses to fix this place up?" Hank shot a look at Hopkins Chandler and then subsided, as though he realized that alienating the Northern Pacific's representative was a two-edged sword.

Forrest Fielding pulled out a pocketknife, knelt, and inserted it into the crumbling foundation. Frowning, he hoisted himself up.

As the group continued through the hotel, Cord showed rooms without enough steam pipe to make the radiator more than a prop. Next, he led the way to the top of the east gable on the hotel's roof, where a widow's walk looked out over the lake and the tops of the lodgepole forest. Noticing the way Laura's skirt clung to her legs in the freshening breeze, Cord thought the roof could have been a pleasant place to while away an afternoon in view of the emerald Absarokas.

He forced himself back to business. "We saw below in the third-floor hall that the roof has been leaking for years."

Hank's narrow nose lifted, as if he smelled something rotten.

The roof had evidently been repaired a number of times, with multiple patches of coal tar and asphalt forming unsightly streaks on the shingles. "Up here, what you see is called V crimp roofing." Cord pointed to the gap where the crown of the roof did not quite meet. "The vertical seams do not form a lock."

"I didn't design this place," Hank said, "just built it."

"The whole building is rife with wiring hazards," Cord went on, "and there aren't enough of the glass globes of carbon tetrachloride to extinguish a blaze of any magnitude."

He could see from the corner of his eye that Laura

listened. What he could not decipher was whether she rooted for him or Hank.

Cord looked out over the lake and saw Hank's steamboat. "I'm sure if we inspected your boat, Falls, we'd find it's a firetrap, as well."

Cord raised a pre-lunch toast to Edgar Young in the lobby bar. "Score one for us."

The meeting had broken up when Hopkins Chandler indicated that he and Norman would take the afternoon and evening to consider the situation and reconvene the next morning.

Edgar smiled. "You certainly showed that Hank hasn't been keeping the place up."

Cord's own grin faded, and the impulse that had sent him to the bar for a celebratory drink evaporated. "Of course, Hank was right when he explained why. The railroad hasn't authorized the funds to keep it together. They're selling to get out from under the upcoming maintenance."

"We have not yet made a firm offer," Edgar reminded.

"That's true."

If Hank did not also deduct the repairs from the price, if he planned to keep on running the place in disrepair, then perhaps the deal might still get away. On the other hand, today's revelations about past inspections had gone a long way toward discrediting Hank.

Something nagged at Cord, though. Much as he had taken an instinctive dislike to the hotel manager, he did not enjoy the process of character assassination. Especially when he didn't have the complete picture.

"Edgar." He set down his glass. "We need to talk about where that letter and report came from."

His banker shook his head. "The less you know about it, the better for you."

Cord's mouth almost dropped open. Edgar had seemed so cooperative. "I'm going to ask you again where you got the information."

Edgar's lips compressed into a line.

Cord slapped his palm on the bar. "See here . . ."

People were staring at them, including the members of the Fielding entourage, coming in to lunch. Laura wore a deep plum riding habit and the boots she had worn on the trail, polished to a high sheen. Even from a distance, he could make out her bruise, becoming a black eye.

Hank stayed close to Laura.

Constance wore the ecru lace concoction he had seen her in last night, the one that made a man look twice to make sure she wasn't naked. Standing without an escort, she met Cord's eyes as though she could will him to join her.

On no account would he walk across to where Hank stood glaring at him. After the argument on the pier last night, and the events of this morning, he had no idea what might erupt in front of Norman Hagen and Hopkins Chandler, who were entering the lobby together.

"Let's get some lunch," Cord told Edgar. Over the meal, he felt sure he could talk the younger man into sharing his source for the mystery documents.

While Cord and his banker took seats at a window table, Laura watched through lowered lashes. He didn't look nearly as pleased as she thought he might after showing Hank up. In fact, he and Edgar seemed to be in disagreement.

Hank shook out his napkin.

Forrest glanced at Cord. "You know, Hank, what he's got is pretty damning."

"They could be forgeries," Hank parried.

"Are they?" Forrest came back.

Hank colored.

Laura studied his discomfiture. "Are you accusing Mr. Sutton of presenting false information? When the things he said about hotel maintenance are true?"

She expected an explosion from Constance in Cord's defense, but she was speaking to Aunt Fanny and not following the conversation at this end of the table. Instead, the rebuke came from her father.

"Daughter!" he snapped. "I do not know what can have gotten into you since we arrived here. I expect your support and loyalty to me in my business endeavors, as well as matters of the household."

She refused to reply, holding his gaze with her

own. Finally, he reached for a slice of bread and began to butter it. Hank studied the menu, though Laura suspected he knew the offerings by heart.

The approach of Sergeant Larry Nevers broke the tension. "Good afternoon, Miss Fielding. I see you have dressed for our outing."

Aunt Fanny smiled. Upon hearing Laura's wish for an equestrian outing, she had altered one of her own riding habits.

Larry bowed. "Shall I escort you to the stables around two o'clock?"

The tension was back as Hank and Cord both scowled from opposite sides of the room.

CHAPTER THIRTEEN
JUNE 26

Cord rode Dante along the lakeshore through a meadow of waving grass. He tried to focus on the beauty of the afternoon, but it was difficult.

Edgar Young had refused to reveal his sources, leaving a dilemma. If Cord could not communicate with Edgar and place his trust in him, should he go forward with him as his banker?

But what else could he do? If he placed his offer on the table in short order and had it accepted, there was no time to arrange alternate financing.

Unless he used the telephone . . . the army had strung lines to the hotel and soldier station . . . to call his adopted father. Aaron would loan him as much as he needed. But Aaron would also know the railroad's attitude toward dealing with those of Indian blood and realize Cord was trying to be something he was not.

"Have pride in both your heritages, son," he always said. "Your father's and your mother's."

A clutch in Cord's gut said he wasn't ready to make a call. It would be tantamount to admitting defeat, and Thomas, his partner in Excalibur, would be sure to gloat that Cord had tried something on his own and failed.

No, Cord would have to go forward as soon as tomorrow, presenting his offer to the Northern Pacific. And he would have to stay clear of Captain Feddors and his accusations in the meantime.

Captain Quenton Feddors thought he was a fool to have taken on the challenge of White Bird simply because the mare had been bred by the Nez Perce. All over the West, they were still bought and sold, traded on the reputation of bloodlines linked to the herd that followed the Nez Perce on their fourteen-hundred-mile flight in 1877.

"Try and throw me?" Feddors hissed through clenched teeth, while he struggled to stay astride the wild gray mare in the Lake Hotel paddock. A shock of his brown hair had come loose from where he'd plastered it down across his receding hairline.

The gray reared again, her shoulder glancing off the split-rail fence. Strong-willed and stubborn, she had an especially long mane and a blaze in the center of her forehead that looked like a white bird flying.

Feddors gripped the reins and noticed that a group of soldiers had gathered to watch their commanding officer's troubles. He really should have reset the stirrups that were adjusted for a taller man, but hadn't wanted anyone to see.

Now, before they flew from his feet, Feddors reached for the thin quirt inserted beneath a strap beside the pommel.

He pulled the whip free, thinking that he had always broken horses the way he managed the weak and lazy men in his command. Swiftly and without leaving any doubt as to who was in charge.

"White Bird!" Sergeant Nevers shouted. He leaned against the fence with one leg propped on the bottom rail, waving his arms and inflaming the mare.

Feddors did not like the young man, with his earnest round face, for the simple reason that he had risen through the ranks faster than he had. He was also humiliated to note his viewers included Laura Fielding, the girl from the stagecoach robbery.

The one that Pinkerton man, Resnick, said was lying.

White Bird turned back and tried to bite Feddors on the calf. He brought the whip down hard.

The animal gave an unexpected twist, and he found himself unseated.

His audience a blur, he fell to land hard on his back in the dirt. The breath knocked from him, he watched the sky spin . . . transported back to the summer of 1877, when the Nez Perce had gone to war rather than to a reservation.

That August he had been staying at Bart Henderson's guest ranch north of Mammoth Hot Springs. Of course, at fifteen, he had preferred riding alone to the company of his father with whom he traveled.

In a meadow in northern Yellowstone, he'd come upon the confluence of two creeks. The sound of rushing water drew him on, up into a thick forest of lodgepole, spruce, and fir. There, a cascading waterfall poured at least eighty feet down tiered steps of lava rock.

Quenton dismounted and approached the pool at its base, feeling the welcome coolness on the hot afternoon. On his knees, hands cupped to drink, he suddenly went still.

Beneath the trees on the opposite creek bank, half-hidden in thick undergrowth, two men watched him from horseback. Both riders appeared to be perhaps twenty years old, with shining black hair divided into braids. They each wore blue trousers that could have been part of an army uniform; stripes of red paint decorated their cheeks and bare chests.

Quenton stood up carefully. He reached for his mare's reins, wishing he hadn't left his Winchester .25-20 in the scabbard behind his saddle. Over his shoulder, he watched the two men, noting their rifles were larger, the Model 1873 Springfield like the U.S. Army carried.

His heart beat faster. At Bart Henderson's, the talk was of little except the band of Nez Perce fleeing though Yellowstone. He'd heard of the battlefields farther to the west, the tribe versus the United States Army, and realized that the trousers and weapons had no doubt been stripped from the bodies of dead soldiers.

Quenton watched with fascination. The Nez Perce controlled their horses without benefit of saddles or bridles, merely by touching their moccasined feet to the animal's side or placing their hands into the horse's mane.

With a shiver, he felt the almost palpable desire to someday be a horseman of that caliber. Sinewy muscles stood out on the men's arms and shoulders . . . he imagined when he finished his growth he would look like that, his scrawny chest and weak white arms transformed magically into manfulness.

Cord returned to the paddock from his after-lunch ride on Dante in time to see Captain Quenton Feddors lose his seat on the back of a well-blooded gray mare. He landed in the dirt, and the gray danced away, still bucking.

Four soldiers in shirtsleeves, who'd been grooming horses, moved to join the group already leaning on the fence. Laura was next to Sergeant Nevers.

Feddors clambered to his feet, knocking a cloud of dust from his uniform pants. "Back to work!" he shouted.

Though one very slim young private, with red hair and freckles, turned away, the others did not.

Feddors raised his whip and started across the paddock after the gray.

The private who'd been leaving put his boot back up on the fence rail.

Catching the mare by the reins, Feddors slashed up and laid open a red welt on the side of her nose.

Cord slid off Dante and went to stand outside the fence beside the sergeant. The whip flashed again, and the abused mare reared.

"By God," Nevers murmured fiercely, "you get him, White Bird."

Her hooves landed harmlessly, and Feddors kept raining blows on her face and neck.

Cord looked around at the enlisted men. A few appeared to be enjoying the spectacle, their expressions taut and their hands jerking as if they were throwing punches. Thankfully, most of the ten or so men looked slightly sick.

Beside Cord, Sergeant Nevers gripped the rail, his knuckles pale. If the captain had not outranked him, Cord thought the young man might have tried to end the senseless cruelty.

"Someone stop him," Laura called out.

At a woman's voice, the men's heads swiveled. But no one made a move to halt the commanding officer's abuse.

In a single motion, Cord placed his hands on the top rail and vaulted over. He ran, out into the paddock toward the fray. Slipping between man and horse, he jerked the reins from the officer's hand. With an almost simultaneous movement, he plucked the quirt from Feddors's fist and threw it across the trampled earth of the paddock.

When he turned his back, he felt an itch between his shoulder blades as though the captain was about to strike him there. Nonetheless, he led the mare to the gate where the sergeant and Laura waited. As Cord passed off the horse, Feddors caught up to him and clamped a heavy hand on his shoulder.

"How dare yew," he sputtered. "What gives yew the right to interfere in mah discipline of an army horse?" The southern influence on his speech that Cord had noticed the other day was more evident.

"How dare you, Captain?" Cord looked down at the hand that still clutched his arm.

Feddors looked around at the men watching him manhandle a civilian tourist.

He held on a moment longer and released Cord.

"White Bird is an 'army horse,' is she?" Cord asked quietly.

Feddors furrowed his brow.

"The only problem with your logic," Cord went on, "is that White Bird here failed to enlist."

A wave of laughter rippled through the watchers, and he noted another woman in addition to Laura. Esther Giles was watching the altercation with an intent interest that chilled Cord; he had no doubt she meant him ill.

"Get out of here!" Feddors waved his arms. Turning back to Cord, he gritted, "I ought to throw you in the stockade at Mammoth for assaulting an officer of the United States Army, you half-breed scum."

Cord's aplomb burst like a soap bubble. Behind him, Mrs. Giles's laugh was as sharp and nasty as a rat terrier's bark, while he hoped Laura hadn't noted the last words.

"I wouldn't do that if I were you," said a voice from behind Cord and Captain Feddors.

Thinking someone had divined from his expression his immediate intent to deck the captain, Cord turned to find Manfred Resnick sitting on top of the rail fence like a jockey in the saddle.

"Mr. Sutton never touched you or threatened you in any way," the Pinkerton man went on, looking sternly at Feddors.

The captain's already-flushed face darkened. "You're defending that red man?"

This time there was no mistake. However in the hell the man had guessed, at his words Laura gasped.

Resnick jumped down from the fence. "I did some checking the other day when you accused Mr. Sutton of poaching and other peccadilloes. He was adopted by Aaron Bryce of Salt Lake City when he was quite young."

"If Aaron Bryce had the rotten judgment to take in an Injun kid, he should get used to folks insulting his . . . ward."

"Son." The word slipped from between Cord's lips. "Aaron Bryce is my father."

Feddors stared at Cord a moment longer. Resnick plucked at his sleeve. "I am sure you would not want to incur the wrath of a man like Mr. Bryce."

"City folks don't carry much weight out heah."

Yet, Feddors permitted Resnick to lead him as he limped away.

Cord felt he should say something to deny the captain's accusations about his heritage, but while he hesitated over telling an outright untruth, the moment passed.

Sergeant Nevers cleared his throat and offered Cord his hand across the paddock fence. "Good show."

He clasped hands with Nevers and looked over his shoulder to be sure Feddors was gone.

"If you hadn't been here and done what I was about to do," Nevers's eyes looked enormous behind his thick glasses, "I reckon I'd be on my way to Mammoth and a court-martial."

"I'm glad I could put a stop to his cruelty. For today, at least."

"If only the little tyrant was throwing his weight around at Headquarters in Mammoth, instead of at his usual post at Lake," Nevers fumed.

Laura and Nevers entered the paddock and walked over to Cord and White Bird. Laura put up a hand to stroke the mare's nose. To Cord's surprise, after such harsh treatment she lowered her head and nickered.

Cord examined the wound on her cheek. The laceration was not deep but had to smart.

Laura looked at Nevers. "This is the horse you told me about. The one you thought I'd like to ride."

"Yes, Miss Fielding. Another day." Gently, Nevers removed the brass military bit with curb chains from White Bird's mouth and went to hang it on a nail in the tack room.

Laura continued to soothe the animal, petting her and murmuring. White Bird submitted to her ministrations.

Cord brought Dante into the paddock and walked him over. The mare tossed her head, then stretched her neck to sniff at Dante's nose.

Sergeant Nevers gestured the red-haired soldier toward the stable. "Private Groesbeck, could you bring me a lead?"

Groesbeck returned with a leather halter that Larry slipped over White Bird's head. As he started to take her into the stable, Laura stopped him. "Could you let me have her for a few minutes?"

Nevers hesitated.

Cord recalled her mounting Dante without fear, her sure seat and good hands. "They'll be okay."

Nevers handed Laura the lead rope. She walked away, White Bird at her heels. They took two turns about the paddock; Laura did not even look down at the mud and muck she walked through, the skirt of her habit trailing. She led White Bird alongside the fence and, before Cord could divine her intention, put a leg up on the boards and vaulted astride the mare's back.

"Watch out," he couldn't help but caution, "she's been sorely mistreated."

From her bareback perch, Laura reached to stroke the long gray neck. "That's precisely why she needs to know all riders aren't like that."

Something swelled inside Cord's chest. His grandmother's gift with animals was long ago and far away, but it did his heart good to see Laura's way with the mare.

From behind the barn strode a tall, slender man in uniform, wearing the insignia of a lieutenant.

The sergeant saluted his superior. "Lieutenant Stafford, sir. This is Mr. Sutton, a guest of the hotel."

Gray eyes were warm in a sun-bronzed face. "Welcome to the park, Mr. Sutton."

"Call me Cord."

"I'm John. My wife, Katharine, and I live up at Headquarters by Mammoth Hot Springs . . . I get down this way during the high season."

Cord wondered if the park's second-in-command was here hoping to keep Feddors in check.

Turning to Larry, Stafford spoke in a lower tone. "Everything all right here?"

One of the soldiers must have told Stafford what had gone on with Feddors. Where a subordinate like Sergeant Nevers might hesitate, Cord dared to speak. "As you can see there on the mare's cheek, your Captain Feddors was a mite enthusiastic with his quirt."

Stafford's eyes met Cord's. "The damage to a piece of good horseflesh is regrettable, but I was referring more to the scene between Feddors and one of the tourists."

"I am that . . . tourist."

Stafford looked surprised. "I was given to understand he was baiting . . ."

"Captain Feddors has a theory that I am of Indian descent."

Nevers made an impatient gesture. "Ridiculous. Anyone can see . . ." He studied Cord's features and stopped.

The silence in the corral was broken only by the wind soughing through the pines behind the stable. In his peripheral vision, Cord noted a pair of buzzards circling overhead.

"The captain has an ax to grind," Stafford said. "Right or wrong, he tells the world the Nez Perce murdered someone dear to him."

Cord tried to keep his face neutral. Men and women had died at the hands of the tribe, that was established.

Stafford went on, "Sometimes it . . . ah . . . colors his view of life. Hopefully, when our new superintendent arrives, Captain Feddors will subside back into the ranks without incident." He touched the brim of his cap. "Mr. Sutton."

At this sign of leave-taking, Sergeant Nevers sprang to attention. The lieutenant returned his salute.

When Stafford was out of earshot, Nevers turned to Cord. "What an understatement. Feddors is the worst officer I've ever seen. Acts as though all the men are worthless instead of saving it for the few who are."

Though they were alone, Nevers glanced around before going on, "I wouldn't be surprised if someday he gets shot by one of his own men."

CHAPTER FOURTEEN
JUNE 26

When Cord approached to assist Laura in dismounting from White Bird, he wore a guarded expression, almost a look of shame.

It must be true, then. Though she'd wondered if he had Indian blood, with his bronzed skin and prominent cheekbones, she had discounted it because of his beard and blue eyes. Flushing at the memory of calling him a savage, she accepted his hand and got down from her bareback perch to the broken ground.

She gave White Bird a last pat on the withers, and Cord passed the mare off to Larry, who spoke of putting some balm on the mare's wounded cheek. She thanked the sergeant for the invitation to ride, and it seemed understood she would go with Cord.

While he escorted her across the muddy paddock with a hand at her elbow, Laura imagined Larry watching them go.

Once away from the stables, they veered along the

shore in the opposite direction from the hotel. She didn't ask, but he answered.

"My grandmother Seeyakoon, 'She Who Spies,' of the Wallowa Nez Perce, loved a white man and bore my mother, Sarah, 'Falling Water.'"

Laura stopped on the path between a pair of eroded-out roots.

Cord halted and faced her. "Though Sarah was courted by Tarpas Illipt, a man of the People, when my father, Franklin Sutton, passed through the mining district—lands stolen from the Nez Perce—it was clear she favored him. A conflict erupted, and her own brother, Bitter Waters, helped drive her from the village."

"My Lord." She looked toward the Wylie Camp. "There's a sign . . . a Bitter Waters tells stories in the evening."

"My uncle." Cord's shoulders squared. "I heard him speak last night before I saw you. He told how Seeyakoon's murder by a white settler helped start the war in 1877."

"Murder." Laura's breath caught. "Surely not . . ."

"Run down in the road."

Her eyes stung. "Did you talk to Bitter Waters? Does he know who you are?"

"He knows me." It came out flat. "But when I tried to speak with him after his . . . performance, he pulled a disappearing act."

Laura touched Cord's blue shirtsleeve, the garment a twin to the one he'd loaned her. "Take me with you tonight. Together, we can be sure he doesn't get away without talking to you." She let her hand rest more firmly.

His arm muscles hardened beneath her fingers. "Why would you want to do that? Now that you know about me," he pulled away, "you'll want to tell your cousin what a narrow escape she had. And, when you tell Hank and he lets Hopkins Chandler know, he and your father will win."

"Why would I . . . ?"

Cord took a few steps off the path as if to leave her, then swung back. "Have you seen that abomination of a poster in the meeting room?"

She had taken a look into all the public rooms of the hotel and been repulsed by the image of the fallen Indian.

"The railroad won't do business with a Nez Perce." His voice gave away how deep his desire to own the hotel, when she'd seen it as a simple business deal.

"You're three-quarters white," she argued.

"That makes no more difference here than it does for a Negro in the South. Even an octoroon is still viewed as touched by the tar brush."

"What about Aaron Bryce? Even in Chicago, I'd heard of him. Surely he can make them see . . ."

"Aaron couldn't fix it so I owned Excalibur, without putting my adopted brother's name on the title," he said bitterly. "Besides, Aaron doesn't know I'm trying to buy the Lake Hotel. I wanted to do this without his help."

They walked a little farther, toward the sod-roofed ruin ahead near the path. Silence once more lay between them, while Laura struggled to absorb what she'd learned.

Lord, if her family knew Cord's heritage, Father would have apoplexy. Aunt Fanny would need her salts for an attack of the vapors.

More importantly, what would Constance do?

Away from the path, stepping over fallen logs, Cord and Laura headed deeper into the dappled shade of forest. He gave the sagging log structure he had noticed earlier a second look. Grass on the sod roof waved in the breeze, inviting one to pause and rest within.

It made him wish he had the right to be with Laura, to take private shelter behind the log walls where no tourist's eyes could pry. How he wanted to tell her he'd given Constance the ring as a keepsake, only a hope of what might develop . . . but honor prevented him from speaking before he'd set things straight with her cousin.

"Look," she breathed.

He did. A drift of smoke rose from the sagging stone chimney.

"No, there." She pointed back toward the hotel.

Edgar Young hurried toward them along the beaten path, his focus on the cabin.

"I saw him out here before," Laura whispered,

"after Hank went into that building."

Cord grabbed her arm and drew her down with him to kneel behind a deadfall. Her wide eyes told him she knew to keep quiet.

Edgar looked around jerkily, his focus passing over them in their hiding place. Cord wanted to duck lower, to put his hand on top Laura's head and press her down.

His banker kept walking toward the ruin, pushed open the door, and disappeared inside. When the sagging door shut as far as it could in the off-square door frame, Cord pushed to his feet.

"Stay here," he whispered to Laura and began sneaking toward the cabin, taking cover from tree to tree. He was pleased to note the windows were boarded; no one could glance out and see him.

On arriving beside the log wall, he crouched. Inside, he detected an indistinct voice.

A look around and he moved toward the rear. As silently as possible, he duckwalked to a section of wall that had begun to collapse, leaving chinks between the logs.

He put his eye to a hole and heard, "You damned fool!"

It was Edgar, gripping the back of a cane chair with a broken seat.

"Some would say." Hank Falls, wearing an improbable suit of buckskin, had his back to Cord in the dimly lit space. He bent to put another log on the fire beneath the leaning chimney.

Edgar stood and watched the taller man thrust at the coals with the end of a charred stick.

"Getting sentimental about your partner?" Something ugly lurked in Hank's tone. "I held off cleaning up loose ends, but he served his purpose when he delivered the papers."

The papers that had cast doubt on his own qualifications?

A twig snapped behind Cord, and he almost shouted. He turned to find Laura, too late to tell her to go away, for he dared not make a sound. She sidled up alongside and peered into the cabin.

Hank, the man who ordered fine wines for the dining room, squatted on his haunches, tending a crude pot of stew suspended on a rack over the fire.

Edgar sniffed the cooking smells. "Squirrel?"

"Killed it this morning." Hank chuckled. "It's against park regulations to hunt."

In that instant, Cord knew that whoever this was, it could not be the elegant Hank Falls.

"You take a lot of chances," Edgar said.

"More than you know."

Edgar reached into his coat pocket and drew out a bottle of Jack Daniels. He removed his outer garment and threw it on another sagging chair over a long black duster.

Cord felt Laura stiffen beside him, as they both remembered the outlaw's garb.

Edgar uncapped the liquor and offered it. "It's too dangerous for you near the hotel, Danny. If Hank were to see you . . ."

Hank's mirror image, except for his garb and demeanor, drank and kept the bottle.

Laura tugged Cord's arm. Getting out of there was a damned fine idea; a rifle leaned against the hearth, no doubt loaded and ready.

Lifting the skirts of her riding habit, Laura lagged by the time they raced out of the woods near the soldier station. Her heart pounded, and sweat ran down her back and sides.

Cord reached the door first and slammed it open. "The outlaw who killed those people in Jackson's Hole. I saw him here in the park."

Captain Quenton Feddors's drawl came to Laura through the open door. "Let me guess, suh. Were you perhaps looking in a mirror?"

Laura shoved past Cord through the tight doorway and confronted the bandy-legged officer. "How dare you? Mr. Sutton has given you no reason to suspect him, yet you insult him at every turn."

She scanned the office, made dark by bark-covered log walls. "Where is Manfred Resnick? We have information for him."

"Here, Miss Fielding." Resnick's voice filtered from the back room. He came out, dressed in his chalk-striped suit.

Larry Nevers, in uniform, followed. He favored

Laura with a smile that was quickly hidden from his commander.

"Please." She focused on Resnick. "The outlaw is in an abandoned cabin not far from here. We both saw him."

Resnick's good eye found Cord. "You saw him?"

"Well, of course, Miss Fielding identified him . . ."

Resnick mirrored the captain's belligerent stance. "I may have been in the back room with Sergeant Nevers, but I distinctly heard you announce that you yourself had seen the outlaw from Jackson's Hole here in the park."

Feddors lifted a hand and toyed with his moustache, a suggestion of a smile at the corners of his mouth.

Resnick turned to Laura. "How is it that Cord knows what the outlaw from the stagecoach looks like?"

She swallowed.

"Could that be because he was there?" Resnick pressed. "Was he the man you traveled with instead of some shadowy folk from Montana?"

"You've got to hurry." She pointed in the direction of the cabin. "The man who shot Angus Spiner is getting away."

Almost half an hour passed while Feddors called up some soldiers from the stable area. They mustered, armed with military issue 1892 Krag rifles and made their way back to within sight of the cabin. The afternoon sun slanted lower through the trees, but the primeval stillness and the warm pine scent were the same.

Feddors gave Laura and Cord a hard look. "You two stay back while we handle this."

She started to protest, but Resnick gestured her to stay put. "If there's shooting, I want civilians well out of it."

"He's right," Cord agreed, though she sensed he wanted to be in the thick of the capture. "Speaking of civilians, there was another man inside. Edgar Young is a banker in Great Falls." He did not mention his association with him.

"Description?" Resnick clipped it out the way he had during his interrogation of Laura.

"Medium height and build," Cord replied, "reddish curly hair. You won't confuse him with the outlaw, who looks exactly like Hank Falls."

Resnick looked at Laura. "You mentioned that before. How do you mean 'exactly'?"

"Now that I've seen him again," she said, "I'm sure they must be identical twins."

Feddors raised a hand and signaled the dozen or so soldiers to surround the dilapidated structure. They obeyed, fanning out silently through the woods.

Laura and Cord stayed where they had been instructed. Anticipation made her toes curl inside her boots. She didn't know whether to hope for a shootout . . . no, the thought of witnessing another killing made her throat tighten.

The soldiers closed in on the cabin. Cord took

her hand.

Feddors raised his arm. His men trained their Colts.

"You in the cabin," he shouted. "We have you surrounded. Come out now, unarmed, with your hands in view."

Silence reigned, save for the chatter of a chipmunk whose territory a soldier invaded.

"I said come out now!" Feddors called. "This is your last warning."

At another signal, the soldiers began to move in. Sergeant Nevers was the man closest to the cabin door, looking back for direction. Feddors nodded, and he kicked the door open.

Gun drawn, he disappeared inside. "No one here!" came his shout.

Laura's shoulders sagged, and she took a gulp of air, having forgotten to breathe. Cord's fingers twisted, and she released her death grip on them.

He frowned. "Maybe they saw us coming and got out the back. Or just finished their business."

"What business?"

"Before you came up, Danny told Edgar I had served my purpose when I delivered 'those papers.'"

"What papers?"

"When you saw me pointing out maintenance problems . . . the clues to that came from some papers Edgar gave me."

"You showed them to the railroad people?"

"I did. It's almost as though Edgar and this Danny are both on my side."

Laura shivered. "Danny's not the kind of friend I'd care to have."

Resnick came to them through the trees. He spread his hands in a "win some, lose some" gesture. With a guarded glance back at Feddors, he directed, "You two come with me."

On the hotel's front porch, he directed them to take seats in wooden rockers, as though they were having a casual conversation. Laura sat, attempting to tuck the dirty hem of the plum skirt under. A breeze blew through the open windows and stirred the lace curtains.

"Let's take up where we left off," the Pinkerton man began. "Mr. Sutton, I've come to believe you were at the stagecoach scene." He pulled out his pad and pen. "The question is, what were you doing there and with whom?"

"I can tell you that," Laura jumped in without thinking. "He saved my life and brought me through the wilderness to this hotel."

Cord laid a gentle hand on Laura's arm. Resnick glanced down at their contact.

"I'll handle this," Cord said evenly. "I was traveling from my ranch in Jackson's Hole toward Yellowstone when I heard shots. I got to the coach and found Laura hiding out in a ravine. There was a gun battle, the man we heard called Danny today, rode away . . . the other man was gut shot."

"You dispatched him with a bullet to the head." It wasn't a question.

Cord nodded, his focus on the wind painting

patterns on the blue lake.

"Did you think you'd be in trouble if you told your story?" Something in his demeanor suggested he referred to Cord's heritage.

"How could he be in trouble? That's all nonsense Captain Feddors keeps spouting."

Resnick looked from her to Cord; she'd spoken too glibly, calling attention to Feddors's claims rather than defusing them.

She tried again. "I asked Cord to keep our journey secret, because I didn't think my father and aunt would take kindly to me spending three nights in the forest without a chaperone. I'm afraid I did make up the story about the couple from Montana . . . to avoid being labeled a ruined woman."

Resnick studied her a moment, his gaze passing over her black eye, then nodded. "There's plenty more you both aren't telling me, but for the moment I'll let it go."

He brushed off his pant legs, which bore some pine duff from the stakeout, and rose. "We'll continue to be on the lookout for this Danny, and I'll speak with Hank Falls about his 'twin brother.'"

Left alone, Laura looked miserably at Cord. "I've made things worse for you."

He got up. "I'm going to find Edgar Young and get to the bottom of this."

She watched him go along the path in a direction that could lead to the stables, to Wylie Camp, or back toward the cabin. Still stunned at what she'd learned about him, she got to her feet in a restless motion.

Manfred Resnick was headed toward the docks, where Hank's steamboat lay snug against the pier. Curious to know what Hank would say about his resemblance to the outlaw, Laura hurried down the slope. Across the Grand Loop Road and down the steep wooden steps to the pier, she shadowed Resnick so inexpertly that he stopped and waited for her at the base of the stairs.

They stood in the shade of the upper deck overlooking the lake, ripples lapping the dock and evoking a sweet water smell mixed with that of damp wood.

Resnick's one-eyed regard took her in. "Did curiosity kill the cat, miss?"

Laura bristled. Seeing "Danny" again had brought back what she'd tried for days to forget. "The outlaw tried to kill me."

"Wasn't the motive for the attack robbery?" he countered.

"I could have been killed," she challenged. "Who are you to say what went on?"

Resnick gave her a reluctant salute. "Very well, Miss Fielding. With you along, the conversation with Falls might take an intriguing turn."

They went along to the break in the rail and stepped onto the well-trafficked lower deck of the *Alexandra*.

At Resnick's first knock, Hank opened the main cabin door. His starched white shirt was immaculate; he'd changed for the dinner hour.

Upon seeing Laura with the Pinkerton man, his blond brows arched. Spreading his hands as though offering to be cuffed, he said, "If I'm to be taken into custody, I'd prefer to be Miss Fielding's prisoner."

She kept her face stony while Resnick nodded toward the interior of the boat. "May we come in?"

Hank stepped back, and they entered the passenger cabin. It was spare, furnished with brown horsehair benches beneath panoramic windows. The wooden deck here was also scarred from many pairs of boots and shoes. Aft, Laura saw an ornate wooden door with a thick brass knob. The varnish was so heavy she could see an almost clear reflection of the three of them.

"Miss Fielding," Resnick began. "Suppose you tell Hank about the man who attacked the stagecoach, whom you saw again near the hotel this afternoon."

Hank's backbone seemed to straighten.

Looking at him, Laura began, "When I first came to the hotel and Mr. Resnick questioned me about my ordeal . . . I told him the outlaw who got away on his palomino looked a lot like you."

She could see from the way his pupils got larger that she'd hit the mark with that one. And, after the first shock, there appeared pain.

"You know it wasn't me," he told her. "You knew the person you saw the other day in buckskin wasn't me, either."

She nodded. "Then who . . . ?"

"We do know it wasn't you, sir," Resnick broke in.

"This afternoon Miss Fielding saw the outlaw again, hiding out in an abandoned cabin. The other man with him called him 'Danny.'"

A little shudder seemed to pass through Hank.

"He looks too much like you to be anyone but your twin." Laura looked at his mirror image in the polished door that must lead to his exclusive private quarters.

In an instant, Hank passed from defensive to enraged. "This is all preposterous." He gestured them to get off his boat. "I have no brother!"

As soon as Laura and the Pinkerton man were gone, Hank strode across the worn floor and flung open the door to his inner sanctum.

His sister stood on the patterned wool carpet near the door. At his entry, she stepped back and almost tripped on the carved wooden leg of a divan covered with gold-threaded pillows.

"You were listening."

Alex's eyes, which matched her lace-trimmed lavender dress, widened. She reached to twirl a strand of her hair, a sure sign she was nervous.

Hank thought that her hair still looked like it had when she was a tiny girl, when Danny used to lift her up to ride in front of him. Danny had always chosen palominos because their manes matched their small sister's crown of shining gold.

"How long has he been here?" Hank slammed the door.

Alex jumped, her usually pink cheeks pale. "Who?"

He stepped closer. "I asked you how long Danny has been here; my brother who destroyed all my illusions about us being two parts of the same whole."

"A few days."

"Well, of course, if he were down south attacking a stage and killing the driver on June twentieth, it would have taken a while to get here."

Alex fiddled with a cameo on a gold chain around her neck. "Danny could never have done what they said," she protested with the certainty of youth.

"You must know better. Danny admitted he was thrown out of the army for embezzling the payroll."

Alex turned away.

He shouldn't tell her what he never had before, but he couldn't stand her continued denial. "You were too young to understand . . ."

The sting of bile rose in the back of his throat, but he told her anyway.

Hank had been with his stepfather, Jonathan, when they'd opened the barn door. The smell of sweet hay, dairy cows, and manure was pleasant in the crisp autumn air. Once inside, they passed down the straw-covered aisle toward the little room Jonathan used as an office. Payroll time after the harvest, and the men who had helped bring in a middling crop of Idaho potatoes were coming in an hour for the season's wages.

Behind the wooden gate of the last stall, Hank

saw his sixteen-year-old brother, Danny, the person he loved most in the world, on hands and knees in the hay. Their hired man who helped in the barns, Frank Worth, knelt beside him gripping an overstuffed cloth moneybag.

On the floor was the empty metal box that had contained the payroll.

Hank nearly retched up his mother's midday dinner of roast beef and mashed potatoes. "Danny," he gasped.

Big, burly Jonathan grabbed Frank Worth and dragged him up. "How dare you?"

Jonathan swung his fist and connected.

In the same instant, Danny launched at his back. "Leave him alone," he shouted in a high thin voice. "It was my idea! To take the money and get out. You've never wanted another man's kids. Frank and I are going to the gold mines."

Jonathan ordered both the hired man and his step-son off his farm and out of his family's lives.

Hank didn't tell Alex the rest.

A year later, at seventeen, he'd traveled to the mining districts in search of his brother. And heard he might be working in Garnet Houlihan's Ketchum, Idaho, brothel.

The rough building was made of new, sawn yellow pine. A heavyset woman held open the front door. "What's your pleasure, son?"

"No, I . . ." Hank stopped on the threshold. The smell of resin was overpowered by a miasma of unwashed bodies, cheap cologne, and the musky aroma of sex.

"Garnet," the woman called. "This boy needs breaking in."

Hank stared at the legs of cots that showed beneath woolen army blankets forming flimsy partitions. Feminine laughter cascaded over the top of one curtain.

A hard-looking woman in her thirties came out of a small office near the entry. She wore a faded rust velvet gown with dirty lace at the neck, her hair an improbable shade of burgundy.

As she surveyed him with knowing tawny eyes, the sound of a man grunting behind a blanket brought Hank's sex to sudden shameful attention.

Trailing a hand down his cheek and chest to brush the front of his trousers, Garnet said amiably, "I believe I'll do the honors meself."

Grabbing his hand, she led him down the narrow aisle to an alcove at the end. A window looked out onto the muddy morass of road beside the Salmon River. Great piles of rock, sifted by miners, lined the once-pristine riverbank. The hills were covered with stumps where trees had been cut to construct buildings and sluices. Men shoveled river sand and gravel into long troughs to check for the flash of color in their pans.

"Ye've struck gold today, me boy," Garnet announced. Sitting in front of Hank on the narrow cot, she opened the front of her bodice. "You can touch 'em."

Despite his aroused state, feeling the fleshy, blue-veined globes was the last thing Hank wanted. But he reached forward woodenly and felt their flaccid softness.

Garnet reached for the buttons on the front of Hank's trousers.

Yet, even as she raised her skirt and tried to draw him down onto the cot, he recalled his mission. "I'm not here for . . . I'm looking for my brother, Danny."

"Ye don't know a good thing when you've got it, boy." Garnet pushed Hank away. "Danny worked here a while, tending bar. I found out he had his hand in the till, and I run him off, I did."

Hank ran down the long aisle that led to the muddy street.

When he heard, a week later, that Garnet had been brutally slain, he couldn't help but suspect his brother. Within the month, a traveling salesman came by the farm and reported someone had seen a palomino tied to the brothel's rail the day Garnet died.

In his elegant cabin aboard the *Alexandra*, Hank clamped down hard with his teeth to keep from being sick.

"Stay away from Danny, Alex."

Between episodes of futile pounding at Edgar Young's door, Cord spent time walking along the lakeshore. The water smells and the scent of heated pine in the afternoon sun made him aware once again that the major draw of buying the Lake Hotel was the wilderness that surrounded it. Sure, he loved Salt Lake City, but in

Yellowstone, as at his ranch, he thrilled to the savory blend of sage and cottonwood, of earth and evergreen.

His gaze skimmed the Absarokas east of the lake, and he noted the telltale plume of wildfire burning through the backcountry. What a mix of contradiction drove this country outpost; fire on the mountain, azure water below. Plain soldiers labored at tack by day and donned dress uniform by evening to dance with the ladies beneath tulip lights. All the while, out among Wylie's tent campers, Cord's own uncle plied the trade of "Injun storyteller."

His cheeks grew hot, and his breath labored with mingled shame and pride. Laura had offered to go with him to see Bitter Waters and to help him speak with the man who shared his blood. But how could he allow her when seeing his uncle in native costume before a tipi would reinforce their different heritages forever?

A passing cloud obscured the sun and darkened the lake's brightness. When Edgar had approached him about buying the Lake Hotel, Cord had had the egotistical effrontery to think the man believed he owned Excalibur outright, that he didn't know Cord's heritage had decreed the encumbrance of his stolid adopted brother's name on the title. At the time, Cord had been too pleased at his good fortune to examine Edgar closely.

But at some level, he'd known since his arrival that there was something not quite right about the banker's manner, a certain quality of evasiveness, along with his unexplained absences. Even so, he would never have suspected mild-mannered Edgar of consorting with a murdering outlaw.

As far as Cord knew, neither Edgar nor Danny had seen him and Laura sneak up and listen to their conversation in the cabin. Yet, the two men had gotten away clean. Coincidence, or had Cord and Laura been seen?

He hadn't told Laura exactly what Danny had said. That remark about "holding off cleaning up loose ends" might explain why Danny hadn't killed him or Laura on the trail. Or later.

But if Cord "had served his purpose," he . . . and Laura . . . might now be targets.

CHAPTER FIFTEEN
JUNE 26

Laura pulled on a pair of Constance's lace-trimmed muslin drawers and sat on the edge of the bed, ignoring the flounced underskirt. From outside her window came the sounds of merriment as coach and wagon tours returned for dinner.

Her thoughts turned to Hank, for no matter his denial of a family relationship with the outlaw, she trusted her eyes. The two men had to be not only blood kin; they were virtually identical except in grooming and manner.

Had it shocked Hank to learn his brother had gone bad? Or did he already know? The pain she'd seen in his expression made her suspect he did. And if they were twins and not just brothers close in age, how especially awful it must be.

Unless Hank were a smoother version of Danny.

At this disturbing thought, she realized that sometime in the last few days she'd gone over to Cord's side.

From his first grudging admission of his parents dying when he was young, to this afternoon's revelation that his grandmother was Nez Perce . . . and had died for it, she'd been touched. He was, as Constance had said, more alive than most people.

Laura pushed off the bed, donned the underskirt, and was studying upon which dress to wear when her cousin came in, as though summoned by Laura's thinking of her. She wore a smart crimson velvet number with a nipped-in waist, and her intent air said she was up to something.

Laura kept her eyes on the bureau mirror and dressed her hair.

"What have you been amusing yourself with this afternoon, while Mother and I were sewing in the lobby parlor?" Constance ran a finger along the lace scarf beneath the mirror.

Laura set Aunt Fanny's hairbrush on the wooden dresser with a clack. "First, you know I went to the paddock to go riding with Sergeant Nevers. Then, while walking in the forest near the shore, I saw the outlaw who robbed the stagecoach." She expected surprise, but Constance's blue stare was impassive.

"We called for help, and though the soldiers gave chase, he got away."

"We?"

Laura reached for the brush again.

"Quite more eventful than embroidery, I should say." Constance put her small hands on her hips. "I had hoped for more than to be left for the day with my mother, especially as I wear William Sutton's betrothal ring."

Doubt and envy stabbed at Laura as it had in the stable. Cord might be playing them both false, as he had been hiding his family secrets. But something tremulous in her cousin's tone gave her pause.

"Tell me, then," Laura challenged. Though it was like biting an aching tooth, she had to know. "What was it like when Cord asked you to be his wife?"

"Wha . . . what do you mean?"

Laura advanced on her. "I mean when and where. Were you on the terrace in St. Paul, or the rose garden, lost in a half moon's magic, when he popped the question? How did he say it?" She dipped as though to go down on one knee. "Did he say, 'Marry me, Connie? I cannot imagine a life without you'?"

Constance glowered.

Laura gripped the silver handle of the brush. "I mean did Cord ever really ask you to marry him *in so many words*?"

Crossing her arms over her chest, Laura focused on her cousin, who met her stare for stare.

She waited.

"All right, he never asked me!"

Laura gasped. If that were true, why hadn't Cord denied they were betrothed?

Constance rushed to fill the silence. "He invited me out West to see his land and to bring Mother, so I believed . . ." Her chin began to quiver. "Why do you call William 'Cord' in that crass way?"

"Perhaps if you knew him better, you'd realize it suits him."

"And you, of course, know him intimately. Since you spent three nights on the trail with him!" Constance's expression was both triumphant and ugly.

Laura's face got hot. "How . . . ?"

"Mother and I were much enlightened by your conversation with Mr. Resnick and . . . William on the porch outside the window where we were sewing."

It was her own fault. No one had forced her to speak up for Cord.

"Eavesdroppers are the lowest of the low," she countered.

"How about liars? How about that kindly couple from Montana that brought you to Yellowstone?"

"How about your lying to everyone who'll listen about Cord asking you to marry him?"

Constance's hands-on-hips formed into fists. "I'm not the one in trouble here. Mother went straight to Father to tell him about you being with a man those nights. You'll be lucky if he doesn't call your 'Cord' out."

"My Cord? I thought you cared for him. How could seeing him called out make you happy?"

Pansy-blue eyes brimmed with tears, and Constance rushed from the room, slamming the door.

Laura entered the lobby, dressed in her best hand-me-down from Constance. The emerald watered silk brought out the green in her eyes, and the puffed peplum at the rear emphasized her waist. In spite of her confidence in her appearance, her chest clutched at what must be coming since her secret was out. All she could do was hold her head high and hope the dressing-down she expected from her father would not be a public one.

The first person she encountered was Constance, who stood alone near the fireplace in her crimson velvet. With sad eyes, she poised with a hand at her throat in a dramatic gesture. Any man seeing her would no doubt be passionately disposed to take on the task of bringing a smile to her tragic countenance.

She broke character enough to give Laura a dirty look.

Going over to Constance and putting a hand on her daughter's shoulder, Aunt Fanny fixed Laura with a chill regard that said she'd taken her breach of truth about the people from Montana badly.

How would she feel if she knew how deep her daughter's deception was?

"There you are." Hank spoke from behind Laura.

She turned and he bowed, his company manners making her almost wonder if the scene on the *Alexandra* with Manfred Resnick had really taken place. At any rate, the closed expression on his hawklike face did not invite her to dredge it up.

From the east hall, Cord made an entrance. His black suit was freshly pressed; his newly shortened hair waved over his brow. In spite of his neat appearance, he bore a scowl that made an arriving male guest step out of his way.

Constance's wilting violet act went into high gear, and she sent Cord a come-hither message. When he did not even look her way, another daggerlike glare shot toward Laura.

A man with apparently a single purpose, Cord stalked straight toward Laura. Only at the last, when his gaze settled on Hank, did she realize she was not his goal.

"Falls. Tell me about your brother."

Hank's narrow nose lifted. "I don't have a brother."

Cord's ringing laugh made the cocktail crowd go silent and look their way. "You'd have me believe you lead a dual life? That you trade in your gray suit for buckskin and hit the trail? That you ride a blooded palomino for your stagecoach-robbing escapades with a fellow named Frank Worth?"

"I . . . I'm sorry. Did you say Frank Worth?"

"Did I not speak clearly? When I, yes . . . I . . . rescued Laura Fielding from Frank Worth and your doppelganger down in Jackson's Hole, Frank was gut shot. I finished him."

Hank gasped.

Laura saw the Pinkerton man sidle around the corner of the fireplace and take up a listening pose.

"Danny got away," Cord finished.

With a visible effort, Hank's features transformed. Back in control, he beckoned Resnick forward. "I suggest that someone find this mysterious 'Danny' before there are any more accusations that I have participated in violent doings." He turned to Laura and placed his palm at the small of her back. "Shall we go in to dinner?"

It did not escape her that Hank's hand trembled.

She wanted to pull away, but her father came up behind her and placed his fingers on her elbow. He gave her a warning look from beneath furrowed brows; she assumed it had to do with her and Cord's secret being out.

"We'll have a nice Burgundy this evening." Hank spoke to the tuxedoed waiter leading the party of him and Laura, along with her father, Aunt Fanny, and Constance, to a prominent window-side table.

He held a chair for Laura and brushed her shoulders while seating her. She looked at his long pale fingers, those of a pampered gentleman, and imagined identical hands pawing through her belongings, stealing her mother's precious cameo.

Hank said he didn't have a brother, but he had a sister. One who might be tripped into answering a cleverly placed question.

Laura turned to Hank. "Why does your sister, Alexandra, not join us for dinner? I have seen her about the hotel several times."

"Yes, we would be happy to see her." Though Forrest's demeanor toward Hank was pleasant, he gave Laura another dark look that said he would deal with her later.

When the waiter arrived, Hank declined the menu. "This evening I think the spring lamb, with wild sorrel and a mint glaze . . . for myself and Miss Fielding."

"Perhaps you might ask what I would like." Laura gestured toward the waiter for the leather-backed menu.

Before Hank could respond, Forrest broke his reach for the breadbasket. "Perhaps you should be happy that the gentleman wishes to order for you."

Laura almost flashed back at him, too, but there was nothing to be gained. She bit the inside of her cheek and put her hands in her lap when the menu was tardily offered.

Hank nodded to Forrest. "Thank you, sir, for calling me a gentleman. At least I am not a boor like Mr. William Cordon Sutton."

Without warning, Constance flared, her dark hair dancing in the light from the chandeliers. "How dare you speak that way about William!"

Before Laura could point out that Constance had denied him this afternoon, Aunt Fanny put a gentle hand on her daughter's just above the garnet ring.

Constance shook off the restraint and fixed on her Uncle Forrest. "William should be with me tonight, but this deal you men are fighting over is spoiling everything!"

Forrest gave his niece an impatient look. "The last time we spoke of the man, you seemed to think something else had come between you." He glanced at Laura.

She reached for the Burgundy the waiter set before her, surprised at how steady her hand was. "I'm not about to apologize for traveling with Cord. He saved me from . . ." She looked at Hank. "Danny Falls."

"That again," he sneered.

Laura's heart pounded. "That again. Unless you wish to confess your role in killing Angus Spiner."

Hank pushed back his chair.

Norman Hagen's hand on his shoulder kept him in place. The big man, elegantly attired in a dark brown suit with a thick gold watch chain, took in the disquiet. "When I agreed to come out here to help sell the hotel, I had no idea how complicated the situation was going to get."

Hank's expression turned from ugly to accommodating. "Won't you join us, Norman? I can have the waiter set another place."

Norman shook his head. "I came to give you a piece of news. It seems my boss, Hopkins Chandler, has been called away on business to Bozeman and will not be back until the day after tomorrow. He telephoned and asked that I extend an invitation to you gentlemen to make an excursion to the Grand Canyon of the Yellowstone in the morning."

Laura noted that Constance's head was up and the old sparkle in her eyes. "Just the gentlemen?"

"Girls," Aunt Fanny chided, "you know the men have important business." She lifted her glass and sampled the Burgundy. "We'll take a tour up to the canyon together one day, just the three of us."

"It's all right." Hank favored Fanny with a smile and put a bold hand on Laura's bare forearm. "You can sit with me in the wagon."

Before she could pull away, she realized Cord stood outside the dining-room doors with Manfred Resnick. With a drink in his hand and an unreadable expression on his dark countenance, he raised his glass to her in a toast. Though the gesture could have been sincere, she felt he mocked her.

Cord watched Norman come toward him from the dining room. Though he had just watched him being cordial to Hank, his instinctive respect for the Union Pacific representative was undiminished as Norman joined him and Resnick near the bar.

"Evening, Sutton. Resnick."

After shaking hands with both men, Norman addressed the Pinkerton representative. "Any progress on apprehending that outlaw?"

Resnick shook his head. "Word travels fast."

"Soldiers talk, especially when they find something more interesting to do than entertain the tourists." Norman looked back at Hank and the Fielding party. "Tempers seem to be running high after Miss Fielding's suggestion the outlaw is related to Hank."

"If he's not," Cord said, "it's the most uncanny resemblance I've ever seen."

"And still at large." Norman stroked his beard and looked at Resnick. "Do you think it safe to take an excursion away from the hotel? Say to the Grand

Canyon of the Yellowstone?"

"As far as we know, Danny's partner in crime died beside the stage. Unless he has a gang we don't know about, he's unlikely to ambush a large party," Resnick replied. "I would think there's safety in numbers."

Norman nodded.

Resnick squinted his good eye and looked toward the lobby door. "If you gentlemen will excuse me, I see someone I need to speak to."

Cord followed his gaze and saw the retreating form of Captain Feddors. It was a good thing he wasn't coming toward them; he would have likely made some bigoted remark. The last thing Cord needed was for something like that to happen in front of Norman Hagen.

As soon as they were alone, he asked, "Could you and I meet with Mr. Chandler early in the morning?" Even as he spoke, he hoped he still had the backing of the bank in Great Falls.

Dammit, where was Edgar?

"I'm sorry," Norman replied. "The reason I wished to speak to you is to let you know Mr. Chandler will be away this evening and tomorrow. He requested I entertain you, Hank, and Fielding with the Grand Canyon excursion I mentioned to Resnick."

Cord grimaced. "I would think Hank's seen the park and has plenty to do keeping up with this place."

"I believe he has agreed to go. In fact, he invited the ladies of the Fielding party, most particularly Forrest's daughter, Laura."

Cord frowned before he caught himself.

Norman cleared his throat. "Something I have been meaning to ask. Word is that you and Miss Constance Devon . . ."

Cord swallowed. He'd seen Constance and Norman together several times in the past few days.

"I wanted to ask you, sir, about your intentions."

He felt like a cad. "That's something I must discuss with Miss Devon before I speak with another."

Norman nodded. "Then may I expect your company on tomorrow's excursion?"

"Certainly."

"I shall see you out front in the morning at eight." He bowed and took his leave.

On his own, Cord looked in again through the dining-room doors. He should just walk in and take Constance out with him. Tell her that he and Laura had been together on the trail before it got to her from another source.

When Cord started toward the dinner table, Laura's mouth went dry. During his conversation with Norman she'd been aware of the several looks both men had given her and Constance.

When he came to stand, not beside her chair, but Constance's, Laura studied her gold-rimmed dessert plate.

"Good evening." Cord bowed and kept his focus

on Constance. "I wonder if you might step out with me for a little while." He looked at the empty sherbet bowl at her place. "That is, if you have finished your dinner."

"I have," she murmured and pushed back her chair.

Forrest Fielding whip-cracked, "Don't you dare!"

Constance sagged back.

Forrest was on his feet. "You low-down cur. You asked my niece to be your wife, yet you have not paid her the slightest attention since we got here. Now I have learned that you compromised my daughter by traveling with her unchaperoned."

Laura broke in, "Would you rather he had left me alone in the wilderness?"

Forrest's face colored. "He could have done any number of things. Waited with you for the stage scouts, escorted you to the town of Jackson, which would not have been an overnight ride . . . things any gentleman would have considered."

Cord faced him. "Whatever you may think of my and Laura's judgment when we decided to travel together, I am here to do the right thing." He extended his hand to Constance. "Are you coming with me?"

Constance studied her uncle's angry face and shook her head.

Cord bowed again. "Then I will speak with you at your convenience." His tone sounded perfectly correct, but Laura sensed anger at her cousin's mealymouthed refusal to go along. Perhaps what she feared was not Forrest's wrath, but what Cord might say about her falsely representing them as engaged.

Cord's regard swept the table at large. "Good evening."

He turned away and left with swift steps.

Laura got to her feet and followed him from the dining room. When her father called for her to come back, she walked faster.

CHAPTER SIXTEEN
JUNE 26

Laura lost sight of Cord in the crowded lobby. Deciding he must have gone out, she headed for the nearest door.

Outside, she stood a moment while her eyes adjusted to the deepening dusk. Upon the opposite hillside, she noticed the glow from the campfire at Wylie's. Remembering her suggestion to go with Cord to hear Bitter Waters, she suspected he'd gone there.

Without going up to her room for a shawl, she hugged herself and moved toward the tipi near the fire. Halfway there, she heard the barker introduce Bitter Waters of the Nez Perce Nation.

Laura had never thought of the tribes as nations, but, of course, that was exactly what they were.

When she reached the outer edge of the campfire crowd, she wormed her way to a place where she could see. Several of the casually dressed campers looked askance at her emerald silk.

Their attention was quickly diverted when a distinguished gentleman came out of the tipi. His dark business suit and white shirt made a startling contrast to his braided hair, breastplate of bone, and colored beads. His powerful gaze swept over the audience and, as his focus came to rest on someone to Laura's left, she located Cord.

The two men looked at one another for no longer than a heartbeat. Then Bitter Waters raised both arms and began to chant. The mellifluous tones sent a chill up Laura's spine.

She moved toward Cord, but stopped. If Bitter Waters saw them together, her idea of helping the two men connect after the program might go awry.

The chant ended and the speaker's focus returned to Cord. "Tonight, I speak a story—no, not a story—the truth of how the Nez Perce went to war against the United States."

Bitter Waters knelt beside the wall of the army tent on the parade ground of Fort Lapwai in western Idaho, a loose assemblage of buildings beside meandering Lapwai Creek. It had been less than a week since the settler killed his mother. Though Bitter Waters had reported the murder, the guilty man was yet to be arrested.

Though his legs ached from squatting, Bitter Waters remained motionless. Many people's future turned on this meeting between the United States government and the Nez Perce chiefs.

Major General Oliver Otis Howard, commander of the Department of the Columbia, stood at attention. The canvas tent walls billowed in the breeze, while he addressed the four Nez Perce chiefs who had come to council. "I have been talking with you for days, but your time is running out."

Toohoolhoolzote, the oldest of the Nez Perce leaders, answered Howard. "Your fort stands within the nation of the Nimiipuu, the Nez Perce People." He crossed his arms over his heavy bronzed chest, a hard look on his deeply lined face. His hair, streaked with gray, hung past his thick neck, down to the waist of his breechclout and leather leggings.

"I know that your bands did not sign the treaty of 1863." Howard appeared to agree. "Nonetheless, you must go onto the reservation that the rest of the Nez Perce agreed to."

The treaty of 1855 had granted the Nez Perce seven million acres in Washington, Oregon, and Idaho, but in 1863, the government had reneged and shrunk their lands to a paltry seven hundred thousand.

"We did not agree," Toohoolhoolzote insisted.

Behind him, three other chiefs of the non-treaty Nez Perce—Heinmot Tooyalakekt, known as Joseph; Allalimya Takanin, or Looking Glass; and Peopeo Hihhih, or White Bird—sat on the grass beneath the open canvas tent.

General Howard rose from the table where he sat with five other representatives of the army. The imposing presence of the barrel-chested, bearded officer seemed enhanced by the empty blue sleeve pinned up below an epaulet with a single gold star; his right arm had been lost in the Civil War.

"Your non-treaty bands are the smallest number," General Howard continued. "There cannot be more than eight hundred people in all your lodges."

Howard's manner had no effect upon the impassive expressions of the chiefs, except for Joseph. He was the youngest and largest of the men, and his strong face beneath his wing of upswept dark hair looked deeply sad. "You would not want to leave your home." Joseph looked up at Howard, who loomed over the seated chiefs.

"You must abide by the will of the majority," Howard told him.

Bitter Waters thought that Chief Hallalhotsoot, known to the whites as Lawyer, had signed the treaty on behalf of the Presbyterian Nez Perce only because his lands were already inside the proposed reservation.

Pushing to his feet, Joseph gathered his blanket around him, despite the springlike day.

"Suppose a white man come and say he likes my horses and wants to buy them. I say, 'No, they please me. I will not sell.' He goes to Lawyer, who says, 'I will sell Joseph's horses to you.' If we sold our land to you, it was in this way."

Perhaps it had happened because the people of Lawyer's lodge abhorred the horse racing, dancing, and wagering Bitter Waters and his friends embraced so enthusiastically.

Howard pointed at Joseph. "I have a petition given me this day by fifty-six settlers of Salmon River County. They tell of Nez Perce tearing down and burning their fences, stealing livestock, and firing pistols for sport."

"These settlers are squatting on our land," Toohoolhoolzote said. "My father and his father before him sleep beneath the land that is our Mother."

General Howard placed a flat hand on top of a Bible that lay near him on the table. His voice rang out, "I am not going to listen to any more Dreamer nonsense or talk of Earth Mothers."

Bitter Waters got to his feet, his head brushing the sloping canvas. Looking down upon General Howard, he pointed in turn. "We have kept the peace for many years, while the settlers have killed thirty of our People." He spoke in Nez Perce, too angry for English. "Only last week my mother was killed like an animal." He spat on the grass before Howard's highly polished boots.

Howard turned to Toohoolhoolzote for translation.

Bitter Waters listened to see if Toohoolhoolzote would translate faithfully or decide with the wisdom of his seventy snows to temper the message. He braced himself to step in and correct the older man in defiance of etiquette.

Toohoolhoolzote repeated it precisely.

The rest of the chiefs rose with a clicking of bone breastplates. The Nez Perce, inside and outside the tent, even the women with babies in arms, also got up. Bitter Waters caught Kamiah's eye, as she struggled to reach him through the colorfully dressed crowd.

The five officers with Howard closed ranks about the general.

"Take these men to the guardhouse," Howard called.

Other soldiers surrounded Bitter Waters and Toohoolhoolzote.

A murmur ran through the crowd like a rising wind. Bitter Waters looked at the pile of stacked arms where the Nez Perce had laid down their weapons.

Toohoolhoolzote faced his captors; his lined face might have been carved from stone. "You may lock me up," his voice dripped disdain, "but behind me are always more of the People."

"You tell your people," Howard ordered, his face flushing, "that you will go onto the reservation within thirty days, or the soldiers will shoot you down!"

Around the Wylie campfire, the crowd erupted with a variety of reactions conveying everything from indignation at the tribe's fate to approval of the Nez Perce being hunted. Through it all, Cord heard Laura's gasp from perhaps fifteen feet away.

He turned and saw she stood transfixed, one hand at her throat. Unaccountably, anger swelled his chest.

What did she know of suffering? Of watching one's parents die, of being taken virtual prisoner by his own uncle . . . of going through the difficult rite of seeking a guardian spirit, then finding a way of escaping it all?

Yet, as Laura's tear-filled eyes met his, he felt a tightness in his chest and wanted to go to her.

Before he could, Bitter Waters continued, "Toohoolhoolzote and I were held prisoner for eight days while the council went on. Then we were released."

Weeks passed, and the men and women of the nontreaty groups pretended the summer sun would continue to shine without incident. Berries ripened, and the young men took advantage of long twilights to spend time with the equally ripening girls coming to womanhood.

Then the chiefs decided their people should move to summer camping grounds to enjoy the balmy June weather. Some reacted with joy, for the annual pilgrimage lifted everyone's spirits. But when Bitter Waters and his wife, Kamiah, left his fine farm near the Wallowa River, he felt they were abandoning it for the last time.

On the river crossing at Dug Bar, deep in the desolate heat of Hell's Canyon, with the Snake running high, even the bravest wondered if they would cross safely. They were right to worry, for hundreds of struggling cattle and horses were swept away downstream into a narrow-walled canyon.

Once encamped in the highlands, far from the reservation lands the United States had decreed as their destination, Bitter Waters went to the council lodge and confronted the elders. "There are only a few suns remaining in Howard's ultimatum."

Joseph responded to his challenge with a long speech. He reminded everyone that their camping grounds were pleasant, and that there was still time for the chiefs to parlay their way to consensus. Bitter Waters had learned to expect Joseph to seek the peaceful solution, but since Seeyakoon's death, he could no longer see the wisdom of turning the other cheek.

"My mother is not yet cold," he declared. "I say that if it is war they want, let us give it to them."

The elders, as had happened so many times before, remained divided.

Bitter Waters marched away from the council lodge, trembling with rage.

Outside, it was pleasant beside a lake in the sun, young men racing their horses on the meadow, and women spreading camas with wilting blue flowers to dry in the sun. He wished that this were like any other year, when the wind would soothe his brow and he would find his wife, Kamiah, take her from her work, and walk with her in the forest.

It had been her sweet strength and the new life that grew within her that had persuaded him not to go after Harding the night he murdered Seeyakoon. "The settlers will lynch you if you kill a white man. You must wait for justice."

Looking around for her, he saw his friend Tarpas Illipt approach, leading a spotted gray. Still in high spirits from racing, Tarpas headed his mount toward the lake for a drink.

"Mind your horse!" A man called Walks Alone waved his arms at Tarpas, but it was too late. The horse had trampled his drying rack, collapsing it upon the shore.

"I have worked hard with my wife, gathering so much camas." Walks Alone gestured angrily.

Bitter Waters had never liked thick-waisted Walks Alone, not since he had set his dogs on him and Tarpas when they were youths stealing apples with Sarah. Smiling at Tarpas, Bitter Waters spoke slyly to Walks Alone, "My wife, Kamiah, is pregnant, but still you do not see me do woman's work."

Walks Alone threw aside the broken pieces of his drying rack. An ugly look took over his features. "Bitter Waters, if you're so brave, why have you not avenged your mother's death?"

Without hesitation, as though this new insult on top of General Howard's ultimatum had torn the shackles of civilization from him, he leaped astride Tarpas's horse, wheeled the animal, and drew his friend up behind him.

At the communal paddock, they picked up another horse. And though he wanted to see Kamiah before they rode out, she would only try to stop them.

By the time they reached their goal, night was overtaking them.

Rifles at the ready, Bitter Waters and Tarpas reined in their horses before the settler's cabin beside the Wallowa. Around the log building, a fence enclosed a plowed square with melons, corn, and potatoes beginning to come up. Beyond was the cleared land awaiting the apple trees Harding had spoken of, enclosed by the rail fence that had cost Seeyakoon her life. Half a dozen hounds lay on the packed earth of the yard, settling in for the night.

"Harding!" Tarpas shouted.

Bitter Waters was glad his friend had called out, for his own throat felt thick.

In the bluish shadows of the porch, the rough wooden door swung wide to reveal Harding with his thick head of graying hair. He carried a pistol, poorly camouflaged at his side.

Tarpas and Bitter Waters slid to the ground.

With a barely perceptible motion, Harding gestured to his dogs. In spite of their apparent somnolence, in a single surge, the pack leaped to attention. They charged, baying.

Bitter Waters stood his ground while Tarpas aimed and fired, picking off two of the dogs. Bitter Waters shouldered his own weapon and took out two more. The remaining animals hesitated and stood in confusion, sniffing at the bodies of their fallen comrades.

Harding raised his weapon, but before he could get off a round, Bitter Waters shot him through the heart.

"It is war," he declared.

Laura pressed her fist to her mouth, for she knew what came next from accounts of the struggle . . . displacement, battlefields, and death. It was easy to miss the human side when reading the dry prose with which history was often related.

But whether the government of the United States dealt with the Navajo, Apache, or the Nez Perce, the record was all the same. Ever since white men had first set foot on the soil of North America, they had broken every treaty made with those who dwelled there before they arrived.

Heedless of anyone seeing, she went to Cord. "I didn't know."

Bitter Waters bowed his head and turned away before his listeners realized he was leaving. He walked to the tipi, threw back the flap, and disappeared inside.

The skin fell back into place.

Cord shook Laura off and strode forward. She gathered her wits and moved, circling behind the tent to head off Bitter Waters if he sneaked out the back.

It didn't take long. No sooner had she left the circle of firelight and entered the forest than she saw a man emerge from the tipi's rear.

"Hold, sir," she said.

Bitter Waters looked surprised, but stopped with a swing of his braids. "My story is complete. For this night."

"There is a man who needs to speak with you. About other parts of your story."

Bitter Waters held her gaze and nodded. "Though the two of you stand apart, you are the woman of Blue Eyes."

Cord stepped around the side of the tipi, too late not to have heard the last words.

Bitter Waters studied the two of them with what looked like compassion. "Sarah stood thusly with Franklin Sutton before she went away with him."

Beneath the older man's scrutiny, Cord was proud to have Laura by his side. But the last thing he wanted was for her to stay and be caught up in his old hurts.

He bent his head and spoke to her quietly, "Let my uncle and me speak together privately."

Her eyes flashed reluctance.

"Please," he said, "go now."

Without a word, she turned her back.

Only after her rapid footsteps retreated toward the hotel could Cord let the mention of his parents churn up the pain. "Sarah stood with my father before you drove her from her People. Before you came in the night and murdered her and her husband."

Bitter Waters shook his head. "I am sure a six-year-old boy might not remember the details, but your father's gun misfired. Your mother died in a terrible accident. And it was not I who threw the blade at

Franklin's chest."

Cord believed he spoke truth, for that was the way the nightmare ran each time it came upon him in the darkest part of the night.

"Do you recall what happened next?" Bitter Waters asked.

The house had burned, but somehow that did not seem to be the answer.

His uncle went on, "I took you up onto my saddle and wrapped you in the betrothal hide Tarpas made for Sarah—which she still kept. Your mother lived between two worlds, as Seeyakoon did when she loved a white man and bore a half-breed daughter."

"As I do," Cord ground out. "When I escaped from the tribe in Yellowstone," he noted his uncle's flinch, "a white man adopted me . . ."

The lines beside Bitter Waters's mouth deepened. "I had taken you in as blood of my blood. You are of the Nimiipuu, the People."

When Cord had heard those words from him as a six-year-old, he'd denied the tribe. This evening, after facing his uncle for the first time in so many years, it was no longer so simple. He bore the scar of the Mormon boy's knife, the brand of "savage." But he carried his *wayakin* of obsidian with him always, as though some part of him did believe.

"I can no longer deny my ties to two worlds, old uncle," he said. "The trouble is that, like my mother, I belong in neither of them."

"Until you accept them both, that shall remain true."

Bitter Waters seemed to evaporate into darkness.

All was still beside the lake, while Cord walked the shore. The hotel lights shined like a beacon.

Two worlds.

When he had conceived the concept for Excalibur, to renovate a decaying warehouse and create a first-class hotel not far from where the Mormon Temple had been under construction for years, his adopted father, Aaron, had invited him into his library. They had sat among the shelves of well-worn books, everything from Cord's childhood favorites of James Fenimore Cooper's *Leatherstocking Tales* and Sir Walter Scott's *Ivanhoe*, to the family Bible.

Being in that room always reminded Cord of what had happened years ago, after the older boys attacked him in the schoolyard.

He'd been lying on the ground, bleeding. Carey loomed over him with an ugly smile, tossing his knife from one hand to another. Then Aaron, blond like Carey, with the most unusual whiskey-colored eyes—no way he would ever be mistaken for Cord's blood father—arrived.

Aaron wasn't as big as Carey, but he came up behind and grabbed him and Levi and knocked their heads together. Then he looked down at Cord and put out his hand to help him to his feet. "Come home, son."

With the knife wound on his cheek throbbing

with each heartbeat, with insults still ringing in his ears, Cord had gone with Aaron into the library. He'd watched the older man open the book of scripture, bound in Moroccan leather, and pull his fountain pen from its stand on his desk blotter.

In neat script, he inscribed the name "William Cordon Sutton" in the Bryce family Bible.

In their Mormon extended family, Aaron's wife, Carolyn, tried to teach Cord to play the parlor organ. Uncle James held forth to instruct Cord in Latin and proper penmanship, and when Cord's adopted sister, Evie, gave birth to a boy, she named him William Cordon. Aaron even seemed connected to the Jackson Hole ranch. It had been his influence, and that of the bishop of the Mormon Church, that had permitted Cord's claim to the land to pass unchallenged.

But the conflicts at Excalibur between him and Thomas had made him ripe for Edgar Young's approach, eager to go to St. Paul and Yellowstone. No, desperate to find a niche where he might control his destiny.

Desperate enough to try to pass for a man without Nez Perce blood.

Beside the lake, he sighed and felt the knots beneath his shoulder blades. How must Sarah have felt, leaving behind her village, her mother, her brother, to go with Franklin? And how did Cord feel this night, meeting his uncle again after over twenty years?

Dismayed that his past had caught up with him? Or, after hearing Bitter Waters tale, ashamed he had denied his mother's People?

Laura hurried back to the hotel, wondering why Cord had not wanted her to stay. Perhaps his uncle's assertion that she was his woman had scared him off.

The more sinister explanation had to do with Constance. Cord had come to the table and asked her to go out with him. Laura had thought, no, hoped his intent had been to break off with her, but she didn't know. In fact, though honor wouldn't permit a gentleman to call a lady's claim to betrothal a lie, there was darker potential.

He might not want to end being the recipient of Constance's favors.

Halfway to the hotel, she remembered Danny Falls lurking about and moved faster.

Upon entering the festive lobby where music played, she saw Constance dancing with Norman Hagen. At least Laura wouldn't have to deal with accusations about following Cord out of the dining room . . . until later.

Her father was in the game room, intent on the cards in his hand. Aunt Fanny was part of a group that included Lieutenant John Stafford.

Laura hurried toward the stairs. She didn't care to run into anyone like Hank or Larry Nevers and socialize. She especially did not want to see Manfred Resnick and deal with more questions.

Once the door of her room closed behind her, she did not turn the light switch. She didn't even look toward her bedside candle, but went to the window and opened it wide.

Somehow, being indoors heightened her awareness of the forest she had walked through. On the dark trail, she'd been closed to sensation, hurrying toward safety and light. Now, she inhaled the perfume of pine and appreciated the call of a wild duck. The bird sounded as if it was laughing.

She deserved to be laughed at. She had no idea who Cord really was, or what he stood for.

CHAPTER SEVENTEEN
JUNE 27

"Good-looking animals," Cord said, his breath making smoke in the chill morning sunlight. He looked over the team of four chestnut horses that would carry them to the canyon.

"Thank you, sir." The stocky young driver wore the uniform of knee-length tan duster, brimmed hat, and dust kerchief. He raised the canvas cover on the wagon's rear platform to check on the lunches.

"Cord Sutton."

"Burke Evans." He offered a hand hard with calluses. "I chose this team because they pull together well and it'll be comfortable for the ladies."

Cord rubbed his hands together and stamped his brown leather boots against the early-morning chill. His head felt cold where his hair was damp from his hasty toilet. "Ah, yes. The ladies."

"And does that make you a gentleman?"

Cord whirled to find Laura, slight and wiry in her

boy's trousers and a white shirtwaist-style blouse beneath her brown wool coat. Seeing her in pants took him back to the time he'd spent alone with her in the forests south of Yellowstone Lake. Though he had not had a chance to clear things up with Constance, he smiled.

Laura's lips did not bow in return.

There were too many folks around, drivers waiting alongside their wagons and guests speculating with interest about the day's sightseeing.

"Come with me." Cord indicated with a jerk of his head for her to walk with him.

"I don't think we have anything to say."

"Please." If he couldn't manage to set things straight with Constance, he'd at least let Laura know it was in the works.

"No." But at the driver's curious look, she seemed to change her mind. Squaring her narrow shoulders, she went with him down the length of yellow board wall and around the corner of the hotel.

There, he shoved his hands into the pockets of his sheepskin coat. "What's the matter with you this morning?"

"Nothing. I am merely going to see the Grand Canyon of the Yellowstone at Hank's invitation." She lifted her chin.

"Hank!" Norman had mentioned that, but, "What do you mean playing both ends against the middle?"

"Me? You came into the dining room to ask Constance to go walking with you."

"You know what I wanted to talk to her about."

"Do I?"

"Look," his blood pressure rose, "I am trying to be a man of honor in letting her know that our . . . association in St. Paul, while heartfelt at the time, has not stood the test of separation and . . . meeting someone else."

"She told me you never asked her to marry you, but you've played along with the betrothal. Were you perhaps planning on asking her soon?"

"For God's sake, Laura." His hands came out of his pockets where he'd been keeping them prisoner, and he trapped her against the wall.

She shoved against him. Her palms on his chest felt warm through his shirt.

"Stop it. I don't want you."

"If you don't," he ground out, "you should have thought twice before you . . ."

"Before I what? I have kissed other men, and I have seen you kiss another woman." Her voice was taut. "The last I heard, it did not have to mean anything."

He pressed his palms against the rough wood to keep from taking her slender face in his hands, especially after she swore it meant nothing.

Her mouth twisted. "Things happen all the time that don't mean a thing. Last night you sent me away instead of letting me stay and meet your uncle."

"There were things that had to be said. Ugly things."

"I can handle ugly. I handled watching you finish Frank Worth. I handled killing a grizzly. You should trust me, especially with what I know."

Pledge or threat, he didn't know. "We should trust each other, but somehow I didn't expect that to mean you wanted to be with Hank."

Laura kicked him smartly in the shin.

He flinched yet spoke softly. "You know some of my secrets, but there are more. Things no one else knows." Close to her lips, he whispered, "You talked of kissing . . ."

From just around the corner, Forrest Fielding called, "Laura!"

She was certain her flaming cheeks must give her away, and she moved quickly away from Cord.

Constance's voice blended with Forrest's. "Have you seen William this morning?"

Cord's eyes bored into hers. He had spoken of honor, and Constance had yet to be told.

Laura straightened her back to face her father. "Good morning," she managed. She felt his sharp eyes missed nothing.

"A pleasant day to you, sir." Cord bowed. He did not touch Laura as they walked into view of the carriages.

"Good morning, William," Constance said sweetly, putting out her hand. Despite her brittle smile, Laura could see the knot of muscle beneath her cousin's ear-lobe.

Constance's outfit made Laura wish she had worn

something prettier than her laundered trousers and a shirtwaist. Her cousin's starched cotton dress, white with tiny blue sprigs of flowers that matched her eyes, was topped by a darker blue pelerine, a short woolen cloak tied with silken cords tipped in rabbit fur. The long fall of Constance's black hair brushed the back of Cord's hand as he helped her up into the wagon.

Inclining his head to Laura, Cord offered to assist her, as well, and she felt the challenge in his eyes. Turning away, Laura saw Hank Falls approaching and smiled brightly. "Good morning."

Hank took her hand, turned it over, and kissed it with a slow warmth that made her want to scrub her palm on her pants. He had dressed for the day in his habitual gray suit, in contrast to Cord's denim trousers.

The driver passed out dusters to protect their clothes, and everyone donned them.

Cord swung up to sit beside Constance, giving Laura a view of the back of his dark head. Hank helped Laura into the rear seat, then pulled his lanky frame up beside her. Forrest Fielding climbed up with an effort and settled into the middle seat, his ample belly hanging over his belt. Norman Hagen joined him with, "It's a shame your sister, Fanny, decided to stay behind."

Cord turned to Norman. "And a pity Mr. Chandler is away."

"Where is Edgar Young this morning?" Norman returned.

No one replied.

Laura leaned forward and put a hand on Norman's shoulder. "It is most kind of you to amuse Constance. I saw you two dancing last night . . . you seem made for one another."

Norman smiled and appeared to lose his train of thought.

The wagon started down the hotel drive. The chestnut team pulled smartly, their hooves raising a plume of dust.

For a few miles, the Grand Loop Road meandered through dense forest, redolent of pine. On their right, the shining silver stream of the Yellowstone River flashed in the sun. Yet, within an hour the peace was shattered, as they slowed beside a cauldron alternately vomiting noxious black mud and swallowing it into an underground chamber. Each emission was accompanied by a stout thud along with a background growl, as though some vile beast were trapped and trying to emerge. Clouds of steam roiled as the vagrant wind shifted, sweeping sulfurous fumes across the road.

Constance wrinkled her nose at the sharp, rotten-egg smell.

Burke Evans turned around on the driver's seat. Nodding his round face at the group, he recited, "When the members of the Washburn Expedition came through thirty years ago, they heard the churning of Dragon's Mouth Spring from the Yellowstone River, a quarter mile away." Burke pointed farther up the hill, where a mud spring boiled and gave off a cloud that wafted more foul sulfur smell down. "Washburn's group named the Mud Volcano, as well."

Laura wanted to get out and walk up the hill, to watch the surging ebb and flow and stand close enough to feel the heat pouring from the earth.

"Oh, drive on quickly." Constance covered her nose and mouth with a corner of her pelerine in a gesture Laura found melodramatic.

A mile farther, thick forest gave way to a vista of broad valley, covered with a sea of grass and sage. The Yellowstone meandered across its floor, reflecting blue sky and fluffy white clouds.

Burke pulled the wagon to the roadside to continue his narrative.

"Some folks believe that thousands of years ago Hayden Valley was a lake." He wrinkled his pug nose and pointed with evident disbelief toward the level tree line that rimmed the valley, several hundred feet above the river. "That was supposed to be the high-water level. Before that, three thousand feet of ice was supposed to be here . . . I can't imagine the snow ever piling that high."

"I believe it," Laura said. "During the Ice Age, glaciers covered a good part of the world."

Hank smiled indulgently and put his hand on her arm. "Look at the Hayden Valley buffalo herd."

Laura looked at perhaps ten or twelve of the big shaggy animals, some lying in grass patches, others grazing. Their tiny-looking feet did not seem as though they could support their bulk.

Cord turned to Laura. "Not twenty years ago

there were thousands of buffalo in this valley. Now there are less than a hundred in the entire park."

She didn't miss how he glanced at Hank's hand on her arm.

The carriage started off, and Burke Evans drove them to the Grand Canyon of the Yellowstone. Though the group could have lunched, as many did, in the dining room of the Canyon Hotel, they stopped to picnic at the Upper Falls.

Seated upon rocks arranged for the purpose, the party opened their boxes to find an assortment of sandwiches, hard-boiled eggs with a folded paper of salt, an apple or orange, and a thick oatmeal cookie. Invigorated by fresh air, Laura ate ravenously, noting that Cord, seated to her left, also made short work of the meal. Constance sat at a distance with Norman.

Hank, who had matched Forrest's slower pace down from the wagon, and was just opening his box, studied the contents with suspicion. "That new Chinaman we hired as cook must have had a hand in this."

"What's wrong?" Laura swallowed the last of her cookie.

"I have distinctly requested that cloth napkins be provided for all picnics. There is naught but paper."

Laura caught Cord's eye and knew he was suppressing mirth, as she was. Within seconds, she gave in and laughed.

Cord joined in. Hank gave them a sharp look.

When they returned to the wagon, Norman adroitly escorted Constance to a seat beside him. Cord swung Laura up and sat next to her, leaving Hank to sit with Forrest.

Burke guided the team downriver where he suggested that a rather strenuous hike would bring them to the brink of the Lower Falls.

Constance's nose wrinkled. "How steep is it?"

"Quite, miss. In places, some folks sit and slide, and getting back up . . ."

"I'm not going." Her hand rested on Norman's forearm. "Won't you stay with me?"

If Aunt Fanny had been present, Laura knew Constance would not have been left unchaperoned, but Forrest ignored the situation, alighting to see the wonders of the park.

Hank balked with a significant look at Constance's ring. "Excuse me, but I was given to understand . . ."

Constance's sudden laugh was the one Laura remembered from when they were both small, the one that meant she was scared but whistling in the dark. "This?" She offered her hand with the garnet, the gold band bright in the midday sun.

The silence seemed absolute, while Laura wondered who would speak next.

Cord stepped forward, leaving Laura, and took Constance's hand. Lifting it to his lips, he kissed it. "A gift from the heart, to a lovely lady."

"But not a promise?" Constance's hand tugged free of Cord's.

"No," Cord spoke softly.

The path through the pines was steep, as advertised. The reduced party of four—Laura, Cord, Hank, and her father—followed Burke Evans as he ferreted out the most stable spots to place one's feet. By the time the trees opened and the river above the falls was revealed, no one had resorted to sliding on their posterior.

They went down a little farther to the flattened area behind a stout rail, and the full impact of the canyon struck.

Stretching for miles, the gorge cut twelve hundred feet into rocks made rotten by the invasion of hot mineral-laden waters. Downstream, the walls of weathered rock rose in elevation so that the canyon deepened. Steep slopes topped with cathedral-like spires had been carved by wind and water into jutting shapes . . . here resembling busts of the heads of ancients, there a woman or man toiling beneath a burden.

Promontories capped in crimson and swathed in broad streaks of mustard, rust, and ochre marked where iron-rich waters had stained the pure white walls. As the mineral-rich zones graded into country rock, there were washes of charcoal, lemon yellow, and all shades between.

Thermal seepage from deep in the earth continued, a steaming stream of water appearing like magic halfway up the canyon wall.

The river that powered the trenching ran swiftly. High country snowmelt poured in a clean green flood to the brink of the cliff, then plunged through the narrowed neck over three hundred feet in a white roar. Below the falls, the river continued on its way, an emerald strand woven with white water.

On the other side of the gorge, Burke informed, it was possible to take a trail equipped with wooden stairs and railings down to the base of the falls on a tour guided by "Uncle Tom" Richardson.

Laura moved to the brink of the precipice, spray dampening her face and hair.

She noted it was not Hank's but Cord's hand that steadied her; she laughed into the wind created by the torrential cascade. She wasn't certain what had transpired above, but she wanted to believe Constance and Cord had parted ways.

The wind lifted a strand of her hair and blew it back into Cord's face. She fought the urge to lean against his chest and look up at the summer blue sky through the clouds of mist, then succumbed. With his support, she lifted her face; the drifting spray made the rock walls look black a hundred feet above the falls. Constantly shifting prisms of color shimmered out of reach but seemed so brilliant she imagined flying through the rainbow like the fishing ospreys.

"Look there." Cord tapped her shoulder and pointed out a hawk tracing lazy circles. As they watched, the bird flew into the gossamer veil and disappeared into a curve of indigo light.

Hank studied her and Cord narrowly from across the observation area. His suit had dust on it from where he'd been leaning against the split-log rail. "Too bad Constance and Hagen decided the trail was too steep."

"Yes," Laura's father answered, so faintly he was difficult to hear over the falls' roar. He'd planted his bulk on a boulder with a view, and his breathing was shallow and rapid. "I'm going to have a devil of a time getting back up."

Laura tried to push aside an instinctive daughter's worry and looked into the rush tumbling over the edge. A large log reached the drop and turned end up to plummet toward the canyon floor. She reeled with a bit of vertigo and leaned against Cord.

"It's time we moved on." Hank took the lead onto the upward leg of the switchback path through the trees.

Laura went to her father. His color was bad, and he sweated in the cooling mist.

"Are you all right, sir?" A furrow appeared between Cord's thick brows.

Forrest got heavily to his feet, brushing aside his offer of a hand. "I'll have to be."

He tried to move faster, but his smooth-soled leather shoe slipped on a root and he nearly landed in a patch of loose obsidian gravel. Falling behind, Forrest reached with a trembling hand to steady himself on the rough bark of one of hundreds of lodgepole pines studding the slope.

"Laura," he called, astounded at how weakly it came out. He could have sworn he nearly shouted, but the sound seemed swallowed up as if his head were swathed in cotton.

She did not turn. Sutton's dark head was bent toward hers.

Forrest looked for Burke Evans, but the young man seemed to have abandoned them.

He bent forward and pushed himself harder up the trail. It hadn't seemed this far on the way down. Though sweat beaded his forehead, the heat of exertion gave way to a coldness that seemed to come from deep inside.

His doctor in Chicago had warned him. No smoking, and Forrest had chuckled at the strange notion. Get more rest, but the doctor didn't understand that in the years since Violet died, work was the only thing that kept him going.

Up ahead, Laura and Cord made the sharp turn of a switchback and she looked back, her green eyes concerned. "Daddy!" She sounded far away.

He put another foot heavily in front of the other and stopped, stunned by a sudden feeling that something slammed into him and then trapped his whole body in a vise. He didn't know how it could be, but he found himself lying on the ground with his face in the dirt.

The rough earth didn't seem to matter; he just needed to lie there until he could catch his breath in this air too thick to draw into his lungs.

A hand took his shoulder and turned him over.

Sutton's blue eyes made nearly a match for the sky bowl above. Forrest looked for Laura in the blurred vestiges of his vision and opened his mouth to tell her of the impossible pressure that bore down and down until he felt he would be pushed into the grave.

Strangely, he thought he heard his wife's voice.

"Did you hear something?" Constance asked Norman. She clutched the side of the touring wagon, her hair swinging over her shoulder, as she looked around the clearing. The sound had been high-pitched, echoing for a fraction of a second before being swallowed by the wind.

Norman scanned the head of the path that led down to the Lower Falls. "I did think for a moment . . ." He shrugged.

She compared the big Swede to William, about the same height but built more solidly, his blond hair, red beard, and ruddy cheeks the antithesis of William's bronzed skin and dark hair.

How dare William show her such lack of respect? This morning when he and Laura had come out from their little hiding place around the corner, the signs had been clear. Both of them had borne the high color and nervous look of someone caught out.

Since she'd met Norman, he'd treated her with the utmost deference, as if she were a china doll.

Now the skin around his eyes crinkled. "You'd turn the heads in my boyhood home of Uppsala, with your hair like black silk."

Flushing at the potential mention of meeting his family, Constance looked away at the Upper Falls of the Yellowstone, at least a mile upstream, cascading into the opening at the head of the Grand Canyon. A cloud of spray swelled above the green forest.

"It's hot in the sun," she observed, careful to keep her voice sweet.

"Let's move into the shade, then." Norman pivoted on his heel and reached up to the wagon seat. He lifted Constance free and swung her into the air.

Along with the sudden sensation of weightlessness, she noticed the golden flecks that floated in Norman's eyes, just at the inner ring of the iris. A sheen of moisture stood on his sunburned forehead, and Constance caught the scent of clean male sweat.

"Oh God!"

Norman's hands seemed to freeze in midair, holding her, as a woman's voice cried out again. Swiftly, he let Constance down onto the rough-packed road beside the wagon. She stumbled as he took his hands from her waist.

Laura emerged from the trees with her hair falling over her shoulders and fresh tears flowing from already-red eyes. Behind her came Hank Falls, his suit jacket slung over his shoulder. Farther back, and looking bone tired from the struggle, William carried Uncle Forrest, a dead weight slung over his powerful shoulder.

Constance's fist covered her mouth, but she still screamed.

Laura clutched the cramp in her side and tried to catch her breath, while Cord took her father to the wagon and lowered him to the floor between the seats. Huffing, for carrying corpulent Forrest Fielding was no mean feat, he straightened and wiped his brow.

A red stain, bright as paint, saturated the back of Cord's shirt.

"Cord, my God. There's blood all over . . ."

"I know."

"I thought his heart . . ."

"No."

"But I didn't hear . . ."

"I didn't hear the shot, either."

The forest hugging the canyon rim could easily hide a marksman.

Norman stepped up to the wagon on the other side and bent to examine Forrest. Constance followed and stood at his side, blue eyes wide.

"Perhaps a poacher," Norman suggested.

Cord made an impatient gesture. "No poacher worth his salt would work this close to a tourist area. As we heard nothing, he must have been shot from downwind."

"You're saying someone shot Uncle Forrest on purpose?" Constance cried.

"Who, pray tell?" Hank's cold gaze fell upon Cord. "Perhaps I should ask you to empty your pockets to find out if you pistol-shot Forrest at close range."

Laura saw the danger in Cord's profile as his clenched muscles turned his scar white. She moved between the two men. "For God's sake, we haven't time for you to fight."

She shoved past Cord and saw her father looked ashen. Cord was beside her in an instant, tearing open Forrest's coat to reveal bright blood drenching a white shirt from left shoulder to waist.

Behind her, she heard Hank's sharp inhalation. Was he wondering what would happen to his backing? For how could her father survive with his heart pumping away his blood?

Cord ripped Forrest's shirt, popping off buttons, to reveal a neat hole welling blood. It appeared to be above and to the left of his heart, but only just.

"I'm going to lift him, Hank. Can you run your hand under his back and see if there's an exit wound?"

Dimly, she heard Hank. "Let someone else." He remained at a little distance, looking as colorless as his coat.

"I've got a good angle to reach under," Norman said from the opposite side of the wagon. "Pick him up now, Cord."

Constance covered her face with her hands.

"Ready, then."

Cord lifted.

Norman's hand disappeared under Forrest's back.

Laura dreaded what he might feel, the sticky slickness of more blood, the ragged edges of a larger exit wound.

"It's dry."

Her shoulders sagged as her father's were lowered back to the dusty wagon floor. Cord pulled a folded navy bandana from his pocket and pressed it over the bullet hole, bearing down with the heel of his hand. "I'll hold pressure."

Norman scanned the forest along the canyon rim. "It would be good to be away from here in case someone is lurking about, but we seem to be lacking a driver."

"Press-gang one from another tour." Cord looked up the dirt road about fifty yards where another wagon was stopped. Though the tourists appeared to be away, two drivers in dusters stood together smoking and talking.

Cord waved and shouted.

"I can drive while you hold on the wound," Norman offered.

But, as soon as he spoke, one man broke away and came running toward them.

Burke Evans looked ashamed for having deserted his guests, but Laura suspected it had happened before. "I'm sorry, folks, I thought you'd want plenty of time to enjoy . . ."

He stopped and stared at Cord's stained shirt, then past him to Forrest lying limp in the wagon. "Gad!"

"Let's get him to the Canyon Hotel," Norman ordered. "There's bound to be a surgeon there."

"Possibly a doctor is on call, sir, but that's not a good bet," Burke Evans reported. "I'll have you to the Lake Infirmary at top speed."

Laura's eyes met Cord's, and she saw in his her own belief . . . that her father might not survive the ride.

CHAPTER EIGHTEEN

Dr. Upshur, a nondescript, brown-haired man in his thirties wearing a white coat spotted with what Cord believed was Forrest's blood, faced the crowd that was waiting for news.

The doctor's gaze roved over the group from the wagon: Constance and Norman, Hank, Cord, Laura, and a goggle-eyed Burke Evans. In addition, because the wagon had arrived behind lathered horses proceeding at a gallop, Fanny, Lieutenant Stafford, Sergeant Nevers, Manfred Resnick, and even Hank's elusive sister, Alexandra, had come to see what was wrong.

"Mr. Fielding is in grave danger, and I know you are all interested in his condition," Dr. Upshur said, "but there are other sick people here, and I cannot have them disturbed." He considered. "His daughter may stay . . . the rest of you must wait elsewhere."

Cord opened his mouth to protest that he was going to remain with Laura, but closed it. If Forrest's sister and niece were willing to accept the verdict, then he must, as well.

Lieutenant Stafford stepped forward. "With your permission, doctor, I'm going to place an armed guard on duty. As we don't know who shot Mr. Fielding or why, we cannot be sure they will not be back to finish the job."

Hank glowered at Cord. "As the only man with a motive, want to show us you're not carrying a pistol?"

Stafford looked pained. "Let's all get out of the hospital as the doctor ordered."

Everyone, except Sergeant Nevers on guard duty, and Laura, left, moving with reluctance the way a crowd will when told to disperse from a wagon accident.

Cord hoped Hank would be ignored, especially as Captain Feddors was not around, but as soon as they were out of earshot of the hospital's front door, Stafford paused.

"What's this about motive?" he asked Hank.

"Sutton wants to stop my purchase of the Lake Hotel."

For a fleeting moment, Cord thought he saw a look of satisfaction on the face of Alexandra Falls, but it vanished before he could be sure. He wished she would leave, but she showed every sign of settling in to listen. Thankfully, Fanny and Constance had walked ahead and were almost at the door to the hotel.

"Come, Lieutenant," Norman interceded. "I know Mr. Sutton, and I don't believe he would resort to violence to achieve a business goal."

"You're taking his side?" Hank's voice rose. "Because you think I'm hiding something to do with that letter and the inspections?"

At Hank's tone, Norman gave him a steady look. "I'm taking the side of law and order. And though I did not previously have a prejudice about the documents, your bringing them up now is certainly suspicious."

Hank turned to Stafford. "None of us in the canyon heard a shot. What if Fielding collapsed because he was fatigued, and Sutton took the chance to shoot him point-blank? The sound would have been muffled."

A glance passed between Stafford and Manfred Resnick.

"Did anyone see Mr. Fielding fall?" Resnick asked. "Was anyone near him?"

"Laura and I were," Cord admitted. "But we were walking ahead looking at the ground, watching our footing. There were lots of roots, stones, and slippery patches." He gestured toward the hotel. "Get Laura out here and ask her if I ran back and shot him."

"I will be speaking with her," Resnick replied. "Did anyone hear a shot?"

"Nope," from Burke Evans. "I'm afraid I left the party to share a smoke with one of the other drivers."

"The wind was up, coming through the treetops like an approaching train, along with the roar of the falls," Cord said. "I didn't hear anything I'd call a shot."

Norman frowned. "Constance and I both heard a high-pitched something, that may have echoed in the canyon below."

Stafford looked around at the group. "Then it is likely that Mr. Fielding was shot from a distance downwind with a rifle."

Hank stabbed a finger at Cord. "Aren't you even going to search him?"

"For what?" Resnick asked. "If he had a pistol, he could have thrown it away along the path, from the wagon, or into the brush around here."

Hank snorted. "Nonetheless, Lieutenant Stafford, I shall speak to Captain Feddors about your failure to properly investigate this matter."

He strode away in the direction of the soldier station.

Esther Giles, looking cool in a white lawn dress, stood outside the log building with Captain Feddors. In female company, the dour officer seemed transformed, smiling.

Hank almost turned away and came back later. But his mission was to present his case against Cord, a smoke screen against his own failings. As Norman suspected, the letter and the inspection report had indeed been sidetracked from the railroad.

It had been just after the grand opening in 1892. Everything was going so well, when he noted the marked envelopes in the postal niche inside the hotel's front door. The first was from a team driver he'd been forced to fire a few years before for sloth. This season, the man had been back in the park working on a road crew outside Hank's domain. They'd run into each other near the front door the day before and had words. Well, words on Hank's side; the driver had been grabbed by two male hotel employees and escorted outside.

Hank's face heated, and he reached for the missive, without thinking that it was against the law to interfere with the post. That was when he noted the larger envelope, also addressed to the railroad, with the name of the inspector at the upper left corner.

It had been so simple to fish it out with the other.

For eight years, he'd felt safe from discovery, but somehow those carefully hidden documents had emerged from a locked bank box. Why had he been so stupid not to burn them?

A peal of laughter came from Esther, and she gave an affected little wave with her pocket handkerchief. From experience, Hank expected the lawn square smelled of lily of the valley . . . the day before yesterday Esther had come to his boat for an afternoon interlude. Her husband, Harold, had taken a fishing tour. Though older than Hank, she had been a pleasant surprise. He'd loosened her Spanish ruby comb and let her long black hair spill over her pendulous breasts.

Hank drew a comb out of his pocket and smoothed back his hair that was falling over his eyes. With his own handkerchief, he mopped his brow.

Finally, he moved forward. "Good afternoon, Mrs. Giles; Captain."

"Hank!" Esther trilled. "That is, Mr. Falls."

He kept his face neutral, bowed to her, and spoke to Feddors. "I wonder if I might have a few minutes of your time."

On the hotel porch, with the sinking sun throwing shadows of the pines across the scrub lawn, Cord settled into a rocking chair. He was exhausted, despite a bath and changing out of the blood- and sweat-stained clothes he'd been wearing when he carried Forrest out of the canyon. Hank might be Forrest's partner, but he'd stood by like a stick that might snap when there was backbreaking work to be done.

It was all Cord could do not to find Hank and take him down a peg. Hell, it would be even more satisfying to smash a fist into his face.

But the high road would be best with Norman and Hopkins Chandler. Let it look like Hank was the desperate one, grasping at straws to save his hotel.

His hotel.

Cord had not thought of it that way before, but from the construction phase on, Hank had lived in this place. He no doubt saw it in a proprietary light, had believed he would go on here as many years as he cared to, in the role of manager for the railroad.

Cord forced his focus back onto his own goal. Hank would get over it, just as he planned to try to get over Thomas Bryce's lording it over him.

Once Cord owned the Lake Hotel, mortgaged

through the bank in Great Falls, he'd sell his half of Excalibur to his adopted brother, Thomas. As the hotel in Salt Lake was larger and grander, he should be able to pay off the loan and take the deed to the Lake Hotel, free and clear. After that, if people found out he had a Nez Perce grandmother, there would be no one legally able to take the property away from him.

The best-laid plans . . .

With Forrest fallen, would Hank plead for more delays? Would his accusations, while apparently not given credence by Manfred Resnick or Norman, influence Hopkins Chandler upon his return from Bozeman?

The day's events called for a whiskey, though what he wanted most was to go over to the infirmary to see Laura.

This afternoon, things had seemed to be falling into place. Constance's staying with Norman once they'd alighted at the first stop had allowed Cord to lunch and share the canyon with Laura. On the walk up toward the wagon, he'd been planning to ask her to go with him tonight to hear Bitter Waters. This time he would introduce her.

As Cord started to rise from his chair and go to the lobby bar, something brushed his sleeve. He turned.

Constance moved her hand from his arm to the back of the rocking chair next to him.

He stood to acknowledge her and, though he indicated the chair next to his, she did not move to sit down.

In spite of the difficult day, she managed to look stunning as always, in a sapphire silk dress beneath a fringed shawl. She had pulled her sleek hair up, emphasizing cheeks pink from the day's sun. Gold earrings danced when she moved.

The only clues to her distress lay in her troubled eyes that mirrored the deepest shade of royal in Yellowstone Lake, and the way she worried an embroidered handkerchief with her hands. "Uncle Forrest is the only father I've ever known. My own died before I was old enough to remember him." She looked out over the water. "If anything happens . . ." She shuddered.

Sweet Constance, Cord thought, so soft and childlike with her emphatic ways. So pampered in her relatives' fine house where he'd met her in St. Paul.

"Who could have shot him?" she despaired. "This West of yours is too wild, too cruel."

Although Cord had a house in Salt Lake City near Hotel Excalibur, he considered his ranch as home. A simple and sturdy log structure, surrounded by three hundred acres that his father, Franklin Sutton, had claimed to mine before the first homesteaders had come to the valley called Jackson's Hole.

It was to his ranch that Cord had always wanted to bring his bride. But somehow in St. Paul, he'd been so caught up in disbelief that a woman like Constance wanted him that he'd forgotten to consider whether his life would be one she wanted to share.

On the day she had stood with him outside the Northern Pacific ticket office in St. Paul, she'd been very quiet. Ornate lettering advertised the Dining Car Line to Cinnabar, Montana, connecting by stage to

Yellowstone Park. Cord had thought she was simply sad to see him leave, but now he remembered how she had peered through the arched windows at the photos of western landscapes and pronounced them stark.

"The West is my home," he had told her.

On the hotel porch, Constance went on, "It's just too difficult, too harsh out here."

Cord sighed. Late June, and it was just getting on to the best time of the year. Constance had no idea what Wyoming was like in winter.

"I thought I could live out here," she went on, "but I was mainly thinking of Salt Lake. I really didn't know how remote Yellowstone was when you said you wanted to buy and manage the Lake Hotel."

His collar felt too tight, and he tugged at the starched material. "Constance . . . Connie, no matter how right it seemed in St. Paul, it's wrong for so many reasons."

He didn't accuse her of fabricating their betrothal.

"I don't know why I decided you'd marry me," she confessed. "I just wanted the fairy tale to be true, the way you swept in and were so different from the men I'd known. By the time Mother and I arrived in the park, I truly believed you would ask me as soon as we saw each other."

Her fingers fumbled at the ring, and he covered them with his own. "No, please. That is my gift to you, for all we imagined. Can't you keep it and feel glad?"

He caught a glimpse of tear sheen in her eyes before she bent her head.

Then she looked back at him frankly, with a hint of the jealous fire he'd seen this morning when he and Laura came around the corner of the hotel. "What about Laura?"

He hesitated.

"You fell for her when you were together on the trail," Constance accused.

Why not admit it? "You're right. I felt guilty about it and held back because of you." His voice rose. "But you shouldn't question what I do from now on since you've made it clear you've set your cap for Norman Hagen."

She flushed.

He was about to tell her about Norman's inquiries for her, but before he could, the screen door to the porch opened.

"Constance," Fanny Devon called from inside. "Laura hasn't left the infirmary even though the doctor won't let her see Forrest."

Her bounteous curves appeared in the doorway. A pearl clasp anchored her dark hair atop her head. "We need to convince Laura to eat something and to rest."

Constance rose obediently.

"William." Fanny greeted him warmly, her voice dropping a full octave.

Cord rose. "Is there any more word on your brother?"

"Nothing yet."

He gestured toward the dining room. "Let's eat something and then take Laura a plate." With the crowd diminished, the doctor might let him join her vigil.

In the infirmary, Laura sat in a straight chair outside the room where Dr. Upshur was operating on her father. He'd warned that when he began probing for the bullet, it would be a critical time. If he severed a larger artery or perforated the top of Forrest's lung, provided the bullet had not already done so, survival was unlikely.

Beyond the hospital walls, Larry Nevers stood sentry, taking a minute every half hour or so to check in with her as darkness approached. Each time he stopped by, it reminded her that somewhere out there, someone might be taking aim at her father again through the lighted windows.

Or at her.

She went to the casement at the end of the hall and pulled down the paper shade.

Coming back, she stared at the closed door of the surgery. Part of her wished that Constance and Aunt Fanny . . . that Cord, were with her, but she knew that even if they were in the same room, everyone waited with their own thoughts and demons.

How awful that in the last few days, her father's primary emotions toward her had been anger and disapproval. Yet, how was that different from the way things had been at home?

From inside the operating room came a clatter. A moment later, a white-garbed nurse came out carrying a metal implement and disappeared into another room. With the surgery door ajar, Laura rose to her feet to peek through the opening.

A moment later, she wished she had not. Dr. Upshur had his back to her, but blood stained the sides of his white apron, making her imagine how much there must be on the front. Her father lay on the table with a cloth over his nose and mouth that she thought must be saturated with chloroform. His shoulder and chest were bare and bloody.

"There, miss." The nurse pushed past Laura carrying the tool and wafting a smell of disinfecting alcohol. Just before she closed the door, her eyes above the mask showed sympathy. "Not much longer."

Laura looked up and down the empty hall and moved toward the desk where they had come in, passing closed doors. From behind one of them came soft voices. When she was in front of another, she heard a long moan.

"Excuse me, please," Laura spoke to the young woman who had earlier appeared to be in charge of hospital files. "Have you a pen and paper?"

"Certainly, Miss Fielding." She turned back and found an inkwell, a fountain pen, and a sheaf of stationery.

Laura went into a vacant room with a table and chairs, closed the door behind her, and pulled the window shade. At last, with the events of the past days crowding her mind, she poised pen above paper.

How terrible it is to wait, while the surgeon's skill and

divine luck decide our futures.

Oh Lord. The hospital's faded walnut table, marked by ink and water, now has a new dark spot, for I pressed too hard with my pen near the paper's edge. Aunt Fanny has always cautioned that a lady does not leave such trails, but whenever I am overcome with the desire to write, it seems I am wrought with dark emotion that does not jive with a lady's rules. How simple it seems for Constance and how difficult for me, a woman who has worn trousers and killed a bear. Now that I have seen this country, the land Cord wanted to show Constance when he believed she might be the one for him, I have trouble imagining returning to Chicago and settling back into my life.

Of course, if Father does not survive, my life, wherever I am, will be vastly different.

As has happened so often in the past week . . . can it have been just over a week since I met Cord? . . . my thoughts turn to him. How safe I felt at his side, in spite of the wilderness around us. How right it seemed to be immersed in nature with him.

It has been so difficult since we arrived at the hotel, first learning that he cared for Constance and having to hide my feelings. This afternoon when she admitted they were not pledged, my heart leaped. If only this thing had not happened, we might be together now.

Father lay in the wagon so quietly that if his chest had not risen and fell, I should not have known he lived. I have not shed a tear, but I sense that inside me there is a great flood waiting for release. If only Father knows how I do love him, how I have always loved him, and wanted him to love me, not for the way I earn my keep, but because he treasures me.

It is as though I am waiting to see if I must weep tears of relief.

Or of mourning.

CHAPTER NINETEEN
JUNE 27

After sharing an uneasy dinner with Constance and her mother, Cord escorted them across the lobby on their way to bring dinner to Laura. He'd selected the dishes himself, deferring to the ladies for agreement: stewed chicken and dumplings, green peas, hot yeast rolls and sweet butter, along with an apple crisp he'd sampled for his dessert.

He held the front door of the hotel open for Constance, Fanny, and a young waitress bearing a tray covered with a white napkin. How odd he had believed Laura was a serving girl.

How was she taking the attack on her father? In tears or braving it out, he would vote for the latter. And how was Forrest faring? Had the bullet been successfully removed, the caliber established? If so, would Hank give up his theory of Cord shooting Forrest with a pistol?

When they started down the path toward the hospital, it was almost full dark. Bats dipped and fluttered in silhouette against the sky. Cord scanned the parking area, almost empty now that the stagecoaches and touring wagons had been driven away for the night.

Fanny followed his gaze. "I heard a big touring group left this afternoon. The hotel won't be booked up again until tomorrow night."

"The manager should make sure that doesn't happen during high season," Cord replied.

A lone figure with an unruly head of hair walked with purpose from behind the east wing, hands in his trouser pockets.

An electric sensation shot down Cord's arms. "Edgar!"

His banker stopped and turned; a false-looking smile distorted his features. Beyond him on a path that led toward the Wylie Camp, but also forked and ran along the shore toward the ruined cabin, Cord saw Hank and his sister, Alexandra. Hank had apparently changed from his road-dusty gray suit into a darker model and wore one of the new-style square crown hats. Upon locking eyes with Cord, Hank took Alexandra's arm and turned her away.

Edgar began walking toward Cord.

Constance laid a hand on his arm. "Mama and I can take Laura her dinner."

He hesitated.

Her blue eyes looked dark in the twilight. "When Edgar didn't show up for the excursion this morning, I sensed something was wrong."

"You guessed right."

With another look toward the hospital where Laura waited, Cord decided to try to get the truth from Edgar again.

"You look like you could use a drink." Edgar approached with quick nervous energy.

Cord agreed, managing to keep a civil tone.

A few minutes later, he waited on the hotel porch while Edgar came out from the bar with a crystal tumbler of amber liquid in each hand. His hair, which had permitted Cord to identify him in the dusk, made a halo against the lighted door to the lobby.

Cord reached for a glass and caught the rich aroma of Jack Daniels Old No. 7. "Thank you."

He took a seat in a wicker-bottomed rocker and motioned Edgar to sit beside him. They had the porch to themselves, an island in the night. A few patches of yellowish light spilled onto the grass from the first-floor windows down the long wall. Across the lake, a loon called; another answered the eerie, laughing cry. Inside the lobby, a string quartet began tuning their instruments for a performance to the reduced guest contingent.

Cord gripped the chair arm. "Where have you been since yesterday afternoon?"

Edgar took a deep draught of whiskey, and Cord thought he saw a tremor in the hand holding the glass. "I had some personal business to attend to. It was . . . inconsiderate of me not to leave you a message."

"Extremely."

"Ye . . . yes."

Cord stopped the motion of his rocker. "You've been nervous as a cat ever since we got here, coming and going at odd hours so I can't find you when I have questions. I don't remember you being this way when we met in Salt Lake."

"I'm sorry." Edgar wet his lips with his tongue. "There are some . . . things that have come up."

Cord turned away, finding the darkened lake more comfortable to look at than his partner's tortured face. As the silence lengthened, he grew more impatient.

"I need to know, Edgar, where you got those papers we showed Norman Hagen yesterday. Did you steal them?"

"We agreed that the less you knew about it, the better." Edgar seemed to have trouble controlling a hitch in his voice.

"I don't recall agreeing to that." Cord drained his drink and set it on the porch floor.

He got out of his chair, placed one hand on each arm of Edgar's rocker, and bent down. "I asked you a question. I want an answer now."

"I can't tell you."

Cord snorted. He straightened and crossed his arms over his chest, ready to reveal yesterday's armed assault on the cabin, where Edgar had been sighted with a killer.

Before he could speak, a movement caught his eye through the lobby window. Hank Falls came out of the nearly deserted dining room, smiling and nodding to the small group listening to music. Hatless, he wore his stock gray suit, still crumpled from the day's excursion.

Cord had to make a conscious effort to shut his mouth. Hank had never changed his suit. Edgar had been meeting with Danny, whom he'd just seen with Alexandra.

"Get out of that chair!" Cord ordered.

Edgar cowered.

Cord grabbed his lapels and dragged him up. Turning Edgar, he pointed. "You see Hank Falls there?"

Only Hank's back was visible as he mounted the stairs toward the second floor, but Edgar nodded.

"Now," Cord went on, "tell me who was impersonating him with Hank's sister this evening. The man you met in secret in the old cabin."

Without warning, Edgar jerked away and took off. He was down the short stairs and running across the lawn before Cord caught up with him.

He grabbed Edgar's shoulder. "You can't get away from me, so you might as well tell me the whole story."

Edgar's face crumpled along with his resistance. "All . . . all right."

Cord thought of propelling him down the lawn to the pier, away from where Hank or other guests might hear, but if the outlaw were out there watching him manhandle Edgar, he might attack. Just the thought of Danny saying Cord had served his purpose made his scalp tingle.

Cord gestured back toward the porch. "How

about you tell me over another drink?"

"Danny Falls is Hank's twin brother." Edgar cupped a fresh glass of Jack between his hands.

"I rather believe I had made that leap." Strung too tightly to sit, Cord balanced a hip on the porch rail.

"Danny ran away from home when he was sixteen because their mother remarried and his stepfather beat him. Hank stayed because he always did things the way Jonathan wanted and was never punished."

Cord suppressed the urge to say his heart bled for Danny.

Edgar swilled whiskey. "I met him in the bar at the National Hotel in Great Falls. We hit it right off. The booth in the back was a good place for talk with a man who drank my brand of booze." He gestured with his glass. "Danny seemed an odd mix of itinerant miner and financial idea man."

"What did he propose?"

"It sounded simple. If I wanted a piece of the pie when the Northern Pacific sold the hotel, I just had to make sure I brought a capable buyer to the table. Danny would supply the rest."

"The documents."

"This past March, we took the train, sixty miles from Great Falls to Helena and back. There was a bit more snow on the ground in Great Falls than in Helena."

Cord made an impatient gesture.

"I'm trying to tell you how it was." Edgar scanned the slope to the lake as though he also feared being watched by Danny. "We went into the First Bank of Helena's vault. I expected the bank official to order him to produce identification. Instead, he clapped a familiar arm around Danny's shoulders and admonished him about staying away from town so long. Then Danny pleaded the loss of his key, the banker laughed, and saw to it his safe-deposit box was opened."

"Let me guess," Cord said. "He took out the letter and the inspection report."

"Under his arm, Danny carried a slim leather portfolio in which he put the papers from the box. It was only when we were leaving that I felt as though I stood upon a trapdoor, for, you see, the bank manager walked us to the door and called Danny, 'Hank.'"

Cord's drink was gone so he crunched ice. "What's his motive in all this?"

"All I'm sure of is that there's bad blood between the brothers, that Alexandra loves Danny best, and that that drives Hank crazy. So when she told Danny the railroad was going to sell the hotel and Hank wanted to buy it, Danny determined he'd thwart him."

"You bring me as a buyer," Cord said. "I produce the papers and discredit Hank; everybody wins."

"Something like that."

Didn't Edgar know Danny was a notorious criminal? He appeared genuinely unaware, even looked relieved at having unburdened himself of what he knew.

"If you went to get the papers in March," Cord

mused, "why did you wait so long to give them to me?"

"Danny only let me have them after we all got here. I had to put two and two together to realize they were the same papers."

"Did you see Danny today?"

Edgar frowned. "I skipped the excursion because he wanted to meet this morning. Then he showed up early and left, something about going up to the canyon."

"The canyon?"

Cord's heart began to thud. He'd considered the outlaw when Forrest was shot, but had been unable to imagine a motive. Maybe it made sense that a bad seed like Danny, who apparently thrived on violence, had grown impatient for victory. If railroad management wasn't ready to award the hotel contract to Cord, then Danny would shoot Hank's financial backing out from under him.

"Where do you suppose Danny is?" Cord spoke as casually as he could.

"You're not going to turn him in?" Edgar still sounded innocent. "Impersonating his brother isn't a crime."

"Is he staying in the old cabin?"

"I . . ."

"This is serious. This afternoon Forrest Fielding was shot in the canyon."

Edgar blanched.

"Tell me where Danny can be found, and maybe you won't be charged." Cord watched confusion war with loyalty to the friend who liked Edgar's brand of booze.

"Do you really think . . . ?" His brown eyes looked uncertain.

Cord lowered his voice. "Danny attacked the stagecoach Laura Fielding was on. I saw him there."

Edgar gripped his drink.

"He's dangerous." Cord leaned forward. "He's using you."

Silence fell.

It ended when the string quartet began to play Bach with sprightly journeys up and down the scale. Edgar tipped up his glass and swallowed the last of the melting ice and liquor.

"I don't know where he and Alexandra are," Edgar said flatly, "but he's been sleeping in the cabin."

"All right. I'll get Manfred Resnick."

Cord left Edgar and found Resnick in the card room. There was no trouble convincing him to lay down his hand.

When they returned to the porch, only a moment later, Edgar was gone.

A fingernail moon was close to setting when Cord and Resnick approached the soldier station. Electric lights shined within the log structure.

Resnick knocked, and Cord dreaded another confrontation with Captain Feddors.

To his relief, he recognized the private who opened the door. The fellow appeared barely old enough to

enlist from the smooth look of his cheeks, though perhaps it went with having pale red hair.

"Good evening, Groesbeck," the Pinkerton man
boomed. "I have urgent business with your captain."

Groesbeck brought his blade-thin body to attention. "I'm sorry, sir, but the captain has gone over to
the Wylie Camp. Something about an Indian stirring
up trouble."

Cord's chest clutched. He followed Resnick toward the camp where lamp-lit tents studded the
hillside. The campfire blazed; Bitter Waters had just
been introduced.

A scan of the crowd for Feddors found him at the
side of the audience, scowling, surrounded by at least
five soldiers.

Bitter Waters came forward. This evening, as
on the first night, he wore traditional native attire, a
breastplate of bones arrayed over his bare chest. Cord
placed himself between the captain and his uncle.

Resnick leaned in close. "Think there'll be trouble?"

"I hope not."

Bitter Waters raised his arms and began his chant.
Gooseflesh rose on Cord's arms at his memory of the
tribe on the trail, people on horseback and on foot, along
with pack animals, strung out over several miles.

His opening complete, Bitter Waters looked into
Cord's eyes and began to speak in his precise accent.

"They say we made the news even in New York
City and Washington, D.C., our eight hundred, with
our two thousand horses. We went to war against

the United States during *hillal*, the season of melting snow and rising waters. At the Battle of White Bird, we won a great victory, routing the soldiers without losses. Traveling toward the land of the Crow in Wyoming, or on to Canada if some chiefs had their way, we camped at a place called Big Hole Creek in southern Montana. Chief Looking Glass decided we would cut poles, put up tipis, and stay over a day. My friend Tarpas Illipt and I rode to the mountains and hunted for game. When we returned that evening, spirits were high. Young boys noisy at their games by the creek, the warriors singing until very late . . .

"We believed there would be no more fighting."

Long past midnight, Bitter Waters surveyed the dark shapes of tipis along the stream and listened to his friend.

"In my dream . . ." Tarpas squinted into the moonless dark of the August night. "I was once again with your sister, Sarah."

She was like a dream to Bitter Waters, as well, her shining dark head and laughing eyes fading into shades of memory. "Sarah has been gone for over seven snows," he cautioned. "My mother, Seeyakoon, told you before she died, Tarpas, it is past time for you to take a wife."

"Tonight, it was as if Sarah and I had never parted." Tarpas's chocolate hair looked nearly black in the starlight glow. "We lay together in my tipi . . . until I saw the Bluecoats storm us."

Two horses splashed through the shallows of the meandering creek. A sudden chill cooled the night wind, and the dogs in camp began a frenzied barking.

"What's going on up there?" Tarpas eyed the dark woods on the hill.

Bitter Waters noted the faint shapes of spooked horses, neighing restlessly amid the clatter of hooves. "We are all nervous, even though the army is far behind us."

"I am always alert during darkness." Tarpas crossed his arms over his chest and rubbed his upper arms. "You know the sun is my guardian spirit, and I cannot be felled in a battle pitched during daylight."

Bitter Waters inhaled the calming smell of freshly cut green lodgepoles. "As my *wayakin* is the sunrise, I am also jumpy during the night."

Though it was still dark, plumes of smoke arose from a few morning cooking fires, while the smell of meat mingled with the nutty aroma of camas porridge.

Tarpas stirred up the fire before his tipi, ruining Bitter Waters's night vision. He saw his friend sit and write something by firelight; before he was through, a faint slate hue began to color the eastern horizon.

"I do not know how or when this letter to Sarah might be delivered," Tarpas told him, "but I have been thinking of her more often since a Bannock scout reported her with the man Sutton and a child in Jackson's Hole this spring."

Fifty feet from him and Tarpas, Bitter Waters made out Chief Joseph's younger wife outside their tipi carrying a load of firewood. She was as slender as a girl, bending to pick up another stick.

The unmistakable crack of a rifle split the still air, reverberating through the clustered tipis. Blood bloomed on the breast of her white cloth blouse; piled sticks tumbled to earth, and she slumped on top of them.

Bitter Waters saw the Bluecoat who had killed her, splashing through the creek into the heart of camp. He could not have been much older than she, his clean-shaven face fearful beneath his brimmed cap.

Tarpas seized his Henry repeating rifle from inside his tipi and turned to face the intruder. He shot, and the soldier fell into the water.

Men and women appeared from inside their lodges in various stages of undress, some towing sleepy and bewildered children. Dark shapes rushed down the hill and into the meadow where the Nez Perce had pitched their tipis. More shots rang out.

An older man stumped past carrying an ax, calling out that he'd lent his rifle to his sixteen-year-old nephew. "Bold Heart," he shouted, but the boy was not in sight.

An elderly man, older than Chief Toohoolhoolzote's seventy snows, sat in front of his tipi, a lazy curl rising from his pipe into the still morning air. A soldier approached and shot him through the chest; a faint smoke swirled up from the dark bullet hole.

Bitter Waters tried to shake off his feeling of unreality and looked around the battlefield. Despite the din of shooting and shouting, he heard the thin wail of an infant cradled in his mother's lifeless arms.

Tarpas said Sarah had a child . . .

A sharp shot and the baby's cries truncated.

Sarah . . . but there was no time to let sentiment sting his eyes. Not when the leaves of the nearby willows were shredded and cut by bullets, not when he and Tarpas had to throw themselves to the earth while the barrage passed.

A soldier pulled aside the flaps of a tipi and a boy of eight or nine fired a pistol, hitting the man in the shoulder. The soldier emptied his Colt into the tent, killing all five children inside.

Tarpas gripped Bitter Waters's arm and gave a keening war cry. Nearly thirty of the young warriors converged on their position as they struggled up from the ground.

"Hold them off," Bitter Waters ordered three of White Bird's band, while he surveyed their weapons, less than twenty rifles and a few pistols.

Reaching to his belt, Tarpas passed his own handgun to the nearest man who was armed only with a knife. "These soldiers cannot be better than those we defeated at White Bird Canyon! Are we going to let them kill our women and children?"

Shouting in a manner that made thirty men sound like seventy, the Nez Perce rallied, their guns making flashes in the dawn. In the creek bottom, men fought hand to hand, using rifles and stout willow branches as clubs.

Bitter Waters saw a sour-faced soldier of the United States scoop out a shallow hole and lie down in it to hide from stray bullets. A woman of the People, already hit and bleeding, took up her dead husband's weapon and fired, killing two of her enemy. Out of ammunition, Tarpas threw down his rifle and drew his knife.

The sky lightened from colorless to bearing the first hint of blue.

Bitter Waters paused beside the stream to catch his breath. All around, it seemed suddenly silent, as the hide tipis brightened in the rising morning light. Behind the hills, he could see the glow that would become sunrise.

The last sense of unreality evaporated when Bitter Waters saw his wife, Kamiah, part the thick reeds of the creek bottom and wend her cautious way downstream away from the battle. The water came up past her knees, darkening her dress and dragging at her. He clamped his teeth against the urge to call out and draw shooting at either of them.

Ahead of her, a clump of willow jerked. Bitter Waters could not ascribe the erratic movement to wind, even had there been a breeze. A soldier rose in her path, lips drawn back to show his teeth beneath a blond handlebar mustache. His gun pointed true at her breast.

Five snows since Bitter Waters took her to wife. And only since they had gone to war had she revealed the new life within her. His wife and child . . . as Sarah was wife and had a child. Should he survive this day, he would find his sister and bring her back to the tribe.

Staring at the soldier who threatened his wife, Bitter Waters prepared to shoot. Before he could move, Tarpas was there, leaping from the brush on the opposite side of Big Hole Creek.

"Here!" Tarpas cried in Nez Perce. "I am here!" Brandishing only a blade, he raced through the water, long legs pumping.

Two guns fired, almost simultaneously.

Bitter Waters lowered his smoking weapon and ran, sweeping Kamiah under his arm and dragging her away.

The soldier's blouse soaked and darkened; his body floated away downstream.

Splashing through the shallow water, Bitter Waters released his wife and dropped to his knees beside Tarpas. A seeping cloud of red stained the clear creek, while the sun crept over the mountain's shoulder.

"We fought back, the battle pitched for many hours." Bitter Waters focused on Cord. "My friend, who loved the mother of Blue Eyes, died facedown in six inches of water."

He raised his eyes to the dark sky. "Kamiah lost our child, so my only blood family is the son of my lost sister, Sarah."

Cord's breath caught at the words meant for him alone.

When it became evident Bitter Waters had finished, Cord sensed a stir, the soldiers making a path through the crowd. He heard a voice, unmistakable in its Southern softness, while at the same time hard and deadly. "Ah'll put a stop to this. Send that Indian back to the reservation where he belongs."

Cord raised his arms to block their way. "Didn't the old man speak truth?" Though it was a small stand he took, it was nonetheless a stand. He looked at his uncle. "I'll try to delay them."

Bitter Waters's lips curved into a smile. Though he did not speak, Cord believed he understood the message that passed between them.

In an instant, Bitter Waters did his disappearing act.

Feddors came to a halt before Cord. "You speak of truth, suh."

He looked down at the bandy-legged posturer. What if he announced Bitter Waters was family? Put an end to the suspense of waiting to be found out?

He did not speak, but let each second of silence give his uncle a head start.

"What do you know of truth," Feddors challenged, "when you're nothing but a lying imposter?"

Cord's fingers curled into fists.

Someone gripped his shoulder from behind.

He wheeled, on the defensive; Manfred Resnick gave him a warning look. "Why don't you let me inform the captain of the latest information on the outlaw?"

Heart pounding, Cord forced his hands to relax.

Moving away from the fire and lighted tents into darkness, his blood continued to roil. Back through the woods, and across a section of pasture, he circled and took up watch a distance from the rear of the tipi. Feddors and his soldiers had gone in the opposite direction, seeking Danny at the cabin.

Though he wanted to follow and see the outlaw apprehended, he tried to figure out where Bitter Waters might be spending his nights. Warning him about the captain's threats was the least he could do.

Unfortunately, all the Wylie tents looked alike.

CHAPTER TWENTY

JUNE 28

Past midnight in the infirmary, Laura gathered the sheaves of paper she had covered with close, cramped writing. Upon those sheets, she'd poured out both her love for her father and her need to be free of him.

A soft knock. "Miss Fielding? You may see your father now." Dr. Upshur looked as tired as she felt.

She started to rise, then stopped. "Have you a match?"

The doctor looked puzzled, but reached to an inside pocket of his jacket and offered a small box. He watched with a frown while she pulled over the soiled plate on which Fanny and Constance had brought her dinner and laid the papers atop it. With a sharp scratch of match head on sandpaper and a sulfur stench, she placed flame to the edge of her journal. Never had she burned her words before, but this night it seemed the only thing possible.

Dr. Upshur studied her over the bright little blaze

until it reduced to ashes, then ushered her down the hall. "The bullet is out, and I've given him morphine. He may not wake tonight, but you may sit with him."

With a shaky hand, Laura turned the knob. The sickroom was all white, the walls and even the wooden floor had been painted. The windows that gave onto the night looked black.

She could see herself reflected in the glass, still wearing her dusty shirt and trousers. Her hair was a rat's nest from the sixteen-mile wagon race from the canyon, her lack of grooming forgotten as she waited and poured her heart onto the pages. Smoke lingered in the hall.

Swiftly, she crossed and pulled down another shade. Out in the darkness, Larry Nevers's lone patrol seemed all but worthless.

Father's face made nearly a match for the sheets. She stood back, her knuckles pressed against her teeth so hard that she tasted the salt of blood. The sting of tears ate behind her eyelids, while she peered into the dark void of death.

They'd all gone on before her: Grandmother and Grandfather Fielding, stern and forbidding folk from whom Forrest no doubt took his ways; her mother's kin, Grammy and Papa, younger and more fun like Violet. And all of it brought back that endless night of waiting and watching for her baby brother's birth . . . while her father's face gradually set into the lines of sadness that had changed him forever. There was no timepiece in this sickroom, but Laura imagined she could hear the seven-foot walnut grandfather clock in the great hall at Fielding House, its golden pendulum marking the seconds.

Dr. Upshur had suggested Forrest might not wake soon, but his papery-looking lids fluttered.

"Daddy?"

He lifted a wavering hand and struggled to speak.

She put a finger to his lips. "Don't try to talk."

He fought the drug, looking at her with sunken gray eyes. "What happened . . . to me?"

Laura hesitated, but he deserved the truth. "You were shot in the canyon. No one saw where it came from."

"Whaaa . . . ?"

She didn't tell of Hank's accusation against Cord. "Maybe a poacher?"

"Hell of a thing." He tried to lift his head. "Things . . . you have to take care of . . ."

Laura forced a brittle smile. "Nothing is as important as having you rest. Everything else can wait."

"A telegram to Chicago . . . tonight. Karl Massey must come from the bank to take over."

Karl, a stocky Indiana farm boy turned banker, was the suitor Forrest Fielding had most often pushed on her back in Chicago. Repeatedly, she'd refused Karl's earnest but dull overtures.

Forrest went on, "Cord won't stop trying to get to Norman Hagen."

"The deal doesn't matter, Daddy. Backing Hank to buy the hotels can't be that important."

"It is. Fielding Bank just lost one of our largest

accounts . . . Silver Star."

Laura knew of Silver Star Meat, had driven past their prosperous Chicago stockyards and smelled their packing plant.

"Other clients are leaving, too," Forrest wheezed. "Things could get so bad that we'd have to sell our house."

"My God." Laura took his hand and squeezed it.

Home, that solid fortress of memory. Decorating each year's Christmas tree, Forrest and Laura always imagined that Violet worked beside them. In their dreams, she was still the slender woman with sleek brown hair drawn back in wings like an angel, frozen forever in a silver frame on the mantel.

"If we make this deal with the Northern Pacific," Forrest rasped, "Hopkins Chandler assured me . . . the railroad will do their Chicago banking with us."

"Will that be enough?" Tears flowed down her cheeks, but she didn't let go of his hands to wipe them away.

"I believe so." Forrest closed his eyes and, for a moment, she thought the morphine had done its work.

"Promise . . ." he whispered.

"Anything."

She reached for a glass of water on the bedside table and brought it to his lips. Forrest opened his eyes, sipped.

"You must help Hank in any way you can," he said with surprising strength.

When Laura came out of the infirmary, her promise to help Hank in his battle against Cord was making her stomach ache. Let that be a lesson never to make an open-ended vow.

Using a hand torch Dr. Upshur had offered to light her way, she began to trudge up the gravel path between scrub brush toward the hotel. While she had been indoors, the air had changed, becoming heavy and hot.

"Laura."

She started at Hank's voice. He leaned against a tree; his alert expression revealing he waited for her. "How is Forrest?" He bent his blond head over Laura's hand.

She jerked away before he could plant another of his insinuating kisses upon it. "Dr. Upshur took the bullet out. It went through his shoulder and missed his heart and lungs, but he needs rest."

To his credit, Hank seemed genuinely concerned. The skin around his deep-set dark eyes looked drawn.

"I have to send a telegram to Chicago, to get some help for you," she said.

"Let's do it now."

He took her arm and led her across the lobby to the business office. The quartet had retired for the evening, and there were only a few people still about.

As there was no one in the office, Hank pulled down a telegram pad, wrote out the message she dictated, and sent it himself. When they returned to the lobby, someone had switched off most of the electric lights, plunging the big room into semidarkness.

"The kitchen is closed," Hank said, "but I can have something prepared for you. Or would you prefer to bathe first?"

She looked down at her dirty pants and lifted a hand to brush back her dusty hair, wondering if she would feel like eating tomorrow.

"If you wouldn't mind," she forced an even tone, "could you have them send a tub to my room? I'm completely done in."

"Certainly." Hank put a hand on Laura's arm. "With your father out of commission, we're partners. You'll let me know of anything I can do for you, and I'll do the same."

Across the lobby, Laura saw Cord, dressed in neat charcoal trousers and a crisp white shirt, watching darkly from the entrance to the east hall. My God, she hadn't thanked him for carrying her father up that steep trail.

Hank shot a look at Cord, a surprising smile spreading over his sharp features. "That fellow is after you, as well as your cousin." Before she could muster an automatic denial, he went on, "Today, I got all the ammunition I need to defeat him."

Cord turned away and disappeared down the hall. Though she wanted to run after him, Laura managed, "What ammunition?"

"All in good time."

At Hank's chuckle, she fought a wave of revulsion.

"There's just one thing before I shoot my magic bullet," he said. "I need for you to use Sutton's attraction to our mutual advantage."

"What . . . ?"

Hank gripped her arm, painfully. "Get him to spill where he got those letters to the railroad."

From the window of his room, Cord watched Hank leave the hotel alone and walk down toward his steamboat.

Going back into the hall, he went toward the lobby. If he asked at the desk, it was certain that the lone night attendant would be reluctant to tell him an unmarried young woman's room number.

Setting that aside, he moved toward the stairs and took them two at a time. On the third floor, he moved down the corridor, trying not to step on any creaking boards. Up here was the Absaroka Suite, with its adjoining rooms. The doors were all identical solid wood with faceted jet doorknobs and glass transoms above.

He stared at each in turn, willing the blank boards to give up a sign. Behind this one, or that, was Laura. In his mind's eye, he opened the portal to find her fresh from the bath, wearing a silk robe that clung to her damp skin. No perfume, just the sweet scent of her that he imagined he caught on every errant breeze.

He'd untie the slippery sash of her wrapper, a pink one to match her sun-flushed cheeks, and slide the robe ever so slowly off her shoulders. Uncover the delicate body he'd seen at Witch Creek.

And each night when he tried to sleep.

With shaking hands, Laura belted Aunt Fanny's rose silk wrapper. Reflected in the bureau glass, her hair hung damply over her shoulders. The bruise at her eye was starting to fade. Going to the bed, she lay down and stared sightlessly at the striped wallpaper until it seemed to dissolve . . .

She stood on the second-floor landing of Fielding House. Behind the door of the master bedroom, Forrest lay propped on pillows, a pale shadow of the robust man he'd once been.

Laura gripped the smooth mahogany rail and looked down upon a middle-aged man in a banker's suit in the marble-floored foyer. He carried a briefcase and looked around the house as if he were estimating the cost of its contents.

She felt two spots of color burnish her cheeks.

The man paused to straighten a Degas, a picture of a seated dancer lacing her ribboned slippers.

"Don't touch that!" Laura's voice echoed in the high-ceilinged hall. Violet had chosen that painting for the occasion of her daughter's first ballet lesson.

"Laura." Forrest's feeble voice barely penetrated the closed door of his room.

"It's all right, Father."

It wasn't. At any moment, the man in the hall would look up at her and say, "I'm here to take the house."

That couldn't happen.

Each room still bore the touch of Violet; here in a Tiffany vase she'd chosen, there in the burgundy silk chairs before the fireplace. A thousand fragments of the years, each a tiny shining facet in the mosaic of time: hiding from her nanny behind the porte cochere and getting a gentle swat on her diapered bottom; learning to play the piano in the parquet-floored, glass conservatory.

Or poised at the top of the marble stairs, a skinny Cinderella hearing the stroke of twelve. Skimming down lightly like a bird, across the foyer and down the lawn to the lakeshore where an imaginary pumpkin lay lonely in the coarse sand.

Cord returned to his room, but did not turn on the light or disrobe. He shoved the sash of the window high and took a seat on the wide sill, while he spun images of his two worlds.

Though many people in Salt Lake City regarded him as Aaron Bryce's charity case, he believed the majority of guests at Excalibur saw him as a gentleman with European roots, as well as a respected local Mormon. He could recount how the angel Moroni appeared to fourteen-year-old Joseph Smith, instructing him to translate the message so that all could read.

How ironic that the leader of the non-treaty Nez Perce also bore the name of Joseph, biblical Joseph of the coat of many colors.

How many colors was Cord trying to wear?

Lightning flashed over the lake, revealing a pair of thunderheads, black towers against a slate sky. Shades of gray, like the fine line he'd walked this evening, trying to protect Bitter Waters from Feddors, but keeping his mouth shut when the impulse to claim his uncle as family struck him.

He reached to his trouser pocket and drew out his *wayakin*. Even in the dim glow from the hallway lighting over the transom, it took on a glassy sheen. As he had done a thousand times, he rubbed his thumb over the smooth surface, hoping the contact would calm him.

In 1877, he'd hated Bitter Waters and the Nez Perce, turned his back on them and all they represented, too youthful and insensitive to even consider their side . . . until he had approached the Wylie campfire.

Another lightning flash, and the thunderstorm looked a lot closer. Silver illumination revealed the lake, whitecaps roiling, while the air around the hotel remained stifling.

Dante hated storms.

The lobby lay quiet before Laura as she descended the stairs, the tulip lights on the redwood columns dark.

She'd sponged off her trousers and put them back on with Cord's laundered shirt . . . in defiance of her family and Hank's expectations.

Stepping across the polished yellow pine floor, she went onto the porch and dropped into a rocker. Pushing it with her foot, she listened to it creak, an empty, aching sound.

The aroma of lake water mixed with that of sage and pine on the rising breeze. A fingernail moon had risen in the east, while a flash illuminated a towering cloud bank to the southeast. And was that also lightning on the high ridges? Surely not, for the orange glow was steady.

It must be the forest fire, visible now by day from the hotel as thin tendrils of white drifting up from the far peaks. Smoke that obscured vision, but hers was coming clear.

Were the bank and Fielding House in danger? She might love her father for swinging her into the air as a toddler while Violet looked on, might wish he were well and whole, but how many times had he manipulated her thoughts and feelings to his advantage?

Hank viewed the hotel as his own. But, as a consummate gamesman, did he deserve the place more than Cord, who had a dream?

In spite of her father's and Hank's assurance of their claims on her, she rose from the rocker.

Just a few steps down the darkened hall, she stood before the heavy door of Room 109. Her blood thudded in her ears.

With her hand raised to knock, she heard the tick of a latch at the far end of the hall. Though she turned quickly, she caught only a glimpse of a tall man with dark hair as he exited and closed the door.

Her father and Aunt Fanny would call her shameless, society would censure, but she went anyway, down the hall, pushed open the door, and stepped out into the night. The faint moon rode in a patch of clear sky.

In the midst of the meadow, she caught a moving darker shadow. "Cord!"

Fifty yards out, he disappeared into the trees. To keep up, she had to pass through the dense grove, arms out before her to stave off the trunks. Another lightning flash revealed him exiting the forest.

The stables lay ahead; he opened one of the tall wooden doors and went inside.

Another bolt from the heavens made the hairs on the back of her neck stand up. Wind swept in off the lake, tearing through grass and scrub, tugging at her hair. She should go back to the hotel.

Moments later, she felt the rough boards of the stable door beneath her hands.

Inside, all was dark.

From down the way, she heard the rasp of a match. Lantern light flared, casting flickering shadows on the walls and into the darkened stalls. She could see Dante's open gate.

"Cord?"

He appeared from behind his stallion, carrying the lantern.

Laura stood at the stall door wearing her trousers and the shirt he'd loaned her at Witch Creek. Her eyes were fever bright.

"Your father?" he asked.

"The bullet's out, and he's still alive."

"The caliber?"

"I don't know."

"Not small, like a pistol?"

Laura shook her head. "No one told me anything." She looked up, her eyes clear green in his mind's eye even in the darkness. "It's like that terrible night when I was ten. We waited and waited while Mama and my baby brother died."

Cord hung the lantern on a nail in the vacant stall next to Dante's, then lowered the flame until the stable was lit by the faintest golden glow. It was warm, with the earthy smells of sweet feed, horseflesh, and manure. The wind whistled up colder and louder through the cracks as the storm took aim at them.

"I hope he pulls through." He meant it, even with Forrest Fielding against him. "Hank accused me of shooting your dad . . . in front of Manfred Resnick and Lieutenant Stafford."

"I know you didn't." Laura's voice was steady.

"I'm hoping you can convince them of that, since you're the only other witness to Forrest's collapse."

"I'll try."

Cord stood where he was, legs apart. "A while ago, I went up to the third floor where your suite is. I wanted to tell you I talked with Constance."

"And?" Her expression gave away nothing.

"She's free to pursue Norman."

That hadn't come out right, especially as Laura had followed him all the way out here in threatening weather. "I mean . . ." He brought his hands out and moved toward her. "I mean we're free, you and I."

For a heartbeat, they gazed into each other's eyes. Gauging, wondering, fearing.

Then their arms went around each other in a grip so tight he had trouble breathing; she probably couldn't, either. Yet, it was such a relief, as if a band around his forehead had loosened. She fit him, the way he'd believed she could the day they went fishing in the lake.

They were quiet for a long time, her cheek against his chest. Then he felt warmth and wet there.

"Hey, hey." He pulled back and tipped her chin up.

"Daddy wants me to help Hank, to keep you from buying the hotel." Tears glistened on her lamp-lit face. "Hank wants me to find out where you got the documents you showed the railroad."

"What do you want?"

Her hand came up; she placed her palm atop his breastbone and spread her fingers. Closing his eyes, Cord thought the intense feeling could have been pain or pleasure.

"Are you sure?"

She nodded. And sealed the bargain by bending and blowing out the lamp.

Cord pulled a saddle blanket from where he'd folded it over the stall railing. Taking Laura's fingers, he drew her into the vacant stall, fanned the covering, and let it settle onto the straw. The mix of faint moon and bright stars spread shafts of silver onto the stable floor, and he saw her clearly, her face aglow.

He drew her down with him onto the blanket. She smelled of lavender soap.

Outside, the weather front swept in. Clouds scudded across the sky, causing the stripes of light to waver.

Then the stable went dark, lit only at intervals . . . more flashes of dry summer lightning, the kind that ignited wildfires.

"No one I know would want me to be here tonight." But all Laura felt was defiant joy. "Not Aunt Fanny, with her outmoded Victorian morality; not Constance, though perhaps she loves me enough to wish me happiness; not Father, who awoke from surgery asking me to promise I would help Hank defeat you."

"Yet, you're here." His lips pressed her forehead.

"This afternoon at the canyon, when you and I were at the brink of the falls, I felt like I was on the highest cloud in a clear blue sky."

He lifted her hair with one hand and moved it to the side of her neck, kissed her in the place where her pulse fluttered. It was right, so right that they shed their clothes and lie together upon the bed of scratchy wool and straw.

The stable creaked in the wind. Thunder rumbled as the gale roamed the land.

"Listen," he whispered. "On my ranch, the wind whistles across the sage like this on stormy nights."

She wished they were in bed beneath a fur robe, miles away behind the door.

"I want to take you there."

Laura twined her arms around him. His eyes looked enormous and dark in the dim light. "I want you to."

To take her to his ranch, to take her . . .

It was supposed to hurt, but she felt only a smooth pressure where Cord fitted into her. "You do me honor," he murmured, "to let me be your first."

Like a string being strummed by a bow, Laura felt the singing inside her. It was as if she and Cord were both instruments, upon which they played. A rough melody at first, that rose and swelled like summer itself, into the sweetest of symphonies.

Liquid, supple and slippery, they moved together in the quicksilver lightning. Sweat slicked their bodies. In the stalls around them, restless whinnies rose as wind gusts beat against the stable. The rain began, drumming on the stable roof and lashing at the walls.

The storm flashed again, and Laura felt as if she became one with the pure light.

Cord must have slept, for he was fighting his way up through blood-soaked darkness, the screams inside him turning to sobs . . . sounds that must have wakened Laura, who knelt naked beside him. He fought the disorientation of returning from that faraway night, the vertigo that traveling from being six years old to the present produced.

Across Yellowstone Lake, thunder rolled hollowly. The rain's pounding had subsided to a patter, dripping off the stable's eaves. Hot tears slid across Cord's cheeks and down his neck.

Laura wiped his wet face with both palms. He took her hands in his, managed a deep breath, and heard it turn into a hiccup.

"It's all right," she whispered.

She didn't understand that it would never be all right for Franklin and Sarah Sutton.

Cord pulled Laura down and wrapped her with him in the blanket. For the second time in a week, he'd returned to that darkest passage of his life, just at a time when he believed fortune had begun to smile. He'd never told anyone about that night, not Aaron Bryce or his family, who'd taken him into their hearts and lives; not Constance, even as he considered making a life with her.

His chest felt as though an iron band constricted it.

Laura's hair, soft beneath his fingers, brought back his father's hand stroking his mother's tresses in their last moments . . . Cord closed his eyes against a crest of pain.

As if he had cried aloud, Laura raised her head. Her eyes shone in starlight that, with the storm's passing, once more slanted across the stable floor.

"It was a dream," she whispered.

"No. It wasn't."

Drawing her head onto a place near his heart, he told her his story.

Laura clung to Cord where they lay with the blanket drawn over them. She had lost track of time while his words painted an orphaned boy raised to riches through the kindness of Aaron Bryce . . . vivid pictures illuminating the man with whom she had cast her lot.

Cord's arm tightened around her. "As long as the hate continues, the blood keeps being shed on both sides."

"There's so much hate. Captain Feddors is horrible to you." She reached to slide her hand over his cheek, encountering the puckered ridge of raised flesh.

He went still beneath her tentative exploration.

"How did you get this scar?"

He fingered the welt. "A schoolyard fight got out of hand. A couple of older Mormon boys got wind of where I'd come from before Aaron took me in."

"And you hate them still."

In the silence that followed, Cord sat up, leaving

her uncovered. He drew his knees to his chest and, though he stared at the stall boards, she believed he saw that far-off battleground where bigotry turned children into monsters.

"I hate that I'm in the middle, neither white nor red. I hate that my adopted white brother, Thomas, has his name on the title of my Hotel Excalibur . . . he never misses an opportunity to point it out. I loathe the supercilious captain who marked me the moment he saw me and won't let it drop. I abhor that poster on the wall of the hotel meeting room, showing the Northern Pacific line built on the back of a fallen red warrior. I despise that my grandmother, mother, and father died senselessly."

His Adam's apple dipped. "And I hate myself for thinking being adopted by a white man would wipe away the stigma of Nez Perce blood."

CHAPTER TWENTY-ONE

JUNE 28

Alex!" Hank tried the brass door handle of the aft cabin on his steamboat. The *Alexandra* lay alongside the Lake Hotel dock, as dawn broke beyond the Absarokas.

The door swung inward.

The cabin bore his sister's touch in the feminine floral wallpaper she'd chosen, lavender sprigs on white. A frilly petticoat frothed on the deck, and her favorite purple dress had been thrown over the top of the wooden wardrobe. A black-and-white cameo pendant with a knot in the gold chain appeared to have been tossed onto the table beside the bunk.

Alex wasn't there.

She might have joined last night's singing at Wylie's tent camp . . . stayed with a young family up the hill, reluctant to walk back to the boat in the dark.

He shook his head. Alex had never been afraid of anything in her life.

She might have met a man at the hotel. Hank envisioned her charming petulant face, challenging eyes, her fall of blond hair, bright gold in contrast to his own dull wheat.

She'd changed and grown a lot in the past few years, but Hank wanted to believe that even at twenty, Alex would resist being swept off her feet by some handsome son-of-a-bitch like Cord Sutton.

Hank left his boat and turned east, following the Grand Loop Road to the soldier station. The rose glow swelled in the east, but the front door of the log building was secured. A check of his pocket watch revealed it lacked ten minutes to reveille.

He could raise the alarm, send the cavalry to search for Alex the way they had looked for Laura Fielding after the stage attack, but Hank had been through this with his sister before. With a sinking heart, he suspected she was with Danny in his lair. Knowing his brother's insolence and daring, he'd probably returned to the abandoned cabin, correctly guessing that Manfred Resnick and Captain Feddors would think that move so foolish they would not bother to post a guard.

The shortest route to the cabin ran though the meadow past the stable, where Hank's shoes became soaked from last night's rain clinging to the grass. While he was some distance from the long building, the stable door swung open.

Feminine laughter spilled into the morning.

Hank stepped with haste into a copse of fir.

It wasn't Alex's girlish giggle but a waterfall's

merry dance, sweet clear music. Hank had tried to draw that unselfconscious laughter from Laura, but had never managed more than a smile from her vivid green eyes.

He looked between needled branches.

In the shelter of the stable door, Laura smiled up at Cord. Wearing those damned trousers she'd affected yesterday, she managed to look incredibly fetching with her hair mussed and strewn with straw. Cord's shirttails were out; her slender arm encircled his back.

Hank told himself he'd asked her to do this, to pump Cord about the letter and the inspection report. But as Cord bent to brush his lips across Laura's, Hank flushed. She was taking her undercover role, if she were acting, way too far. At any rate, Hank's assessment of Laura Fielding, Chicago lady, had been flawed.

If she would spend a night with a man in the barn, she was probably the kind of woman who'd do it for him, as well. Of course, she would, especially after he revealed what he knew about Mr. William high-and-mighty Sutton.

When Cord bent his rumpled head to kiss her, Laura wondered if anyone might be watching them come out of the barn. But all seemed quiet as they parted, he to saddle Dante and take him out, she to hurry back to the hotel.

Reaching her room without running into anyone,

she faced herself in the mirror. Lord, anyone who saw her must be able to tell she was not the same, with her high color and hair mussed by Cord's hands.

Her former existence felt far behind.

She thought of calling for a bath, but didn't want to see the boys who brought the tub and water. Instead, she ducked down the hall to the bathroom and filled the thick white china pitcher that matched the washbasin.

Stripping down, she soaped a cloth and washed her breasts where Cord's moustache had left patches of pink around the nipples. Down her stomach where he'd laid his cheek and she'd dared to think of bearing his children someday. On to the tender flesh where they'd joined several times during the course of the night. She rinsed the rag and her skin, then wrung out and hung the cloth on the hook on the side of the dresser.

Then she brushed her hair, getting out the straw and sweeping it into a knot at the nape of her neck. Despite the demure style, she felt certain everyone who saw her would know what had happened.

In defiance, she donned Constance's emerald silk dress with sweeping skirts, though it was clearly meant for evening.

"You're up early," Hank told Laura, pushing off the white wall of her father's infirmary room. With a raised brow, he took her in, from the tortoiseshell comb in her hair to the tips of Aunt Fanny's satin slippers.

Forrest, propped on pillows in bed, looked some-what better than he had the night before, though he greeted Laura with a weak wave. A thick pad of ban-dage covered his left shoulder. Hank, dressed even at dawn in a suit, bowed over her hand, giving a close-up of the narrow, knife-like bridge of his nose.

"I trust you slept well." He sounded cold. "Did you get a chance to find out about that matter we dis-cussed?"

Forrest watched them from bed, a puzzled expres-sion on his drained face.

Laura shrugged.

"You were going to try to find out where Cord got those letters to the Northern Pacific," Hank pressed.

"I haven't seen him." She avoided Hank's eyes and reached to plump her father's pillows.

"I daresay," Hank snorted.

Forrest subsided back onto the freshened mound.

A soft knock sounded at the door. Hank moved to open it as though he were part of the family.

A young woman in the blue-striped dress and white apron of a Lake Hotel maid dropped a swift curtsy. Her brown hair was pulled back so that not a strand was out of place; her pink cheeks glowed with abundant good health. "I have a telegram for Herr Forrest Fielding," she said with a German accent.

Laura pushed past Hank to take the flimsy enve-lope, thanked the young woman, and closed the door. She offered the telegram to her father.

LINDA JACOBS

He gestured it away. "Read it for me."

Going to the window, where a patch of sunlight spilled in a square onto the floor, she opened the envelope and glanced at the sender's name. "It's from Karl Massey." It would be well nigh intolerable when Karl arrived and both he and Hank vied for her attention.

Dear Sir, I regret to inform you that I will be unable to join you in Yellowstone, as I am this day resigning . . .

Laura swallowed.

. . . my position as vice-president of the Fielding Bank.

In an even tone, she read the opening lines aloud.

And continued, "I am joining Fred Whitehouse at First Illinois. I feel that I should also inform you that the accounts of Ramsey Tool and Die and Sears Roebuck will be changing banks along with me."

"Sears," Forrest muttered. "I'd never thought of them leaving."

Stop.

Laura raised her eyes to her father's stricken face. Though she had not wanted Karl to come courting, he'd been a major asset to the Fielding Bank.

She went to the bedside. "Whom else can I send for?"

He shook his head. "Someone's got to manage the accounts we still have. With Karl gone, I don't know who I'd choose to come out here."

"There must be somebody."

Forrest's face changed from the color of chalk to a pinker hue. "There isn't. And if you'd paid attention to Karl, kept him in the family, I wouldn't be in

338

this fix."

Laura felt as though all her blood was rushing to her head. "Don't even think of blaming me for your business and your personal failures. You've treated me like a serf all these years, and I imagine you did the same to Karl and all the other promising young managers you've had trouble holding on to."

"Daughter, you know I . . ."

"I know you're an impossible tyrant!"

Hank pulled out his pocket watch and pressed the lever with his thumb. "This is all charming, but time is running out with the railroad. Hopkins Chandler wants to meet after lunch to decide where we go from here."

"Does he think Fielding Bank will withdraw because Dad's injured?"

Hank's nearly colorless eyebrows came together. "He very well may. The railroad can decide at any time not to sell their Yellowstone property at all."

Forrest tried to rise, but grimaced. "I can't get up."

"Laura will have to help me," Hank said.

"No!"

"I want you with me in the meeting today," Hank went on as if she had not spoken.

"Shall I define the word *no* for you?"

She turned to the window and spied Cord riding into the woods astride Dante. Man and horse moved in accord as though they had become a single creature. The thought of sitting with Hank on the opposite side of the table from him made her queasy.

"I have something to say that will be of great interest to you." Hank gave a low chuckle and followed her gaze out the window.

"What could possibly interest me? I don't know a thing about the deal."

While Cord and Dante disappeared behind a steam cloud rising from a fumarole, Hank finished, "It's not about the deal; it's about Sutton."

Cord took Dante on his morning ride, reflecting.

He'd known his share of women.

Those from the less affluent side of Salt Lake didn't care about rumors, just hoped for a Cinderella story that might send some of the Bryce fortune their way. He'd met others while traveling the continent, like the sophisticated Frenchwoman he enjoyed until he found out she was cheating on a husband. And the Tuscan daughter at a vineyard where he lodged for a month. That one had boosted his ego, making love with him in the hayloft and in the stone chambers of eleventh-century ruins.

His discovery of Laura exceeded it all.

He'd spoken the truth about wanting her at his ranch. To have her in his bed, in his life . . .

To have her accept his heritage where society did not.

Cord turned Dante's head and rode to the administration office of the tent camp. He dismounted and looped Dante's reins over the wooden rail out front.

Inside, the candy-striped tent resembled a conventional office, with metal desks scattered over the raised-board flooring. This early in the morning, the only person about was a thin-lipped man in his midtwenties with a receding hairline. He kept his head down over a stack of paper until Cord cleared his throat.

"Help ya?"

"I'm looking for Bitter Waters, who does the campfire program in the evenings." Cord made his voice impersonal.

"Popular fellow this mornin'. Soldiers from the Lake Station in here lookin' for him, too."

Cord looked over his shoulder through the open tent flap. "How long ago?"

The Wylie man pulled out a cheap steel pocket watch. "Fifteen minutes?"

"What did you tell them?"

"He's been usin' the tents what ain't rented for the night, movin' from one to anuther."

"Which one is he in?" Cord tried to keep his impatience hidden.

"He come in last night and looked at the list to see what was open. There was at least twenty. I dunno which he took."

Cord turned away. It wasn't fair that Bitter Waters had to live like a vagabond in order to deliver his story of the Nez Perce War.

Outside, Cord stood before Dante and stroked his face; the big head lowered to sniff his pockets. "You had oats this morning."

Still smoothing his stallion's nose absently, he studied the array of tents on the hillside. All was quiet, as it lacked a few minutes till seven. Breakfast and the eight o'clock coach departures would bring out a crowd.

Suddenly, his hand froze in the act of petting Dante. Between the tents, in full uniform, marched Captain Feddors with a trio of soldiers Cord didn't know.

"Spread out and cover the main paths to the dining hall, the bathing tent, and the privies," Feddors ordered. "The old Injun will come out of his sleeping tent for one of nature's calls."

Before he could be recognized, Cord loosed the reins from the hitch rail, stepped around, and placed Dante between him and Feddors. He walked as slowly as possible away from the tent camp toward the lake.

As the sunlight grew stronger and the night chill began to dissipate, the dewy cobwebs brought back a fragment of memory. Of his uncle saying sunrise was his *wayakin*, that he rose at first light each day to absorb the wisdom of his guardian spirit before the damp burned off the grass.

High in the Absarokas, when the Nez Perce were fleeing, Cord had wakened at first light with a start. The canvas wall of Bitter Waters's and Kamiah's improvised shelter stretched over his head. His legs and feet were freezing where he had slid out of the tent on the slope during the night.

"Boy!" a deep voice hissed. "Blue Eyes!"

He twisted and stared across at the buffalo robes where Bitter Waters and his wife slept. They were empty.

"I knew with them eyes you had to be white," the voice behind the drape went on.

Cord rose and threw back the canvas to discover Cappy Parsons, the miner the tribe had kidnapped to guide them through the mountains.

"It was my tough luck to have been grabbed." Cappy belched. "I was looking for gold south of Cooke City when I wandered into the park. Ran into them Nez Perce, and they held me prisoner along with those other tourists they picked up by the Firehole River." He gestured for Cord to crawl out of the tipi. "I'm getting out of here. Thought I'd take you back to decent folk where you belong."

Even at the age of six, Cord's face had grown hot while his silence lied for him.

"I got nothing for a kid, but in a few days' ride we'll find people with wimmen and milk cows."

When they found settlers, Cappy Parsons wandered on, leaving Cord to make his random way from settlement to settlement until he wound up in Salt Lake City. There a Mormon charity led him to the attention of Aaron Bryce.

If Bitter Waters and Kamiah had not risen before dawn, Cord's life might have been very different.

He mounted Dante and nudged him forward, seeking a place where the lakeshore faced the rising sun.

It didn't take long. On a promontory, dressed in his dark suit, Bitter Waters raised his arms to the morning sky. The only obvious difference between him and someone like Hopkins Chandler was his braids.

The lake was a mirror, the morning sky an almost impossible blue, rain-washed from the storm. The sun, above the horizon, transformed from lemon to diamond bright, blinding . . . There might have been two suns, one in the sky, the other mirrored in smooth water.

Cord reined Dante in, dismounted, and ordered him to stand. He walked through the trees toward his uncle, putting his feet down with care, the way the man he approached had taught him ensured silence.

About ten yards from the bank, Cord stopped. He listened and heard Bitter Waters murmuring what must have been a morning prayer. Something in the timbre of his voice made Cord touch the obsidian in his pocket.

It transported him back to early morning near his parents' cabin, watching his mother go onto her knees and plunge her hands into a lively foot-tall cascade of falling water.

The waterfall represented her guardian spirit, she had told him. When he was older, he would spend time in the wilderness finding his own. Her message, so oft repeated, had been the reason he had taken his pilgrimage seriously when Bitter Waters set him upon it.

Why, then, for all these years, had he used his obsidian as a sort of lucky piece, something to worry with his hands when his mind was seeking solutions?

This morning, he gripped the stone and felt as though its warmth came, not from his skin, but from its being born of fire. His throat thickened the way it did when he heard the national anthem, or when the Mormon Tabernacle Choir sang the hymns of Christmas. Within him mingled the blood of mighty traditions.

Bitter Waters turned. "There you are," he said as though he had known Cord was behind him all along.

Cord resisted the urge to wipe his brimming eyes.

His uncle noticed, as his sharp regard had taken in all the nuances of a six-year-old's emotion. "You have questions." He moved to sit on a thick and twisted silver log and gestured for his nephew to rest beside him.

Cord looked over his shoulder in the direction of the Wylie Camp. "I came to warn you at last night's campfire. The captain running the park is looking for you, says you're a troublemaker with your stories."

Bitter Waters smiled. "So my story . . . my truth, has pinched."

With another glance back the way he had come, Cord moved toward the log. "I saw them this morning searching the Wylie Camp."

"Then they will find me. And I will move on, back to the reservation at Nespelem in the state of Washington."

"This fellow Captain Feddors is a real hard case. He could hurt you."

His uncle nodded and patted the log. "Then sit,

for we may not have much time. I would tell you the rest of my story."

Cord folded down, rested his elbows on his knees, and looked out over the water. A little breeze kicked up and ruined the perfect, mirrored surface.

"I would tell you of Camas Meadows, where our rear scouts watched as General Howard and the soldiers made camp in an area we knew well. Chiefs Ollokot and Toohoolhoolzote plotted a night raid to steal their horses."

Cord shifted on the log so he could watch Bitter Waters's face.

"Later in the day, there was a skirmish. No Nez Perce were killed. I do not know about the men of the United States."

How strange to hear what Cord thought of as his country named as enemy.

"I heard we managed to make off with only mules, but I had already gone on my own pilgrimage. I took two men and crossed Teton Pass to find Sarah and her son . . ."

This time, Cord did not burst into a diatribe about his uncle killing his parents.

"I took you in as my son. One morning in Yellowstone when I was at prayers and Kamiah was building the cooking fire, you disappeared . . . the white miner was gone, also."

"I went with him on my own." Cord did not let his gaze waver.

"To the life of a white man. The story I told, I

wish it could speak to your soul."

"I heard you." Cord's heart came close to softening, but . . . "Tell me about your driving my mother from her home."

Bitter Waters lips set. "That would take many suns. Know that it is a story with many rights and many wrongs."

The back of Cord's neck prickled. The crackle of a pinecone was faint; he saw that Bitter Waters had heard before him. First, the cone, then small limbs snapping, and hoofbeats approached from along the shore.

"They are coming for me."

"I won't let them . . ."

The look Bitter Waters gave Cord told him he had no recourse against a soldier's gun.

Cord put two fingers to his mouth and whistled, aware that it would erase any doubt as to their location. From behind, he heard the quick thuds of Dante's hooves.

"Take my horse." He rose and snagged the reins, putting a soothing hand on Dante's withers. "There, boy."

Bitter Waters was on his feet. "I . . . not your fine animal."

"Take him and get out of here," Cord instructed. "Where is your horse?"

"Tethered in the meadow back of the Wylie Camp. A fine Appaloosa with the brand of a rising sun."

"Hey!" called a male voice.

"Yiiii!" Another spoke to his mount.

His uncle gripped his sleeve. "I will hide in the woods as long as you need and trade for my horse."

Cord swallowed. He didn't know if he could trust Bitter Waters not to bolt right away, taking Dante, the finest horse and one of the best friends he'd ever had.

Bitter Waters barely touched Dante's side, slid his foot into the stirrup, and looked down from the saddle. Cord handed up the reins with a thick feeling in his throat. "Meet me at noon, where your horse is tethered."

"Halt!" Captain Feddors's voice was unmistakable. Cord turned to face him.

"Well, if it isn't Mr. Sutton with his friend, the Injun." Feddors rode a good-looking bay with a silky black mane and tail. He focused on Dante. "That one of them-there Nez Perce horses?"

Dante shifted his feet and neighed. Bitter Waters controlled him with ease.

Behind Feddors, Sergeant Larry Nevers rode White Bird. Her cheek bore the scar of the whip.

Feddors leaned back in his saddle and shifted his gaze to Bitter Waters. "I heard about you, old man. Stirring up trouble among the tourists with your stories about the Nez Perce War."

Cord stepped between Dante and Feddors's mount. "Last I heard, they weren't stories."

Feddors stared down at him and fingered his moustache. With a deliberate motion, he lowered his right hand to his side. His pistol holster unlatched with a snick.

Larry Nevers gave an audible gasp.

The Colt slid out of the leather; Feddors raised the shining silver gun and looked at it with affection. "Bitter Waters has been telling stories. Anybody want to hear my story? About the Nez Perce War?"

On the train and the stage to the world's first national park, Quenton Feddors got to know his father, Zeke, in a way he never had before. By the time they arrived at Bart Henderson's ranch just north of Yellowstone, Zeke was speaking to fifteen-year-old Quenton of the lingering pains of Reconstruction as though he were already a man.

On the train, they heard about the Nez Perce. How General Howard tried to catch them for months and lost them in Yellowstone.

On August 31, in the northern reaches of the park, two Nez Perce braves on horseback had surprised Quenton in the woods beside a waterfall, both men painted up and carrying rifles. Sneaking away undetected, he raced to McCartney's Inn at Mammoth to spread a warning. The small log building nestled against the hillside at the head of the meadow below Mammoth Hot Springs, a towering cone of travertine marking the track into the yard.

On a boulder before the building rested a man in army blues. He rose and introduced himself as Lieutenant Hugh Scott. "Stay back," he advised, but the curiosity of youth impelled Quenton forward.

A bearded young man lay on the porch, clutching a sheaf of sheet music in his hand. Quenton read at the top of the crushed score that it was by Mozart. Fresh blood stained the worn wooden boards.

"Shot by the Nez Perce," Scott told Quenton. Richard Dietrich was a music teacher from Helena who had studied in Germany. With two bullets through him, he wasn't even cold yet.

Feddors raised his pistol and pointed it at Bitter Waters.

Cord's throat threatened to close, but he managed, "This man had nothing to do with Richard Dietrich's death." He hoped that was true.

Before he finished his sentence, something like recognition spread over Feddors's mean features. "Sergeant Nevers," the captain said, "Ah believe ah have figured something out. Our Mr. Sutton's Indian blood is not Crow, Bannock, or Shoshone." He showed his yellowed teeth. "He's a fuckin' Nez Perce!"

Cord's two worlds collided. His fate was sealed, as it had been since his birth.

"That's right," he said evenly. "This man you are threatening is my uncle."

"That so?" Feddors's pistol did not waver.

"Yes." The second time, it came out easier.

"Captain Feddors!" said a voice from the forest. Cord didn't dare take his eyes off the Colt to see who had arrived.

"Lieutenant Stafford." Feddors solved the problem. "You're not needed heah."

From the corner of his eye, Cord saw Stafford dismount, Colt in hand. "Sir, as your second-in-command, I must back you and Sergeant Nevers up." He looked at Bitter Waters astride Dante. "What is this man's offense?"

"His offense?" The captain's aim did not waver. "This man has been inciting the tourists about the Nez Perce War. Getting things stirred up all over again."

"Bitter Waters is kin to me," Cord broke in. "He has spoken the truth of history."

Stafford's solemn gray eyes flicked over Cord, his commanding officer, and back to Bitter Waters. "Let him leave the park in peace. He will agree not to return."

To Cord's surprise, his uncle inclined his head in answer.

Feddors glared at Bitter Waters a little longer, then shrugged. He holstered his pistol with what Cord believed to be pretended indifference.

"Go on," Stafford directed.

Bitter Waters rode away with slow dignity. Several times, Dante looked back over his shoulder as if bewildered at being given away.

Stafford looked at Feddors. "There is a telephone message for you at the station, sir."

Cord took the opportunity to walk, not ride, away.

What had he been thinking to entrust Dante to the man he'd always blamed for his parents' death? He knew so little about Bitter Waters.

Except what the heart could discern.

His mother, Sarah, had always had a lilt in her voice when she spoke of her childhood family. Her older brother had taught her to call in waterfowl; to play games with a ball and stick; to dig clay from the creek bank, form it into shapes, and let it bake in the sun. Only when Franklin Sutton came and loved her had the trouble began; a story with so many rights and wrongs that Bitter Waters declared would take many suns to tell.

With an ache in his chest, Cord recalled the way Dante had trembled when he handed over the reins. He saw the intelligent brown eyes with their long black lashes, and recalled the contrast between the velvet nose and the few longer, coarse hairs when he stroked his muzzle. He counted the hours till noon and prayed Bitter Waters stuck around.

In preparation, Cord circled around the Wylie Camp and located Bitter Waters's tethered Appaloosa. At his approach, the animal tossed his head, pawed, and snorted.

"Shh, shh," he murmured. "You're a good boy." He should have taken the time to find out his name. To be sure he had the right horse, he checked the brand and found the rising sun.

Within minutes, Cord was leading him down to the lake for a drink. He walked him, then retethered him to the staked rope. Offering his hand, he let it be sniffed, and promised to return later in the day with Bitter Waters.

Between now and then so many things would be decided.

The next time Cord saw Laura, she would proudly and publicly accept him, or she would not. With the bullet out, her father would improve, or he would begin to develop the fever and infection that presaged decline and death. Edgar would show up beside Cord at the late-morning meeting with the railroad, or he would have fled in the night.

Hell, what was the use in even showing up at the meeting? Why not just wait till noon, get Dante back, and ride?

But, no. He wasn't going to run as Feddors hoped. He'd stay, attend the meeting with his head high. Hopkins Chandler and Norman Hagen had a clear choice to make.

Hank had behaved deceitfully, hiding the evidence of his past mistakes. Cord had to plead his personal record, his integrity . . . and the fact that in the new century there was no reason not to do business with the adopted son of prominent Aaron Bryce. After all, he was still the man who had created Excalibur.

One who just happened to have a newfound pride in his native roots.

CHAPTER TWENTY-TWO

JUNE 28

Cord nearly choked on his lukewarm coffee when Laura entered the hotel meeting room at ten-thirty with Hank. Dressed almost gaily in emerald silk, she nonetheless had dark circles etched beneath her wide green eyes. Two spots of color stood out, high on her otherwise pale face.

Norman Hagen, who had been tapping the table and running his fingers through his bushy red beard, smiled kindly. "How is your father?"

"Until he is better, I will represent the bank in these discussions."

Norman nodded.

Cord started a slow burn. How could she waltz in here with Hank after what had happened between them last night?

"We'll wait for Edgar a minute more," Norman suggested, though Hopkins Chandler looked displeased.

Laura took a seat. Her bent head revealed the nape of her neck, with an escaped lock of hair. The tendril curled to just below her collarbone, where a shadow defined the delicate hollow beneath the bone.

Cord stared at her, and she suddenly seemed to find her fingernails fascinating.

Norman studied the wall clock and looked apologetic. "I guess we should begin without Edgar."

Cord did not argue.

"Even with Forrest struck down . . ." Hank cast a challenging look at Cord, "the Fielding Bank will still partner with me in funding my purchase of the Lake Hotel."

"What do you say, Norm?" Cord ignored the implied accusation and used the familiar version of Norman's name that he'd adopted this spring in St. Paul. He still hoped for a quick decision; perhaps Hopkins Chandler would leave the park before hearing any slurs against his heritage. "When do you anticipate making a decision?"

"Hold on," Hank demanded. "I have new information that bears on Sutton's eligibility to purchase the concession."

A creeping cold took hold of Cord. Surely, Laura couldn't have . . .

Hank rose. "The United States Government and the Northern Pacific have gone to a great deal of trouble to clear the Crow, Blackfoot, and Shoshone out of Yellowstone Park."

Cord set his jaw.

Hank paused to light a cheroot, while anticipation deepened. Inhaling through pursed lips, he blew the smoke across the table into a cloud over Cord's head.

"I have learned," he announced smugly, "that William Cordon Sutton, despite his fancy name and blue eyes, is really a Nez Perce."

Cord was on his feet, looking at Laura with a rage so palpable she felt as if he had struck her. His sleek hair gleamed in the light, and Laura thought that Sarah's hair must have been like that, a blackbird's wing glowing in the fire that had consumed her.

Laura fought the lump in the back of her throat and forced herself to look at him. "I didn't . . ."

Hopkins Chandler's expression was ugly, as he glanced at the railroad poster of the fallen red man. "If this is true . . . Mr. Sutton . . . ?"

Laura watched Cord draw himself up and make a formal bow. He addressed the room at large, "For the second time this morning, I am taken to task for the blood of my people."

His angry gaze met Laura's and held. "And for the second time, I must confess—no, announce with pride—that I am of the Nimiipuu, the People."

Then he wasn't looking at her anymore, but at Hopkins Chandler. "If that eliminates me from your consideration as a buyer, then there is nothing more to be said."

He stalked from the table and left the room. The firmness with which he shut the door behind him was not quite a slam.

Laura wanted to go after him, but Norman leaned forward, both hands flat on the table. "I don't see why," he addressed his boss, "there couldn't be a shift in policy. It is the twentieth century and Cord—that is, Sutton—is only one-quarter Nez Perce. His association with Aaron Bryce . . ."

"Yes," Laura agreed.

"This is ridiculous." Hank glared at her. "You're supposed to be on my side."

She got up. "I agreed to come, because Father asked me to. I am here to represent that if you should be chosen to buy the hotel, Fielding Bank will back you." Her eyes met Norman's and he nodded. "But I cannot deny I want Cord to win."

Hopkins Chandler slammed his palm atop the table. "Everyone shut up!"

Everyone did.

"Hear this, and hear it good. This afternoon I am leaving for St. Paul and telling the home office that there is no one to whom I could recommend selling the hotel."

Twenty minutes before noon, Cord waited and watched near Bitter Waters's tethered Appaloosa. The blood was still raging through his veins.

He'd trusted Laura with his secrets. And only a few hours after they had parted from sharing everything that was right and good between a man and a woman, Hank had come to the table armed with all he needed to defeat him.

As the minutes ticked toward twelve, Cord scanned the woods for his uncle's approach. If he'd bolted for the park boundary, Dante was many miles away. While there were people to whom horseflesh was simply that, Dante was . . .

A faint shush of moccasin on leaf, and Cord turned.

Bitter Waters stood with his weight balanced on both feet, a bag over his shoulder, and Dante's reins light in his hand. A little boy's impulse to run and throw his arms around his stallion's neck seized Cord. "I fed your Appaloosa and watered him."

The older man replied, "I had no feed, but Dante cropped sweet grass and drank from the lake while we waited for the hour."

"That is all I might ask."

This was wrong. There was so little time, there was no time, and they spoke in stilted tones.

Bitter Waters handed over Dante and walked to his mount. He bent and pulled up the metal stake and chain. "I thank you."

Cord swallowed. "I . . . we are family."

His uncle's face softened. "That is what I have always hoped to hear from you. Speaking of family," he gestured toward the hotel, "you will take the woman as wife?"

This morning, when he and Laura had left the stable, he might almost have considered it. Now, he shook his head. "She is set upon a different path."

Bitter Waters stowed his tether and chain in his bag. He moved, lithe and quick for an older man, and mounted his horse bareback. "Something you must learn, Obsidian."

Cord waited.

"Your *wayakin* is hard and tough, but also brittle and easy to break."

Bitter Waters nudged his horse. "Always honor your people, the Nimiipuu, as well as your father's, and as for the woman . . ."

He started to ride away, but looked back a last time. "You must find a way to change her path."

Though the morning had dawned clear, rain was once again threatening when Cord approached the hotel porch. Intent on his mission of pounding on the door of Forrest Fielding's suite, and camping out in the hall if no one answered, he almost walked past Laura as she exited the lobby.

"There you are." He gripped her wrist.

"Let me go!"

He didn't loosen his hold. "Not until I have some answers."

The lake roiled beneath the overcast.

"What do you mean by spending the night with

me and then coming into the meeting on Hank's side?" Cord pressed.

A pair of elderly women fled the weather, their bee-tled brows telegraphing disapproval as they passed.

Laura jerked free. Cord stepped closer; she retreat-ed until a porch post at her back stopped her. "What could I do? Father may be dying, and he begged me to help Hank."

The wind rose; a few fat raindrops landed on the porch. Laura's skirt billowed.

Cord took her by the shoulders, his thumbs fram-ing the hollow at the base of her neck. "How you could have faked . . . ?"

He stopped at the sight of Constance running up the drive toward the hotel. One of her hands was raised to shield her silken hair.

Laura had her back to her cousin's approach. "Faked?"

Constance bounded up the stairs onto the porch, brushing raindrops from her face and her pretty cre-tonne dress, printed with pink flowers. Her blue eyes went wide at the sight of Cord apparently manhan-dling her cousin. "William! What are you doing?"

"I am trying," he gritted, "to have a conversation with Laura."

The weather whipped up off the lake in earnest, a tearing gust swept chill rain in under the overhang.

"Talk about this," Constance challenged. "That ugly Captain Feddors keeps telling everyone you're a Nez Perce."

Let it all be in the open, then. "It's true."

He straightened and stepped away from Laura.

"Yes, it's true," Laura echoed. Cord couldn't tell if she meant to support him or cut him down.

Constance's chest heaved; she struggled to pull off the ring she'd agreed to keep. Clutching it, she raked the stone down Cord's right cheek.

He sucked in his breath. The slash mirrored the scar on his left; he felt once more as though he'd been sliced with a knife.

But he refused to flinch, just raised a hand and touched the trail of blood.

"To think I trusted you." Constance's voice caught.

Laura ducked away, slammed the screen door open, and disappeared into the hotel.

"You low-down cad!" Constance held out the garnet in trembling fingers.

He made no move to take it.

"I was so happy when you gave this to me." She laughed, a bitter note.

It sent him back painfully to St. Paul and a rose garden in spring; their mingled laughter had marked their retreat from the dinner party into the softness of evening. The perfume of roses had filled his head, along with the carnation scent he'd come to associate with her soft white skin.

On the porch, the rain came down harder, blowing in and splattering their shoes. He'd thought it was too good to be true the way she'd let him off the hook without a fight.

"You lied to me about who you are. You lied to everybody!"

Cord started to say he hadn't lied, but he'd already concluded the sin of omission was as great as an outright falsehood. "I'm sorry for that, now."

"Take it." Constance offered the ring again. When he still did not accept it, she made a move to slip it into his pocket.

Cord wiped his bloody hand on his trousers, took the garnet, and laid it carefully on her palm. "All I can say is I'm sorry it couldn't have turned out better."

Constance ran until the breath burned in her chest, and she kept on running, heedless of the rain streaming down her face and soaking her pink-flowered dress.

Lightning split the sky, and she dodged, as if it would pick her out above the scrubby sage and meadow grass. The rain came down harder, silver sheets blowing sideways across the field. Almost to the shelter of a copse of fir, she turned her ankle on a tuft of sod.

She went down, full length in a patch of wet earth.

The tears started again, welling up from that place they had begun the other day when William had kissed her savagely and then turned away. Thunder rolled through the meadow, and she opened her hand, looking down at the ring smeared with fresh earth.

What was worse, learning he cared for Laura and keeping her head up, or finding him to be a lying masquerader who'd tried to fool both her and her cousin?

She lay in the dirt, while the deluge began to let up. Though she knew she should rise, she didn't have the spirit for it.

Suddenly, incongruously, a waft of smoke came to her on the wind.

Constance raised her head and looked into the copse.

Sheltering from the weather with a shoulder against a tree, Norman Hagen drew on his cigarette. He shielded the flame from the drips that made it through the needled canopy. Though not as wet as she was, his thick hair curled in the humid air.

"What are you doing out here in the rain?" she asked, knowing she looked a fright.

"I could ask you the same thing." His cigarette made a crimson rose against the dark day.

As if continuing a conversation they had started the last time they were together, he smiled. "It's done, then?"

"The storm?"

"The storm is abating, but I was referring to your relationship with Cord Sutton. I take it you're upset because you didn't know about his background."

Constance pushed herself up onto hands and knees and tried to brush dirt from her dress. She succeeded in smearing it into more mud. "Of course, I'm upset. He didn't . . ."

"He didn't let a lot of people know, and I can't say I disagree with him. Does it really matter so much to you that he's Nez Perce?"

"Not so much that, but he should have told me if . . ."

"If you were the one for him, he might well have."

He reached into the pocket of his brown vicuna jacket. "Smoke?" He extended a pack of Richmond Straight Cuts.

Constance shook her head, declining the harsh filterless tobacco. "Laura knew."

Norman nodded. "He would have told her."

The last of her sobs turned into a hiccup.

"You look like a drowned rat." Norman threw down his cigarette and pressed it into the soft earth with his boot heel.

Constance felt tears start again, and she wiped her face with the backs of her hands. She'd imagined Norman found her desirable.

He burst out laughing, a big merry sound that seemed to bounce back and forth between the tree trunks. Kneeling before her, his eyes were kind. "I was laughing because you have managed to get mud all over your pretty face."

He drew a silk square from the breast pocket of his jacket and scrubbed her cheeks. Taking her dripping hair into his hands, he squeezed the water from it. "I can safely say I have never wrung out a woman's hair."

She smiled through her tears.

"Come on." He offered to help her to her feet.

Extending her hand, Constance realized she still held the ring. "I don't need this."

Norman plucked it from her palm. "When I first met you in St. Paul, I thought perhaps you and I . . ."

He used his pocket square to clean the stone. Then he bowed and handed back the ring.

Constance took it, but her gaze was on Norman's face. "You thought . . ."

"Let's discuss that later," he said. "Now, I think you should get cleaned up and let me take you in to lunch."

CHAPTER TWENTY-THREE

JUNE 28

When the rain subsided to isolated drops and dripping off the eaves, Laura left her room where she'd barricaded herself. Wearing one of Aunt Fanny's shawls over emerald silk, she made her way downstairs, past the dining room occupied by the last luncheon stragglers, and into the dim east hall to Room 109.

Without hesitation, she rapped.

Cord had to believe she hadn't been the one to tell Hank. She'd explain how she went to the meeting because she promised her father, never intending to say anything to undermine Cord's cause. To prove it, she'd tell her father about them, that she'd chosen her man and it wasn't Hank Falls.

She knocked again. "Cord! If you're in there, open up!"

All was silent, within and without. It was the time of day when guests had checked out and their replacements weren't due until the cocktail hour.

She pounded with her fist. Beneath her assault, the portal swung open.

The bed was made. There was no sign of Cord's saddlebags on the luggage stand. The top of the bureau was clear.

Laura advanced into the room and found nothing in the drawers or on the windowsill.

But wait. Peeking from beneath the bedspread was the sparkle of black glass: Cord's obsidian, the guardian spirit without which he might be open to harm.

"Miss?"

She jumped at the tentative voice from the hall. "Miss, if you're looking for the man who was in this room . . ."

"Yes."

"He checked out a little while ago."

The young man from the desk held the door and gestured for her to come out. She hesitated, then bent to grab the stone.

"What's that?" he asked in a suspicious tone.

She closed her hand over it. "Just something Mr. Sutton would want. I'll hold it for him."

He shook his head and held out his hand. "Everything that's left in a room is given to Mr. Falls. His strict orders."

Laura's fingers clenched. The stone warmed, as did her courage.

"It's just an old piece of rock." She opened her hand so the young man could see and closed it.

She turned toward the door and almost bumped

into Captain Feddors's stocky chest.

"Here," he said. "Let's see this rock Sutton has left behind."

On instinct, she clenched her fist and thrust her hand behind her back.

Feddors laughed. "You dare to defy me? A'hm the law and ah say to show me what you've got."

Laura looked up and down the hall, but there was no one. Of course, if there had been, what guest or employee would help her defy the ranking officer in the park? Yet, feeling the stone in her hand almost glowing, she was loath to part with it.

"What do you care about a rock?"

"Nothing. But when a rock becomes someone's magic, someone ah despise, then ah'd best take that magic away from him."

Laura recoiled. How could Feddors know she held Cord's connection to the spirit world?

The captain took her arm, using his fingers like pincers. Her hand opened, and the obsidian dropped to the boards.

He scooped it up. "Lots of Injuns use this kind of stone to ward off evil."

His laugh followed Laura as she hurried down the long hall and out into the gray afternoon. Within a few yards, she regretted the gown and thin black satin slippers. The smooth soles slipped in the mud, and the hem of the dress dragged over wet roots on the path. Droplets fell from the trees, making a soft sound where they landed on pine needles. When the wind picked up, they showered down, wetting her face and hair, and spotting her silk skirt.

Nonetheless, she pressed on toward the stables.

Cord had to be here. He couldn't have packed his saddlebags and be gone already.

To save time, she left the path beside the lake and cut through the meadow. Soon her skirts were soaked above the knee from the long grass and thigh-high sage. As the wet aroma rose, it reminded her of the morning she'd fought her way out of the Snake River.

Yes, this land was wild and filled with dangers. But she didn't want to go back to Chicago. She wanted to find Cord and stay with him, to see his ranch.

She reached the stable and pulled open the door. "Cord!"

The door at the opposite end of the stable was closed, the tackies evidently having taken shelter elsewhere during the storm. The interior was darker than it had been the morning she'd come to visit Dante and seen Constance slide her arms around Cord. Strange, how that no longer mattered.

"Is anybody here?"

No human voice replied, but a dozen large heads poked out over the stall gates. The horses nickered for an apple or oats.

Dante did not appear.

Laura walked the length of the barn, in case he'd been moved to another stall. She paused to stroke White Bird's nose, then carried on. When she reached the far end, she was forced to admit that both Cord and his horse were gone.

How could he have ridden away without finishing what he'd called their "conversation"? More a shouting match, but if someone cared enough to shout, they should care too much to walk—ride—away.

Laura went back to White Bird and examined the whip cut on the mare's cheek. "You've been hurt, too, girl. I'd take you home with me if I could."

With a last pat on the soft nose, Laura left the stable.

On the way back, she crossed the meadow on a path that ended at the hotel staging area for wagons and coaches. Parties were arriving back early, no doubt having skipped some sights during the rain.

Laura passed the carefree tourists on her way to the infirmary. She should be sorry for yelling at her father this morning since he was an invalid, but she wasn't willing to accept any part of the blame for his business troubles. If he'd let her come into the bank years ago, it might have been different, but expecting her to marry the right man to keep him tied to the company while she continued to manage the household . . . why, if she had married one of Father's choices, he'd have managed to maneuver her husband into living at Fielding House.

If . . . when he recovered, he'd have to hire somebody to take care of things in Chicago, because she was going to find Cord, no matter what it took.

Dr. Upshur reported Forrest was just dropping off into a good sleep, the first healthful and natural rest he'd had since the drugs used for surgery had worn off. The doctor had checked the dressing over his wound a few minutes ago and found it clean, with no sign of pus or infection.

"In fact, he's doing so well he'll be able to travel in two or three days," Dr. Upshur went on. "Provided his business here is complete."

"It's complete, all right," said Hank from behind Laura. "Hopkins Chandler is leaving in a hired hack before dark so as to overnight at the National Hotel at Mammoth. That way he can catch the morning stage to the train up at Cinnabar."

Dr. Upshur moved away discreetly and went into another patient room. In her present mood, Laura felt like telling Hank it was fitting the railroad wouldn't sell to him, either. Disloyal as it might be to her father, she wished Cord might have won.

She glanced at her father's door. "Does he know?"

"Not unless you told him."

She shook her head. "And I shan't tell him now. The doctor says he must rest."

Hank jerked his head toward the outer door. "Shall we go, then?"

Once they were outside, she tried walking fast toward the hotel to get away. Hank kept pace with her.

Realizing she would have to be more direct, she stopped. "You know your brother probably shot my father."

Hank matched her stare for stare. "You know your lover is the best candidate to have popped him with a little pepperbox or the like."

"He never . . ." Then, because Cord's leaving stung, "He's not my lover."

Hank smiled. "I am most gratified to hear you say that, whether or not it is true. As he has ridden out of both our lives, you must join me for supper aboard the *Alexandra*. Not the victory celebration I had hoped for, but perhaps we can console one another."

The last thing she wanted.

But there were too many mysteries. Had Danny shot her father? Was it coincidence that he'd attacked her coach in Jackson's Hole? Why did Cord's banker seem to be in cahoots with a criminal?

If Hank were Danny's brother, he must have some of the answers.

And though she shouldn't care about helping Cord, she suddenly decided to trick Hank into helping her get his obsidian back from Captain Feddors. With its uncanny quality of heat, it might bring her some kind of luck . . .

If nothing else, it would be something to remember him by.

By early evening, the lake was still unsettled from the storm. Quick waves licked the *Alexandra*'s hull, as Hank led Laura on-board.

She'd changed from the water-spotted green silk, eschewing the pink dress with lace and the striped taffeta in favor of a plain serge skirt and white shirtwaist. Hair pulled up in a tortoiseshell clasp, no toilet water or cologne. She might plan to enlist Hank's aid, but one thing she did not intend was to inflame his senses.

Leaning against the railing, he looked at her with intent dark eyes, his blond hair stirring in the breeze. The sun, which had emerged around four o'clock, peeked from beneath a bank of clouds on the far shore of Yellowstone Lake. High in the Absarokas, the smoke of the wildfire they'd all been watching had grown to a plume that billowed into the evening sky like cumulus.

"Shouldn't the storm have put that fire out?" Laura asked.

"This afternoon's rain probably passed it by . . . or it burns with such fury that a short dousing could not extinguish it. Ever seen a forest fire up close?" Hank used his hands to pantomime leaping flames.

"Sometimes in Illinois grass fires creep for miles, but I've never seen anything big."

"Pity," Hank murmured, close to her ear. "I have found that so much fire can be frightening . . . and beautiful."

Laura tried to imagine the torrent of heat and sound, sweeping through the forest.

"I heard that the fire lookout reported new smoke late this afternoon." He pointed to the northeast. "Near Nez Perce Peak."

"Nez Perce?"

"A big ugly mountain, treacherous climbing . . .

story is, at least part of the tribe camped in a high valley there on their way through in 1877. This was after they shot a white man named George Cowan, kidnapped a tourist party, and traded some worn-out nags to them in exchange for their fresh horses."

Laura suppressed a retort.

His hand tightened on her arm. "Let me show you my modest little berth."

He took her in through the spare-looking passenger cabin and opened the ornate door to his quarters. From the gold-threaded embroidered pillows on the carved divan, to the striped burgundy armchair, fine silks and brocades dominated. She recognized the carpet as a Persian Heriz, a complex pattern of reds and blues that radiated outward from a central diamond.

She looked further and flushed. Behind a Chinese screen ornamented with a cavorting dragon and the Great Wall, stretched a wide bed covered in sleek black satin.

"Like it?" Hank asked with pride.

Laura dragged her focus away from his "modest berth" and swallowed. "It's not what I expected. Not what a woman would select."

"Alexandra did a wonderful job of decorating for a man."

"A single man." Laura emphasized the second word. "I suspect you make a habit of entertaining women who are passing through."

Hank went to the Chinese bronze oil lamps one by one, trimming the wicks with care, rehanging them on their brass hooks, and lighting them. Sandalwood incense wafted on the cooling air.

Footsteps on deck preceded a knock.

"Our dinner," Hank said.

The waiter looked familiar, the young man on whom Cord had spilled salad in the hotel kitchen. Working efficiently, he put out covered plates.

She turned toward the open window framed in velvet and watched the lake darken. When Hank closed the door behind the waiter, she heard a click.

A moment later, the pop of a champagne cork was followed by a faint effervescent fizz.

Handing Laura a crystal flute, Hank clinked his glass against hers. She swirled the champagne in her mouth and turned the bottle in its silver bucket of ice. "Veuve Clicquot Ponsardin," the label informed, "since 1772."

"I've noticed the cutthroat trout is your favorite," Hank said.

She recalled him trying to cut Cord's throat in the meeting this morning. "You're very sharp, Hank."

How and when could she steer the conversation toward Danny . . . or Cord's *wayakin*? She'd have to be careful, say she wanted it for herself.

Hank lifted the silver cover from a serving platter. A whole trout lay in a white wine sauce with wild mushrooms and shallots. Beneath the fish, a bed of rice was tinged yellow with expensive saffron. Alongside appeared another delicacy, tinned white asparagus.

Hank pulled out a chair for her. She sat slowly,

reluctance in her limbs.

He served the trout onto china that was clearly finer than the hotel's best. The nearly translucent porcelain was tinted lavender, hand painted with tiny purplish forget-me-nots. Even with the masculine appearance of the room, Laura recalled Alexandra's penchant for purple and thought she'd indulged her own taste in the china.

Laura touched the gold rim, and Hank smiled. She reached for her fork and tasted the trout. "This is lovely, Hank," she murmured, looking at Limoges.

"Not half so lovely as you."

Laura hid a grimace. Any other time or place, she would have appreciated the china and the dinner.

With her fork halfway to her mouth, she said, "You know, it's the strangest thing. This afternoon, I was in the hotel hallway and one of the staff found something left behind in Cord Sutton's room . . ."

Hank pushed back his chair and came to her, drawing her up.

"It was a piece of obsidian, really beautiful . . ." Speaking lightly, Laura tried to pull away.

He shifted his hands, sliding them up to hold her shoulders hard enough to assert his claim. "I know we should finish dinner," he pulled her closer, "but I seem to have lost my appetite."

"Hank." For the moment, she gave up on the obsidian. "I've never given you any ideas." She tried to maintain a reasonable tone.

With a suddenness that shocked her, his lips

mashed hers. His tongue twisted against her teeth, as he tried to insinuate it inside her mouth.

She pulled away and he lost his hold. "Hank, no."

He was big enough to do whatever he wanted to her.

Dragging her back into his arms, he pleaded, "Laura, let me show you how it can be for us." He bent to kiss the place where the high collar of her blouse met bare skin, then loosened the clasp that bound her hair.

So much for her plans of managing him into answering questions. "You know I don't want this."

Gripping her shoulders, he propelled her toward the Chinese screen and the black-covered bed.

She shoved his hands away. "I said, no!" The cabin door looked far away. "I'm leaving."

"Stay," Hank whispered. He took her glass and set it with his on the table beside the bed. His breath came fast against her ear. "Since the first night I saw you," he whispered hoarsely, "even in men's clothes . . ."

"Let me go!"

She pushed at him, hard. He overpowered her and threw her onto her back on the bed. Her breath whooshed out.

Hank straddled her. His hungry eyes took in her mussed hair and her breasts beneath the blouse's soft white ruffles.

Up until this, she'd thought he was enough of a gentleman to heed her refusal. Now, he appeared wild in the lamplight, his blond hair in disarray . . .

He looked like his brother.

Tugging at her blouse, he scattered pearl buttons,

then tore at the delicate ribbons of her camisole. The silk ripped.

"I saw you come out of the barn with Cord this morning," Hank said thickly, "with straw in your beautiful hair."

Forrest had been no fool, saying what a prize his daughter would be.

Hank's blood surged, as he pressed Laura down on his bed. Though she struggled beneath him, he clamped his thighs more tightly. She might pretend not to want it, but he'd seen how the morning light illuminated the flush of a woman who'd been more than satisfied.

Tonight, it was his turn.

He folded back the silk and exposed her delicate breast. The sight set Hank to comparing her with other women he'd had. Those conquests, delightful as they had been, paled in comparison to the exquisite challenge of Laura Fielding. She produced a heat that exceeded any he'd felt before. No matter whether she wore her boy's clothing, emerald silk, or this evening's plain skirt and shirtwaist . . . if she danced divinely in his arms or raised her arms willingly to another man, he had to make her his.

"Laura," he gasped, "just let me . . ."

She got a hand free and jabbed the side of his neck with her nails. The sharp pain sent him into a rage.

"You little whore." He'd thought she knew the game. "You'll let him, but . . ."

She slashed up again and raked his cheek, coming close to his eyes.

Forrest Fielding had told Hank about Laura's willful ways. And that it took a firm hand to deal with her.

Hank dodged her attempt to knee him in the groin and fumbled with the buttons of his flannel trousers. Grabbing one of Laura's wrists, he collected the other and pinned both hands on the bed above her head.

CHAPTER TWENTY-FOUR

JUNE 28

Cord listened to Yellowstone Lake lap at the pilings beneath the pier. He should be long away from here, but . . .

Early this afternoon, after Laura and Constance had run from him in opposite directions, he'd struck off toward the stable to calm Dante through the latest storm. He'd not gotten halfway there before Captain Feddors blocked his path, his hand on the grip of his Colt.

Cord tried to look around without being obvious. They were alone in the driving rain.

"Heard you've been found out. No more thinkin' you'll buy the hotel and throw your weight around here."

Cord attempted to sidestep and was blocked again.

"No more sniffin' round those women from Chicago." Feddors spit tobacco juice over the tops of Cord's boots.

Rage nearly blinded him. All he wanted was to get his hands around this asshole's neck and squeeze until he saw his eyes go opaque.

That was what the captain longed for, waiting with his gun at the ready.

"Guess that old Injun took off to save his hide." Feddors tried another tack. "Yer uncle."

"That's what I said."

"Mebbe you oughta take a message and follow him."

If this was a contest in illiterate speech, Cord decided he'd win. "Reckon I oughta."

"You don't, and you'll wish you had," Feddors finished. He pulled his weapon and gestured with it for Cord to get on with his getting on.

He headed toward the stable, arriving soaked and dripping. As soon as the rain let up, he saddled Dante and rode him around to the front of the hotel. Then he cleared out his room.

It only took a few minutes. His good black suit, a couple of white shirts, charcoal slacks, denims, and blue cotton shirts . . . all went into his leather saddlebag.

When everything was in, he stood for a moment with a nagging sense of leaving something behind. Checking his bureau drawers and the shaving stand turned up nothing.

In conspicuous view of anyone who might be taking note, he checked out, and loaded his saddlebag, his small pack, and his sealed rifle. Then he'd ridden into the woods, left Dante tied to a tree, and circled back on foot.

Looking for Laura.

She might have been the one who told Hank, but something in her stricken expression when he'd accused her on the porch had him risking his life to be sure, hiding out at the base of the bluff where the pier met the water. After full dark, he'd risk looking in the dining room and lobby windows and decide if the coast was clear to go inside.

He shook his head. Feddors might have ordered his men to be on the lookout. The only one Cord believed he could trust not to turn him in was Larry Nevers . . . but even that wasn't a given. Larry had stood by and let Cord rescue White Bird.

Perhaps the answer lay in Laura visiting her father in the infirmary. If he lay in wait in the trees along the path, he'd be able to see if she went there, hopefully alone.

He peeped out from under the pier. A couple walked along the edge of the Grand Loop above, the woman's arm through the man's.

Cord waited until they passed, then looked again. Seeing no one, he started up the steep bank toward the road. When he was halfway to the top, he thought he heard something off toward Hank's steamboat. Reaching the bank above, he saw a glow in one cabin window.

The steamboat rocked, and a wash of wave slapped the dock. Cord turned toward the infirmary.

A scream split the night, raising the hairs on his

arms and the back of his neck. On instinct, his hand
went to the horn-handled hunting knife he'd strapped
to his belt after the encounter with Feddors.

Another scream, this one choked off in the middle.
Between the dark curtains of the steamboat's cabin, a
shaft of yellow lamplight penetrated the darkness.
There was no other sign of light or life in the marina.

Cord ran to the stairs, down them, and along the
dock. There was no outer door to the lighted cabin,
and the portal to the passenger cabin was locked. He
rattled the knob and another cry came from inside.

He butted his shoulder against the water-swollen
wood and bounced off. Moving to the curtained window with its tantalizing wedge of light, he found the sash
lifted. Raising it higher, he parted the velvet drapes.

On the opposite side of the opulent cabin, half-
hidden behind an elaborate Chinese screen, a man and
woman lay entwined on the rumpled bed. Hank was
recognizable by his thin shoulders and blond hair. He
was coatless, his starched white shirt half off, pulled
down over one arm. His round white buttocks were
bare, his suit pants around his knees.

Sandalwood incense played a light note. The
woman's dark hair spread over brocade pillows shot
with gilt thread.

Cord felt a twinge in his groin. He hesitated,
wondering if he had imagined the frightened tenor of
the scream, or whether it had merely been exuberant
love play.

"No, damn you!" The woman beat her fists against

Hank's chest and heaved her body beneath his.

Cord put together the voice and the small ravaged face. "Laura!"

He leaped through the window and knocked over the dinner cart. Silver covers clattered and bounced. Lavender china shattered.

Staggering, Cord stumbled over a champagne cooler. It tipped and the bottle landed on its side. Effervescent gold pooled on the carpet.

Hank rolled off Laura and leaped up. His pants hobbled him; his thin penis shriveled. Laura pulled her skirt down, but the torn sides of her blouse hung open.

Cord crouched and kept his weight on the balls of his feet, hoping to God Hank didn't have a tiny derringer secreted somewhere.

Hank curled his thin lips into a sneer. Silver flashed in the dimly lit room as he pulled a stiletto from a sheath on his calf.

Reaching for his knife, Cord shouted, "Get out of here, Laura!"

Hank thrust forward.

Cord leaped aside, but the blade's tip slit his sleeve.

Laura scrambled off the bed and ran toward the door.

Cord circled warily, then swiveled and kicked up between Hank's legs.

Hank managed to grab Cord's foot. Both men went down, swearing.

Cord landed on his face and heard the clatter of his knife on the deck beyond the Oriental carpet.

He strained to reach it.

Hank flung himself onto his back. Expecting the sharp pain of the stiletto between his shoulder blades, Cord rolled and twisted in Hank's grasp.

Hank emerged on top, straddling Cord's thighs with long legs. He raised his blade.

Cord intercepted the knife hand on the descending stroke.

The stiletto slashed his forearm. His muscles trembled as he worked through the pain and strained to hold the knife away from his chest.

Hank smiled.

Cord brought his free hand up in a slashing blow. Hank fell back with a scream, his nose dripping blood. His hands came up to clutch his face, and he lost his grip on the knife handle.

Snatching the weapon, Cord reversed their positions, pinning Hank to the carpet. Both men gasped for breath.

With the stiletto in his hand, Cord lowered it until the tip of the blade rested a quarter inch from Hank's bare chest, just above his heart.

Hank's bloody hands dropped to his sides and he watched, breathing shallowly so as not to contact the steel.

"As you and others have so succinctly pointed out," Cord said softly, "I am a savage."

He let the blade touch flesh.

Hank's chest rose. A spot of blood appeared.

"Easy," Cord cautioned. "I wouldn't want you to

hurt yourself."

He barely raised the blade off skin. "You see, if anyone is going to hurt you for what you were doing to Laura . . ." he lowered his voice to a whisper, "I'd like for it to be me."

"What in the name of God is going on?" growled a deep voice.

Norman Hagen lifted Cord off Hank with strong hands and dropped him onto the deck. "I was having a cigarette by the water . . ."

Hank curled into a fetal position, his arms and legs protruding awkwardly. He held his hands over his rapidly swelling face.

Cord half-crawled to the nearby bed, still holding the knife. His cheekbone throbbed where he'd impacted the deck, right on the cut Constance had inflicted with the gemstone. He pulled himself up to sit on the edge, feeling himself start to shake while the pulse-pounding rush of the fight ebbed.

Laura stood just inside the door beneath a bronze lantern. She held her torn blouse together at the neck with one slender hand, her lamp-lit taffy hair spilling over her shoulders in tangled waves.

Hank groaned and pushed himself up on trembling arms. His knife-thin nose canted to the side and dripped blood on the fine carpet. "This savage," he told Norman, pointing dramatically, "came through the window while I was entertaining Laura Fielding and attacked me."

Norman's sharp eyes took in the remains of dinner

and the champagne bottle, lying on its side with a few precious inches of liquid still inside. Two glasses, half-full, sat on a table beside the bed. Norman raised his blond brows at Laura.

Hank looked quickly at Cord. "You saw her. She was begging for it."

"I screamed bloody murder," Laura said flatly. She spoke to Cord, her eyes enormous in the lamplight.

"Look what he did." Hank brushed back his hair that had fallen over his bruised and swollen face. "My nose is broken."

Cord grimaced and rolled his own bloody sleeve back to reveal the stab wound in his muscular forearm. "If I'd lost the fight, I'd be lying on your deck in a pool of blood."

"That's enough." Norman took Cord by his unin-jured arm and pointed him toward the doorway. "I'll walk with you back to the hotel so everyone can calm down."

Cord looked for Laura, but she was gone.

"I'm not sure what happened tonight," Norman told Cord as they walked away from the dock. "There's bad blood soiling this whole deal."

Cord looked Norman in the eye. "The fight hap-pened because I thought Hank was raping Laura. I still believe it."

Norman looked as though he were gathering his

thoughts; he reached into his breast pocket for his Richmond Straight Cuts. "I think most people would find that difficult to believe of Hank."

"You saw her blouse was torn."

"Still, it boils down to 'he said' and 'she said.'"

"And what I saw."

"You're not what anyone would call a disinterested observer. And you seemed a bit more interested in the situation than prudence might dictate."

"What's your point, Norm?" Cord asked tersely.

Bending, Norman struck a match on the heel of his shoe. Cupping the cigarette in his hands, he put the flame to it, inhaling the smoke. "I have no problem with you or who your parents were, but perhaps this is not the time or place for you to publicly fight for Laura Fielding's hand."

Cord winced as he involuntarily clenched his fist.

"That's a nasty cut." Norman checked out the bloody forearm. Then he looked toward the steamboat. "My advice to you is to leave here tonight, before Falls comes after you again."

Sound advice, for more than one reason; he didn't tell Norman that Captain Feddors had a place earmarked for him in the Mammoth stockade.

"What happened to you?" From the cabin doorway, Alexandra took in Hank's bruised and swollen face, his torn shirt, and the blood he hadn't wiped from the decking.

It was approaching midnight. He'd mourned the loss of the Veuve Cliquot with a Napoleon cognac. His broken nose still swelling, it throbbed unmercifully even after he'd drunk the liquor.

"I had a fight," he said.

"I see that." Alexandra tossed her cape onto the damask sofa. Advancing into the opulent room she had decorated, she set one of the bronze incense lamps swinging with a flick of her finger. Coming to the bed, she peered at Hank's wounded face. "Did you go after Danny?"

"You mean, did your brother go after me?"

"Danny is your brother, too. Is he all right?"

"How should I know?" He stretched for his glass of cognac on the bedside table. It was empty. "I was fighting Cord Sutton."

Alex slumped down on the satin covers piled at the foot of the bed. "Don't you know how much Danny would give for just one moment of your precious time?"

"I went looking for you both this morning at that old cabin. That would have been a moment of my time, enough to settle the score."

"Not to fight each other," Alex pleaded. "For an hour when you would share a meal with him without thinking he's some kind of monster."

"He is a monster, a thieving, conniving cheat. He's been here in the park, not to visit you, as you seem to think, but hatching a plot to destroy my hopes of owning the Lake Hotel."

Alex's back straightened. "All right. He hates you. Because you've been against him forever."

The pain in Hank's face grew worse. "It's not just me he hates. He hates everything and everyone who's decent." He shouldn't go on, but . . . "I've reason to believe he murdered a woman who ran him off a job for stealing . . ."

Alex's pupils dilated.

"And I've learned he attacked the stagecoach down in Jackson's Hole last week."

"That's not possible." She sprang up, her hands over her heart.

"He was identified."

"He would never . . ." Her beautiful face turned ugly. "Danny's right. He's been right all along. You'd say anything to turn me against him."

She was so young; Hank tried to protect her. She might cross Danny in some innocent blundering way and end up like Garnet Houlihan.

"You tell *your* brother . . ." his voice was flat, "if he comes near you again, I'll kill him."

Almost midnight and the musicians had packed away their instruments. The sounds of guests walking the hotel porch and talking on the lawn had died away. Hank was still aboard his boat, unless he'd swum away; Cord had seen no sign of him from his hideout.

From the shadows, he'd watched Captain Feddors lock the front door of the soldier station and retire to the sleeping barracks.

With the wound in his arm burning, he mounted the short stairs to the hotel's rear porch. Across the boards and inside the darkened lobby, he walked quietly but with purpose, so as not to look suspicious to the night clerk. A glance assured him the young man was absorbed in his dime novel.

Three flights and Cord was in the hall, looking up at the light square of the transom over a room in the Absaroka Suite.

His hand went automatically to his pants pocket where his obsidian usually rested. It wasn't there.

His heartbeat accelerated, for in the last few days he'd come to believe it was far more than a lucky piece. Rather, it was a talisman, some piece of the planet that Cord Sutton was meant to shelter while it guarded him in turn.

A quick mental inventory said he'd not seen it in his room this afternoon when he packed.

With a creeping dread, he thought what an awful day it had been. Had he brought on this chain of events by misplacing the symbol of his guardian spirit?

Cord almost turned away and went down the stairs, but he'd come for answers. He'd almost been ready to believe Laura's story about coming to the meeting with Hank because her injured father asked it.

He stepped up to the only room with a light burning, took the faceted doorknob in his hand, and made a mental inventory. According to the hotel plans, there were three bedrooms in the suite. Forrest was in the infirmary, so Cord was either about to try Laura's door or the one Constance shared with her mother.

The knob turned smoothly.

Inside, Laura stood naked beside the china washbasin, scrubbing herself with a washrag.

Cord closed the door behind him and leaned against it. "Could we finish our conversation?" His voice was hard.

She turned to him with a disbelieving expression and flung the wet cloth at him, hitting him squarely in the face. "That's my answer to your thinking I was on Hank's side."

Retrieving the rag with the arm Hank had stabbed, Cord winced. Despite that, he pitched the rag accurately back into the white china bowl.

"If you're not on his side, how did you manage to end up in his bed? Sure, you screamed when things got too rough, but he could scarcely have dragged you to his pleasure nook."

Her glare said she wished she had another cloth to throw. Instead, she reached for a rose silk wrapper and knotted it firmly around her. "How dare you? You checked out of the hotel, and I had every reason to believe you'd left without saying good-bye."

"So you went straight to him."

"Yes, I went on-board Hank's boat with him, but I was trying to get some answers, not to . . . not to . . ."

Cord's knife wound had begun to bleed again.

The sight of it made him queasy, the way he felt when he recalled the sight of Laura's hair spread over Hank's fancy pillow.

"If I thought Captain Feddors would believe me and not Hank, I'd try to get him brought up on charges for attacking me," Laura despaired.

Blood splattered the shining wood floor. Cord collapsed on the bed. This was wrong, baiting her when he should have known from the fright in her screams that she didn't want Hank.

"I'm sorry," he managed. "Little dizzy."

Gray spots started at the edge of his vision.

Laura's fingers trembled while she unbuttoned Cord's soiled white shirt and slipped her hands inside. Gently she pushed the cotton off his shoulders, catching a whiff of the sweat he'd worked up during the fight.

"I'm sorry, too," she murmured. "I was terrified when you and Hank started slashing at each other."

When she tried to slip the sleeve from Cord's arm, she found the shirt plastered to the wound. Going to the bureau, she found the manicure scissors Aunt Fanny had loaned her and cut away the material.

Fresh blood mingled with a blackening crust, the deep puncture already growing dark around the edges. Carefully, she washed the cut with lavender soap and poured from a bottle of White Heliotrope perfume.

The sting of the alcohol seemed to revive Cord. He

shook his head as though to clear it. "I . . . shouldn't," he muttered, "have doubted you."

Tearing one of Constance's petticoats to make a clean bandage, Laura tied it on carefully. Then she pushed at his shoulders for him to lie back on the bed.

A few steps to the door and she turned off the overhead light, plunging the room into darkness relieved only by a faint glow from the night sky. Sitting beside Cord, she lit a candle on the night table.

Then she climbed onto the bed, slid her hands into his hair, and massaged his temples with soft circular motions. Of course, he was angry and suspicious. She would be, too.

She wanted to ask why he'd checked out and then stayed around, but she could do that later. For now, she continued to stroke his head.

From the window, she could see Hank's steamboat at anchor beside the dock, starlight glinting on the golden flames that topped the stacks. How vile and ugly Hank had turned out to be, not the opposite of his outlaw brother, but a mirror image.

She looked down and found Cord watching her with renewed alertness.

CHAPTER TWENTY-FIVE

JUNE 29

A woman's scream ripped the fabric of Laura's sleep.

Opening her eyes, she found a red glow suffusing the ceiling of her hotel room, and she smelled smoke. Her heart surged, but she forced herself not to move until she knew whether it was safe to get up or if she needed to crawl.

A look around revealed the candle beside the bed had nearly burned down; its faint glow did not begin to compete with the fire she realized was not in her room.

"Cord?" she asked of the rumpled bed beside her.

She patted his empty place. A look around the room, which was getting brighter all the time, showed that sometime after they'd made love, he'd put his clothes back on and left.

Getting up naked, she went to the window and parted the curtains.

On the slope between the hotel and the lake, guests who had worn silks and tuxedos for dinner emerged from the building. Women's hair tumbled loose from their pins, and they clutched their shawls over batiste gowns. A heavyset man worked at tucking his nightshirt into his trousers.

Beyond the Grand Loop Road, flames from Hank's steamboat leaped into the night.

From next door, Laura heard Constance's voice, "I'm going . . ." and Aunt Fanny's reply, "We'll stay here where it's safe."

Laura opened the wardrobe and put on the first thing that came to hand, the water-spotted emerald silk. On with the black slippers, and she took no time to comb her hair. Moments later, she ran across the lobby, still buttoning the front of the dress.

As she went out the door, an explosion aboard the steamboat caused fire to bellow out in a flaring arc. The flames caught a uniformed soldier in the bucket brigade.

He staggered back, arms flailing. His shirt blazed in the brisk wind.

Two other men, silhouettes against the fiery night, grabbed the burning man. They tried to slap out the flames, but as he began to scream, they shoved him off the dock. One leaped into the lake after him.

A chorus of shouts cleared a path, and a group of men dragged a fire hose to the scene. In less than a minute, it was set up, the canvas hose sending a stream of lake water in a tall arc onto the burning boat.

Even so, the dock burst into flames. Some of the rowboats and little sailing vessels went up, the heat too intense for anyone to move them to safety.

Laura started down the slope toward the water, scanning the crowd for Cord.

Hank awakened choking.

He started to sit up and encountered heat. In his somnolent and semi-drunken state, he somehow managed to hold his breath and roll off his bed onto the rug.

Christ, his boat was on fire!

He tried a breath of somewhat cooler air and choked on the stench of kerosene, more than any spilled lamp could supply.

He pressed his nose to the Heriz and began to crawl on his belly. He'd drifted to sleep in his gray trousers and torn shirt; the wool rug was scratchy on his bare chest.

Though the smoke was getting to him, he had one more cabin to visit. Hank couldn't let his little sister die.

Despite the firefighters' efforts, the upper deck of the *Alexandra* began to collapse. In eerie slow motion, half-hidden by a steam cloud, the craft came to pieces. Laura pictured the flames licking the lacquer off Hank's Chinese screen while the black bed burned.

Another, larger explosion aboard sent out a wave of heat that seemed to push at Laura. The deafening blast drowned the cries from the throng crowding the Lake Hotel lawn. Burning debris rained.

Laura brushed glowing embers off her gown and slapped at the sudden hot stab when one fell onto the back of her arm.

"Hank!" a woman cried.

She turned to find Alexandra Falls, bundled in a violet velvet robe against the night wind. She looked even younger than Laura remembered; golden hair tousled like a child's and smudges beneath her eyes. While her namesake burned down in the night, she stifled a sob. "Oh God, Hank."

Laura stared at the burning wreck, half-hoping the man who'd tried to force himself on her had died a dreadful fiery death, yet . . .

She stepped closer to Alexandra. "Was he . . . ?"

Alexandra turned on her. "He was asleep. He was drinking. Oh God." A shudder went through her, and she kept looking around.

She looked so broken up over her brother that Laura found herself comforting her. "You don't know he didn't get out. Wait and see before you give up."

It seemed to take a long time for the steamboat to burn. Bits and pieces of the structure continued to glow, metamorphosing from bright flame to crimson embers.

Watching for Cord, Laura saw Hank before his sister did. He staggered up from the lake, wearing his torn white shirt and gray trousers, dripping wet from head to pale bare feet.

"Hank!" Alexandra cried. Her expression froze as though she were seeing a ghost.

"Alex, thank God!" he croaked. Shuffling faster, he winced as his feet encountered stones.

He threw his arms around his sister and pulled her against him. "I couldn't find you . . ."

Laura took a step away, hoping he wouldn't see her. As brother and sister embraced, she could see that Hank's nose had stopped bleeding, but it had swollen alarmingly. Above his bruised eyes, a soot streak marred his forehead; others painted his cheeks and neck. "I searched until the heat drove me overboard."

The *Alexandra* burned down in the night with only a few feet of smoldering hull above the waterline. Hank patted his sister's shoulder; she stifled a sob and buried her face against his chest.

The sound of boots on the crushed stone drive announced the arrival of Captain Feddors and Sergeant Nevers. Laura wondered who was guarding her father.

"Sir!" Feddors clipped out briskly to Hank, then inclined his head toward Alexandra. Removing his gold-braided cap, he revealed his receding hairline. "My condolences on the loss of your boat. Did one of your lamps . . . ?"

"I smelled kerosene, too strongly." Hank was stopped by a fit of coughing that doubled him over. He spat a wad of phlegm onto the ground and took a ragged breath. "Cord Sutton . . . earlier . . . broke my nose."

Dread crept over Laura, as Feddors came to attention like a dog sniffing out a trail.

"Arrest him," Hank got out before choking again.

"I thought Sutton was gone." Feddors reached into his pocket and displayed an irregular dark shape on his palm. "His room was cleaned out, except for this."

Before she thought, Laura stepped forward, palm out. "Let me have that."

Feddors laughed and flung the rock into the darkness, where the scrub brush grew thick near the hotel wall. He looked toward the smoldering ruin of the *Alexandra*. "You may rest assured that we will find and arrest Sutton, whatever it takes."

Laura tried to move away casually. In the morning light, she'd find Cord's stone, but right now, she needed to warn him. That is, if she could without leading Feddors to him.

The captain turned back to Hank. "It's a piece of luck that Mrs. Giles . . . I guess we can both call her Esther, can't we?" He chuckled. "Good thing Thomas Bryce told her his adopted brother was Nez Perce."

Laura stopped. Though Cord had spoken of Thomas laying claim to Excalibur, it hadn't sounded as if he knew his so-called brother would betray him.

Mouth dry, heart pounding, she wandered up the slope and into the lobby, lighted in the middle of the night. All the way, she imagined she felt Captain Feddors's eyes on her back.

She went through the building and out the other side, past the employee dormitory. There, she lifted her skirts and ducked into the darkness beneath the trees. Though she'd been to the stable earlier and found Dante gone, she had to start somewhere.

Laura approached the long building from the rear. All was quiet outside; it felt very different from going there by day, or when she had followed Cord through the darkness. When she pulled on the heavy wooden door, the hinges squealed, something she'd not noticed before.

Inside, the smell of horses and hay smote her. On swift feet, she found the stall where Dante had been stabled. "Cord!" she hissed. She wished she had a stub of candle, or the lantern they'd used last night.

"Cord!" she cried again, her eyes straining to pierce the blackness.

At a sudden unmistakable footfall in the straw behind her, she jumped and almost shouted. She'd left the door open so there'd been no warning from the squeaky hinges.

"Let's see what we got here." Laura recognized Captain Feddors's voice.

A match flared and illuminated Dante's empty stall along with Feddors's face, his sparse goatee of straggling hairs adorning his chin. Acquiring her arm in an iron grasp, he mimicked, "Cord!" in a weak falsetto and shook the match out. Only an inch or so taller than she, he appeared as a solid darker mass against the night. By the smell of smoke sour on his breath, she knew he'd brought his face close to hers.

"Cord did nothing!" Laura struggled to get her

arm free. "It's crazy what Hank's accusing him of."

She stopped short of calling the captain crazy for believing it.

He kept his grip. "It's no use trying to protect Sutton. He tried to kill Hank Falls earlier and came back to finish the job."

"That's all wrong. Hank tried to . . ." Laura's face flamed.

Feddors pulled her along with him. "Let's just go and talk about that for a bit."

Outside was black and silent. Where were the rest of the soldiers and the people who had watched the *Alexandra* burn?

Beside the darkened soldier station, Feddors fumbled the key from his pants pocket. He shoved open the thick log door and dragged Laura across the threshold.

In the weak light of a dying fire, he pushed her down into a hard wooden chair. When he trapped her, both hands on the arms, she recognized a note of liquor on his smoky breath. "You were giving Hank some trouble?"

He had the same filthy note in his voice as when he'd spoken of Mrs. Giles. Did he, too, plan on taking Hank's violent approach?

"I wasn't giving Hank half the trouble I'll give you if . . ."

An electric light came on in the rear of the building. "Who's there?"

Feddors swore.

"Mr. Resnick!" Laura called, unable to keep the

relief from her voice.

The Pinkerton man appeared in the rear doorway wearing a striped nightshirt.

"I'd forgotten you were bedding down in here." Feddors's tone was pleasant, as though he'd not just sworn at finding out Resnick was on the premises. "You've slept through a spectacle. Sutton tried to murder Falls by setting fire to his boat."

Resnick's expression went from dull to sharp.

"That's not true," Laura objected. "Hank was . . . raping me! I screamed, and Cord came to help. They fought . . ." She stopped, for one could interpret this as a case against Cord.

Feddors turned away from Laura and stirred up the embers in the grate. He fed in kindling from a copper bucket beside the hearth, and the fire burst into renewed life.

Resnick looked at her. "Are you all right?"

She nodded . . . as right as one could be with all that had happened.

He disappeared briefly and came back wearing trousers and a shirt. Crossing to Laura, he bent close, fixing her with that one eye that almost had greater impact than two. A perceptive man, he'd discerned the connection between her and Cord and must be wondering if Cord had resorted to arson in avenging her.

Resnick glanced at Feddors, who still knelt to tend the fire, and spoke to her. "Did you help Cord Sutton burn that boat?" His voice was colder than in any of their previous encounters.

"I was asleep in my room when I heard the commotion."

"Where is Sutton, then?"

"I don't . . ."

Feddors slapped his knees and rose. "He'll have to be tracked down."

Resnick did not break eye contact with Laura. "Then I suggest you gather some men and start at once. I'll question this one."

Feddors hesitated, but apparently the prospect of the chase was more attractive.

As soon as the door closed behind the captain, Resnick straightened. "There isn't any time. Tell me what you know."

"Cord fought Hank, but he'd never burn his boat."

"Where's he gone, then?"

"I don't know. Feddors caught me in the stable; Dante's not there."

"Are you sure Cord isn't guilty?"

Laura sucked in her breath. "He was with me in my hotel room when the fire went up."

She believed that, didn't she?

Aunt Fanny sipped tea from the service she'd ordered up to the Absaroka Suite. "This is cold," she said disapprovingly, smoothing her black dressing gown.

"What do you expect at this hour?" Laura set her cup aside with unsteady hands. It had still been full dark when Manfred Resnick escorted her to the hotel and knocked on Aunt Fanny and Constance's door. Now, the barest gray brightened the eastern horizon.

Being in the family suite, safe and warm against the chill, was almost dreamlike, but two things spoiled the idyll.

As hopeless as the quest might be, Laura needed to be out looking for Cord.

The other issue was a woeful snivel coming from the divan, where Constance sat amid a pile of ruined paper handkerchiefs. Apparently, the news had spread like wildfire among the guests that Cord was accused, tried, and convicted of arson and attempted murder.

Fanny looked at her daughter, whose turquoise robe bore tearstains. "Unlike some people," she glared at Laura, "she's still got her reputation to consider. After all, Constance was engaged to that lying pretender, more's the pity."

Laura waited for her cousin to admit she and Cord had never been pledged, but Constance came off the couch like a little whirlwind. "I will not have you insinuating I'm the only one who made a mistake with William. We were all taken in by him, you more than anyone, Mother!"

"Constance," Laura warned. "We don't know he burned Hank's boat."

"Of course, we do. William's motive is that he can't stand losing the hotel to Hank."

"Hank's not getting the hotel, either." Laura bit back telling them about Hank attacking her and

Cord's rescue; she'd realized with Resnick that it set up a more heated motive than a failed business deal.

Laura looked out the window at the growing light. From the direction of the stable came a group of mounted cavalry. Captain Feddors was in the lead, with Lieutenant Stafford, another fellow Laura recognized as Private Arden Groesbeck, and two soldiers she didn't know. They appeared intent on their mission to find and bring Cord to justice.

Setting aside her cup and saucer, Laura rose. "I'm just going to lie down a while."

Once in her room, she looked for her trousers. They weren't on the floor where she was certain she'd left them along with Cord's shirt, a pair of step-ins, and a petticoat. A search of the wardrobe revealed that housekeeping had not hung them up. No sign of them in the bureau drawers.

Laura knelt and looked under the bed. Nothing there, including her boots, which she knew she'd set side by side next to the metal upright of the frame. She went back to the wardrobe and saw that Aunt Fanny's riding habit was no longer there.

Ten steps later, she was back in the suite's drawing room.

"Where are my trousers? And my boots?" she accused her aunt. "What have you done with them?"

Fanny sniffed. "I made some decisions for you, Laura. You haven't been making good ones for yourself lately."

The grass was covered with dew, a million tiny cob-webs bridging the stems. Steam rose from the hot pools beside the hotel drive. There was no sign of the posse; they'd evidently ridden off.

But when Laura, hurrying in the green silk dress and thin slippers, had nearly reached the stable, she saw a man astride a well-blooded palomino, wearing buckskin. She ducked into the fir copse she'd followed Cord through the other night.

So Danny Falls was still about, riding openly as though he, too, had watched the men from the soldier station ride away.

While she watched, he drew rein and looked to-ward the dock, where an eddy of pale smoke rose from the still-floating ruined hulk. Hank stood on the bank with Alexandra. Though he still wore his torn, soot-stained white shirt and gray trousers, she had changed into a lavender dress.

Danny smirked like he had at the stagecoach when he'd discovered her little pistol and pocketed it.

Laura waited in the trees, impatient to be about her mission. But she dared not move as long as Danny was in the area.

In a few minutes, Hank and Alexandra turned away from the wreck, went up the slope and into the hotel, no doubt for the breakfast Laura was skipping. Once they disappeared from view, Danny made a click-ing sound with his tongue and nudged his palomino into motion.

As soon as he was out of sight, Laura raced across the meadow to the stable. As quietly as she could, she opened the door and went inside. This early, the interior was dim and cool.

"Help you, miss?" one of the stablemen called.

Taking a breath of the manure-scented air, Laura tried not to act rushed as she walked down the aisle. When she reached White Bird, she put out a hand and petted her on the withers. "I'd like to have this one saddled and take her for a morning ride."

Hopefully, Feddors hadn't put out any orders that she was not to have a horse.

The tackie, dressed in denim and a plaid shirt, hesitated. "White Bird is one of the army mounts."

Laura tried to appear relaxed. "Yes, I know. Sergeant Nevers wanted me to try her out."

The stableman smiled with teeth white against his chocolate skin. "Sure thing, miss. But if you don' mind my sayin' so, you need to wear something a lil' warmer."

"I'll just walk her over to where I'm staying and change," Laura lied.

"Sure thing. Sure thing. Jus' take a little while."

A few minutes later, Laura accepted the reins, along with a heavy canteen.

"You should take a lunch, too." He offered a paper sack from a box that must have been sent down from the hotel kitchen.

"That's a good idea, but I should be back before

long." Nonetheless, she accepted the bag.

The first question was which direction Cord would go. North led toward Mammoth and Feddors's fabled stockade. Southwest along the lakeshore was beside a busy road; busier with the *Alexandra* no longer in service. If Laura wanted to hide, she'd go east through the passes until she was out of Captain Feddors's jurisdiction.

Trying to appear casual, she rode slowly until she was out of sight of the stable. Then she urged White Bird to a quicker pace, following the lakeshore trail until she reached the place where the Yellowstone River flowed north out of the water body. There she drew rein and looked around.

The path continued to the north along the riverbank. The Grand Loop Road ran close alongside.

She looked at the ground for tracks, but there was no way to tell which way Cord and Dante might have gone. At this rate, she might as well turn back.

CHAPTER TWENTY-SIX

JUNE 29

The posse passed the abandoned cabin and pushed on to the north. Larry Nevers rode on the right flank, closest to the Yellowstone River.

He felt a little sick. He'd liked Cord Sutton from the moment he came into the soldier station. In his opinion, the best thing Sutton had done was publicly humiliating Feddors.

Or the worst.

Hopefully, they were on the wrong track, but Larry doubted it. If the army were after him, he'd swim his horse across the Yellowstone and go east through the mountains.

Ahead on the short stretch of the Grand Loop Road they were following, there seemed to be a commotion. A tourist wagon had stopped and the group was out, pointing and staring down toward the river. When the posse drew closer, the driver stepped into the road and waved his arms.

Without slowing, Feddors ordered, "Nevers. Deal with this."

He hated to do it. If they caught up to Sutton, he wanted to be there.

"Sir, yes sir!" he clipped out, slowing his horse. "Trouble with the wagon?" he called to the gray-bearded driver.

A nearby woman wearing a ridiculous feathered hat gestured toward the Yellowstone.

The driver grimaced. "One of the passengers hollered at me to stop. Saw what looks like a body."

Larry handed his reins to the driver and went to the edge of the road. Down the slope to the riverbank, he side-footed until he got a look at what appeared to be a man washed up on the opposite shore.

Cord wiped sweat from his brow as he rode. He'd boldly followed the Grand Loop Road past the outlet of the Yellowstone, north along the west riverbank, and crossed where it ran placid and shallow above the rushing cataract of LeHardy Rapids. Heading back over marshy ground, he'd caught his first glimpse of the men trailing him in the broad meadow west of Ebro Springs.

Last night, he'd hidden in the trees along the shore and watched Hank's boat burn with a fierce satisfaction. And stayed around long enough to know he'd be hunted down as the arsonist.

Now, on the east side of Pelican Valley, he angled along the southern edge of the trees at the base of Sulphur Hills, surveying the terrain and considering options. The shortest distance out of the park as the crow flew would be to head up Bear Creek on the west slope of Mount Chittenden and make it out through Jones Pass.

But the Bluecoats came on through knee-deep grass beside the shining waters of Pelican Creek. The stream meandered in tight loops, seeming to echo and reecho itself between the abandoned loops of previous courses.

His pursuers reached a particularly nasty stretch of bog that held a few feet of water and were forced to slow. But they were close, too close.

If Cord hadn't lost his *wayakin*, would this streak of rotten luck be running?

He pulled his Colt and looked at the wax seal Sergeant Nevers had attached to it. Yellowstone's laws against guns did not seem to consider what threats a man might find there. Cracking the sealing wax, he used his knife to cut the tape around the trigger. Then he took some ammunition from his saddlebag and loaded the revolver, one chamber at a time. One more offense wouldn't change Feddors's mind about him if he were caught.

Men pointed in Cord's direction and veered toward him.

His only escape now would be the wooded slopes on the northern side of Pelican Creek. He'd never be able to cross the open valley to get up Bear Creek.

From behind, he heard Feddors shout, "Shoot the sum bitch before he gets away!"

Cord's shoulder blades tensed; he waited for the impact of bullet on flesh. After it was done, it would be justified as a guilty man fleeing the scene, a man who attempted to murder Hank by burning his boat.

A bullet whined past his ear. Another plugged his saddlebag.

Lying out flat along Dante's neck, he spurred him on toward the thick forest that ringed the valley. It was just a matter of yards, but it looked like miles as another bullet grazed the side of Dante's neck, plowing a dark red furrow.

Laura chafed against returning to the Absaroka Suite, to having a bath and dressing in the feminine clothing her aunt had left in her wardrobe. To lunch in the charming dining room with a view, while she wondered if Cord had been hunted down like an animal.

Admitting defeat was the last thing she wanted, but she was no tracker.

As she turned White Bird back toward the hotel, a sharp crack, followed by a rising pitch rang out on the other side of the river. She jerked the reins. "Sorry, girl."

Soldiers? Shooting at Cord? Who else had guns when the tourists were prohibited a working weapon?

Of course, there was someone else who defied all rules, cooking squirrel with his rifle propped beside the fire.

Another volley of shots went off.

Laura looked over her shoulder toward the infirmary where her father lay. As she'd written in her burned missive, at some level she loved her parent.

Even so, she turned White Bird to face the Yellowstone.

Another shot sounded.

She urged the mare to the edge of the water. The memory of being swept up by the Snake made her breath come fast . . . thinking of bone-chilling cold and a tangle of deadfall almost made her turn back.

"Let's go, girl." At her direction, White Bird waded in.

Laura caught her bottom lip in her teeth as the water rose over the mare's flanks. She couldn't do this . . . Water rose, emerald silk floating slimy against her legs.

Her knees were wet, her thighs. White Bird's feet left the bottom. The water was around Laura's waist and trying to float her.

She gave up sidesaddle and gripped the horse with both legs. Leaning forward, she wrapped her arms around White Bird's neck.

This wasn't working; they were being swept downstream the way Dante had. And above the splashes of White Bird's swimming, there came a more ominous sound. Somewhere around the blind bend of the river, there were rapids.

White Bird struggled to keep her nose above water.

Though every instinct told Laura to cling to the animal, she slung her leg back across and lowered herself into the water on the down-current side. With a death grip on the saddle horn, she made sure the reins were around her arm and took her weight off White Bird.

Would Cord be proud if he could see her? Was he alive to care?

White Bird's hooves took purchase on the bottom; then she was swept on a little farther.

Finally, she struggled and found footing. With Laura hanging on, a drag on the saddle, she staggered out of the river.

Laura let go and landed on her feet. With no time to waste, she remounted and rode in the direction of the shots.

Dripping wet, she should be freezing. She should be thinking about what she'd do if whoever had a gun decided to take a bead on her.

She pressed on.

Ahead, suddenly, there was light. A valley, covered in lush grass opened up between the lake and the forest, stretching to the east. A stream meandered across its floor.

And a cavalryman on foot led a horse with a man's body slung across its back.

Laura recognized the soldier. "Sergeant Nevers! That is, Larry."

Was that Cord?

"Miss Fielding." He doffed his cap. ". . . Laura. What are you doing out here?" He looked with disbelief at her soaking clothes; even her hair was wet.

"I . . ." She could say she was taking a ride, but who would ford the Yellowstone for sport? "I . . . heard shots."

Her heart raced while she waited to know.

Larry gave her a steady look. "You were afraid the posse had shot Sutton." His tone said he knew about her and Cord.

"He's not . . . ?" She stared at the man's motionless legs, not long enough to be Cord's, she saw that now, ashamed to be so relieved. "Who is he?"

"I don't know."

Laura brought White Bird closer and took in the brown suit, matted brown hair, and pale forehead. "That's Edgar Young, Cord's banker."

"Looks like there was a knife fight and someone dumped him in the river." Something in Larry's face changed.

"Will he be all right?"

"He's breathing."

She looked at the motionless form. A person in this condition often never woke, or if they did, they were changed in some monstrous way. If that were true of Edgar, he might not ever be able to tell what happened.

"I saw you this morning," she told Larry. "Riding out with Feddors."

"The rest of them have gone on. I stopped to take care of . . . Edgar."

Laura focused on Larry's eyes, enormous behind his spectacles. "Cord is a good man. He couldn't have burned Hank's boat, and he would never have fought Edgar."

"I'd like to think that's true."

As soon as Larry headed toward the infirmary with Edgar, Laura surveyed the valley and the mountains. She saw no one.

Now that the rush of fording the river had passed, she began to shiver. But there was no time to build a fire and dry her clothes as she and Cord had done after their dunking in the Snake. Had there been, she had no matches. Her sack lunch had gone down the Yellowstone; all she had left was a full canteen.

This was crazy. She had to turn back.

But there, on the other side of the valley, barely visible above a rocky cliff, she believed she spied the head of a black horse.

Laura stood up in the stirrups and waved both arms.

The figure of a man appeared on the bluff. He wore the blue of Cord's denims and cotton shirt. For a moment, he stood without moving.

Then he ducked out of sight.

This was the sheerest folly, waiting for Laura when he was hunted by a man who wanted nothing more than to kill him outright.

After evading the posse in the forest, Cord had reined Dante in on a promontory, where he would have sworn his Nez Perce uncle, Bitter Waters, had rested his tired horse back in 1877. Pelican Valley lay behind in the flats, rocky slopes ahead. Here, the tribe had surveyed the valley, looking back for signs that the Bluecoats were still in pursuit.

Thankfully, the posse had made a turn to the southeast and headed up Bear Creek, clearly understanding Cord would have gone that way to get out of the park as soon as possible.

If Laura got here soon, they might thread the needle through Mist Creek Pass and come out into the Lamar Valley ahead of Feddors and his men. He would follow the route he remembered traversing when Cappy Parsons had taken him to find women and dairy cows.

Laura and White Bird reached the upper end of the grassy valley. The day had heated up; flies buzzed around the bloody marks on Laura's skin where a few bold mosquitoes had braved midday for a feast.

Though it would be only a little way up through the forest to where she'd seen Cord, Laura had to rest the mare before the climb. The stout girl was a workhorse, but the treacherous footing in the wetlands had winded her. Thankfully, there'd been abundant fresh water and the horse had drunk her fill.

She loosed the reins and let the mare crop sweet grass, for once they got into the pine forest there would be nothing for her.

A look around the valley floor confirmed no sign of Feddors and his men. If this were a case of vigilante justice, and she prayed it was unfounded . . .

Yet, Cord had left her bed, either before the fire broke out or afterward. There had been doubt in Larry Nevers's eyes when he spoke of someone dumping Edgar in the river.

A flash of the night she and Cord had spent together in the stable came back. "I hate that I'm in the middle, neither white nor red . . . I loathe that supercilious captain who marked me the moment he saw me and won't let it drop. And I hate myself."

How far would a man go if he hated himself and so many others?

Pushing aside her doubts, she urged White Bird forward. Would Cord have waited or had his ducking out of sight meant he was long on his way?

To her relief, he came to her on foot. His eyes were bloodshot, his hat and clothing dusty from fast riding. "Are you all right?"

She nodded.

He reached to help her down, his hands at her waist. "What are you doing out here?" He took in her ruined silk. Though dry, it bore the shriveled look of having been through a clothes wringer without ironing.

"Looking for you. Feddors has made up a posse . . ."

"I've already been shot at, thanks." He gestured bitterly toward Dante.

Laura sucked in her breath at the raw red scar across the side of the stallion's neck. Though no blood ran, the furrow was at least a half-inch deep and crawling with flies Dante kept tossing his head to avoid.

"I heard the shots." She tried to sound matter-of-fact. "That's when I had White Bird swim the river."

"You might have been coming to view my body."

Laura took a steadying breath. "Dead or alive, I was going to find you."

For a moment, they looked at each other, last night and the night before swimming to the surface of consciousness. They had to get through to his ranch, and she was ready for whatever it took.

Somewhere along the way, she'd lost the mind-numbing terror that had marked her first encounter with a raging river, the screaming rush when the grizzly had attacked at the brink of Lewis Canyon. There were more important enemies.

"I saw Danny this morning, riding around the hotel on his palomino, bold as brass since the soldiers were out after you."

"This gets better and better. I suppose you believe I burned Hank's boat."

She hadn't been certain, but faced with Cord's injured expression, she did know. If she hadn't believed in him, she wouldn't have swum the Yellowstone.

CHAPTER TWENTY-SEVEN

JUNE 29

L arry Nevers stood guard outside the Lake Infirmary. With one shooting victim inside, and
Edgar Young another victim of foul play, he took up
his post as naturally as breathing.

Not long after Edgar was brought in, Manfred
Resnick showed up, his hands and clothing sooty from
examining the wreck of the *Alexandra*. "Definitely
arson," he reported. "Somebody went on deck and
splashed around a load of kerosene, then must have
overturned a lantern."

"Somebody?"

Without answering, Resnick went into the infirmary. Though Larry had no backup watch outside,
he went in, also. From the start, he'd felt something
about blaming Cord Sutton wasn't right. Talking with
Laura had cemented it.

Dr. Upshur stood guard in his own way, putting
up a hand to stay anyone who would enter the room

he had Edgar in. "He's in grave condition and I won't have him . . ."

He was talking to Resnick's back, for the Pinkerton man pushed past and went to Edgar's bedside. "A man in grave condition needs to unburden himself of who harmed him," Resnick said over his shoulder.

Larry thought the words "before it's too late," hung on the air.

Resnick peered with his one good eye at the unconscious man. Wasting no time, he dug his thumbnail deeply into the nail bed of Edgar's index finger.

The hand jerked back.

Resnick grabbed it and repeated the maneuver on another finger, and another.

The third time, Edgar groaned.

The fourth, he rolled his head on the pillow and his eyelids fluttered.

"Edgar!" Resnick called.

"Uhhhhh . . ."

"Who hurt you, Edgar?"

His eyes blinked, unfocused.

"Edgar?"

His head lolled back.

"Cord Sutton? Was it him?"

Edgar's eyes closed.

"Not Cord?" Larry hoped.

Resnick was no longer hurting him, but holding his hand in a supportive grip.

Edgar lay still and silent, breathing evenly as he had before.

Before Resnick could try anything else to awaken him, Dr. Upshur tapped his shoulder. "I must insist."

Larry followed the Pinkerton man outside. Though he was supposed to take charge, he deferred to him. "What do you think?"

"Sutton fought with Falls last night, but that was apparently over Laura Fielding." Resnick stroked his chin. "And while he might have gone back to finish the job, she says they were together when the boat went up." He pulled out his tiny pad and pencil. "I haven't had a chance to question her about the business of her father's shooting, but I'm certain she'll back him."

Recalling a conversation he'd overheard between Resnick and Feddors, Larry asked, "Do you think she's lying this time?"

Resnick shook his head. "If she had any inkling a man had shot her father, she'd have gone straight to the authorities."

"What about the outlaw?"

"I used the company resources to check. A Daniel Patrick Falls was born the same day, same town in Idaho, as Henry James Falls, who goes by 'Hank.'" Resnick made a note. "When Hank denied having a brother, that proved there was trouble between them."

"Edgar was meeting Danny. Couldn't he have hurt him, rather than Cord?"

After another scribbled notation, Resnick lifted his head. "Possible, even probable."

"But they're hunting Sutton."

"I was afraid you'd gone." Constance stood in the open doorway of Norman Hagen's room.

Norman turned from folding a shirt into the open valise on his bed. "I was supposed to leave yesterday evening with Hopkins Chandler."

"You stayed . . . ?" She wanted him to say he had remained for her. But she'd waited in vain for him to resume the topic he'd introduced yesterday in the rain. When they went in to lunch, he'd been the consummate gentleman. And last night, though she'd hoped Norman would appear to dance with her, she'd been stuck with Private Arden Groesbeck.

"I'm taking the noon stage." Norman's hands fumbled his folding.

His saying it out loud made it feel final. The mirror on the wardrobe door reflected him, a big, bearded man with eyes that looked back sadly. She was there in the glass, as well, wearing her sapphire silk dress she believed accentuated the blue of her eyes. Unfortunately, those eyes were rimmed in red.

"It's awful," she blurted. "Everyone thinks William burned Hank's boat."

He dropped the shirt in a wrinkled ball. "Do you?"

"I don't know," she answered tearfully.

Norman had been weighing the pros and cons for

hours, ever since he'd seen the flames and his first thought had been of tearing Cord off Hank, of knives and blood. But now he said, "I don't think he did it."

He took a step toward Constance, feeling overly warm in his traveling suit of brown wool. An impulse to pull her inside his room and into his arms seized him.

The feeling wasn't foreign. He'd felt it when he swept her off the high wagon at the canyon. And again when he'd found her crying prettily in the rain over Cord Sutton.

She pushed off the door and came to him. "I'm glad you don't think William did it." She sniffed.

Norman considered and discarded the idea of offering her his handkerchief. Reaching carefully, he interrupted the path of a tear on its way down her cheek. Her skin felt soft as velvet beneath his thumb. He told himself not to do it, but he bent and pressed his lips to the sweet flesh near the corner of her eye.

"God help us, sweetheart," he whispered. "Maybe some day I can catch you when you aren't crying about someone else."

She sucked in her breath. "No," she said. "No." She placed her ringless hands on his lapels. "I'm crying because everything is so crazy. Because I think Laura's taken a horse and ridden out looking for Cord. Captain Feddors and his men are out there, too, and I'm afraid . . ."

Norman drew her into his arms.

Though they needed to be on their way, Laura and Cord were forced to wait a while to rest White Bird. They kept away from the edge of the bluff, and after she told Cord how she'd spotted Dante earlier, they tethered both horses farther back in the forest.

Sitting with Cord on the slope, Laura said, "Down by the river, I ran into Larry Nevers. He had Edgar Young slung over his horse, near to death."

"What happened?"

"Larry said a knife fight. He was found washed up on the riverbank."

"Dammit! Feddors will put that on my ledger, as well."

"Not if Edgar wakes and tells his story."

Cord was silent for a moment, staring out toward where the Yellowstone bisected the forest. "Poor son of a bitch."

Reaching for his two-quart metal canteen, he uncapped it and offered it to Laura. "I waited for you, but the way you're dressed, you'll have to go back."

Laura plucked an Indian paintbrush and shredded the red flower, ripping off one petal at a time. She hadn't come this far and risked so much to give up the dreams she'd woven. "There's no place else I should be."

Cord set the canteen on the ground. "You know Feddors and his men are after me. Want to join the lynch party?"

"I can't believe you did anything wrong." After all her agonizing, the words came out easily. "I don't think you're capable of rising from my bed and going out to kill someone."

A ghost of a smile flickered across his lips. "The way one feels after making love doesn't exactly fit with murderous rage." He put a hand on her forearm below the pleated upper section of her dress sleeve. "What happened to your field clothes?"

"Aunt Fanny decided they didn't become a lady and took them. I'll get by."

"Quit trying to argue with me." She felt the puff of his exasperated breath on her hair. "Running away will make you look like an accessory to whatever crimes I'm charged with. When I asked about the lynch party, I meant you could end up hung along with me by vigilante justice."

Across the valley, she caught a flash of blue coats, men on horseback coming back down toward them.

She pointed. "If we don't both want to hang, I suggest we get out of here."

Mounting up on Dante and White Bird, they rode under forest cover up the slope to the divide between the Pelican Valley and the Lamar. Afternoon light turned lemon, then golden, as they outran their pursuers in their quest for the eastern park boundary.

In the valley of the Lamar, almost ten miles from where they met up, Cord drew rein.

Laura followed his gaze.

The skyline on the valley's opposite wall was dominated by a massive peak. Its crown was conical, bare of trees and other vegetation. Below the tree line, the mountain dropped away rapidly, except for three sharp spines of dark rock that formed ridges. The west side facing Cord and Laura sported enormous blocks of talus.

"That's Nez Perce Peak, named because some of the tribe took that route."

"Were you with them?"

He nodded. "There's a canyon, treacherous and full of deadfall, *ananasocum*, Bitter Waters called it, that divides Nez Perce from the mountain to the north." He pointed out the deep gash. "They'll never follow our trail through there."

The last red alpenglow lit the peaks of Nez Perce and Little Saddle Mountain to its north, when Cord and Laura entered the canyon. A wave of déjà vu settled over him.

Twilight came down fast between cliff walls of black rock no more than two hundred feet apart. It looked as though a giant had played a game of pick-up-sticks; scattered deadfall made the going nearly impassable in places.

With the visibility almost nil, Dante's hoof loosened a stone. It tumbled and bounced down behind him, narrowly missing White Bird's knee, gathering speed until it burst with a sharp sound like a rifle shot.

"It's getting too dark to ride," Cord admitted.

When he climbed down from Dante's back, Laura also dismounted. With night falling, he thought she should be getting ready to dance in that silk dress, not running for her life. He let his gaze stray to her narrow waist and thought about Bitter Waters's advice to marry her and start a family.

Pulling his spare canteen from his saddlebag, Cord shared the last of his water. A sip for him and Laura; then he poured some into his hat for Dante and White Bird. They still had a little in Laura's canteen, but they'd need to find some running water here in the canyon.

It might even be safe to slow down during the night and rest the horses, for below in the Lamar Valley he saw the unmistakable glow of several campfires.

"Why have they stopped?" Laura asked.

He chuckled. "Because they're lousy trackers? Must've lost our trail along with the light."

"So who's that ahead?" She peered into the depths of the canyon.

Against the fading light, there was a brighter glow, up in the chasm.

"I don't know." Keeping his voice low, Cord pulled his Winchester from the scabbard beside his saddle.

"Should we stay here and hope they don't see us?" she murmured.

If they didn't move on, they'd be trapped between whoever it was and the posse. It was even possible some of the soldiers had managed to get ahead of them this afternoon using a flanking move.

"That's no good," he replied. They had to get past, if they were going to make it through the pass Cappy Parsons had led Cord through.

"Wait here." He handed his Colt to Laura.

Though his heart was racing, he took a steadying breath and started up the ravine, walking silently the way Bitter Waters had taught him. Ahead, a campfire flared in the lee of a steep rock face.

When he drew closer, he paused and listened, but heard no voices.

By the time he got near enough to hear the snap of a burning stick, he made out the shape of a large pale horse. A man crouched, laying another log on an already adequate fire.

Cord pulled his rifle to a ready position.

He ought to shoot Danny Falls in the back. The world would be a better place, and there'd be one less peril to dodge.

Danny put on more wood.

Cord put the Winchester to his shoulder and placed his cheek hard against the stock's comb. An easy shot, with his target a prominent silhouette.

Like being at the range.

He focused on his stance and tried to slow his breathing. All the while, he mentally prepared. Danny was a cold-blooded killer. He'd seen him in action, been shot at himself at the coach. If Danny had burned the steamboat, and who else could have, he'd meant to kill both Hank and Alexandra.

And Edgar.

Cord moved his finger toward the trigger and felt the curve of metal beneath his index finger.

He drew in his breath . . . held it . . . focused on Danny's back . . .

Let out half . . .

What was he doing? So far, Cord was innocent of the charges leveled at him. Did he want to explain shooting a man in the back?

He took up the slack in the trigger, held, and relaxed the pressure with a sigh. Lowering his weapon, he soft-footed his way back to Laura.

"It's Danny Falls," he whispered.

Laura had thought having one's heart leap into one's throat was a saying. But hers felt like it was choking her, its wild erratic beating like the wings of a captured bird. She stared at Cord, unable to make a sound. That was a good thing. Inside her head, she was screaming, while it all flooded back: Angus Spiner's slow-motion fall from the high seat to his last bed in the spring snow; Danny's satisfied smile when he pocketed her little pistol; his avaricious sneer as he pawed through her things.

Her hand tightened on Cord's Colt. Danny was just there; she'd gladly go and shoot him.

"I thought about it." Cord touched her shoulder. "That's what separates us from outlaws."

He looked back the way they'd come, where the

soldiers camped. "We've got to get past him tonight. Get up into the high valley between Little Saddle and Nez Perce, where the going's easier."

The last thing she wanted to do was to move.

"If he comes toward us, we'll both blast him," Cord directed.

Laura managed to nod.

They set off. She followed Cord and Dante, leading White Bird with a slack rein while they picked their way over the broken ground by feel. They couldn't afford to loosen another stone.

Though they hugged the right side of the canyon, as far as possible from Danny's camp, the smell of roasting meat made her mouth water. She didn't see anyone beside the fire.

Slowly and silently, one step at a time. Cord was keeping to where the earth was soft and duff-covered in order that the horses' hooves not make noise. Laura tried to place her feet where he did. It seemed to take forever, but at last, the firelight began to fade behind them. Relieved, she looked down to find the next quiet place to step . . . from the corner of her eye she saw a shadow flit between trees.

It must be an owl.

The incline steepened. Her dress clung to her armpits where she sweated, even in the night wind. In the hand that wasn't holding White Bird's reins, she clutched the Colt.

Ahead, Cord stopped and put out a hand. Laura went still, and both horses stopped. White Bird's hoof touched a stone with an audible scrape.

From the corner of her eye, Laura once again caught motion. Before she could turn to see what it was, something seized her.

It took a fraction of a second to know it was a man's long arm, sliding around her throat. And a laugh that sounded like Hank when he'd pinned her on his bed.

Heart racing, her knees turning to water, Laura nonetheless clutched the Colt and tried to point the barrel up over her shoulder at his head . . .

"No, no, no." He disarmed her with a single move and pressed the barrel hurtfully against her temple.

She sensed Cord trying to bring his Winchester up.

Beside her ear, she heard the hammer being pulled back, one click . . .

Two.

Laura wanted to shout at Cord to shoot.

Three.

Even if she was at risk.

Four.

Cord lowered the Winchester.

"Let's all go over to my fire, shall we?" suggested Danny Falls.

CHAPTER TWENTY-EIGHT
JUNE 30

It must have been past midnight, as the night chill came down in earnest. Cord sat with his head tilted back against a sapling, his arms bound behind him and around the trunk. His sheepskin coat lay nearby; he wished Danny had let him give the wrap to Laura, who lay huddled in a miserable bundle too far from the fire to get any warmth.

Danny had feasted on roasted rabbit he must have shot earlier in the day, but had offered neither food nor water to Cord or Laura. He'd tethered Dante and White Bird near his palomino.

Tilting a compact ceramic jug that smelled of liquor, Danny drank, his prominent Adam's apple bobbing, one, two, three times.

"Tracked you all day," he said.

Four times.

"Got the jump ahead in the boulders and deadfall." He moved with deliberate steps toward Laura.

"Shouldn't have brought a woman to slow ya."

She struggled to a sitting position. Her hands were not tied, but a loop around her waist secured her to a fir.

Danny reached to twine a lock of her hair around his finger. "Pretty." He spoke softly, eyeing Cord.

Laura's knotted hair clung to Danny's finger, and he jerked, yanking the hank out by the roots. In the firelight, Cord saw tears shine in her eyes.

With a chuckle, Danny traced the curve of her breast beneath filthy green silk, still puckered after being wet earlier. She kept her head averted.

"Take your hands off her," Cord demanded. He imagined that he threw Danny to the earth and ground his boot into his face.

"Got to you with that?" He turned from Laura, seeming to lose interest in her. "The shoe's on the other foot." His face was ugly. "You killed my partner, Frank. In fairness, I should return the favor."

Cord started to speak, but Laura burst out, "Was it fair what you did to the stage driver? For a paltry valise of women's clothing."

"You think Frank and I are small-time operators who go around robbing stagecoaches?" He shook his head. "No, no, no."

Cord shifted his aching shoulders and tested his bonds as he'd been doing for hours. His knife had gone into Danny's pack. This time, as he swept his bound hands across the ground, he uncovered the tip of something hard and sharp.

Danny drank again. "I'm not as dumb as Hank thinks. I set my high-livin', too-good-to-talk-to-his-twin brother up to lose his fancy Lake Hotel."

"I guessed that much," Cord said.

"Got eyes and ears all around. Frank was in a bar in Jackson, found out from the fellow runs the stage station that a Laura Fielding would be on the Yellowstone run."

Cord craned his neck trying to see the ground.

"Queer," Danny mused, "gal traveling alone, but that name matched the bank the railroad told Edgar was backing Hank."

There. Cord felt the adamantine surface of obsidian.

He strained, his shoulders aching, and managed to touch it with the tips of his fingers. It wasn't a knifepoint or arrowhead, but a piece of material that had been worked into a single sharp edge and then abandoned without being finished.

Danny's laugh was a chilling arpeggio. "What better . . . dis . . . discouragement for a man investin' than to lose . . . his daughter?" The drink was getting to him.

"You didn't *know* it was the right woman?" Laura looked horrified.

He shrugged and took another drink. "Fair bet."

"Why did you hurt Edgar?" Cord demanded, using an angry jerk at his bonds to scoot over an inch where he could better dig at the stone flake.

"Edgar hadda bring . . . lousy Nez Perce." His

voice slurred.

"That's no excuse to try to drown him," Cord said.

"Bastard tried . . . fight me. On yer side . . ."

Danny reached with drunken precision to lift Cord's Colt from where he'd set it on a log. He stumbled a little and then straightened up.

Cord managed to dig out the obsidian, but his nerveless fingers loosened, and it fell from him.

Danny lined up the sights, and Cord looked down the barrel of his own gun. As if from a distance, he heard Laura's intake of breath.

Stretching, he managed to take the glass between his frigid fingers again. It was cold, as well.

From ten feet away, Danny's dark eyes looked enormous behind the weapon.

The obsidian began to warm in Cord's fingers, taking heat from his hand or giving it, difficult to tell. He kept his face impassive.

"Better let . . . army . . ." Danny glanced down the canyon.

Before Cord understood, he lifted the gun, pulled back the hammer, and fired it into the black sky.

Laura flinched. Cord's ears rang. Getting a better grip, he got the sharp edge against the rope and started sawing.

"They'll blame ya . . . Edgar . . ." Danny let the Colt down beside him.

Cord saw Laura notice. He gauged the length of the leash that held her and thought it might work.

He sawed harder.

He'd seen Bitter Waters, working a like piece of volcanic glass one night around the Nez Perce campfire. Pointing out the fires of the army scouts only a few miles away, he had declared, "God is with the white man, but not with us!" The black glass had broken in his hands, and he had thrown it to the earth.

Though the magic hadn't worked for his uncle, Cord believed. He might have lost the piece he'd treasured for so many years, but the spirit had rewarded him with another chance on the same mountain peak.

One of the layers of rope parted. He started working the next. The posse would have been alerted by the shot and by now were mounting up.

Laura was on the move, scooting closer to Danny, who didn't seem to be paying her any attention. Rather, his dark eyes studied Cord with drunken intensity. "I'll . . . hafta leave . . ."

He returned Danny's dark gaze and tried to work the sharp edge against his bonds without making it obvious. Sweat gathered in his armpits.

Laura was looking at him, questioning.

He didn't dare look back with Danny staring at him. As a cover for his motion, Cord spoke. "The army is after me for another piece of your work."

Danny raised a brow.

The final rope parted.

"Burning your brother's steamboat." Cord wriggled out of the rope while keeping his shoulders as still as possible.

"Burning his boat?" Danny put his hands on his

knees in preparation to rise. "Gotta get outta here . . ."

Laura's hand was within three feet of the Colt. Danny was looking toward his palomino.

"Go!" Cord shouted. He straightened his shoulders against a shaft of pain and shoved awkwardly to his feet. Danny turned toward him with a dumbfounded look.

Cord dove across the clearing, knocking him off his heels onto his back.

Laura surged to the limit of her tether but wasn't able to reach the Colt.

"The hell?" Danny hollered, drawing a little four-barrel pepperbox from his pants pocket.

With his arms on fire from blood surging back into them, Cord slashed backhanded at Danny's wrist. The impact felt rubbery, but the little gun flew to the side.

Danny was out from under him, staggering up as Cord scrambled to regain his footing.

From the corner of his eye, he saw Laura snatch up the weapon that had landed within her reach.

Danny didn't see, thank God for drink. He crouched on the balls of his feet, hands out to fight Cord. The Colt lay behind him.

Cord shook out his arms, all pins and needles, and tried to bring up his fists.

Laura was studying the little gun.

Please, let it be loaded.

And let her know how to use it.

"Look out, Cord!" she cried.

Danny turned toward her voice. Cord feinted out of the line of fire, and, with the barrel only a few feet from Danny's chest, she pulled the trigger.

The little gun went off with a sharp snap. A stinking sulphurous cloud floated up.

Blood stained Danny's buckskins around a black exit hole Cord could see beneath his right shoulder. Grabbing Laura by the throat with one hand, Danny jerked the pistol from her and placed the barrel against her temple.

With Danny's back to him, Cord didn't hesitate. Pulling back his arms, he swung his clasped hands like a club, connecting solidly with the back of the outlaw's head.

Danny went down like a felled pine.

Laura stared at him. "Is he dead?"

"Out." Cord ran back to the sapling where he'd been tied and picked up the wedge of obsidian.

He came back to Laura and severed the rope that bound her.

Hoofbeats sounded from down the canyon, along with shouts. Men were coming, holding flaring torches aloft.

"Let's get out of here." Cord went to Dante's head and untied him. He looked around, but didn't see his Winchester, or his small pack with food. As a last resort, he tried to locate the little pepperbox that might contain three more cartridges, but it was lost in the shadows thrown by the fire.

Laura had the Colt in her hand, on her way to

White Bird.

Intent only on speed, they pointed their mounts blindly into the black depths of Nez Perce Canyon.

Within a hundred yards, Dante became stuck in a bottleneck where the trees grew too closely for him to pass. Panicked, he threw himself forward, wedging himself more tightly between the pines.

Cord remembered seeing an old woman of the Nez Perce beat a stuck horse with a stick until it reversed out of the blind alley. He placed a comforting hand on Dante's flank and spoke softly, backing him out.

Within a hundred yards, it had happened twice more.

Behind, he heard a commotion of voices as the soldiers no doubt went to Danny's fire and found him.

Cord urged Dante on, Laura riding beside him. But the terrain forced them to proceed slower and slower, until they reached a place where deadfall blocked the horses.

Dismounting, Cord felt his way along to the right until he found passage. Dante followed, one faltering step after another.

"Cord?" Laura hissed.

"This way." He hoped she could follow the sound of his voice.

Ahead, he made out a faint graying of the night. Straining his eyes, he moved forward.

There was open space ahead, he realized. In fifty feet, he was out of the forest. A sliver of rising moon and the Milky Way illuminated that here the cliff edge that had bounded the chasm gave way to the vast field of jumbled rocks they had seen from below. The talus pile continued up perhaps a thousand feet and intersected one of the great rock spines leading up several thousand more feet to the top of Nez Perce Peak.

"The horses can't do this." Laura patted White Bird's neck with a hand that was a paler shade of gray than the night.

Cord ran his hands over Dante's coat. In addition to the bloody furrow left by a soldier's bullet, new wounds seeped from his frightened plunging against the trees. The big horse whimpered, a thin tentative sound.

Putting his arms around Dante's neck, Cord closed his eyes. He remembered his first sight of the colt, all spindly legs and foam-flecked coat. Born on a crisp autumn morning, Dante had staggered valiantly to his feet beneath his mother in half the time it normally took a newborn.

"What are we going to do?" Laura asked.

Cord looked back the way they'd come. Torchlight winked through the forest behind them, drawing closer.

He pressed his cheek to Dante's velvet nose. He sensed even in the night that Dante watched him with keen intelligence.

"We'll have to leave the horses," he said in a matter-of-fact voice. "The soldiers will find them and take care of them."

"But . . ." She looked back.

The Army of the United States pursued as relentlessly as they had in 1877.

Laura smoothed her hand along White Bird's shoulder. Cord thought she was crying, as she slid off White Bird and faced the wall of rock.

Staggering beneath her bone-numbing exhaustion, Laura pulled herself up onto another boulder on the seemingly endless climb. She could barely see Cord above her, a dark silhouette against a bank of clouds streaming over the ridge from the east.

Her entire being focused onto the next rock, where she would place her hands and feet, and whether she would be able to drag her weight up. Her throat was parched, and her heart pounded fiercely.

After leaving Dante and White Bird at the edge of the boulder field, Laura and Cord had come no more than halfway up the talus pile, headed for the spine of the ridge.

"The other side is covered in forest and the going will be easier." He reached back and helped Laura up onto the next ledge. She felt the sticky wetness of blood between their clasped palms; the sharp volcanic rocks had sliced open both their hands.

She wanted to tell him she couldn't climb another

foot, that he must go on and leave her to save himself, as they'd left the horses.

"This is a good sheltered place to stop until dawn," he said. "We've both got to rest or we'll never make it to the top."

"What about the soldiers?"

"They must have lost our trail again," Cord said. A study of the rock pile they'd scaled did not show anyone climbing after them.

Laura looked around. They were in the lee of the wind, but since they had stopped climbing, she could already feel the night air chilling her sweat-dampened skin. Cord had his sheepskin coat, while she wore nothing but her dress, torn and ripped from the climb. If only there'd been time to check Danny's camp for blankets, water, or food.

Below in the canyon, Laura could see the light of the bonfire. For a moment, she thought she smelled smoke, but it must be her imagination.

Cord seated himself in a sheltered hollow. "Come sit."

Laura hugged herself, staring back the way they had come. "I hope White Bird and Dante . . ."

"Don't think about it," Cord ordered. "You're shaking with cold, and in a little while I will be, too, unless you get down here and share some body heat."

A nasty gust eddied onto the ledge, and she gave up on what was behind them. When she came to shelter with him, he slid his coat off and wrapped it around them both.

Impossible to think that only a few weeks ago Chicago had been her world: petty jealousies between her and her cousin, worrying what her aunt thought about her wardrobe, daydreaming of getting out from under her father's thumb.

Cord's embrace tightened, and he winced.

"Your arm hurts?" She wished she had clean warm water, fresh bandages.

He stroked her hair, gently touching the sore place where Danny had pulled some out.

Laura studied the moon, intermittently visible behind a bank of low scudding clouds continuing to sweep over the eastern ridge in waves. The flat sheen of Yellowstone Lake lay far below to the west, cool waters masking the surface of the volcano beneath.

In the Lamar Valley, the fires the soldiers had smothered sent up pale smoke.

Cord pointed. "The campfires of the People cast their glow into the cloudy skies as we moved through these mountains. Horses dragged travois loaded with precious possessions, painted hides, silver jewelry, and ceremonial breastplates . . ." He trailed off, seemingly lost in memory.

As Laura watched the sky, she detected the faintest crimson in the east. "It can't be morning."

"It isn't. Rest while you can."

The wind began to strengthen, its moan rising as it crested the ridge above. While night wore on, it gusted so strongly she and Cord heard the crack of trees breaking above. The leaves and pine straw in their hollow swirled and took flight.

Lightning split the sky at intervals, but there was no rain in this dry, cold front. In fact, the nagging smoke smell grew stronger, making her recall what Hank had said last evening about a new forest fire on Nez Perce Peak.

With their backs against rough rock, Cord and Laura huddled in each other's arms, her head against his chest. Hours passed; neither slept.

Sometime before dawn, Cord bent his head and whispered, "We'll get through this."

Without food or water, and with miles of back-country ahead, Laura wondered if they might not be forced to give themselves up to survive.

But Feddors and his men had already taken shots at Cord. Would the captain, who acted irrational, if not outright crazy, allow Cord . . . or her . . . to be taken alive?

CHAPTER TWENTY-NINE

JUNE 30

Laura did sleep, for Cord's voice awakened her. "First light."

It was hard to tell, but there did seem to be a barely perceptible brightening. Of course, the moon was overhead and perhaps that made a difference.

The wind picked up from higher on Nez Perce Peak, sorting what looked like mist into wispy trails. Across the canyon lay Little Saddle Mountain, another sharp peak ringed with treacherous blocks of talus. The air appeared clearer there.

Laura extricated herself from Cord's arms and studied his beard-stubbled, bruised face. The fresh wound, where Constance had cut him with her ring, made a match for the ancient one. Getting to her feet, she scanned the long blocky slope of boulders that she and Cord had climbed in darkness.

At the base, two blue-jacketed army men were ascending on foot. The rifles slung over their shoulders made her aware she and Cord were armed with only a single pistol.

Cord pushed to his feet. "I don't like the look of this."

Thick fingers of a strange-looking fog billowed over the top of the ridge. With them came the strong stench of burning.

They began to climb. It seemed as though it might have been better not to rest, for Laura's muscles had tightened like a leather bridle soaked with horse sweat. The cut flesh on her palms had stopped seeping, but as soon as she stretched for a handhold, the wounds reopened. Her thirst, which had abated somewhat during the cold night, returned to her parched throat.

From his pocket, Cord brought out a flake of obsidian, smaller and thinner than his *wayakin*. He took the narrow edge between finger and thumb and broke off a bit. "Put that under your tongue, and it'll help your saliva come." He put another piece into his mouth and pocketed the rest.

"Where did you get that?" she asked.

"Last night I found it right below my hands. Used it to cut loose."

Laura felt the stone warm in her mouth. If his guardian spirit had sent another helper, perhaps they might get out of this.

Foot by foot, hour by hour, she and Cord narrowed the distance to the ridge. Though the soldiers came on behind, they heard no shouts to indicate they'd been spotted in the smoke haze that grew thicker as they climbed. Rather, there was an ominous sound from the other side of the ridge, like one of the Chicago trains approaching the station.

"The wildfire must be right over there," Laura finally admitted aloud. The quaver in her voice frightened her.

Cord started to touch her and stopped, looking at his torn palms. "We can probably get around it." He pointed east. "You can't see from here, but the Lamar circles back around and is only a few miles down there. We'll be drinking from the river before the soldiers even think about getting up here."

"I hope so. What will we do for food, since you can't shoot anything without giving us away?"

"Tomorrow I'll show you how to dig camas roots."

"What are they?" She wrinkled her nose.

"They're starchy and not very interesting, but we won't starve," Cord remembered. "The Nez Perce used them for everything from making mush to eating them raw."

"I wish we had some now." She smiled wanly.

As they pulled toward the top, the smoke billowing above them grew darker and thicker.

"Soon we'll be slipping and sliding down a slope of pine needles, faster than we could run," Cord proposed. "From the sound, the fire's to the north, opposite of the way we want to go."

Up over the last boulder and they found themselves on a knife-edge, overlooking a steep, northeast slope studded with pines. An ancient, twisted tree reached gnarled limbs into the smoky morning sky. It seemed to grow from a cairn of boulders that men might have made; perhaps the Nez Perce had made a monument here during their passage.

But there was no time to wonder, with all the sense of accomplishment at scaling the slope, all the optimism Laura had based on the obsidian crashing.

A blast of heat hit them in the face.

The rumble became a roar. Great tongues of crimson-and-orange flame leaped voraciously upwards. Tall pines torched as the fire front threw off fireballs that rolled upward and then disappeared into the white-hot sky. Thick smoke rolled blackly off the two-hundred-foot wall of fire, sweeping across the slope toward them, faster than a horse could gallop.

Cord looked over his shoulder, back the way they had come. Feddors led Lieutenant Stafford, climbing more nimbly than Cord would have expected. Of course, the man was driven by his demons.

Thankfully, he wasn't in rifle range yet.

Perhaps if Cord put up his hands, John Stafford would be able to influence Feddors to accept his surrender. That way, at least Laura would be spared.

He turned to her and saw she was gauging the speed of the inferno and the distance.

"No!" he cried.

She took off along the ridgetop heading up the

mountain. Away from the fire, but it was burning up-hill.

"That's no good!" Cord shouted. "Laura!" He realized she could not or would not hear him.

He ran after her.

The terrain fell away so steeply on either side that the pines on the slope seemed to be growing on a vertical wall. A sudden wind shift brought the smoke sweeping up over them in a choking cloud.

The dragon's roar grew ever louder, punctuated by the sharp snap of limbs exploding and the louder reports of tree trunks blowing apart.

Cord's thigh muscles ached as he ran uphill after Laura. Catching her was harder than he'd thought, but from the terrified look of her face when she glanced back at the fire, she was running on pure adrenaline.

A sudden sharp whine near his ear. My God, Feddors was within range.

Cord found his own surge of pure terror, caught Laura's hand, and plunged off the ridge onto the forested slope. Immediately they were knee-deep in a patch of coarse, icy snow.

He saw Laura's ridiculously thin slippers sucked from her feet with the first two steps, but he dragged her on. They half-wallowed, half-fell down the sixty-degree incline.

A dead limb caught Cord in the face. He kept pulling her.

He smashed a shoulder into a tree and grunted in pain.

Heat at their backs told him they weren't going to make it.

Unless . . . a cluster of lava boulders at least thirty feet on a side. He stumbled down to the landmark, threw Laura into the lowest crevice, and fell on top of her. They'd probably be cooked, their hair afire and the liquid boiled out of them, but it made the only shelter in sight.

The wildfire raged, roaring through the treetops. Below on the slope, a fir exploded. Burning bits of wood showered them.

Cord rolled over and clawed at the loose pile of rocks. Impossibly, the gale force wind felt freezing cold as it swept toward the inferno.

The wind shifted, and became a hurricane. The banshee wail crescendoed while ovenlike temperatures came down on them. Cord held his breath; his next one would draw searing gases into his lungs.

Frantically, he worked at the rocks on one side of Laura, trying to burrow out a place for her, even though he knew it was hopeless. The fire's glow grew so intense that he closed his desiccated eyes and saw brilliant orange through his lids.

Even blind, he kept on digging.

Suddenly, he felt a shift, as though the earth tilted. Laura fell away beneath him.

The plunge felt endless. She fought a sickening weightless feeling that reminded her of when she fell out of an apple tree at Fielding House when she was twelve. In a fraction of a second, she landed on her chest and stomach with the breath knocked out of her. Then, instead of lying flat on solid earth like the lawn beneath the apple tree, she slid headfirst down a cold and slippery slope.

Crashing to a stop, she felt a sharp pain and wondered if she had broken her arm. The blood pounded in her head, and she stared up at the glowing light.

"Cord!" she screamed.

Only the dragon answered.

Sudden heat flared on the back of her legs, and she twisted her head to find her skirt aflame.

Before she could move, a heavy weight crashed into her. "Jesus, Laura!"

Cord leaped up to roll her over, packing wet snow over the burning cloth and the backs of her legs. The stench of singed silk mixed with the smell of smoke.

Within moments, the air grew warm and suffocating.

Cord yanked her up and struggled away toward the darkness. Her twisted right arm was agony as he dragged her farther into what Laura felt certain would be their grave.

Stumbling barefoot over jumbled blocks of scoria that cut like knives, she gasped, "I can't make it."

Cord tripped over a boulder and they went down together on the rough, rocky floor.

Laura worked her pained arm and felt the heat of

the burns on the back of her legs. She tried to speak, but her throat was raw.

Cord swiveled his head toward the light of the flames that still roared. The look on his sooty face was of defeat, something she never thought she would see in him.

It grew hotter and dryer as the fire sucked the air out of the cave. Gauzy gray gathered at the edges of Laura's sight, turning rapidly darker. She reached weakly for Cord.

He lay still beside her. Had he blacked out?

She put a hand onto his chest and felt every muscle tense. He raised a hand. "Feel that?"

The faintest hint of cool air barely brushed her face. Gradually, the breeze picked up to become a steady wind blowing from the depths of the cave toward the fire.

"There must be another entrance," Cord murmured.

Laura drank in the sweet air in great gulps, filling her parched lungs. For a long moment, they lay catching their breath, then pushed up to sit on the rocky floor.

"What is this place?" She eyed the dark rock walls and piles of boulders on the cavern floor. It seemed to go off in one direction only, a long tunnel leading deeper into Nez Perce Peak. The walls and ceiling of dark rock had an odd smooth texture.

"A lava tube," Cord answered. "Molten rock flowed through and left the tunnel behind."

Within minutes, the firestorm had passed. Yet,

they could hear it rumbling on through the forest like a freight train.

With the cave air clearer, though still smelling scorched, Laura struggled to her feet and picked her way barefooted back to the cone of ice on which they'd landed. It appeared that winter snows had sifted in through the hole in the roof and accumulated in a drifted pile. The insulating effect of the porous lava was such that the fire above had softened the snow, but not melted it.

Cupping both hands, she shoveled the coarse dirty coldness into her mouth. Cord dug in and took a huge bite, then rubbed some on his face, smearing the soot into streaks. Reaching again, Laura soothed the cuts on her feet and the burns on the back of her calves with handfuls of crisp iciness. She decided her arm wasn't broken, as the first acute agony diminished.

Cord came to her and pulled the piece of obsidian from his pocket. "It's the closest thing I have to a knife."

Bending, he used the sharp edge to saw what remained of her skirt off at the knee. Then he ripped off the puffed peplum that covered her behind and fashioned two wrappings for her feet.

He helped her to sit on the rock floor, avoiding the roughest patches. Now that the fire had burned past, a damp chill came from the partly melted cone of snow. The walls of the lava tube were cold against the burns on the backs of her legs. Though she'd eaten snow, her stomach was painfully empty.

"By now, Feddors and his men must believe we're dead," Cord said.

"If they do, they'll be well on their way back down the mountain. Especially, if Danny survived, they'd need to get him to a doctor."

Gently, Cord drew her closer. "If we make it out of this hell, I don't want to live without you."

Her chest grew tight. "*When* we get out of this, I'm not going back to Chicago."

"I wouldn't let you." He smiled and smoothed his hand down her back. "We'll have all the time we need. To watch the sun set on Blacktail Butte after the shadow of the Tetons has brought dusk to the ranch." His eyes gazed fondly upon that faraway scene.

She wanted all that, and more. But she happened to look at the cone of snow and take in what the fire's heat had done to the height of the icy mound. The top was at least six feet below the jagged edges of rock. The ceiling inside the tube was smooth where liquid lava had slid past.

Getting out of here was going to require wings.

"Don't worry," Cord soothed. "We'll figure something out."

He wished he felt as confident as he tried to sound, while he looked around and thought. Pushing to his feet, he peered up at daylight through the hole they'd fallen in, no more than four feet wide and a little longer. If they didn't get out before nightfall, even starlight would not penetrate the darkness below.

"I think maybe before we get too upset, I'll do a little investigating for another way out." Cord wished for another torch, but the embers he'd seen above had gone dark. He had no matches; they were in his small pack, left behind at Danny's camp.

Laura started to get up, but he put a hand on her shoulder. "Without shoes, you should stay here."

Without the benefit of light, Cord began to feel his way down the dark stone corridor. He kept one hand on the wall and one on the ceiling, moving forward one careful step at a time.

The illumination that picked out differences in topography on the cave floor and walls gradually dimmed, then vanished. This was where a man had to ride hard on his demons.

He reached to his pocket and touched the obsidian that had saved him and Laura beside Danny's fire. Surely, it would help get them out of here.

The blackness ahead became absolute. Cord turned to look back and found that the gentle curve of the tunnel had taken him out of sight of the light.

Men weren't supposed to get nervous in the dark, and he normally did not. So why did he feel as though his next breath was so difficult to draw?

Ignoring his claustrophobia as best as he could, he forced himself to stoop and go on when the rock ceiling lowered. But though he poked and crawled around in total darkness for at least an hour, he could not find a way through the narrowed opening. Had he been thinner, perhaps he might have shimmied on his belly into the tunnel, but with no light, he did not dare enter what was most likely a blind gut.

At some point, he realized the obsidian he'd found in Danny's camp was no longer in his pocket.

Defeated, he turned back. As he went toward where he had left Laura, he saw first a spark that might have been imagination, then a steady dot. Finally, the walls on either side of him began to silver.

When he could see Laura, she was on her feet. "Any luck?"

"Air gets through. We don't." He shifted his feet and some loose lava rock made a hollow clinking.

Looking away toward the cone of snow and the dead pine, he noted that she'd been busy while he was gone. Signs of a struggle were evident in knee-deep prints in the icy slush and the little tree lay canted at a different angle.

"I tried to set it upright to make a ladder, but it kept getting away from me," she said.

"Let's try together."

With the thickest part of the broken pine jammed into the ice for stability and the top resting against the side of the hole above, about two feet protruded into daylight.

"You go up first," Cord told her.

She shook her head.

"Go on," he said. "It might not hold my weight."

With a shudder, she refused again. "I want you at the top to give me a hand up. And if it breaks under my weight, I don't have the strength to pull you up."

"All right." He checked to make sure his Colt was secure in his holster.

With determination, he stepped up onto the cone. His leg went in to above the knee. Painstakingly, he climbed up another few feet until he was at the apex of the little snow mountain.

He grasped the trunk in one hand. The dry bark tortured the cuts on his hands. Grimacing, he transferred his weight from standing on snow to dangling from the ridiculous little dead Christmas tree.

Hand over hand, he made it up another few feet. The trunk was now less than three inches in diameter, something he could easily break over his knee. He looked up; about four more feet and he could get his elbows onto solid rock and drag himself home.

Three feet.

He braced himself for what he would see outside. Charred forest . . . ash . . . Captain Quenton Feddors with his gun trained.

Two feet, the same number of inches the pine trunk had narrowed to. He tried to feel lucky.

One foot.

Crrrack!

"Oh God!" Laura said.

"No!" cried the six-year-old inside him.

The pine snapped in two and dropped him on his

hands and knees in dirty slush. He crouched there, taking in the reality of being doomed to slow starvation.

Without hesitation, he drew his Colt.

"What are you doing?" Laura's eyes went wide.

He raised the muzzle and drew the hammer back the trademark four clicks. "If anyone's left on this mountain, we have to signal them."

"Cord . . ."

He fired through the hole into the sky.

Hours passed. Each time Cord shot to attract attention, there was a "discussion" between him and Laura. By the time the light was fading from the sky and they were facing their first night below ground, she finally agreed that, even captured, Cord stood a better chance than he did in this premature grave.

"It's too bad we can't burn some of the pine," he said. "Get some smoke rising."

"Why can't we?"

"No matches."

Laura reached to the bodice of her dress and drew out the small piece of obsidian he'd given her to hold in her mouth. "Can you use this as a flint?"

"Perhaps if I chipped it against my belt buckle."

Laura moved to help him snap the dead pine into kindling.

With a fire laid, Cord removed his belt and turned

his attention to some thin slivers of bark. He knelt with his face close and chipped the glass against metal.

Nothing happened.

The second time, there was a small spark.

Cord tried again; this time the spark flared to brief life on a fragment of bark and sputtered out.

He sat back on his heels to rest a moment.

Then he leaned down and starting chipping obsidian against metal rapidly, while blowing a light, but steady stream over his work. A few more flashes . . . a piece of bark flared and settled into a diminutive flame.

Laura sat against the wall and watched as the pile of pine caught. Smoke eddied and curled, then finally coiled up and out the hole.

Cord restrung his belt and sat beside her, but she could feel his restlessness. She tried to start a conversation about what they'd do when they got out of here; it fell flat. Finally, she leaned her head against his shoulder and let the fire's hypnotic influence fascinate.

So beautiful and so deadly. It gave warmth and life . . . but did Cord see his parents' cabin inside every flame? Would some part of her forever cringe back because of the dragon whose breath had almost seared them?

For good or ill, their little beacon did not last long. The pine snapped as the fire's teeth devoured it, until nothing remained but orange, then crimson embers. Finally, she and Cord sat before a bed of cooling white ash.

What were the chances their signal had looked

any different from the smoke that was probably still rising from the remains of the forest?

The light faded, and the chill from the rocks began to be uncomfortable.

Cord pulled out his Colt again. "Last one."

As Danny had fired one shot to attract the soldiers before, now the fifth and last bullet in the revolver exploded into twilight.

Sending up their final signal to the world on the surface seemed to take the heart out of Cord. Laura, seated on a relatively smooth patch of rock floor, gestured for him to join her.

When he moved slowly to sit beside her, she wished she could tell him it would be all right. But what were the chances the soldiers were still out there? Even if they were on the mountain, the sound of the Colt must be muffled from down here.

"We've done what we could," he said, putting an arm around her and drawing her against his side.

Defeat came with exhaustion. "I don't think I've ever been so tired." The last hint of light was suddenly gone, and they were in total darkness.

"Must be cloudy tonight," Cord observed, without interest.

She put her head against his chest and closed her lids to stop her eye muscles from straining. His heartbeat beneath her ear was strong and steady.

This floating feeling of unreality reminded her how she'd slept against his shoulder on horseback after the stagecoach attack, wrung out in the aftermath of terror.

This time, instead of sleeping, she sat awake while minutes and then hours ticked past. No sounds came from above, save the occasional crack and thud of a burned tree succumbing to the roving wind. Sparks of color played tricks on Laura both when her eyes were open and closed, but no torchlight appeared to brighten the blackness.

Once, as they waited for a dawn that seemed forever in coming, Cord's lips brushed her hair, and she knew he was awake, as well.

"I love you," she said.

"I knew I'd fallen for you," he replied, "when I couldn't bear to put you on Hank's steamboat. I needed those last hours beside the lake before never seeing you again."

How long did they have this time? He'd spent their last bullet . . .

She'd heard people could live for a number of days, maybe close to two weeks, without food. And they had the slush pile to drink from, however long it lasted.

All she wanted was go to sleep and hide there while death crept up on them both. If she went first, she'd have someone with her . . . but how could she leave Cord to set her lifeless body aside and curl up alone to die?

Tears sprang to her eyes. It wasn't fair; having finally found each other, they should have their whole lives to look forward to.

Cord's chest heaved; he was weeping, also. Mourning those sunrises and sunsets on his ranch, giving up wondering what ancestors their children might resemble, saying good-bye to being a part of the human chain that linked each parent to immortality.

Knowing he loved her was the cruelest irony, when they had no hope.

CHAPTER THIRTY

JULY 1

Constance woke at dawn in the room she shared with her mother at the Lake Hotel.

If she had once believed Cord was the man for her, she now saw the error of her ways. With him, there had always been a sense of something held back, while Norman embraced her with what felt like his soul.

Throwing back the covers, she got out of bed and went to the window. The lake was just beginning to reflect the palest gray from the eastern sky. Out there somewhere, Laura and Cord were being hunted, while she remained here doing nothing. It made her ashamed of the way she and Laura had fought since coming to Yellowstone. Sure, there had always been a tension between them, their spats and jealousies . . .

Most of the time, things had evened out. For every time Constance had been chosen to sing solo soprano in the choir, Laura had won the blue ribbon for jumping her horse over the tallest and widest obstacles. For every prize Constance had won for her preserves and comfits at the Evanston Ladies' Club, Laura had seen samples of her poetry and journaling printed in their monthly newsletter.

Whatever Cord had held back, things to do with his family . . . and later, to do with Laura . . . none of that mattered. As surely as Constance and Norman enjoyed the precisely pruned shrubs and formal garden of Como Park in St. Paul, Cord and Laura both belonged in the chaotic country of Yellowstone.

Constance stared out at the wilderness that had swallowed them and prayed Laura's toughness would bring her through.

Deep down, she loved her as though they were sisters.

Norman Hagen left his room when sunrise silhouetted the Absarokas and turned the dark waters into a lake of fire. He'd planned to see this dawn on the train.

Walking down to the pier, he saw that sometime during the night, the remains of the *Alexandra* had sunk. Tough break for Hank; there'd been a deal of money in that boat, and Norman hated to see anyone's investment turn sour.

Yesterday afternoon in the lobby, he'd come upon Hank still wearing his tattered clothing and drawing stares from arriving guests. Aware of the image the railroad wanted to project in their hotels, and, not incidentally, feeling sorry for Hank, Norman offered him a shirt and trousers. They were about the same height, and though Norman was thicker in girth, Hank had been able to cinch up his belt. Someone must have taken pity on his sister earlier in the day, for she wore a lavender lace-trimmed dress instead of the violet robe Norman had seen her in during the fire.

Their lives had changed, as had his.

Today, he planned to ask Constance to marry him. And he intended to make sure Forrest Fielding understood that, despite the hotel deal falling through, Norman would use his influence to be sure the Northern Pacific threw some banking business Fielding's way.

All night, Sergeant Nevers had kept his vigil guarding the infirmary and the two men who'd been attacked. At times, he wondered why he bothered, for there was a quality in the stillness around the hotel that said no one was abroad in the night.

Every half hour, he checked in at Edgar Young's bedside, but by dawn the patient had not made any coherent sounds. He did moan occasionally, and Dr. Upshur had indicated that perhaps there was hope. As for the other patient, with the coming of morning, Larry heard Forrest Fielding demanding breakfast and a bath and reckoned he was much improved.

Larry decided to go over and check in by telephone with Headquarters. They could send over some fellows from Norris Station to reinforce the reduced staff here.

He checked out with Dr. Upshur and left the infirmary. Though he started to take the most direct route, when he was near the hotel he stopped and looked toward a clump of brush not far from the wall.

Stepping out into the hotel drive, he gauged the distance to the thicker vegetation. He turned and looked down toward the pier where the *Alexandra* had been docked, again thinking distance. He picked up a chunk of gravel and, trying to mimic Feddors's trajectory, pitched it.

It disappeared into the thicket, just as he'd watched Cord Sutton's obsidian fly out of sight into darkness. Apparently, there was something special about the stone, at least to Laura Fielding, who had wanted it badly.

Larry headed for the scrub and started looking. It didn't take long to find the distinctive piece of black glass, shiny side up and glinting in the morning sun.

Manfred Resnick had already dressed and was drinking coffee before a lively fire when the soldier station phone rang. He went behind the wooden desk, sat in the straight chair, and answered, identifying himself as being with Pinkerton's.

The male voice over the wires sounded tinny. "This is Private Arden Groesbeck calling from Headquarters."

"Yes." Resnick recognized him as one of the members of the posse from Lake.

"There's no danger at Lake," Groesbeck said. "Last evening, Sutton was sighted up in the Absarokas, miles from there. He and the girl had abandoned their horses and set out on foot."

"How did you get back to Headquarters so fast?" Resnick sipped his coffee. "Did you apprehend them?"

"No, but Feddors and Stafford are still up there. We found Danny Falls shot beside his campfire and were ordered to try to get him to the Fort Yellowstone hospital before he died."

Resnick hung up and went to tell Sergeant Nevers he was moving his investigation to Mammoth.

Since the burning of the *Alexandra* had disturbed some guests enough to make them leave, Hank slept in a vacant room on the hotel's first floor. His sister was a few rooms down the hall.

Yet, when he came out in the morning and tapped on her door, she didn't answer. After knocking louder and calling, he pulled out his master key and found the room empty.

Thinking she must already be up and at breakfast, he started in the direction of the lobby. Before he'd taken more than a few steps, he heard the door at the other end of the hall open.

"Hank!" Alexandra gasped.

He turned to find her wearing a white dress embroidered all over with tiny violets. She might have looked fresh and lovely, but her expression was one of horror. "I was out walking and ran into Manfred Resnick, on his way to find us."

Long ago, Hank had been able to feel his brother's presence, no matter how many miles separated them. When Danny had broken his arm wrestling a calf for branding on a neighboring ranch, Hank had abruptly become ill.

This morning, though some deep instinct told him the news was of his brother, he had no inkling whether Danny was alive or dead.

Cord opened his eyes to a brilliant silver-white light accompanied by a dreadful hissing. He leaped up, Colt in hand.

A peculiar acrid smell came from the light that glowed brilliantly on the smooth rock walls and the rough boulders on the cavern floor. It twirled slowly, a disorienting circling of bright and black darkness.

Behind him, Laura gave a muffled exclamation. Cord stood his ground though he felt dizzy and disoriented; he'd wakened from a sleep so deep he might already have been dead.

The man on the rope reached the floor of the cavern, his knee-high black leather boots touching the floor. His blue wool coat, decorated with a double row of silver buttons, was smeared all over with pale ash, as were his trousers. A pair of crossed sabers peeked from beneath the carbide lamp strapped to his hat with a leather thong. Cord recognized Lieutenant John Stafford, gray eyes hard in his leathery face.

Stafford drew his sidearm, a .45 caliber Colt. "United States Army, Mr. Sutton."

Here was the rescue Cord had hoped for, a way out of dying underground without seeing the sun again. But where was his elation, as he lowered his own weapon and bent to put it on the rock floor?

The officer continued, "You're under arrest for the attempted murders of Hank Falls and Edgar Young."

"As well as shooting Danny Falls." With a sinking heart, Cord recognized Captain Feddors peering in through the hole, the morning sky above. He had his Krag aimed at Cord's heart.

"I shot a wanted killer . . . in self-defense," Cord spoke before Laura could, to protect her.

"Is Danny . . . ?" she began.

"He wasn't talking when we found him," Stafford offered. "Groesbeck and the others took him to the fort hospital in Mammoth."

"Danny confessed to hurting Edgar," she declared. "He tied us to trees and was threatening us."

Stafford kept his pistol ready. "How did you escape?"

Cord's hand started toward his pocket and stopped. "I found something on the ground and used it to cut the rope around my wrists." He lifted his face toward the daylight and Feddors. "A shard of obsidian."

He could have sworn the captain shrank back, as though a man with two guns trained on him might yet manage to work some kind of magic.

But he recovered quickly. "I congratulate you, Lieutenant Stafford, on triangulating yesterday's gunshots and discovering the cave." He glanced at the ashes of their fire. "Looks like they were sending up smoke signals."

When they roped Cord up into the light, he looked away down the mountain. As far as he could see, green forest had given way to a landscape devoid of color. A layer of white ash covered the ground, and smoke curled up into the cloudy gray sky. The blackened skeletons of burned trees still stood. They might remain upright for another forty years, until the restless wind brought them down. Fire still ate at the hearts of the largest lodgepoles, crimson embers glowing within the charred exterior. To the southeast, small flames worked the slope, orange tongues licking their way through the undergrowth in the still air of morning.

With a glance at Feddors, Stafford bent and lifted Laura to his saddle.

"What do you think you're doin'?" Feddors protested.

"As a Southern gentleman, sir," Stafford's voice was bland, "I know you'd never considering making Miss Fielding walk under such conditions." He gathered the reins, his elbows on either side of Laura.

Perhaps because the lieutenant had put him in the position of being a boor, Feddors turned away with a look of studied nonchalance.

Something in the set of his shoulders said Stafford had better watch his back.

By dusk, they had long since left the scorched earth behind, come out of the mountains, and made their way down the Lamar River Valley. Cord had never been here, but knew where he was from studying maps.

Though there was a stage station at Soda Butte, Feddors did not stop. Cord was glad Laura was riding, for the marshy bottoms along the river made for difficult walking.

Finally, near dark, they came upon a camp of about twenty soldiers. Feddors took charge, ordering that his and Stafford's horses be fed and watered. Cord studied the remuda of mounts with the troop, but neither Dante nor White Bird was among them. There was no sign of Danny Falls's palomino, either.

The smell of biscuits, beans, and coffee made his stomach cramp. He swallowed around the dry spot in the back of his throat. Another step and his ankle turned in the soft earth of a burrow.

He went down and lay, hearing the pleasant sound of running water. In his mind's eye, he immersed himself fully in the cold river, drinking deeply and soothing his parched tongue.

Though there were at least ten tents pitched, Cord was left outside on a rough wool army blanket. His handcuffs prevented him from swatting the bloodsucking mosquitoes swarming up from the boggy bottom. He recalled Sergeant Nevers's description of the forced march a poacher had endured along with a horsewhipping . . . he hoped to get off that lightly.

Feddors could make a powerful circumstantial case, citing the fight with Hank in the case of arson, and suggesting Cord became enraged with Edgar when the hotel deal fell through. The added spice of his being Nez Perce, and proud of it, would no doubt prejudice the circuit judge further.

Wait.

In Yellowstone, the Army was the law. And Feddors, at present, was the commanding officer. There was no requirement that Cord have a lawyer or judge. Like the common poacher, he could be dealt with under military justice. And when he'd arrived at the soldier station to have his weapons sealed, Feddors had practically accused him of poaching the game he and Laura had found at Lewis Canyon, as well as the bear.

Wide-awake beneath the open sky, he despaired of finding a comfortable position while he tried to ignore the quiet voices of two sentries who'd given up walking the perimeter for playing cards.

With an ache in his chest, Cord wondered which tent Laura was in. He'd seen her earlier, sitting on a camp stool bathing her feet in a pan of water, and then wrapping them in linen strips from the camp first-aid box. Lieutenant Stafford stood observing, so Cord assumed it was on his orders.

God, how he wanted to be free, to walk with her in the peaceful silence of evening, with her hand tucked beneath his arm. He'd point out where forests turned to stone passed the eons, up on the long shoulder of Specimen Ridge.

If . . . when . . . he got these charges dropped and was free to come back to the park, he'd take her to see a whole cliff of obsidian that stood sentinel over a shallow lake. Jim Bridger, one of the early trappers and explorers of Yellowstone, had written in the 1840s of shooting mistakenly at the reflection of an elk in the mirrored volcanic glass. It had been hyperbole, but effective.

The camp grew quiet; the sentries put away their cards. Only the Lamar made a rushing sound. Cord located his old friend, the Big Dipper, pointing perpetually at the North Star. Beyond the horizon, a silver glow signified that the moon was about to rise.

The stillness was broken, a coyote sounding staccato barks, followed by a single mournful howl. Another answered.

Cord imagined the band roaming free in the night, up on Amethyst Mountain. From where he lay, the peak was a black shadow hunkered down at the rim of the world.

CHAPTER THIRTY-ONE
JULY 3

The soldiers from the Lamar camp climbed the last steep switchback out of Gardner Canyon, a few miles the northern boundary of Yellowstone. Laura looked over her shoulder for Cord, but all she could see was the broad, blue-coated shoulder of Captain Feddors where he rode behind her.

This morning, when Stafford had offered his hand to help her ride with him, Feddors had instead taken her up into his saddle. His fetid breath sickened her.

Or perhaps she was already sick with the agony of the third day of Cord's ordeal, being forced to walk in handcuffs the forty-some miles from Nez Perce Peak to Headquarters. She felt certain that if Lieutenant Stafford had not taken her part, Feddors would have ordered her to walk, as well.

Thank God, they were almost to Mammoth. She looked ahead at the late-afternoon sun illuminating Mount Everts on the opposite side of the steep-walled river gorge. Flat-topped, the long mountain had broad gray bands of rock running along its side, layered with green grassy slopes.

They topped the rise and Fort Yellowstone lay before them, neat rows of buildings painted uniform beige and covered with red tin roofs. Laura saw a pair of long stables, across the road from two other T-shaped windowed buildings she supposed were barracks. In front of those, facing the parade ground, were four two-story duplexes that she suspected housed the officers.

A quarter mile away, on the west side of the valley, the terraces of Mammoth Hot Springs shone white in the shadow of the mountain. Streaks of orange and rust algae marked the pale stone.

Below the terraced hillside and directly across from the parade ground stood the five-story National Hotel, built of dark wood with a shingled roof. On the verandah, Laura saw rows of rocking chairs filled with people whiling away the last of the day.

Feddors turned his horse onto the Fort Yellowstone parade ground, and Stafford followed.

A troop of mounted cavalry drilled, hooves thudding on the packed earth. The horses had been brushed until they looked burnished, and the soldiers' polished black boots and crossed swords on their forage caps reflected the glow of the setting sun. Women stood with their children in front of Officers' Row, watching the spectacle and waiting for the men to be freed for the evening.

The laughter and applause suddenly stilled, and a murmur rose at the sight of their commanding officers' filthy uniforms, the tattered remains of Laura's dress, and Cord, soot-blackened, in handcuffs.

A cannon boomed from atop the rounded contours of Capitol Hill overlooking the fort, while the clarion call of "Taps" sounded. Captain Feddors rose in his stirrups to salute the lowering of the colors.

Once the last notes faded, he dismounted. Laura slid off before he could help her.

He gestured at Cord, who looked as though at any moment he would fall down. "Take this man to the stockade."

Laura's gut churned.

"The woman, as well."

Lieutenant Stafford intervened once more. "I'll take her to my home. Katharine will see to her."

Feddors bristled. "She's an accessory to Sutton's crimes . . ."

"There's no evidence of that . . ."

Laura cut off Stafford's mild reply. "There's no evidence against Cord, either."

And nothing in his favor, unless Danny Falls lived and was willing to tell the truth.

The home of Lieutenant John Stafford and his wife was one of the big tin-roofed duplexes facing the parade ground.

Katharine Stafford, a rotund woman who smelled of baking bread, had a dusting of flour on the front of her black serge skirt. Kind blue eyes took in Laura's ruined dress, her scratches and insect bites, and the dirty rags on her feet. Though Lieutenant Stafford had seen to it her feet were bathed and bandaged the night before last, there had been no other chance to clean up.

Laura was grateful the dutiful officer's wife asked no questions except whether she would prefer to eat or bathe first. Her skin crawled, and she felt even worse than the evening she'd washed in the hot pool at Witch Creek. Moreover, she felt sure she'd not be able to get a mouthful past the lump in her throat.

While Katharine boiled water and prepared a tub in a front bedroom, Laura looked out the window between sheer lace curtains. The pale monument of Mammoth Hot Springs stood out against the gathering night. Smoke rose lazily from a fumarole in the middle of the parade ground. Tourists wandered from the springs down to the hotel.

Katharine drew the rolled shade over the window. "You have soap," she itemized, passing chore-reddened hands over a transparent glycerine bar that smelled of roses, "and a towel."

A thick, but rough-looking cloth lay folded on a stool beside the tin tub of steaming water. An oil lamp sat beside it with a box of matches, mute testimony to the fact that Fort Yellowstone did not have electricity.

"Mercy me," Katharine mused. She ignored

Laura's inability to hold up her end of the conversation. "What am I going to get you to wear? You'd go swimming in my clothes."

She snapped her fingers. "There's a little ole gal, just about your size, who got here this afternoon. She's staying next door in the vacant superintendent's house with her brother."

When the door finally closed, Laura stripped off her filthy rags and lowered herself gingerly into the hot water.

Her injured arm throbbed. Her flayed feet and the torn palms of her hands stung when the soap touched them. The burns on the back of her calves felt hot, and the red welts of insect bites itched wildly.

As she began to soap herself, surrounded by the delicate aroma of roses, a wave of anger rolled over her. It wasn't fair that she enjoy this luxury while Cord was imprisoned.

Too late, she wished they'd made love in the cavern, but at the time, it had been impossible. Neither she nor Cord had been able to do more than mourn the life they'd imagined together.

Since their capture, Cord hadn't asked her to do anything to help him, probably fearing Feddors would thwart whatever he asked. But she believed he would want her to contact his father in Salt Lake City.

Before she could rise from the tub, a knock sounded on the door.

Streaming water onto the rag rug covering the plank floor, Laura reached for her towel. Wrapping herself hastily, she went to the door. Surely Captain Feddors would have more couth than to interrupt her while she was bathing.

"Who is it?" she asked carefully.

A female voice answered, sounding younger and more delicate than Katharine Stafford. "You needed something to wear?"

Laura opened the door a scant inch and peered through.

Alexandra Falls, her golden hair perfectly coiffed, stepped up to the doorway. She wore a white voile dress embroidered with tiny violets and carried the deep purple dress Laura had seen her wear at the Lake Hotel.

Clutching her towel with one hand, Laura swung the door wider.

Alexandra studied Laura with violet eyes. "They phoned the Lake Soldier Station yesterday that they had found Danny . . . Hank and I came at once."

"He's not . . ."

"Alive . . . barely."

Though Laura had wanted Danny to live because of Cord, she hadn't realized how relieved she'd be to learn she hadn't killed a man.

Alexandra walked in and dumped her dress over the arm of a mohair divan decorated with lace doilies. "I came for Danny, but . . . I believe Hank came after you."

Laura's heart sank. He was probably already in Captain Feddors's office asking him to string Cord up.

"He knows about you and Cord, but once he's out

of the way, Hank's sure you'll get over it."

The twilight filtering through the white window shade had a sudden nightmarish quality. Hank wanted Cord dead and he thought she would "get over it"?

Alexandra turned her head and a small pendant swung free of the neckline of her dress. Hanging from a braided gold chain, a woman's sharp white profile was drawn finely against black onyx.

Laura almost gasped aloud. Yet, why should she be surprised? Danny Falls would have given Violet Fielding's cameo to the little sister he loved.

Like Cord with his obsidian, like the cameo had been to Laura before she lost it, Alexandra clearly viewed it as a charm that might save her favorite brother.

Though she wanted to rip it off her neck, Laura decided to bide her time.

Shutting Alexandra out of her room at the Stafford's, Laura lit the lamp and dressed in haste.

As she'd hoped, when she came out of the bedroom, lamp in hand, Alexandra was nowhere in sight. Thankfully, in front of the door sat a bottle of witch hazel to clean her wounded feet and hands, Epsom salts and a foot pan for soaking, and fresh linen for bandages. Beside the first-aid supplies sat a well-worn pair of black felt slippers that looked too wide but would work with her feet wrapped.

When she once more left the bedroom, muted

voices came from the kitchen, along with the aroma of meat, onions, and a warm smell of baking potatoes. The light from that room was stronger.

Though Aunt Fanny had taught Laura a lady did not eavesdrop—what had she and Constance been doing in the Lake Hotel lobby?—Laura set the lamp on a walnut drop-leaf table and moved closer.

"We brought in a man accused of arson and attempted murder." John Stafford's voice was low and controlled. "You wouldn't notice, but apparently he's of Nez Perce blood and Feddors has dredged up . . ." He paused. "Feddors shot at him to stop him getting away."

"If he were fleeing . . . ?" Katharine's tone suggested he must be guilty. "The woman?"

Laura waited for her to want her out of the house.

After a moment of silence, broken by the sizzling of meat in a skillet, she heard Katharine. "She cares for him?"

"From what I've seen, yes."

Laura stepped closer. In the light of a kerosene chandelier, Stafford took down a blue-and-white enameled cup from a shelf beside the polished black woodstove. He poured coffee from a matching pot set toward the stove's rear.

"You said he was accused . . ." Katharine dumped the beefsteak onto a white china platter.

"Feddors thinks he's guilty."

"You don't."

Laura moved into the doorway. "Cord's not guilty,

Lieutenant," she declared, looking up into Stafford's intent gray eyes.

"Call me John." He pulled down another cup and filled it for her.

She took the coffee. "I told you Danny bragged about trying to kill Edgar Young."

"But why?" John stirred in sugar from a china bowl decorated with pink roses. "He and Edgar were meeting together in the old cabin as though they had a common interest."

"They did. Having Cord buy the hotel out from under Hank was one more skirmish in the war between brothers." She held the hot cup by the handle and blew on the liquid. "Only when Cord turned out to be 'unqualified,' it backfired. Danny went into a rage at Edgar's apparent incompetence."

"Time for supper." Katharine brought plates to the table along with a loaf of fresh-baked bread. John snagged the meat platter, while she opened the stove door and pulled ashy baked potatoes from the coals. He brought over knives and forks, and pulled cloth napkins from a drawer. Last, he got down a syrup pitcher, decorated with the roses that must be Katharine's favorite, and filled it from a five-gallon wooden keg.

Laura watched their well-rehearsed routine and imagined her and Cord preparing dinner.

The three of them sat. John and Katharine bowed their heads while he said a rough but heartfelt prayer. Laura hadn't prayed in a long time, but she sent up a silent entreaty for Cord.

When the plates were passed and filled, she finally realized how hungry she was. After nearly three days without food, and only picking at camp beans last night and this morning, the succulent aromas invited her to attack the simple yet tasty fare.

"More bread?" John asked, after a silent interval of everyone putting laden forks to their mouths.

Laura swallowed a bite of the rich and yeasty loaf, soaked in syrup. "Do you suppose that Cord . . . ?"

"I'm sure Feddors would love to starve him," John said, "but prisoners always get an ample, if simple meal. If you like, I'll stop by and make sure."

"Lieutenant . . ." Laura began carefully, ". . . John. It's been my impression that many of the men don't care for Captain Feddors."

His sun-roughened face took on a neutral expression. "A lot of soldiers despise their officers."

"Cord Sutton is a gentleman, and he owns a fine hotel in Salt Lake City." Her words tumbled out. "Won't you please help him?"

The gray of his eyes changed to that of a winter sky. "I may deplore Feddors's attitudes, but I must uphold the law. Mr. Sutton will face his accusers in a proper hearing."

Defeated on another front, she rose and took her plate to the drain board. "In addition to the rest of your hospitality, could I borrow a little money for Western Union? I need to send a telegram to Cord's family in Salt Lake City."

"Go over to the hotel," John suggested. "If you try

to do it from the superintendent's office, I'm sure Fed-dors will make sure something happens to divert it."

The summer evening was cooling as Laura made her way across to the National Hotel. Stars already spangled night's canopy, and she found it amazing to be in a place without electricity in 1900. Muted illumination barely spilled from the upstairs rooms. The porch lamps were gas, as were the lobby chandeliers, their glow soft and golden.

Inside the lobby decorated with red, white, and blue bunting for the Fourth of July, Laura went to the desk. "Telegraph," she requested.

The receptionist pointed to a closed door next to the dining room. Though Laura went and tried the brass knob, it did not turn. She knocked impatiently, garnering curious glances from guests.

Finally, the door swung open slowly. Laura felt sure that the young man wearing a rumpled shirt and suspenders had been asleep at his post. His curly red hair was ruffed up on one side, and his freckled cheek bore a crease from where he must have been lying on the desk.

Laura pushed into the wardrobe-sized office. An enormous rolltop desk dominated the room. "I need to send a telegram to Salt Lake City." She reached for the message pad and bent over the desk to write.

Aaron Bryce
Salt Lake City, Utah
Army in Yellowstone has taken your son Cord into custody. He is falsely accused of attempted murder. Send telegram immediately Washington or wherever commander above this garrison resides. Most desperate urgency. Laura Fielding.

"I can't send this," the young man protested.

Laura looked at him in disbelief. Was everyone in town a pawn of Captain Feddors? "What's wrong with it?"

"Salt Lake is a big place. Without an address, there's no way this could be delivered."

"Aaron Bryce is a wealthy man. The people at the telegraph office will know who he is," Laura said with a confidence she did not feel.

"I'm sorry, miss." He looked nervous, as he had obviously read the message.

"Look," she said reasonably. "What do you care if I waste my money? Go ahead and send it."

Taking the paper, he bent dutifully over the key and tapped out her message. She watched restlessly, willing the wires to sing with her words. Surely, the Aaron Bryce who'd taken an orphaned child to his heart would be able to help him.

She realized the operator was speaking. "You're Laura Fielding, then?"

"Yes."

"There's a telegram came about an hour ago," he said, "addressed to you at the hotel. You weren't registered . . ." He shrugged.

Reaching into the cubbyhole labeled with the letter *F* above the desk, the operator handed over a thin envelope.

She took it carefully, as if it would burn her. She'd never seen a telegram that brought good news.

Deciding to read it in private, she turned slowly and walked out, passing between the barroom and the hotel office with its wide bay window fronting the porch.

Taking a deep and measured breath, she slit open the telegram.

By gaslight, she read: *Arriving Mammoth tomorrow's morning stage stop Leaving Lake at dawn stop Your father Constance Norman Hagen stop You will take afternoon train from Cinnabar to Chicago with us stop Army says you are well and that Cord is in custody stop Thank God Constance saw through him as she will marry Norman Hagen stop.*

Your loving aunt Fanny.

Slowly, Laura stepped off the porch. She headed across to the darkened parade ground, clutching the wrinkled paper. The message might as well have come from Venus. With everything overturned in Laura's life and now Constance's, Fanny persisted in her straight-laced ways. She and her brother, Forrest, would clearly always be well suited to one another.

Putting this reminder of the world she used to inhabit aside, Laura looked over at Fort Yellowstone. The windows of the big houses on Officers' Row glowed with lamplight. Farther down, the stockade made a darker shadow beyond the Headquarters building.

Imagining Cord behind barred windows, lying on a hard cot, if, indeed, he had a bed, brought fresh tears to her eyes. Having sent the telegram into the void, there must be something more she could do.

She would go to the stockade if she thought there was any chance of Feddors letting her see Cord. Failing that, she hurried off the edge of the cleared area where the cavalry drilled. Her sore feet protesting, sage and scrub grabbing at her ankles, she crossed the road and approached the fort's hospital, lying in a field beyond the neat layout of the rest of the fort.

CHAPTER THIRTY-TWO

JULY 4

Larry Nevers was alone at Edgar Young's bedside in the Lake Infirmary when the injured man died. If he'd known time was so short, he'd have wakened Dr. Upshur, who had bedded down around midnight in a room at the rear.

Near the end, Edgar's eyelids had fluttered and he twisted in bed, grasping at the covers. "Uhhh."

Larry had moved closer. "Yes, Edgar?"

"Daaaa . . ."

"What's that? Danny? Are you talking about Danny Falls?" Hour by hour, hoping Cord Sutton wasn't guilty, Larry had waited for this. "Did Danny stab you?"

Edgar appeared to panic. He managed another gasp. On the exhale, he seemed to grow smaller.

His chest did not rise again.

Larry shouted, "Dr. Upshur!" as the light of life in Edgar's eyes burned out.

His military boots clomping on the wood floors, Larry rushed into the hall.

How silly to run for a doctor when the patient no longer needed his skills. In fact, there were no patients left since Forrest Fielding had been moved to the Absaroka Suite, in preparation for what would no doubt be a difficult journey home.

Once the doctor was alerted, Larry was out the door. From the soldier station, he phoned the superintendent's office at Fort Yellowstone.

It took five rings. "Captain Feddors."

Larry had expected a private on night duty. "Sir, Sergeant Nevers at Lake. Edgar Young has died."

"Did he say what happened to him?"

"No sir."

Feddors did not exactly chuckle, but made a noise that sounded over the humming wire as though attempted murder turned to the real thing gave him pleasure.

As soon as he hung up, Larry called Norris and asked them to have a fresh horse waiting when he got there. Then he hurried to the stable.

Danny Falls lay on a narrow metal cot in the Fort Yellowstone hospital.

Laura pressed her palms against the rough plaster wall, holding herself up as she had been for hours. Alexandra occupied the only chair in the room, while

Hank paced, pausing now and then to press his sister's shoulder.

After refusing Alexandra's shrill request to leave and mind his own business, Manfred Resnick had cited his position with Pinkerton, as well as Danny's near-certain guilt in the matter of the stagecoach attack, and stayed. He leaned against the wall, hands in his suit pockets, his one eye bearing its usual quiet watchfulness.

Dr. Liam O'Malley, a grizzled man with white hair and ruddy cheeks covered with spider veins, shook his head. He held a flaring lamp to examine the darkened edges of Danny's wound.

"Thirty-seven years ago I marched off to Georgia, sewing the guts back inside men after Sherman spilled 'em," O'Malley mourned. "When will we stop finding ways of killing each other?"

He looked over his shoulder toward the ceiling. "Live or die, it's up to the Lord, as I've done all I can."

Laura looked from Hank to Danny, thinking how uncannily alike they looked in one heartbeat and how different in the next. Hair of exactly the same shade lay damp and stringy over Danny's brow, where he sweated with pain. Hank's hair had been slicked back with his inevitable pomade. Both men had the same rapier-thin bodies.

Alexandra went to Danny, pressing her fingers to the pinkish froth at his lips as though she could push his blood back inside. He heaved beneath her touch and worked his mouth.

"Don't talk," she whispered.

Laura looked to Hank. Much as he'd denied his brother, his eyes were tear bright, as well.

"Tired," Danny told Alexandra. He looked to Laura. "Tell what I done."

"No!" Alexandra said. "I don't want to hear any of her lies."

Laura pushed off the wall. Reaching to the lavender neckline of Alexandra's dress, she jerked forth the cameo. The delicate chain snapped, but she had her prized possession back in hand. "This belonged to my mother," she declared. "I saw Danny rooting through my things at the stage. He took it and gave it to you."

"That's impossible," Alexandra continued her denial.

Manfred Resnick came to Laura. "You sure this is the same piece?"

She let him take it. "Look on the back. It says, 'To Violet, upon the birth of our daughter Laura— Forrest.'"

The Pinkerton man examined the jewelry. "Sure does say that." He looked at Alexandra. "If Danny gave it to you, you must surely have known he didn't come by it honestly."

"I thought it was an estate piece he'd bought for me." Alexandra's voice trembled.

Hank stared at his sister. "When are you going to face the truth about your precious brother?"

She was looking at Danny.

The door opened to admit Captain Feddors. "Edgar Young has died," he announced.

"I . . ." Danny nodded again at Laura.

"Danny killed him. I told you that."

Feddors reddened. "That true?" he asked gruffly.

"Ye . . . yes," Danny got out.

Alexandra's violet eyes went wide.

Hank's face flushed. "I was sure Cord tried to kill me." His eyes sought his brother's. "Who burned the steamboat?"

"You said you would kill Danny if you saw me with him," Alexandra wailed.

Danny looked at her.

"I asked," Hank gritted angrily, "who burned the *Alexandra*?"

Danny began to choke. Blood bubbled from the corner of his mouth.

For a moment, he seemed to be having some kind of seizure, his eyes rolling up.

Feddors shouted, "Doctor!"

O'Malley appeared so quickly it was evident he'd been waiting just beyond the doorway. He moved swiftly to the bedside and placed his fingers onto the side of Danny's neck.

After a long moment, the doctor shook his head.

Laura couldn't breathe. She'd killed him, sent the bullet that lodged in his lung and drowned him in his own blood. She had to keep telling herself he'd been ready to murder her and Cord. Had murdered Angus Spiner.

Dr. O'Malley moved back and glanced at Alexandra. She had her face covered, her shoulders shaking.

Hank stepped forward, gathered his brother's pale

and slender hands, and crossed them on his chest. With care, he pulled up the sheet, covering the blood and Danny's gaunt white face.

"Captain Feddors, you must let Cord go," Laura demanded, following the bantam officer from the hospital. Hank accompanied them, while Alexandra remained beside Danny's body with Manfred Resnick.

Feddors kept walking without answering. In the deep silence of two a.m., not even insects seemed to be awake. The only movement in the fort was a faint wisp of steam rising from a fumarole, picked out by moonlight on the parade ground across the road. The windows of the houses on Officers' Row were dark.

When Hank continued to tag along, Feddors turned and looked at him. "You, I can't figure," he said. "If I let Sutton go, you don't get the girl."

Hank reddened from the tips of his ears, the flush spreading across his face.

Fearing he would leave, Laura put a hand on Hank's arm. "Don't let him rile you. You may despise Cord, but you must tell Feddors that Danny burned your boat. Alexandra told him you'd threatened to kill him, and that's a far more powerful motive than Cord ever had."

Hank looked down wearily at her hand on the sleeve of his ill-fitting white shirt. Even in near darkness, his narrow face appeared to bear the brunt of the

long vigil and his brother's death. "I may have said I
wanted him to stay away from Alexandra, but . . ."

How typical of him to dissemble in front of the
law. How like his brother.

Though it would have been satisfying to break out
into renewed accusations against him for attacking her
on his boat, she needed him on her side. "Alexandra
may have been exaggerating," Laura allowed. "But in
there . . ." she nodded back toward where Danny lay,
"you seemed to doubt Cord did it."

She twisted the lavender handkerchief she'd found
in the pocket of Alexandra's purple dress, then realized she was knotting the chain of the cameo she'd
also stashed in there.

Feddors picked up his pace as though finished listening.

Laura hurried after him to the red-roofed frame
building of the stockade, with its barred windows. He
opened the front door to a small spare room with a
desk, wooden chairs, and a potbellied woodstove. A
sleepy-looking enlisted man sitting guard gathered
himself to his feet, tucking in his rumpled shirt.

Feddors regarded him with disgust. "Soldier, you
are out of uniform."

The young man grabbed his cap from a nail and
put it on.

"Ah get so tired of lack of discipline . . ." Feddors
went on.

"Captain!" Laura said from the door. "I have not
finished speaking with you."

With an angry glance at her, Feddors told the soldier, "Wait outside."

Fearful of being alone with Feddors, Laura glanced behind her and was actually relieved to find Hank still with them. Perhaps Alexandra was right that in his warped way, Hank was still after her. For, with the same insinuating manner he'd showed in formal dining at the hotel, he put his hand at the small of her back and escorted her to one of the straight chairs.

"You know, Captain," Hank said evenly, "I owe Laura here an apology."

"How's that?" Feddors asked.

"I may have been a bit . . . enthusiastic when she came aboard the *Alexandra* for supper. I'm sorry if she misconstrued . . ."

"Sorry that *I* misconstrued is not what I'd call an apology." Laura's cheeks heated. "Feddors should find a place for you in his stockade for what you did to me . . ."

Hank's back straightened, and she knew she'd lost whatever advantage she might have had with him.

The captain pulled open a drawer at the bottom of his desk. "Damned women," he cursed, bringing up a small silver flask. "Driving me to drink in the middle of the night."

Hank pulled out his pack of Old Virginia Cheroots and offered it to Feddors, who took one. Hank lit his own, elegant hands moving deliberately, and reached over to give Feddors a light.

Continuing their exaggerated little ballet, Feddors passed Hank the flask; he drank.

"So what's your verdict, Hank?" Feddors retrieved his liquor and tipped it up. "Your brother burn the boat or that Injun I've got locked up?"

"Danny never admitted it."

"He died in the middle of being asked!" Laura leaned forward. "You saw Danny confess to murdering Edgar. I watched him kill the stage driver in cold blood, so we know what kind of criminal we're dealing with." She turned to Hank. "He not only came to Yellowstone with Edgar and a plan to thwart your dreams . . . the stagecoach attack was aimed at killing me . . . so Father wouldn't want to invest in the West where his daughter died."

"You expect me to believe Danny told you all that?"

"Edgar told Cord about their plot to discredit you. And yes, Danny said his partner found out I'd be on that coach and intended to kill me. Just ask Cord."

Feddors slapped his palm on the desk and Laura jumped. He looked at Hank. "She and Sutton had days in the wilderness to perfect their story. Of course, they'd both say the same thing."

Hank shook his head. "Even if Danny decided to murder me, he'd never have risked it with Alex aboard. She was the only person he ever cared about." He looked pained, for weren't identical twins supposed have the ultimate bond? "All this talk of the boat is moot. Your lover killed my brother."

She took a breath. "I shot Danny."

Feddors burst out laughing.

Hank gaped. "You?"

"He was drinking. And left the little gun he stole from my valise at the stagecoach within reach of where he tied me," Laura argued. "You've got to let Cord go. It makes no sense to hold him without evidence."

"Hank," Feddors said, "you ever heah such nonsense?"

Laura's desperation grew. She turned on Hank. "You're just doing this because you hate Cord for knocking you out of consideration for the hotel, because he fought you . . ." she ticked her fingers, "and because you have some cockamamie idea that if Cord is out of the way, you do 'get the girl.'"

Hank inhaled smoke.

"And you . . ." Laura turned on Feddors. "You don't know anything about Cord except that he's Nez Perce. Why do you hate the Nez Perce so?"

"You want to know why I hate those murdering savages?" Feddors drank again. "Ah'll tell you."

On the other side of a cell door, Cord lay looking at the barred sky through a window and listening. Though he'd known Laura was tough, having weathered two harrowing treks through wild country with him, he'd not realized how fiercely she'd fight for him.

It drove him crazy to be pinned up, so close to her and yet behind that invisible barrier between his father's world and his mother's. Feddors believed in his heart that Cord was a "murdering savage," and he was telling Laura and Hank why.

For over an hour, Cord listened to Feddors plow the ground he'd gone over beside Yellowstone Lake while he held a pistol on Bitter Waters. The tale of how an innocent lad was frightened beside a waterfall by a pair of Nez Perce braves riding bareback, wearing the spoils of war and carrying Army Springfields, of how he rode to Mammoth to sound an alarm and found Lieutenant Hugh Scott securing the site of the murder of musician Richard Dietrich.

But there had to be a better reason for Feddors's hate, unless he was truly a madman.

Cautioned by Lieutenant Scott to be careful, Quenton rode down Gardner Canyon toward Bart Henderson's, where he and his father were staying. Fast water rushed over his calves when the mare reluctantly swam the river. On either side of the stream, towering cliffs of buff volcanic rock rose. The shelf of loose talus narrowed, the rock wall rising nearly straight out of the riverbed, and Quenton was forced to ford again.

Ahead, the valley opened onto the broad plain where the Gardner joined the course of the Yellowstone. The small rough outpost of Gardiner sat at the juncture of the two rivers. Riding down the dusty street, Quenton thought the cluster of log stores and saloons looked deserted.

"Best get inside, boy," a voice called from behind a

wooden shutter. A rifle barrel protruded from a narrow slit. "Injuns about."

Quenton urged his mare into a gallop out of town toward the northwest. He rode along the flat grassland beside the incised valley that marked the Yellowstone until he found the cutoff where Stephens Creek joined the larger river. He turned his mount to follow the slower-moving waters. Clear and shallow, the stream meandered through open land toward the wooded slopes bounding the valley.

Quenton's heart pounded as he recognized the rough cairn of stones that marked the corner of Henderson's land. Here along the watercourse, towering cottonwoods grew close to the edge. He rounded a bend and stopped.

Curling tendrils of smoke rose from the ruined hulk of the ranch house. Though Quenton cupped his hands and shouted, the sound seemed to flatten and be swallowed up by the waving golden grasses.

The only answer was the cry of a hawk.

Dismounting, he moved quietly through a copse of trees toward a saddled but riderless horse cropping grass beside a leaning outhouse.

If the Nez Perce were about, he would probably end up like Dietrich. The .25-20 he carried wouldn't be a match for the Army Springfields he'd seen in their hands.

At twenty-five yards, Quenton became certain the lone horse was Nellie, the chestnut his father had been riding for the past few days.

A creaking sound came from the wooden out-house beneath a lone cottonwood. The wind moved the door on its tired hinges. Dry mouthed, Quenton approached and saw something on the ground, keeping the door from closing.

He crept closer, clutching his rifle in trembling hands. A man sprawled facedown where he had fallen from the seat. His trousers bunched around his ankles, the white of his buttocks contrasting with the crimson stain that covered the back of his blue cotton shirt. Quenton would have known the black hat with silver braid anywhere.

"The Nez Perce shot my father!" Feddors shouted. "Killed him in the goddamned crapper! While I was standing there over his body, they swept back through the field and took Nellie away with them."

Though Laura had a lump in her throat at the end of Feddors's reminiscence, she couldn't let that matter. "They could have killed you, then, but they didn't."

Feddors shook his head.

She kept trying. "The Nez Perce, what's left of them, have never been able to go back to their homes in Wallowa Valley. They were treated shamefully, and you should be satisfied that they've been punished. Killing Cord won't bring back Richard Dietrich . . . or your father."

Feddors looked to Hank. "She doesn't understand.

A Southern man never forgives . . . or forgets."

Laura bowed her head. A single tear escaped and ran down her cheek. "Just let me see Cord. That's all I ask."

Hank pushed back his chair with a rasp and unfolded his long frame. He walked out, his leather heels making sharp sounds on the wood floor.

Feddors pushed to his feet and came to Laura. "Let's go."

She started to move around the desk toward where the cells were, but he took her by the arm and turned her. Trying to pull away, she said, "I thought you were taking me to see Cord."

"I am merely escorting you out." He propelled her to the door. "I really cannot stand a woman's tears."

As she went out into the deepest part of night, Feddors addressed the soldier who stood at attention when he came out. "Private, I need for you to round up six men with their rifles. There's going to be a hearing this morning, and there may be a sentence to carry out."

CHAPTER THIRTY-THREE

JULY 4

Laura went up the stairs to the rear porch and let herself into the Staffords' kitchen. At three-thirty a.m., all was dark, but someone had left a candle and matches on the clean kitchen table. A little heat spilled into the chilly room, the banked coals waiting for morning.

She lit the candle and started down the hall toward the front bedroom where she'd bathed and dressed. Halfway there, she stopped before the door of a room that served as a combination parlor and office. The pigeonhole desk was open, paper and an inkwell in view, along with a cup of pens.

Being sure to move quietly, Laura went to the desk, took down writing materials, and began to journal what had happened since she and Cord left the Lake Hotel. Time passed without her noticing, and at half after four a faint light was coming through the lace curtains.

Another hour passed, and the morning light overpowered the candle. Laura blew it out and kept writing.

The sight that greeted us on the east side of the divide was astounding. Like the raging heart of a furnace, fire swept toward us through the tops of the trees, leaping from one to the next in the space of a single heartbeat. I know not how far we ran along the knife-edge to the north before we dropped down onto the steep slope. Trees exploded as though hit by cannon fire. Sound poured over us like nothing I have ever heard, a full-throated hollow roar that struck terror.

I wish I could say we were saved through action on our part, some clever sleuthing of cold cavern air, but we fell into our refuge without seeing it. In a dank lava tunnel with a cone of dirty snow unmelted from last season, smoke nearly suffocated us.

We lived, yet are guaranteed no more and no less than anyone who takes their hold on life for granted.

On the hillside below Mammoth Hot Springs was the fort cemetery. According to Dr. O'Malley, who had talked incessantly all the time he spent in Danny's room, Private Thomas Horton of the 22nd Infantry had been the first serviceman buried there in 1888. In the past twelve years, civilians had been added, including Isaac Rowe, who in 1899 had been struck by lightning on the jumbled rocky narrows of Golden Gate Pass above Mammoth.

Death, it seemed, lurked anywhere and everywhere.

Laura imagined the six soldiers Feddors had

rounded up, smoking cigarettes while their rifles were stacked against each other, awaiting orders to execute a prisoner. They wouldn't ask who Cord was or where he came from.

How would their wives or sweethearts feel if they were shot for no reason, their mothers, sisters, and friends bereft because a blind bigot abused his power?

What time will the hearing be? As it is already first light, I shall not go to bed. And as soon as reveille sounds, I will be sure John Stafford knows what happened. Surely, if he is present at the hearing, he can ensure that cooler heads prevail.

Constance had decided the West was too hard, but Laura bowed her head and thought that life . . . and death, in this wildly beautiful land, would be enough if she could be with Cord.

Behind the Staffords' house, inside Fort Yellowstone, shots rang out.

Lieutenant John Stafford came running down the stairs into the hallway of his house. Laura was on her feet, waiting for him. "During the night," she told him, "Captain Feddors called up some soldiers with rifles to stand by for Cord's hearing this morning."

She followed John to the kitchen window. He pulled aside the white lace curtain and looked out over the yard facing the main body of the fort.

A steady stream of enlisted men poured onto the

covered porch of the hundred-thirty-foot barracks, some still buttoning their uniform blouses. Normally no one came out in the morning before they were ready to pass inspection.

The wooden pendulum clock on top of the pie safe said it was five past six. "It lacks fifteen minutes until Boots and Saddles and another ten until Assembly at six-thirty," John said. "What can be going on?"

Katharine Stafford appeared in a chenille robe, her dark hair tumbling from a heavy coil. "From what you've said about Feddors," she glanced at Laura, "maybe he decided to skip the hearing."

"You two stay here." John reached for the belt hanging just inside the kitchen door and strapped on his Colt.

"Wake up, Sutton," a harsh voice grated.

Lying with his back to the door of the cell in the Fort Yellowstone stockade, Cord wasn't asleep. Not after hearing the dawn volley of shots echo over the fort.

He'd heard every word during the night, including Captain Feddors's order that a firing squad be called and that they sight in their weapons as soon as daylight permitted.

Carefully, he rolled over on the bunk and put his bare feet to the cold floor. Running a hand through the filthy dark stubble on his chin, he thought longingly of hot lather and a barber with a well-stropped razor.

"Get dressed!" The slender young man in the open doorway could not have been more than twenty, with brooding eyes that turned down at the outer corners.

Reaching for his socks and boots, the only items of clothing he'd taken off, Cord found his wounded hands shaking. He got to his feet, moving slowly for all his muscles ached, and went to urinate in the bucket in the corner. He'd used it before, and the odor was rising. He cast a longing eye at the water pitcher he'd emptied hours ago.

The soldier handcuffed him before taking him outside. The sun had not risen, but Cord looked gratefully at the dawn sky over the flat top of Mount Everts. The sparse grass growing on the rocky earth outside the stockade was heavy with dew.

"Guard!" the soldier barked.

Six men with 1892 Krags marched from behind the guardhouse. In unison, they snapped their weapons to their shoulders and fell in around Cord.

"Forwaaaaard march!"

The sharp accent on the last syllable made Cord jump as though someone had fired one of the weapons. He swallowed and tried to calm the pounding of his heart.

Reveille had not yet sounded. The neat red-roofed buildings of Officers' Row lay silent in the crisp morning air. They crossed between the canteen and the long barracks, the smoky smell of woodstoves, frying bacon, and baking biscuits wafting from the canteen's kitchen. Enlisted men milled on the barracks porch and in the yard, clearly roused by the early shooting.

Cord wondered if any of the armed soldiers had a wife waiting at home, with whom they could awaken every morning, the way he wanted to wake with the sweet warm weight of Laura beside him.

The rising sun caught him in the eyes, while the steady cadence moved them past the first of the stables. The ground before the long red-roofed building was ruined where the footsteps of men and horses' hooves allowed nothing to grow. Cord heard the soldiers' boots fall on hollow ground, as if the very bowels of hell lay beneath Yellowstone.

Where was this hearing he was supposed to have? He expected reasonable men like Lieutenant Stafford would be there, that he'd have a chance to tell his side of the story. Even during the long night in his cell, staring out through the bars at the slowing revolving stars, he'd held on to the fierce belief that his innocence could not fail to shield him.

Cord had always wondered how a condemned man managed to meet the hangman without dissolving into a shivering mass of what was once human. Looking at the youthful soldiers carrying their rifles, it did not occur to him to beg for a mercy that was not theirs to offer.

Sergeant Larry Nevers heard shots from the direction of Fort Yellowstone while his horse galloped the road down through The Hoodoos. The great jumbled blocks of limestone, fallen from an earlier, more massive series of hot-spring deposits overlooking Mammoth Valley, were a sign that he was only a short distance from his destination.

He'd ridden through the night, stopping only at Norris for the arranged fresh horse because something told him Cord Sutton needed help.

Hank Falls knocked on the door of Alexandra's room in the vacant house awaiting the arrival of the new Yellowstone superintendent. "Alex," he called.

After the terrible night, he'd lain down only an hour ago, but with the dawn he'd been disturbed by shooting somewhere behind the house. It forced him to admit he was wide awake, and he pushed his tall frame to a sitting position on the side of the bed. Studying the planes of his face in a shaving stand on the dresser, his mind flooded with images of his brother, a thin ascetic mirror Hank would never gaze into again.

"Alexandra!" Hank tried the knob.

It opened easily to reveal his sister, asleep with her golden hair spread over the pillow the way it had when she was a little girl. She looked so innocent when she slept.

Hank left her and turned toward the stairs. He went down, through the hall and kitchen, and out the rear onto the high back porch. Behind the identical duplex next door, Lieutenant Stafford's wife stood looking toward the barrack and stables.

"What's going on?" he called.

"That shooting," she said, her eyes concerned.

"Practice?" Hank suggested, but even as he spoke, he remembered that it was against the cavalry's regulations to target shoot in the park.

"Maybe it's something to do with the Fourth, but the celebration's not till later." She frowned. "The only crimes the garrison deals with are poaching and defacing the formations . . ."

And burning the *Alexandra*.

Hank took the wooden stairs down from the porch three at a time. He hurried behind the large double barracks, where soldiers had gathered between the fort shop and the stables.

Looking around, he spied Lieutenant Stafford entering the near stable, followed at about ten paces by Laura, wearing Alexandra's dress.

"John!" Laura called, as he went in the side door of the long building. "Wait."

He turned. "I told you to stay with Katharine."

"Did you think I would?" she challenged.

"I suppose not." Even in the gray light inside the stable, she saw that he might have been amused.

"What are you doing?" she asked.

"I got a look at what's happening. Cord's being

taken under armed guard to the place behind the stable where Feddors whipped the poacher. As there's been no hearing, I don't know if Feddors plans a trumped-up story of Cord attempting escape, or the like, and plans to whip him before holding a hearing . . . or if he's lost all concern for losing his commission and hopes to order an execution."

Laura swallowed. "Wouldn't he end up in prison?"

"If the evidence holds in Cord's favor."

"Cord would still be dead," Laura pointed out.

John turned and started walking up the aisle between stalls.

She started to follow and stopped. That enormous black head, bending over the gate to sniff at her . . .

"Dante!" She ran her hands over his face, and he nickered softly. "John, wait. This is Cord's horse." Stretching her neck over the next gate was White Bird.

He looked back. "We found him with the palomino and the gray near Danny Falls's camp. Arden Groesbeck and the others led them down when they brought Danny." He shifted his weight, seeming impatient.

"What are we doing in the stable?" she asked.

Sergeant Nevers galloped his lathered horse into the Fort Yellowstone yard and slid off, landing on the run. There was a crowd of men, and there was Cord Sutton being marched by a group of soldiers carrying rifles.

He saw Arden Groesbeck and hurried to him.

"Just got in . . ." he gasped for breath. "What's going on?"

Arden shook his head. "Not sure."

Larry spied Captain Feddors waiting in the space between the two long stables, in the spot where he'd tethered the poacher to whip him.

The armed squad swept Cord past the long stable. Ahead, he saw the beige wall at the end of the other stable coming toward him in slow motion. My God, did Feddors intend standing him against that wall and ordering him shot? He fought a wave of nausea by biting down hard, until the warm salt taste of blood swam in his mouth.

Looking at the forested peak of Sepulcher Mountain to the west, Cord longed for home in Jackson's Hole, to ride Dante again through the pungent sage. To watch the sun place its rosy finger upon the peak of the Grand Teton, spreading down until the mountain's full majesty was bathed in lemon morning light.

Close at hand, to his right, came a sudden deafening report.

The soldiers escorting Cord stopped and swiveled their heads, looking for the source of what had to be gunfire.

Kablam, again.

Cord's guards dissolved into a milling crowd,

pointing their weapons in different directions.

The third shot clearly came from inside the stable, along with shrill whinnies and thumping as horses reared and plunged. Cord watched in disbelief as a small door in the long wall of stable swung open. Not three feet away, a hand beckoned, a swift urgent movement.

His sense of inevitability shattered, Cord ducked through the cavalry's confusion and into the relative darkness of the stable. Behind him, someone slammed the stable door and rammed a wooden bar in place.

"Sutton!" A man unlocked Cord's handcuffs and slipped them off.

Cord flexed his wrists.

He recognized Lieutenant John Stafford, urging him toward a large horse standing calmly despite the pandemonium of the others.

Vaulting onto the animal bareback, Cord found instinct overcoming the slow way he felt his mind working. There must not have been time to saddle the horse, but he gathered the reins in his lacerated hands.

He looked to down to see Stafford holding a Cavalry Model .45. The officer glanced up at the light leaking through three bullet holes in the stable roof. "I'll see no one follows you. Get out of the park and meet me at sunset where the Gardner joins the Yellowstone."

At the far end of the stable, the big door opened to admit a rectangle of morning light. Beyond, he saw an expanse of packed earth that ended in scrub and some trees on the rim of the drop-off into Gardner Canyon.

Soldiers pounded on the door Cord had come through, the bar jiggling. He heard shouts from the other side.

"Go!" Stafford ordered. Finding his seat, Cord suddenly recognized the familiar shape of the horse beneath him.

"Go, boy," he echoed.

Dante sprang forward powerfully. Cord marveled his stallion's wounds had been superficial enough to permit his essential strength to prevail.

They surged toward the light at the end of the stable. A swelling feeling rose in Cord's chest as he recognized Laura holding the door.

Out into the stable yard, he steered Dante toward the lip of the drop into Gardner Canyon. He'd seen on the way up that it was a steep hill, treacherous going for a horse, but not by any means a cliff edge. Dante's hooves pounded the bare turf as he swept out from behind the stable and across the open ground of the fort.

A chorus of cries rose behind, men shouting.

Cord's heart hammered.

So close . . .

A bullet whined past his ear.

Larry Nevers watched in disbelief as Feddors fired a second shot from his Colt at Cord's retreating back.

Before Larry could move, Arden Groesbeck launched himself at the captain. Feddors must have detected it from the corner of his eye, for he side-stepped. Arden landed on his side in the dirt.

"The prisoner is getting away!" Feddors shouted.

Though several of the men with Krags hesitated, a few started to raise their weapons toward Cord and the black stallion.

Lieutenant Stafford stepped out through the stable door into which Cord Sutton had disappeared. "No one shoots anyone here."

Though the squad looked relieved, Feddors lifted his Colt again. "If nobody else will apprehend an escaping criminal . . ."

He fired again into the distance, but as far as Larry could tell, Sutton had escaped over the edge of the hill behind the fort.

At his feet, Arden Groesbeck fumbled out his weapon. Before Larry could stop himself, he gasped, "Arden, no."

Feddors stepped forward smartly, placing his boot on top of Arden's wrist. "You may not threaten your commanding officer." It seemed to happen in exacting slow motion, as the captain raised his Colt and pointed it at the helpless private's forehead.

In the same instant, Larry Nevers and John Stafford drew their sidearms.

CHAPTER THIRTY-FOUR

JULY 4

Hank cringed at the double tap that reverberated through the fort, especially after the other volleys.

He hurried behind the large double barracks where a crowd gathered between the south and north stable buildings. When he drew closer to the milling soldiers, some with their suspenders dangling, many without blouses, he realized discipline had broken down. Though it was twenty past six, no one was sounding Boots and Saddles, and none of the men appeared to be getting ready for the morning inspection and drill—very strange for the Fourth of July, when he would have expected an extra effort at ceremony.

Rather, the soldiers talked in excited tones, looking at something out of sight to Hank behind the end of the building.

"Trying to escape," he heard.

Hank shouldered his way into the group and rounded the corner. With a shudder, he saw an army blanket drawn over a man lying on the ground. The drab wool was soaked with blood.

"Who?" he managed.

No one answered, but he saw Sergeant Nevers of the Lake Station staring down at the body with a sick look on his face.

Hank approached and saw Lieutenant Stafford place his hand on Nevers's shoulder. "It's all right," he said in a fatherly tone. "I think you saw that there are two bullets in him, one of them mine."

"Had it coming," said Arden Groesbeck, also from Lake. "He'd have shot me, I swear, you shoulda seen the look in his eyes . . ."

Hank couldn't stand it. He stepped through the circle of men, knelt, and lifted the blanket with care to expose the dead man's face. Broad forehead, sparse brown hair, and goatee . . . someone had closed Captain Feddors's eyes.

To Hank's surprise, he felt relieved it wasn't Cord Sutton.

As soon as Laura realized Feddors was down, she ran across the hoof-beaten ground behind the paddock toward where Cord and Dante had disappeared from view. To get to the drop, she crashed through brush and small scrubby trees.

At the edge, she was rewarded with the sight of Cord on Dante. The horse was side-footing his way down the last of the rocky slope above the highway. As Laura watched, they reached the route and galloped out of sight down Gardner Canyon.

He was once more on the run, this time to freedom.

When she turned back toward the stable, her elation vanished. A man was dead.

A man who'd brought it on himself, but she felt the same sense of waste she had when she'd stood behind Cord and watched Frank Worth's hungry eyes go vacant.

Slowly, she walked back, skirting the crowd where she saw Hank talking with John Stafford and Larry Nevers. Thankfully, a blanket had been put over the man who'd allowed decades of hate to smolder inside him.

If she and Cord were fortunate enough to make a life together, would he be able to put this experience behind him?

Three hours later, Laura stood behind John Stafford's house with him, Larry, and Hank. Silently, they watched a group of soldiers led by Arden Groesbeck and observed by Manfred Resnick load Captain Quenton Feddors into a wagon for his last journey . . . to the Fort Yellowstone cemetery. A wooden casket had been put together hastily in the fort's shop, for the Fourth of July promised to be a scorcher and the body would soon become ripe.

"Doesn't he have any family?" Laura asked.

Manfred Resnick turned away from the wagon and joined them. "According to his service record, he's alone in the world. Maybe if he'd had someone, things would have turned out differently."

Hank made a noise in his throat. He'd had a brother, and what good had it done him?

Larry Nevers stepped up beside Laura and pressed something into her hand. "I looked around in the bushes near the Lake Hotel and found this."

She looked down at the familiar shape of the obsidian Cord had brought down from Nez Perce Peak as a child. "Thank you," she murmured, rubbing her thumb over its smooth contour and placing it into her pocket with the cameo.

"That the damned charm of Sutton's? The one Feddors threw away?" Hank asked. He turned on John. "What kind of officer are you? Shooting Feddors when you thought he was going to kill young Groesbeck is one thing, but what were you thinking to let a prisoner go free?"

It was all Laura could do not to hit Hank on his still-swollen nose.

John nodded to Alexandra Falls, who appeared on the rear steps of the superintendent's house. He spoke mildly, "Sutton is meeting me this evening . . ."

Hank made an impatient gesture. "Let me tell you about Santa Claus. Sutton won't stop running till he's in Salt Lake hiding behind Aaron Bryce."

"He'll meet John tonight," Laura said hotly. "I know he will."

John continued, "As I was saying, as acting superintendent, I can then address any outstanding questions."

Alexandra approached and slipped her arm through Hank's. Over her white dress with violet embroidery, she wore a cape of gray wool against the morning chill. "What questions?" she asked with wide-eyed innocence. "What are you talking about?"

John smiled, as a man will at a pretty young girl with her blond hair burnished and caught up in a jeweled snood.

Manfred Resnick spoke up. "I imagine John might have been about to say . . . there is still the matter of the burning of the *Alexandra*."

If Laura had not been looking directly at her, she would never have seen it. Just before Alexandra's long lashes swept down to cover her eyes, there was a quick hot blaze of malevolence. In addition, her hand upon her brother's arm went tense for the time it apparently took her to notice and relax.

"Yes," she murmured, "my poor brother's boat. This Sutton man must have done it."

Laura started to argue again that Danny had set the fire. But before she could open her mouth, she realized that on his deathbed, he'd told the truth about the stage attack and about Edgar Young. Why would he have held back this one confession?

Alexandra kept her eyes cast down, toying with the ties on her cape.

Laura gasped, taking in Alexandra's dress, her accessories, and the dress she herself had been loaned.

"No," she said. "Neither Cord nor Danny burned the steamboat."

Hank looked at her in surprise. "I'm sure you're not suggesting I torched it myself."

"No. Look at what you're wearing, Hank, something borrowed, because all your clothes burned. Now look at your sister; she's still got a wardrobe, enough to even loan me a dress."

Alexandra's head came up and she glared at Laura.

"She tried to kill you, Hank, because you threatened her favorite brother. But she miscalculated when she didn't let her clothes go up in smoke."

"She's crazy," Alexandra said at Hank's ear.

Manfred Resnick put up a hand. "She's right. A woman would notice such things, just as Pinkerton taught me to. Last night I phoned from the hotel to the soldier station at Lake, and I've gotten a return call—a valise filled with women's clothing was stashed in the abandoned cabin where Danny was staying."

"I didn't . . ." Alexandra began.

"Women's clothing that was predominately various shades of purple," Manfred finished.

"Alex?" Hank sounded bewildered.

"I hate you!" she shrilled. "When you said you would kill Danny, I . . . splashed the kerosene . . . even spilled my perfumes . . ." She turned and started to run across the grounds of the fort, toward the hotel, where a clatter of hooves announced a stagecoach coming from the park interior.

John Stafford and Manfred Resnick each caught

Alexandra by an arm. "Hold on," John said. "I don't think you're going anywhere."

From where she stood behind Officers' Row, Laura saw the spectacle of the stage's arrival.

On the long veranda, a dozen people watched as the driver brought the stage to a jerking halt and stood, sweeping off his hat decorated with an American flag. Thick dust on his tan coat showed how fast he must have driven the early-morning run.

The driver opened the coach door with a flourish and bowed. Norman Hagen stepped out first, then turned back to assist the ladies.

Fanny Devon and Constance alighted and stripped off their dusters. Fanny waved her paisley shawl as though she were cleaning a rug, while Constance brushed at the dirt on her dark skirt. Forrest Fielding did not alight, but Laura saw him through the open window, his shoulders wrapped in a plaid woolen traveling blanket.

Though she'd thought she despised them all, she broke into a ragged run. Waving and calling, "Daddy! Constance! Aunt Fanny!" she arrived pell-mell and pulled herself up through the coach's open door.

He was weak, his arms holding her with only a fraction of his former strength.

"Child," Forrest whispered, and she wished she could be a child again, when life was simple and, in bedtime stories, everyone lived happily ever after.

Aunt Fanny reached in through the coach window to clasp Laura's hand. "Thank God you're here."

Laura found tears in her eyes. After all she'd been through, believing she and Cord were going to die, she was amazed how the bond of family lifted her spirits. After helping her father down and to a chair on the veranda, she even found her arms wrapped around her cousin while they cried on each other's shoulders.

"I'm so sorry," Constance said, "for everything." She pulled back and her blue eyes searched Laura's. "Is Cord . . . ?"

"Cord has been exonerated of all charges." Laura's eyes moved to Fanny and Forrest's faces. "Danny Falls murdered Edgar Young, and Hank's sister burned his boat."

Constance gasped. "There's got to be a story there. You can tell us all about it on the train."

Forrest pulled out his gold hunting case watch and opened the lid. "The Northern Pacific leaves from Cinnabar at four." It was at least ten miles to the small town at the end of the line, north of Gardiner.

Laura stalled. "You really should rest some more before taking on the train trip. There should be something going on for the Fourth of July later, maybe they'll even have fireworks."

With a sidelong glance at her brother's slack profile, Fanny said, "I think he'll do better lying in a berth. We cannot afford to miss that train."

Perhaps they could not, but Laura decided, "I

won't be going with you."

She had an appointment at sundown. And though night would be falling, she viewed it as the dawning of the rest of her life.

CHAPTER THIRTY-FIVE

DECEMBER 25, 1900

On Christmas night in Salt Lake City, nearly a hundred happy relatives of Aaron Bryce swarmed through his big brick house off Temple Square.

In the kitchen, a dozen folks who'd sworn at two o'clock they would never eat again, made turkey sandwiches. In the parlor, plump, gray-haired Aunt Charlotte played the piano with earnest enthusiasm, thumping out "What Child Is This?" in a martial rhythm. Aaron's children and grandchildren gathered before the fire and sang in joyous cacophony, their music seeping through the closed door of the quiet library.

"Son," Aaron said, "you've been in another world since you got here."

It was true, Cord realized. He'd sleepwalked through Christmas, hardly heard the Mormon Tabernacle Choir's hundred voices raised in praise of the Lord. He'd partaken of the communion service, mechanically passing the bread and water to the next hand.

"Tell me," Aaron said in the deep voice that had always invited confidence. "Have you decided what you're going to do . . . after Excalibur?"

Though the strain between Cord and Thomas had lessened since Cord had sold him his share of Excalibur, there was still a dynamic tension.

Cord looked into his father's loving eyes, regretting the silver that had invaded his blond hair. "I've been thinking about doing something new at the ranch. There's been some talk in Jackson's Hole that tourists from the East might care to come out, ride horses, eat fine food . . . Laura has even threatened to learn to cook."

"That sounds fine, so why the long face?" Aaron brought his cup of hot cider and sat in the biggest leather armchair in the room. Through the years Cord had watched him seated comfortably in that chair, his head bent to listen, first to his own young children and then to nieces, nephews, and finally grandchildren on his knee. Cord had been seven when Aaron had taken him from the Mormon Agency for Orphans, too big for such games.

Aaron waited patiently.

Outside the shining mahogany door, someone started the gramophone, and the words to "O Holy Night" reminded Cord of the stars shining brightly as he'd held Laura on Nez Perce Peak.

"I guess it's nerves," he cleared his throat. "You remember when you got Laura's telegram and came to Mammoth on the Fourth of July . . . when John Stafford married us that evening, we thought the fireworks went off just for us. But I'm just a little nervous about having another ceremony in the Tabernacle tomorrow."

"Because?"

"Because the one thing I learned last summer is not to pretend, in any way, to be someone I'm not."

"The bishop will be disappointed to find out you're not a Mormon anymore." A hint of twinkle lighted Aaron's eyes.

"That's not what I mean. I guess I keep thinking of Bitter Waters, wondering what he's doing, how he feels . . ."

The library door burst open, and a laughing Laura launched herself at Cord, landing in his lap. "No fair hiding out in here talking man talk," she admonished. "Aunt Fanny, Father, Constance, and Norman have arrived."

"Then we'd best all go and greet them." Cord dropped a kiss on Laura's forehead.

Over the top of her head, he smiled at Aaron, who said, "As to that matter we were discussing, I think you know there's only one way to find your answer."

CHAPTER THIRTY-SIX
JANUARY 5, 1901

Early January snow drifted against the row of small squalid houses on the Colville Reservation in Nespelem, Washington. The creaking wagon in which Cord and Laura had hitched a ride from the railroad siding at Columbia Junction rolled on.

Watching the retreating buckboard, he looked around. Laura gripped his hand.

The taciturn Nez Perce driver had let them out in front of a fine home, contrasting sharply with the rest of the leaning, unpainted structures. Fronted by a long porch, the well-built white house had a sign in front that identified it as Superintendent Stillwell's Residence.

Cord moved their valises to the roadside, went up the stone walkway, and knocked.

A pair of small blond girls with identical pigtails and ruffled pinafores answered the door. It took him a moment to realize that they were not twins, but perhaps a year or two apart in age.

"Is your father or mother home?" Cord asked gently.

The older of the girls looked sad. "They have gone to the Dreamer Church with Chief Joseph to prepare for a funeral."

"I am sorry," Cord said gravely. "Perhaps you can direct me?"

"Just there." The girl leaned out the screen door and pointed to the largest building toward the end of the street.

Cord thanked the girls and headed back into the wind, pausing to wrap his muffler more snugly about his neck.

"I hope we haven't come at a bad time," Laura murmured.

They passed the first of the small homes, and he found himself forced to reconsider his impression of squalor. Glass windows gleamed brightly; lace edged the curtains inside. On either side of the stoop, beds had been laid in which wild roses had been cultivated, though they stood dry and dead against the winter blast.

A boy of perhaps ten years came out of one of the houses wearing brightly colored clothing that had clearly been mended a number of times. When he approached, Cord noticed the child's face was shiny clean.

Cord reached into his pocket and extracted a pack of Adam's pepsin gum. Beckoning the boy, he pressed it into his palm.

At the end of the street, the small, wood-framed Dreamer Church looked like any other, with a bell tower above its steeply sloping roof. Cord held the door for Laura and entered on a chill gust.

Inside, it was warm, with a steaming smell of damp winter clothing.

Cord might not have recognized Chief Joseph. The big man still wore his draped blanket, but the crest of crisp black hair Cord remembered fell in graying hanks beside a face set in lines of sadness. Deep furrows ran from the base of his nose to the corners of his tight-lipped mouth, and his eyelids drooped, making his once-flashing eyes look small.

His one ornament a tall hat decorated with eagle feathers, Joseph stood at the front of the small chapel before an open coffin in which a Nez Perce woman of perhaps forty or fifty years lay. She wore a beaded headdress and a royal-blue wool dress, also beaded in patterns of red and silver.

A white man with thinning hair sat on the front bench with bowed shoulders.

Cord set his bag in the anteroom and removed his hat. He helped Laura with her coat and hung it on a peg, then put his beside it.

Joseph looked toward them.

"I'm sorry to intrude at such a time," Cord said slowly. "I'm looking for a man named Bitter Waters."

"Who seeks Bitter Waters?" Joseph asked.

"My name is William Cordon Sutton. Once, long ago, Bitter Waters taught me something of family."

"You are not Nez Perce," Joseph said.

"Am I not?" Cord walked down the church aisle,

reaching into his pocket. Carefully he drew out a glistening piece of black obsidian and offered it on his open palm.

Recognition dawned on Joseph's features. "You are Blue Eyes, the brave young man who found his *wayakin* during the dark days of our flight for freedom."

Cord nodded.

"I believe Bitter Waters has gone to the sweat lodge, but he will want to see Blue Eyes." Joseph looked at the older white man, who rose.

"I'm Superintendent Stillwell." They shook hands. "I will go and find Bitter Waters."

When he had gone, Joseph stepped away from the coffin. "Let us sit someplace."

He led Cord and Laura to a small room at the side of the chapel. There, he motioned them toward scarred wooden chairs with bright clean cushions, stepped into the church kitchen, and returned with mugs of steaming coffee. "You must get warm after your travels in this weather."

Smiling at Laura, he removed his elegant hat and set it aside. "I wear this for our festivals to remind the People of their heritage. In New York, three years ago, I walked through the lobby of the Astor Hotel in full buckskins. They laughed and called me savage, thinking I did not understand."

Cord had read in the papers about Joseph's trip to the East, accompanied by Buffalo Bill. He sipped coffee and, putting an arm around the back of Laura's chair, settled in to listen.

"My father, Tuekakas, sent for me when he was dying," Joseph said. "He told me, 'Always remember that I never sold our country. You, my son, must never forget that.'"

Cord felt as though he were tumbling back into the past. He wondered what Joseph thought of his running away to the white world with miner Cappy Parsons.

"You are fortunate to have been far away when we surrendered at Bear Paw in Montana. We were taken by flatboat down the Yellowstone and Missouri to Fort Linden. There we were welcomed by the town and assured by General Howard's men that we would be returned to our homes." Joseph's direct dark eyes came to rest on Cord's. "General Sheridan ordered us loaded onto freight cars and taken to Fort Leavenworth. One hundred of our four hundred survivors died there of malaria and other sickness."

"If I had been with you then," Cord told him, "I would not have spent so many years without knowing what is left of my blood family."

"We try to keep tradition alive," Joseph said. "I have a house of wood that the government built for me. It is drafty and too far from the church and school, so I live in my tipi."

"You keep tradition," Cord observed, "but the children learn English and study at the white man's school."

"The old ways are passing," Joseph replied in a resigned voice. "When I traveled to New York and saw its wonders, I knew we must prepare the youth to live in that world."

Cord felt the wall between his two worlds crumbling. He could honor both his heritages, as he had when he and Laura had exchanged vows in the Mormon Tabernacle last week, and then had come here.

"The Colville Reservation will never be our home," Joseph went on. "We will put Kamiah into the earth here, but someday it is my hope that she, and all of us, may sleep in the valley of the Wallowa."

"Kamiah?" Cord's heart began a slow thudding. "If that is indeed the Kamiah I knew, then I must tell you a good woman has been lost."

The church door opened to admit a blast of cold wind and Bitter Waters. His hair was wet. "I came as soon as I rinsed my sweat in the waters of the stream." Over his arm, he carried a soft-looking hide. "I also stopped by to get this."

Laura gave a muffled exclamation at the sight of the intricate artwork on the hide. Men with bows hunted deer and elk from the backs of fine sleek horses. "It's beautiful."

Cord swallowed. "Believe it or not, that belonged to my mother."

Laura smoothed her hand over a painting of a tall young man offering a stringer of salmon to a slender, dark-haired girl. "How did it come to be here?"

Cord put a fingertip carefully to a patch of beads. "I last saw it in my uncle's tipi the morning Cappy took me away. It was painted for Sarah by her suitor, Tarpas Illipt, the one who died in the creek at Big Hole."

"Did you tell me why they never married?" Laura

asked.

"The young man's father forbade the match, because she was half-white."

Bitter Waters shook his head. "There has been much trouble in our family, people taking sides and staring across a line drawn in the sand."

He looked toward his wife's coffin. "She would have raised you as her own." His eyes shone with tears. "You have come too late for Kamiah, Blue Eyes, but . . ."

Bitter Waters went to Laura and reverently placed the marriage blanket around her shoulders. "It is not too late for me to welcome the newest member of our family."

EPILOGUE
APRIL 1901

Cord awakened when the first rose finger of dawn lighted the spire of the Grand Teton.

Outside the wide glass window of his and Laura's bedroom, a lone elk bugled. Stretching his neck out long, the bull shook his head, shaggy with the thick coat of late winter. Several inches of fresh snow had fallen during the night, piling cleanly on top of the already-deep drifts against the cabin's wall.

Last night, the dream had come again. The soldiers had walked him between Fort Yellowstone's stables and centered him against a whitewashed wall.

Once he'd heard his mother say that if you dreamed you died, you would. Each time Cord awakened in a cold sweat, he wondered if the firing squad might still have the power to kill him. But he believed with each day he was safe and happy, these dreams would pass, as the nightmares of his parents' deaths had ceased to visit him.

Putting his arm around Laura's waist, Cord savored her softness. He remembered waking alone so many nights. He'd watched the sunrise on the mountains, the bright gold of aspens seeming to mock him, and the winter desolation that had matched the loneliness inside a man between worlds.

This morning, he felt only contentment as he watched the rosy glow spread down the mountains, while bluish shadows lay deep in the valley.

Cord blew warm breath on Laura's neck. Before he could draw her closer, she tossed back the covers and went to the window, a silhouette against the brightening world. He followed and bent to kiss her.

"Come," he murmured, attempting to draw her back to bed. She looked delicious naked, save for her mother's cameo on a braided chain.

Over her shoulder, he saw Dante come from behind the barn and pause to allow White Bird to catch up. "You might say White Bird went AWOL from the army," Cord chuckled.

"I can't wait until she foals." Laura's lips curved into a smile, and she took his left hand, looking down at their matching gold wedding bands.

Reaching to the bed, Laura wrapped the softness of Sarah's marriage blanket around her. Cord went to the woodstove and lit the fire he'd laid last night. He clattered the stove lid back into place and joined her again at the window, waiting for the fire to overcome the chill air sheeting off the glass.

Drawing Laura against his side, he felt something

different about her, a lushness and languor. A certain fullness that caused him to dream . . .

In just a few years, their son might push his way with chubby hands through the summer-fragrant sage between the ranch house and the Snake River, playing in the same yard where Franklin Sutton and Sarah had watched over Cord.

Rose illumination turned lemon as the Tetons shifted and blurred beneath the constantly changing light. Just when Cord thought they remained the same, the wind would come up on the high peaks, blowing a veil of powder down another canyon.

AUTHOR'S NOTE

I have tried to recapture the experience of Yellowstone at the turn of the twentieth century, the stage tours, hotels, tent camps, feeding garbage to the bears . . .

I was surprised to discover that the Lake Hotel had phones and electricity in 1900, while Mammoth, seemingly closer to civilization, still lacked power. And there was a bar in the Lake Hotel despite the prohibition of alcohol in the rest of the park.

It is true that the Lake Hotel did have maintenance problems, and the Northern Pacific decided to unload it around the turn of the century. There were rival buyers, and the sale was postponed until 1901. Otherwise, I have written a complete work of fiction around that event. My apologies to the descendants of whomever might have been interim Yellowstone Superintendent in the summer of 1900, as I was unable to unearth a name and I did not intend to paint a real man a villain. The harsh treatment of poachers and tourists who defaced the geological formations is rooted in fact—there is an historic report of a poacher being force marched to Mammoth and horsewhipped. There were also a number of stagecoach robberies in the park.

As for the flight of the Nez Perce, the chiefs and generals, the victims Richard Dietrich and George Cowan, Lieutenant Hugh Scott, and Superintendent Stillwell are real history and personages. My other characters are fictitious.

I have remained wherever possible true to fact and some of the characters act out events reported by history. Meetings between the Nez Perce and the U.S. Army at Lapwai, along with the Battle of Big Hole, have been recreated through recorded eyewitness accounts.

There are various versions of the route the Nez Perce took through Yellowstone and some apparent controversy surrounding it. Some say the tribe split into two groups, and that one went through the Absarokas where I have placed my story.

Though there were summer wildfires in 1900, they were not on Nez Perce Peak for an excellent reason. While there is a Nez Perce Creek named for the incidents of 1877, I have planted a fictional mountain in the eastern ranges of the park. This youthful volcano played an "active" role in my previous books, *Summer of Fire* and *Rain of Fire*.

SUMMER OF FIRE
LINDA JACOBS

It is 1988, and Yellowstone Park is on fire.

Among the thousands of summer warriors battling
to save America's crown jewel, is single mother Clare
Chance. Having just watched her best friend, a fellow
Texas firefighter, die in a roof collapse, she has fled to
Montana to try and put the memory behind her. She's
not the only one fighting personal demons as well as the
fiery dragon threatening to consume the park.

There's Chris Deering, a Vietnam veteran helicopter
pilot, seeking his next adrenaline high and a good
time that doesn't include his wife, and Ranger Steve
Haywood, a man scarred by the loss of his wife and baby
in a plane crash. They rally 'round Clare when tragedy
strikes yet again, and she loses a young soldier to a
firestorm.

Three flawed, wounded people; one horrific blaze. Its
tentacles are encircling the park, coming ever closer,
threatening to cut them off. The landmark Old Faithful
Inn and Park Headquarters at Mammoth are under
siege, and now there's a helicopter down, missing,
somewhere in the path of the conflagration. And Clare's
daughter is on it . . .

ISBN#1932815295 / ISBN#9781932815290
Gold Imprint
US $6.99 / CDN $9.99
www.readlindajacobs.com

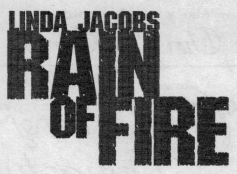

LINDA JACOBS
RAIN OF FIRE

The world's largest volcano does not reside beneath Hawaii's mountains, or in Washington state, but Yellowstone National Park. Past eruptions have darkened our continent and covered it with a blanket of ash that smothered both plant and animal life. Now the supervolcano, with its earthquakes and geysers, is monitored on a daily basis for signs of the beast reawakening.

As a terrified child, geologist Kyle Stone watched her family die in the 1959 Hebgen Lake Earthquake near Yellowstone. Fighting a lifetime of fears, she is one of the scientists with a finger on Yellowstone's pulse. When a new hot spring appears overnight in the park and a noted naturalist is scalded to death, Kyle mounts an expedition into the Yellowstone backcountry to unravel the mystery. Accompanying her are Ranger Wyatt Ellison, former student and friend, and Dr. Nicholas Darden, volcanologist and former lover. More than just a volcano is heating up.

Amid personal conflict, earthquakes uprooting the land, and poison gases killing wildlife, Kyle finds herself in the unenviable position of convincing park officials to evacuate Yellowstone before tens of thousands of people die. As the earth shudders, Kyle must also choose between past and present, and defeat her darkest terror simply to survive.

ISBN#1932815279 / ISBN#9781932815276
Gold Imprint
US $6.99 / CDN $9.99
www.readlindajacobs.com

Also by Linda Jacobs, writing as

Christine Carroll

Children of Dynasty

Eight years after her breakup with Rory Campbell, Mariah Grant, sole heir of her father's construction company, returns to San Francisco from self-imposed exile. Her father is ailing, the business is floundering and in danger of being devoured by an arch rival; Mariah's expertise is desperately needed.

Rory Campbell, also the sole heir to his father's construction giant, realizes that in spite of the intervening years, Mariah still heats his blood to boiling. Trouble is, their fathers — men once as close as brothers — are now, mysteriously, sworn enemies. Their businesses are battling, and fraternizing with the competition is considered consorting with the enemy.

Then there is a deadly, and suspicious, accident on a Grant skyscraper, killing Mariah's oldest friend. But was he the target? Will the elder Campbell stop at absolutely nothing to bring Grant down and keep his son from rekindling forbidden fires?

The war is on. Empires are at stake . . . lives hang in the balance . . . and the time has come for . . .
The Children of Dynasty

ISBN#1932815422 / ISBN#9781932815429
Contemporary Romance
US $6.99 / CDN $9.99
www.readchristinecarroll.com